beauty born anew

A Novel
by Michael Mitton

Part 3 of the Dorchadas Trilogy

An Amazon self-published book

ISBN: 9798597777481
Imprint: Independently published

First published February 2021
Second impression March 2021

Readers of *The Face of the Deep* wrote:

Enticing, penetrating, poignant, believable, entertaining.

I would recommend the book to anyone who struggles to reconcile the concept of a loving higher power with the mess and pain so evident in our beautiful but fragile world.

Readers of *The Fairest of Dreams* wrote:

This book's beauty is found not only in the way the story is told, but in the truths that it conveys to all who pick it up. This book holds together the tensions found in life - tragedy and healing, suffering and restoration - and watching the way Douglas walks through these deeper questions with courage, humour and hope, causes faith to rise in the reader for the journey that lies ahead of them.

As well as enjoying the story, I was reminded about my own spiritual journey in a way that stirred and renewed me.

PREFACE

It was a daunting task setting out to write Volume 3 of this trilogy. After the dramatic events at the end of Volume 2, how would the story gather momentum again? Were the characters of the novel exhausted after their exertions in the previous two novels? I did what I usually do before writing a novel, which is to spread out a large sheet of spare wallpaper on the floor and start sketching out ideas. As I did so, the characters (who have become good friends to me in the last few years) let me know in no uncertain terms that they had plenty to say in this further volume. Soon new characters arrived, and those on the edges of the last novels took up their positions for a more prominent role. And so there emerged another story of human struggles coming into contact with the surprising wonder and puzzling mystery of the light of God.

Most of what needs to be said by way of a preface for this book was said in the preface of *The Fairest of Dreams,* so I won't repeat myself. But I will point out two appendices at the end of this book, which might help you before you embark on this novel. The first is a summary of *The Fairest of Dreams,* for, if your memory is anything like mine, you will need help recalling the main events of this previous novel in the trilogy. I have also provided another appendix which is a list of the main characters who appear in all three books, in case you need help in remember who's who.

The title of this novel is taken from Pope Francis' *Evangelii Gaudium* (The Joy of the Gospel). Pope Francis is known perhaps as much for his humanity as his holiness. He is down to earth in the sense that he is not only comfortable in his own human skin, but he also knows much about the sheer and desperate struggle that life presents for many of his fellow humans, and he is therefore a deeply compassionate man. Yet, despite his acquaintance with the sorrows of this world, he is a man of extraordinary hope. This hope is rooted in a profound conviction that the resurrection of Christ has released a life-giving power that is available to each and every human who walks the face of this earth. If the main characters of this book could step out of the pages and come and chat with us over a cup of tea or glass of Guinness, I expect that, sooner or later, they would be telling us that this power is something worth discovering for our pilgrim wanderings through this precious life that has been entrusted to us.

However dark things are,
goodness always re-emerges and spreads.
Each day in our world
beauty is born anew,
It rises transformed
through the storms of history.

Pope Francis
Evangelii Gaudium

CHAPTER 1

Alice Morwenna Fournier lay on her back in the succulent, green headland meadow and gazed at the hazy blue expanse that stretched before her. Gazing at the sky was one of her favourite occupations. At this particular moment, the great life-giving star, that was over ninety million miles from Earth, had emerged from behind a large cumulous cloud and was blazing its light and heat on this part of her planet. If Alice were to stay lying in this meadow for several more hours, the Earth would have revolved sufficiently for the sun to disappear from view, and the dark of night to arrive. Then, if Alice were to stay here in this meadow, and if the curtain of the clouds remained open, she would be able to delight in the vast splendour of the milky way. In the days when her eyesight was good, she loved to come to such a place as this, far away from urban lights. She would lie on her back and would study the ribbon of starry light set in the dark mystery of the immensity above her. Or was it below her? That was the kind of question Alice loved.

Here where she lay was her favourite place - a cliffside field near the little coastal parish of Morwenstow, on the eastern edge of Cornwall and only a half an hour's drive from her home town of Bideford in North Devon. Or a two-hour cycle ride, as it had been on this bright April day. Well, just over two hours, if you included the very welcome cider and pasty break at Hoops Inn. In the old days she could cycle here in much less than two hours, but in those days, she had two good eyes to steer her around the lanes. It was trickier with her sight as it was now. Her mother was not at all keen on her cycling this distance. And she certainly would not tell her Aunt Mavis who would have had a seizure at the thought. But neither of them understood the way she had learned to see nowadays. She saw far more than either of them realised.

Yet she could not deny the gradual deterioration in her eyesight and that subsequently her days of cycling were numbered. However, she was determined to have this one last ride to her favourite place on earth. She had propped up her bike in the church porch, and had walked the familiar track to the cliff top. Familiar, that is, to her and to her father when he was alive. This was their track, and this was their spot. She pressed the palms of her hands to tufts of fresh, Spring grass as she continued her inspection of the blue yonder. She breathed in the briny sea air, and recalled how her father had brought her here on her seventh birthday.

'This, my little girl,' she remembered him saying, 'is the very place where Morwenna built her home. Oh, and such a home it was. Filled with praising angels, and saints who prayed so much that their knees were permanently black with Cornish mud.'

'And just who was this Morwenna, Pa?' she enquired.

'Well now, let me tell you, my poppet,' he said, curling his strong arm around her and holding her tight. She had heard the story of her namesake a hundred times, but this was their little game. She would always pretend she had never heard of this Celtic saint, so she could hear once more the story that never failed to delight her.

'Morwenna of the light, as I likes to call her,' said her father in his story-telling voice. 'Why now, do you see, young Alice, that horizon over there,' he said, pointing far beyond the teaming surf to the thin line of the horizon.

Alice squinted her eyes and held her slender hand up to her forehead, 'Yes, Pa, I can see the horizon.' She smiled in anticipation.

'Well, there is always something exciting beyond the horizon. And beyond that one, young Alice, is the beautiful and blessed land of Eire. One day I shall take you there, that I surely will.' He squeezed her again as she continued to study the horizon.

‘Well, one day a young lady called Morwenna - she got the call, Alice. And the Voice says to her, “Young lady, the dear people of Kernow need you. They need you, and it is time for you to go to them.” You see, we were the land beyond her horizon, Alice. We were her adventure.’

Her father’s face lit up as he chuckled at the thought, and then continued, ‘And sweet Morwenna says to the Voice, “But, Lord, how can I go, I have no boat.” And the voice says to her, “Oh, yes you have, Mistress Morwenna. Look up to the old oak tree whose great and ancient branches are giving you welcome shade today.” And she looked up at the old oak tree and, as she did so, the wind blew a great gust, and a huge leaf fluttered off from the top of that dear old tree. Down, down, down it floated,' At this, her father would wave his hand imitating a falling leaf and let it rest on Alice’s head. It always made her laugh. 'Down it came. She had never seen such a thing in her life. Just like your regular oak leaf, Alice, but this one was ginormous - so beautiful too. My, you had never seen such a thing! Well it was clear, this was to be her boat, and she dragged it down to the coast, got herself in it, and looked to the sky and called out “Blow, O blessed Spirit! Blow!” And straight away the northerly breeze blew upon the boat and blew that dear maiden over the horizon to the shores of our beloved land here.’

‘And what did she do here, Pa?’ asked the eager Alice, looking up at her father, half closing her eyes to shield them from the bright sky beyond her father’s gentle face.

‘Well now, my poppet,’ said her father looking back out to the sea. She came to tell the people about the Christ - the God who became one of us so we could live with glory and wonder in our hearts all our days. She settled exactly here, my love. Just where we are sitting now. “The Raven’s Crag” they called it. Though, in time, they started to call it “Morwenna’s Holy Place”, or “Morwenstow”.

'And tell me about the stone, Pa,' said Alice, pulling at the grass beside her and throwing it up for the wind to play with.

'Ah, the stone, Alice. Yes, the stone,' said her father with a smile. 'Well now, one day our young Morwenna goes down to the beach - just down there, Alice,' he said, pointing to the curve of beach below them. 'There - can you see it, my love?'

'Yes, Pa - I can see the very spot where she found the stone,' cried Alice with excitement.

'Yes, my pretty. You can see the gap her stone left. Well she picks up that great stone - God knows, Alice, the angels must have helped her, I reckon, because it was no light stone. And she brings it all the way up here and pops it down on the very place where she wanted her church to be built. And do you know what, Alice?' he asked, looking down at the bright curls on the head of his daughter.

'No, Pa,' said Alice, though she knew exactly what was coming next.

'Well, just as she puts the great stone down on the ground, a mighty spring of water gushes out from the hillside and a wonderful well of fresh water appears.'

'So that the people could enjoy the waters of eternal life,' said Alice smiling back up at her father, pre-empting the very words he would always use to finish this story. But on this occasion her smile quickly turned to a frown as she said, 'But Pa, I have always wanted to know one thing.'

'What is that, my sweet?'

'Why did you give me her name as my *second* name. I would like to have it as my first. I want to be "Morwenna Alice."

'Ah, well now, my love,' said her father, his face showing more than a hint of sorrow. 'That would have been my wish. But your lovely mother had her heart set on calling you "Alice" because she loved those books of the Wonderland and the Looking Glass.'

'Hm,' said Alice thoughtfully. 'Yes, Pa. I do love those stories very much. But I love the story of Morwenna more.'

'Well, then, my sweet. Never forget your name is Morwenna, and as far as I'm concerned you are as beautiful, special and blessed as the Morwenna who came to this land on her oak leaf.'

That conversation was nearly forty years ago now, but as Alice lay in the grass she remembered it as if it were yesterday. How she adored her father, even in her teenage years when she tried her parents' patience considerably, and even he had his moments of being irritable with her. No matter how turbulent her world, he was still the same, kind-hearted, steady fixed point in her life. To most people in town, he was the reliable plumber who said little as he went about his work repairing burst pipes and installing boilers. He was a regular at St.Mary's Church. He loved the building and would often be found on a Saturday doing the odd repair job for the very grateful Vicar. But to Alice, his talents were far more than those of a plumber and odd-job man. He was the fount of all wisdom, the collector of ancient stories, the healer of breaches, the heart of gold and, not least, the consummate teller of hilarious jokes. Though jokes usually only she found funny. Her mother seldom laughed at them. In fact, her mother seldom laughed.

As she lay on this favourite spot on earth, she wept at these precious memories, and little pools of water formed above her closed eyelids. He never did get the chance to take her to Ireland. Her world was so shockingly darkened on that dreadful day of the accident. It was a blustery Tuesday in November. She was in the University library researching for a project on quantum physics. He was driving to nearby Northam to fix a leaking kitchen sink. One moment he was driving down the A386, and the next he was with the angels, his body a broken mess inside the tangled wreckage of his van. How she managed to complete her degree, she never knew, but complete it she did. And with a First. But, with the tragic loss of her father, her life slipped off its steady course and many years of inner lostness followed. But in the last couple of years she had been making her steady way back on to the kind of course that her father would have wished for her.

She sat up and the moisture from her eyes drained down her cheeks on to her purple T-shirt. She breathed in and felt her innate resilience. She had survived that bereavement, and she had survived her divorce with Georges, and, to be fair, she had reached middle age reasonably intact. Yes, she had her scars and there was much that was unresolved in her life, not least her relationship with her mother. But then, this was life. Some things might never mend. And she had lovely Aunt Mavis. Thank goodness for Aunt Mavis, who had been so kind to her.

And then there was Douglas Romer, the former Vicar of Mavis' church in Sheffield. Handsome, interesting, honest and very likeable. Perhaps even very loveable. But not available. She had learned much of his story from Mavis. Clearly, he had made a much better choice in marriage than Alice had. His love for his wife was unusually deep. Alice felt more sadness rising as she thought of his desperate hurt. And Mavis had told her of the shocking news that Saoirse had been deliberately killed because she was on to an illegal arms dealer. It all sounded too horrible for words. And just recently Douglas had been involved in a bad car accident. No, the poor man did not need to have his heart troubled again. And yet, and yet… It was hard to get him out of her mind.

And there was another thing. In one conversation with her, Douglas had mentioned that he had met a curious fellow in Dingle. He had said this man claimed that he used to be an angel, a claim that Douglas confessed he was now inclined to believe. Alice wasn't sure quite how to respond. Douglas was clearly a little embarrassed about owning up to such a bizarre possibility and he quickly changed the subject.

For Alice, the idea of a man claiming to be an angel in human disguise was far from bizarre. For she had also met an Irishman who claimed to be an angel during the time when she was living in France. She was bruised, literally, by her marriage, and Marseilles had become a very lonely place for her. Then one day, he turned up in a coffee shop. He just sat down at her table and chatted with her. Her sight was failing at the time and she could not see him so clearly but, during the conversation, she saw with a different kind of eyesight. It was hard to explain, yet it was as clear as day to her: she knew without any doubt that the man sitting opposite to her sipping at his coffee *was* an angel. Curiously, it did not feel at all unnatural.

She met him several times and he introduced her to a couple of friends of his. She had never dared tell anyone about it. People would never believe her, for the friends in question had been dead thousands of years. But dead or not, they certainly changed her life. That's how she got on to Jesus. Her old Pa would have been so pleased. He had always said that she should not copy his faith, but find Christ for herself. And this she certainly did. She had intended to share all this with Douglas, but somehow there never seemed an opportune moment, not least because her Aunt Mavis was often with them when they were together, and Aunt Mavis would certainly have nothing to do with angels wandering around in this world disguised as humans.

The sun that had been shining warm on Alice's face, momentarily disappeared behind a cloud and she opened her eyes. 'So, what happened to you?' said Alice out loud. 'What happened to you, you angel of heaven, who once helped me so much?' She cast her gaze across the sea in the direction of Ireland. 'Have you settled beyond the horizon in your favourite land now?' She turned her eyes back to the sky and said, 'Or has your time come? Has He freed you from your mortal dwelling place? Are you now exploring out there in the deep, deep blue, in the domain of the stars?'

At their first meeting, she had told him about her two names and her love for Morwenna. She asked about his name. He told her his name and explained it was the Gaelic word for darkness. An Angel called Darkness made complete sense to Alice. No, never could she forget the angel, who had come to her aid, and whose name was Dorchadas.

CHAPTER 2

March ended by hurling another wet storm over the Dingle peninsula. But on the first day of April the clouds had hurried off east, and in their place a bright and warm sun bathed the soggy land, and the streets of Dingle town shone like polished glass. The local people never seemed to mind the storms and rain, but Douglas Romer could not deny that he always preferred sunshine to clouds, and warmth to cold. He looked out of the window of his room at St.Raphael's Guest House and watched the sunlit street below gleaming in the Spring sunshine.

In recent days he had felt remarkably content. The events of that extraordinary day in January of the memorial service and the dramatic car chase now seemed a long time ago. Yet the recollection of those moments that followed the accident, when he and the others stepped into that deep memory, were as vivid as if they had happened yesterday. He only had to close his eyes and his mind would take him back to that darkened sky, the blood-stained soil, the rough-hewn wood, the gaze of love, the touch on the shoulder, the tender and familiar voice. Each and every part of that memory brought peace to his soul. Though he still missed his beloved Saoirse, the grief no longer suffocated him. His injury from the accident was healing well and he could now laugh and cough without it hurting. In all kinds of ways, he was healing. And he felt alive. Truly alive.

And yet, he was also troubled. Less than a week ago he had come across this strange girl called Grace on the seashore. She started talking about death. He could cope with that. But then she started talking about the death of someone he had grown to love very much - Kathleen Griffin, who had also shared in that deep memory experience at Golgotha. Kath, whose life was now coming together after much pain; Kath, who was meeting up with Peter and could have such a good future with him.

According to Grace, this Kath had a terminal cancer and would soon be entering the valley of the shadow of death.

Douglas was roused from his thoughts by Elsie calling him from the hallway: 'You'll need to get yourself downstairs now if you want your breakfast, Douglas. I've got to head out very soon.'

'Just coming,' called Douglas, and soon he was down in the dining room. There were several other guests staying in the house now and Douglas missed the days when it was just him and Elsie at breakfast. However, no matter how busy the Guest House, Elsie always had time to have a chat with her favourite guest, whom she now viewed much more as a member of the family than a guest.

'Someone said they spotted Dorchadas in town yesterday,' she said, as she handed Douglas his breakfast.

'Oh, really?' said Douglas. 'That's great news. I'll head down to the Presbytery later and see if he is there.'

'Aye, but you know what he's like,' said Elsie collecting a large pot of coffee and bringing it over. 'And one other thing to tell you about, Douglas: my sister's back in town.'

'Oh good,' he replied, pleased but also a little nervous. He looked up at Elsie as she was pouring the coffee and asked, 'Elsie, do you mind if I ask you - Is Kath well?'

Elsie paused and looked around the room. It was clear this was not a subject she wanted others to hear about. She put down the pot, and held her hands firmly together. 'Why do you ask, son?' she asked, and her eyes started to fill.

'I won't trouble you now, Elsie. But, you know. Her cough... I was just wondering.'

Elsie picked up the pot of coffee again. 'She'll be very glad to see you, Douglas,' she said, trying to return to her business-like self.

'I'll get up there this morning,' said Douglas and gave her a reassuring smile.

'Now, I'll be fetching your eggs. They're a fine batch this week,' she called to one of the guests, as she made her way out of the dining room. Only Douglas saw her remove her glasses briefly so she could wipe the moisture from her eyes.

*

As Douglas brushed his teeth after breakfast, he felt a stab of anxiety in his stomach. He had been hoping that Grace was wrong about Kath's health, but Elsie's reaction made it clear that Kath was far from well. He knew he needed to go to see her. But before he left his room, he stood before the broken crucifix in his room, and gazing upon it he spent several moments in silence. This had become his new way to pray. In the old days he used so many words, but now he felt he just needed to come into the Presence and wait there. In the silence, his soul was praying for his friend Kath, who could be very seriously ill, and for her sister, Elsie, who had looked so worried. He then grabbed his coat, sped down the stairs, opened the front door but could go no further because, who should be standing there on the point of pressing the doorbell, but his angel friend Dorchadas, who had clearly returned from his wanderings.

“Well now, you seem to be in a mighty hurry this morning, Douglas, that you do!’ said Dorchadas, placing his hands on his hips and smiling broadly.

‘Dorch, you’re back!’ said Douglas laughing, and the friends tightly hugged each other, both delighted to be together again.

‘So, were you dashing out to see your old friend, Dorchadas on this fine April morning?’ said Dorchadas, still grasping Douglas’ arm.

‘Actually, Dorch, no. Though I did hear you were back in town.’

‘Ah, well, I know when I’m not wanted,’ said Dorchadas, releasing Douglas’ arm and pretending to look hurt.

Douglas smiled. ‘Look, I was actually going to see Kath, but I can go later. I’d love to catch up with you now.’

‘Well, Doug, I think that would work well as it happens. I have just been up to Kath’s myself, and Peter is there at the moment and he told me Kath has gone off to fetch provisions for the café and won’t be back ’til later. So, what say you we find ourselves a nice coffee?’

Douglas felt pleased and was hopeful that he might now have Dorchadas’ company on his visit to Kath. And, as it turned out, the two friends would need most of the morning to catch up.

They quickly found a welcome coffee shop and settled themselves at the table and ordered cappuccinos. ‘So, what’s been happening to you, then?’ asked Dorchadas, studying his friend carefully.

’Plenty. But I’m keen to hear about you, Dorch. Last time I saw you was… you know, in that place.’

‘Aye,’ said Dorchadas, as a young waiter placed the two drinks in front of them. Dorchadas placed his hands around his mug. He stared at the delicate pattern of a leaf on the frothy surface of his drink. 'Amazing how they do this, Doug, don't you think? These beautiful patterns with the milk?'

'Dorch, don't change the subject please,' said Douglas, who was acquainted with Dorchadas' occasional tendency to avoid a tender subject.

Dorchadas played with the top of his coffee for a few moments then said, 'I never thought - you know, Doug. To be in that holy place. I knew I had to take you all there. Though, to be fair, Doug, I wasn't expecting that I'd get there by tumbling down the hill in that rust bucket of yours.'

'Sorry, Dorch,' said Douglas, looking for a moment like a naughty child.

'Are you getting some new wheels, Doug?' asked Dorchadas.

'Well, Elsie, bless her, got in touch with her nephew, and he's bringing another car for me this week sometime.'

'Do you think the doors will open this time?' asked Dorchadas, smiling broadly.

'I'm hoping so, Dorch,' said Douglas. 'Now, back to your story please.'

Dorchadas sipped his coffee and looked out of the café window, and then continued. 'I knew where we were, straight away,' he said, his mind vividly recalling the scene. He looked back at Douglas. 'You must have been so shocked, Doug, when you realised where we were.'

'I was, Dorch,' said Douglas.

Dorchadas looked back out of the window. 'It was cold, wasn't it? And so dark. I was so grateful that Antonio was there.' He looked back at Douglas and smiled. 'Felt like we were in the hands of a good friend, didn't it?'

'Yes, it did,' agreed Douglas.

‘I want so much to know what happened to everyone, Doug. I’ve not heard anything yet.’ Dorchadas frowned as he looked at Douglas.

‘But Dorch, what happened to *you*? Please tell me.’ Douglas sipped his coffee and looked hard at his friend.

‘Yes, I will tell you, Doug,’ said Dorchadas and he took a long sip of his cappuccino. ‘You have become such a good friend to me, you surely have. I really don’t want to hold anything back from you. Well, as I suspect you discovered, Golgotha is both a terrible and a glorious place. Did you see something of the glory, Doug?’ Dorchadas looked at Douglas with eager anticipation.

‘Oh, yes, Dorch. I did,’ said Douglas with conviction.

‘And Kath, Kevin and the others from the accident who were there, God bless them. Did they see the glory?’

‘Most of them, Dorch. Yes.’

‘Most, but not all?’ said Dorchadas, his frown returning.

‘I will fill you in, Dorch. I promise. But I want to hear about *you*.’ Douglas was starting to feel impatient. He was longing to know what happened to Dorchadas, who was separated from the group in the deep memory experience of Golgotha, and had only just reappeared back in Dingle.

‘Yes, Doug, yes,’ said Dorchadas, recognising his friend’s eagerness to hear his story. He drained his coffee cup and placed it carefully back on its saucer. ‘Well, as you know, I was led away from those sad crosses. I can tell you, I felt so bad at leaving you there. I wanted so much to stay with you and Kath and Kevin, but it was clear that Tony had received clear instructions and I was to leave you in his hands.’

‘Well, he did care for us well, Dorch.’

Dorchadas smiled. ‘It was one of the reasons why we had to meet him beforehand, Doug. I knew he would take care of you.

But I had to move on, though, the truth is, I wasn't sure where I was supposed to go. It was clear I had been called to accompany you to Golgotha, but I'd not been told what I should do after that, so I just walked towards the crowd of onlookers. What a crowd they were, Doug. I mean, some of them were raging and swearing at the crosses. Others were laughing and mocking and making rude gestures. And some were weeping and wailing. And quite a few just stood silent, struck dumb by the horror of it all. I was looking across at all them human faces when, all of a sudden, I saw a face I recognised, and it wasn't human. Guess who it was, Doug.'

Douglas raised his eyebrows and said, 'I really can't imagine, Dorch.'

Dorchadas also raised his fulsome eyebrows and said, 'Why it was the chief, himself. The Archangel Gabriel. Just standing there in the crowd and looking hard at me.'

'Gabriel? At Golgotha?' exclaimed Douglas.

'Well, where else did you think he'd be?' said Dorchadas. 'Not that any of the humans saw him there, of course. But there he was there all right. Make no mistake. He's taller than me, you know. So I couldn't miss him in the crowd, and he beckoned me over. So, I made my way through the crowd and he reached out his hand and took hold of mine and within moments we were in a different place. A beautiful place actually. So beautiful, Doug, that it would make you cry even to think of it, let alone visit. Well it certainly had me weeping, at any rate.' Dorchadas reached out for his coffee cup and then saw he had already finished it, so withdrew his hand.

'Another?' asked Douglas.

'In a moment, Doug,' said Dorchadas. 'Let me just finish this.' He breathed in a long breath before continuing. 'Well, he and I had a wee conversation. It's curious, Doug. I knew that Christ had fully forgiven me. And John, when we met him in the cave that time, had told me that the angels had also forgiven me. But I couldn't quite believe that bit of it, you know. I'm a stubborn fool at times, honest I am.'

Douglas smiled warmly and said, 'Yes, Dorch, I suppose you are.'

Dorchadas shrugged his shoulders and then his eyes reddened. 'Well, here I was, a junior angel, and a failed one at that, now in human form, speaking to the head angel and, I know this will surprise you, Doug, but to be honest with you, I felt really nervous. I finally discovered what human nervousness feels like. It's not a good feeling is it?'

'No, it certainly isn't, Dorch,' said Douglas, who had known too much nervousness in his own life.

'Well, Gabriel invited me to sit down on the lovely grass with him, and I was fully expecting a kind of end of term report to tell me I'd made a pretty bad fist of things during my time as a human. I know, I know, what you will say, Doug, because you're kind. And lots of people have said kind things about me. But when I look at the years I have spent in this world, I can see I've too often made a mess of things. And also, I sometimes think, I've enjoyed myself far too much. I mean, I've probably had a little too much of the Guinness for one thing. And I've eaten far more of Mrs McGarrigle's treacle pudding than I should've. And things I've said that I shouldn't, and wrong advice I've given. So much of that. I mean, I got plenty wrong with you, Douglas, didn't I? I should have been far wiser than I have. I've really not had a great record.' Dorchadas looked down at the table and shook his head. He then looked up at Douglas and said, 'But do you know what Gabriel did, Doug?'

'No, Dorch. Please tell me,' said Douglas, intrigued by this story of the conversation between an angel and the archangel.

'No word of a lie, Doug,' said Dorchadas, leaning towards his friend and tapping the table with his forefinger. 'He went through every single person I was sent to help in this world - every visit I have made across the continents and through the ages. He knew of every one of them, and I can tell you, Doug, there have been a fair few. So, we were there for some time.'

'Well, what did he say about them, Dorch?' asked Douglas, eager to hear the Archangel's assessment of Dorchadas' work on earth.

Dorchadas was quiet for a few moments, and Douglas noticed an expression on his face that he had not seen on his friend before. It was an expression of coyness. Dorchadas was playing with his empty coffee cup, running it around his saucer. 'Well, Doug,' he said, with his eyes filling with moisture. 'He said I had done an excellent job with each and every person I had met in this world. He told me a little of what had happened with each person after I had left them. How their lives had changed. How they had found peace, love - you know, all the things we hope will happen for souls in this world. And he said he was delighted with what I had done. Delighted, Doug!'

'Well, that's brilliant, Dorch! Congratulations!' said Douglas and smacked him on the back. Then he added, 'And no mention of the Guinness?'

'No mention of the Guinness, Doug,' said Dorchadas and chuckled. 'I was chuffed, I surely was. And so pleased to hear those reports of them dear people that I tried to help as best I could. And mightily relieved to be honest.' He continued to smile for a few moments, but then the smile quickly vanished and he looked up at Douglas. 'But that wasn't all, Doug. There was something else he said.'

'Oh?' said Douglas.

'Douglas, he told me that my work as a human is just about done.' He looked at Douglas and added. 'This means the Dorchadas that you see sitting in front of you now, won't be in this world for too much longer. I'll be heading back to my old form. You know - a proper angel.'

Douglas was not sure quite how to respond to this. It felt like a reinstatement, so he wanted to congratulate his friend. But he was also aware that the Dorch he knew and loved would therefore not be with him much longer, and that made him feel deeply unhappy.

Dorchadas looked down at his empty cup and then looked back up at Douglas and said, 'I suppose it will be like dying in a way. And the truth is, Doug, I have come to love living in this world here as an eejit ex-angel. I do love this world so much, Doug. And I love you humans. I have loved living in this world as a human. I feel like I have become one of you and, to be honest, I don't want to leave. But leave I must.' He pressed his lips tight and nodded his head. 'Should have done a worse job with you all, shouldn't I?' he added and laughed.

Douglas laughed as well, but he felt genuinely sorry for Dorchadas and did not know quite what to say.

'Doug, I don't want you worrying about it,' added Dorchadas, typically thoughtfully. 'I'm going to be fine, I know I will. It just takes a bit of getting used to, that's all. I knew it would have to happen one day. But I mean, who wants to leave lovely coffee shops like this?' He laughed again, then looked serious and said. 'Actually, Gabriel told me that Christ felt the same. He loved being with his friends so much that he was none too keen to leave when his turn came. Except, of course, he is still here. But, you know what I mean, Doug. He just felt at home as a human.'

'Will you be wanting more coffee, gentleman?' The voice of the young waiter startled both of them.

'That would be grand, Martin,' said Dorchadas. 'Same again for you, Doug?' he asked, looking at his friend.

'Please,' said Douglas.

When the new cappuccinos returned, Douglas filled Dorchadas in on all that had happened with each of the group who had gathered in the deep memory of Golgotha following the accident. All through his narration, Dorchadas listened intently, so much so that Douglas had to remind him to drink his coffee. Douglas never tired of remembering these sacred stories.

'Can I just get one thing clear, Doug,' said Dorchadas after he drained the last of his coffee. 'It was not just your man, Niall, who was after you, but this Gerald from England as well? The one that was the arms-dealer?'

'Yes, that's right, Dorch. Two of them after me!'

'So, you were not wrong, then, Doug. And there was me thinking it was just your paranoia getting the better of you!'

'Yes - this was the one time in my life when I had a good excuse to be paranoidal!' said Douglas, laughing.

Dorchadas also laughed, then his expression changed as he said, 'But what about your man, Gerald. What became of him? Did he make it to those crosses?'

Douglas always found it difficult to speak about the fate of Gerald. Through an extraordinary experience of grace at Golgotha, Douglas had found a place to forgive the man who was responsible for his wife's death and he genuinely wished Gerald could have reformed. Whereas everyone else in that little group was utterly transformed by their experience at the crosses, Gerald clung to his craving for power and refused to yield to all that was being offered him.

Dorchadas' expressive face could not hide the deep sorrow he felt. 'Ah, Doug, I am so sorry to hear this. The man was given every chance, wasn't he?'

'Yes, he was, Dorch. I don't quite know what this means for him. I'm not really sure about things like hell or purgatory these days.'

‘No, son. All that is in His hands. But it sounds to me as if Gerald was growing less and less human. In fact, it sounds like he had been diminishing for years. Dark things like greed and bitterness can do this. Humanity drains bit by bit until there is nothing left. And what about his dear wife? said Dorchadas, looking up at his friend.

‘She’s very impressive, Dorch,' said Douglas. 'She was very upset, of course, by Gerald's death, but she was completely transformed at Golgotha. She's back in the UK now and has lots of meetings with the police and security services as they investigate all of Gerald's murky dealings with arms and finance.'

'Is she in trouble with the law, Doug?' asked Dorchadas.

'I don't know - all that is being investigated,' said Douglas. 'But she is remarkably at peace about it all. She's even willing to lose the big house that once meant so much to her. As I say - an utterly transformed person.' Douglas went on to tell of the subsequent reconciling conversations he had had with Saoirse’s parents, and the memorial mass on the beach. Dorchadas was delighted to hear these reports.

It was lunchtime by the time they left the café and, as the sun was shining, they decided to buy a sandwich and made their way to the harbour. They sat on a sun-warmed wall and watched a group of tourists boarding a boat that would take them out into the bay in search of the local school of dolphins.

‘So Dorch, I now need to speak to you about Kath,’ said Douglas struggling to release his sandwich from the grip of its wrapper.

‘Yes,’ said Dorchadas turning to Douglas. ‘We must talk about Kath. And the young girl who told you about her.’

CHAPTER 3

'Do you know Grace, then?' asked Douglas, his face betraying his surprise.

'I do, Doug,' said Dorchadas.

'So, who exactly is she, Dorch? And how does she know about Kath? And how did you meet her?' Douglas was full of questions about this mysterious young teenager whom he had last met a week ago on the seashore, when she informed him that Kath had cancer.

'You can ask her yourself,' said Dorchadas looking over Douglas' shoulder. Douglas turned around and, sure enough, sauntering along the quay was the slight figure of the young teenager that Douglas had met on two or three occasions during his time in Dingle.

'You guys not going to see the dolphins?' called Grace as she approached them.

'Not today, lass,' said Dorchadas smiling at her.

Grace walked towards them, kicking some fishing rope to one side as she approached. She seated herself on a tangled pile of fishing net that was next to them. She pulled off her baseball cap momentarily and brushed back her hair, before replacing the cap on her head.

'So, you two know each other?' said Douglas looking at both Grace and Dorchadas in turn.

'Oh aye, we've met a couple of times recently, Grace, haven't we, lass?' said Dorchadas and munched his sandwich.

Douglas was frowning and said, 'Well, can I just get one thing straight. Exactly who are you, Grace?'

'You not told him?' said Dorchadas, his mouth full of cheese and ham.

'I sure did,' said Grace with a frown. 'I told him I was Jerry's girl. He should've guessed from that.'

'Well, to be fair, I don't think he knows the man as "Jerry",' said Dorchadas.

'Jerry Who?' asked Douglas, feeling increasingly irritated.

Dorchadas pulled a piece of stray watercress from his mouth and said, 'Well, Doug, I guess you would know the man as Jairus.'

Douglas recognised the biblical name and feeling a little deceived by the girl, said, 'But when we first met, I asked you if you were from the bible.'

'Well, I didn't deny it, did I? You got any sandwich to spare?'

Dorchadas passed her his second sandwich. Douglas thought back to their first meeting in the playground. It seemed such a long time ago now and he didn't have a clear recollection of it.

'So… let me get this right,' said Douglas, putting his hand up to his head. 'Your father is Jairus, and you are the daughter that Jesus brought back to life.'

'That's the one,' said the girl. 'Cool sandwich, Dorch. Thanks.'

'OK. So, have you moved to Ireland? Do you live here now in this time? Is your dad here?' Douglas had so many questions.

Grace swallowed hard on a piece of the sandwich, then looked at Dorchadas and said, 'Do you want to explain, or shall I?'

'It's your story, lass,' said Dorchadas. 'Go ahead. And Doug, in case you are asking, I've only met the girl recently. I hadn't met her when you first bumped into her, so put aside all your conspiracy theories.'

‘Thank you, Dorchadas,’ said Douglas with some sarcasm in his voice. He turned to Grace. ‘All right, young lady. Tell me all about it.’

Grace shuffled on the netting to make herself more comfortable. The boat carrying the tourists revved its engines hard and Grace waited until it had chugged away from them. ‘Don’t think they will see the dolphins today. Dolphins are like that - love the tourists most days, but sometimes they just want to be left on their own. We all like a bit of peace and quiet sometimes.’ She turned back to Douglas and said, ‘Anyway, you want my story, so here it is. No, I’ve not moved to Ireland. You and Dorchadas are the only people who have met me here. I’ve come because I was called. The first time, I was told I was not to tell you who I was. You weren’t ready to hear then. So, I made out I was a bit stroppy as you called it.’

‘Well, you played the part perfectly, if I may say so,’ said Douglas.

‘Actually, it’s not difficult for me. I know, I came back from the dead, but when you’ve been to the other side, it’s hard to settle back in this world again. Though I do like this travelling, I must say. And I like being Irish as well.’ She smiled at Dorchadas who nodded back to her.

‘Well, of course I know your story in the bible,’ said Douglas.

‘Preached on it a few times, I expect?’ mumbled Dorchadas, finishing his sandwich.

‘A few times, Dorch. But never mind that - I’d like to hear it from you, Grace. Can you tell me what happened?’

‘Sure, I can,’ she said. She closed her eyes for a few moments as she called to mind the extraordinary events of that day. ‘So, I was just twelve years old. As you know, my dad was called Jairus, and I am sure he would have been called Jerry here in Ireland, don’t you think?’

‘For sure,’ said Dorchadas, brushing crumbs from his jeans.

‘Thanks, Dorchadas,’ she responded. 'He knows much more about this land than I do. Anyway, my dad was in charge of the synagogue. So, people knew him and they loved him actually. He was a nice dad.’ She smiled a warm smile as she remembered him. ‘I got ill, as lots of us did at that time. I didn’t think it was much, but I could see my mother was concerned. I remember getting really hot, and she was rushing to the well to get some water to cool me down. I started to feel pretty weird and then I started seeing things. “Hallucinating”, I think you call it. It was pretty scary. I know at some point, I lost consciousness. But, just before I did, I heard my parents talking. “We are losing her”, I heard my mother say, and I then started to feel really frightened. I heard my dad say something like, “That rabbi, Jesus from Nazareth, is in the area. He can do miracles, I will go and fetch him.” “Then fetch him quickly,” I heard my mother cry and I think that was the last thing I heard before I went unconscious.’

Grace paused for a few moments. A flock of seagulls started squawking overhead as a fishing boat was making its way into the harbour. She looked up and smiled at them. “Noisy creatures, aren’t they?’ she said.

‘So you then… died?’ asked Douglas, eager to hear more of the girl’s experience.

‘Yes,’ replied Grace, turning her attention from the gulls back to Douglas. ‘My father rushed out and found Jesus, but on the way to our home He got held up by another healing He had to do - a lady just down the road from us who had been sick for years. We became good friends afterwards as it happens, but at the time she was not my da’s best friend at all, because she stopped Jesus getting to me while I was still alive. By the time He eventually got to our house, I had been dead for a while.’

‘Did you… you know, remember anything about being dead?’ asked Douglas, aware of just how strange his question sounded.

'Very clear,' said the girl. 'I felt myself slip out of my body and I sort of floated up to the ceiling and just stayed there for a time. I don't remember feeling anything really. It just felt normal, like. Funny to say that isn't it? But I was just there looking down at myself, and I thought I looked very peaceful. I thought I looked rather nice, to tell the truth. Then I saw my mother come into the room with the wet cloth. But when she saw me, she knew I was dead. She dropped the cloth on the floor and rushed over to me and then grabbed me and sobbed and sobbed. I was watching all of this but I still didn't feel anything. I mean, as I think about it now, I feel so sad and upset for my ma, but at the time I was just floating in this place of absolute peace. That's what it was - absolute peace. Then a door opened near me, and I stepped through it into - well I guess you would call it a garden.'

Here Grace looked down for a few moments and shuffled some pebbles and shells with her feet. Douglas heard her sniffing and she seemed upset.

'Don't worry,' said Douglas. 'Don't tell me if it's difficult.'

'She's all right, son,' said Dorchadas, touching Douglas lightly on the arm.

Grace sniffed hard and looked up at Douglas. Despite the fact that her face was flushed and her eyes wet with tears, she looked completely radiant. 'The trees, Douglas... You have never seen trees like that. And the sky. My, the sky...' She looked out to sea, blinking hard. 'There are colours there that I didn't know existed. And creatures... such gentle creatures...' She paused for a few moments, then looked at Douglas and said, 'Don't suppose you have ever stroked the mane of a lion, have you, Douglas?'

'I can't say I have, Grace,' said Douglas smiling.

'You should hear what they have to say,' she said and chuckled. 'Never thought I'd hear a lion speaking to me.' The fishing boat moved past them, taking the flock of seagulls with it. She glanced up briefly. 'Have you ever wanted to fly with the birds, Douglas?' she asked, turning her head to one side as she looked at him.

'Yes, many times. And once or twice I have in my dreams.'

'Well, then, perhaps you know a little of what that garden is like. I have never known anything so beautiful, so free, so full of light, so... Well, there are no words really. Anyway, I was allowed that glimpse.' She paused again, and removed her cap, brushing back her ash brown hair. 'I then heard a voice. It was such a beautiful voice, and I heard it coming like a voice calling across the waters. It came from such a long way off, and yet it was a voice that I knew belonged to this garden. It was a voice I would have travelled the world to hear and I knew I wanted to find it wherever it was. I sort of floated towards it. It only spoke once, but the sound of it held in the air, and I felt it would stay there for as long as I needed it to. The closer I got, the more I heard what it was saying. I heard the voice say, "Little girl, get up!"'

Grace looked out to the sea for a few moments, then turned her face back to Douglas and said, 'And I was back in my bed. I woke up, and I knew that I had come back from death. And, sitting on the bed holding my hand, was a man who I had never seen before yet I felt I had known all my life. It was He who was saying, "Get up". I knew He belonged to the world I had just visited. He somehow smelt the same. Curious that, don't you think? Anyway, as soon as I opened my eyes, my ma squealed with delight and came and hugged me, drenching me with her tears. My da also hugged me so hard I thought he was going to send me back up to Paradise.' She laughed, and Douglas and Dorchadas laughed with her.

'I was hungry, you know,' she said. 'I suppose dying must make you hungry!' She giggled, then added. 'He knew I was hungry because he told my parents to get me some food. Nice of him to think of something like that, wasn't it?' She adjusted her position on the fishing net, and looked out to sea.

'What a very wonderful experience,' said Douglas. He felt his comment in no way did justice to the experience Grace had just described.

'It's the right word, Douglas,' said Grace, turning back and looking at him with her mahogany eyes. 'Wonder. You know, so many humans have forgotten what it is to wonder. If you have lost your power to wonder, you are only ever going to live half a life at the most.' She bent her head a little as she looked at Douglas. 'I hope you never lose your ability to wonder, Douglas,' she said, and Douglas could see it was not just a sentiment she was expressing but a very sincere hope.

'I really hope I don't, Grace,' he said.

'It's what I brought back with me from that land. And I felt homesick for that garden for the rest of my life on earth. And I had a long life, Douglas. But it wasn't the kind of homesickness that meant I was never at home in this world. Quite the opposite in fact.' She frowned for a few moments, and fidgeted on her netting. She then looked back up at Douglas. 'When you get a glimpse of that world, you are given new eyes. The things of this world start to catch light- they remind you of the things of that garden. And you want to do all you can to make this world like that garden. That's why lots of the saints you read about got on so well with the animals. They had seen a bit of what animals can be like when they lose their fear and we lose our fear. Those stories don't surprise me at all. They don't surprise you, do they Dorch?' She looked across at Dorchadas who was listening intently to her.

'No, lass. I've had good times with lots of animals during my time as a human,' responded Dorchadas. 'I guess I take it a bit for granted now. Not been near a lion mind you, so have yet to try the mane-stroke.'

'Yes, well I look forward to hearing about that if you do meet one,' said Douglas, smiling warmly at his friend.

They were all silent for a few moments and watched the buzzing life of the busy harbour. Then Douglas said, 'Grace, tell me. When we last met, you told me about Kath. How do you know about her?'

'Ah, well... Let's just say that I see things. And that's one of the reasons I'm here - to tell you about the things I see. I've come to give you not just the gift of wonder, but the gift of hope.'

'And is there anything else you can see?' asked Douglas.

The girl smiled a winsome smile, 'You wanting me to tell you your fortune now, are you, Douglas?'

Douglas smiled back. 'I get your point, Grace. What you have told me about your experience and what you know about Kath is very special. I'll hang on to those.' He shifted his position on the increasingly hard and damp wall, then asked, 'So, what happens to you now, Grace?'

'I'm done here, I think,' she said and she rose from her fishing net seat. 'It's been nice meeting you, Douglas.'

'Yes, you too,' said Douglas as both he and Dorchadas got up from their wall.

'And you know,' added Grace, looking up at Douglas, 'because of Him, we don't need to be afraid of death. We'll feel the grief, of course. And many tears. But not fear. You are going to be a great strength to Kathleen. And you will see things. Quite brilliant things, I think. Well, I'll be on my way now.' She waggled her fingers as a wave to the two men and then skipped down the quay dancing in and out of the various ropes, buoys and other obstacles as she went.

'God's speed to you, lass,' said Dorchadas raising his arm to wave to her.

'That's quite a few now, Dorch,' said Douglas folding his arms.

'A few what, Doug?' asked Dorchadas looking quizzical.

‘A few of your bible friends that I’ve met,’ said Douglas.

‘Oh aye, a fair few, Doug. In fact, I think you now hold the record! You should become a saint at the end of this!’ Both men laughed.

‘Well, Dorch, I can’t put it off any longer. I’m going to see Kath. Are you joining me?’

Dorchadas was just about to agree when there was a ping on Douglas’ phone and, when he glanced at it, he saw it was a text from Kath. ‘It’s Kath,’ he said as he opened the message.

‘So, what does she say, Doug?’ enquired Dorchadas.

‘Well if you want it exactly as she writes it, she says, “Here u want 2 c me. Cant do 2day. Can u looj in tomz morn. Will be on then. Luv Lath xx”.’

‘Ah, I think I get the gist of that,’ said Dorchadas. ‘Well I guess that answers it for today, then,’ So the two men spent the rest of that bright April day sauntering around the town of Dingle and, at Father Pat’s insistence, Douglas joined Pat and Dorchadas for dinner at the Presbytery.

When Douglas returned to his room that evening, he decided to catch up with his journal.

Journal 1 April

Been another interesting week. Last week I was down at the beach when I bumped into a girl called Grace. Seen her around a few times in recent months. We had a nice chat. Up until then I assumed she was just a regular schoolgirl. Only it turns out she wasn’t. Far from it! She claimed to know some very disturbing news about Kath. Said Kath had cancer - in fact, she suggested it was pretty serious. Didn’t know what to make of it, and have been very disturbed about it. Couldn’t check it out with Kath cos she's been up in Adare with Peter, though is back now.

Anyway, great thing today. Dorch is back! So nice to see him again. Sounds like he's been around for a few days. So we had a good catch up and I filled him in on what we all experienced at Golgotha. He then told me his story - at Golgotha he met with Gabriel. Extraordinary. Though rather wonderful, actually. It was a sort of end of term report on his work on earth since he became a human, and I would say he got pretty much top marks. Well, that's certainly the score I would give him. But the worrying part of it is that it looks like Dorch might be summoned back to being a proper angel again soon. Rather sweet how he said he'd really prefer to remain a human now. I expect that's why he got top marks - he has given himself so fully to those of us he's helped. He's become one of us. Well, we went down to the quay (beautiful Spring day today), and who should come along but this girl Grace again. Turns out she is also a bible character - Jairus' daughter. I suppose I should have guessed when she told me her dad was called Jerry. She told me her story. Such a beautiful description of the world she visited when she died. And then Jesus called her back to this life.

I've had to think a lot about death these past couple of years or so. When I lost my faith, I got to assuming that when we die, that's it. Lights out and the door of all life firmly closed. Before that, I held the official line, of course: Jesus died and rose again so we could all get to heaven, kind of thing. And those not saved ending up in hell. But then Saoirse died and she didn't have much time for Christianity, and I couldn't bear to think of her in hell. Got even worse when Niall thought she was in purgatory because of me. Well, all that changed for me after my Golgotha experience. So, when Grace told me her story, it wasn't difficult for me to believe it.

But I'm thinking about it now. Something about the way she told her story. Something she said. She didn't say something like 'Heaven's great, you'll love it.' But more 'Heaven's great, and let its life affect how you live in this world.' That's not how she put it, but it's what I heard. She talked a lot about wonder. The purpose of any encounter we may have with heaven is to release wonder in us - that ability to see the world with awe. Funny, because when we first met she kept saying life was a dump. But she said that was just to put me off the scent, as it wasn't the time for me to guess who she was then.

But it fits with my Golgotha experience. It was the cross, not the resurrection - and yet, I could feel something like resurrection life released there. I think we all did. Must think more about that. Anyway, tomorrow Dorch and I go and visit Kath who could well be dying. Feels desperately sad to me, because her life in many ways is only just getting going. So glad Dorch will be with me.

CHAPTER 4

On the following day a grey sky replaced the bright blue of the day before. Douglas had not slept well. He was growing anxious about seeing Kath, now that he had gained further evidence that Kath was seriously sick. At breakfast he decided to say nothing about Kath to Elsie, who was busy anyway with some new arrivals to the Guest House.

After breakfast he went down to the Presbytery to collect Dorchadas and, just as he was arriving, he saw Kevin making his way also to the door.

'Kevin,' called Douglas as he arrived.

'Why there, Douglas,' said Kevin. 'It's good to see you. Has your new motor arrived yet?'

'Elsie says Jonny's delivering it tomorrow, Kev.'

'Well, be sure to bring it along to the garage so I can check it out, won't you, now?' said Kevin.

'You're a good pal, Kev,' said Douglas. Then he added, 'So what brings you to the priest's house today?'

'Well, Doug, I think you've heard that my mammy's not well.'

'Yes,' said Douglas.

'I saw Dorch last night,' said Kevin, 'and he said you were both heading up to my mother's this morning. So, if it is all the same to you, Doug, I thought I'd join you.'

'Of course,' said Douglas and, in fact, felt relieved to think of Kevin being there with them.

Dorchadas soon came to the door and the three men made their way up to Kath's Coffee Shop. It was still before the 10am opening hour when they arrived and the door was locked, so they knocked and awaited a reply. In a few moments, after much clanking of locks and some shouting of voices from inside, the door was opened and Douglas was surprised to see that they were being greeted by a tall, somewhat muscular-looking woman, who stood in the doorway staring blankly at them. For a moment, Douglas wondered if she was someone Kath had recruited to help her in the café, but then Kevin said, 'Sis, I didn't know you were here. When did you come?' He went towards her and gave her a brief hug, and she offered a limp response.

'Douglas, Dorchadas,' said Kevin turning to the two men. 'Meet my wee sister, Nancy. Nancy, meet my two great friends, Dorchadas and Douglas.'

Kevin had mentioned to Douglas that he had two sisters who used to visit him when he was in prison, but he had never said very much about them. So, at first, Douglas was surprised to suddenly be presented with one of them. She was certainly nothing like he expected her to be. He guessed her to be in her early forties. She had a similar build to her mother, but none of her warmth. Her straggly, greying dark hair fell untidily to her shoulders. She looked at the two men from behind her thick-rimmed glasses and said, 'Come in. Mam's expecting you.' Douglas gave Dorchadas a quizzical look. Dorchadas in return raised his eyebrows and shrugged his shoulders. They entered the café which was distinctly gloomy until Kath came down the stairs in a cloud of vape fumes and switched on the lights.

'Dorch and Doug, God bless you,' said Kath and warmly greeted her two friends and her son. She looked up at Dorchadas and said, 'My, Dorch. It's good to see you again. We were wondering where you had got to.'

'Aye, I'm back for a wee while now, Kath,' said Dorchadas and smiled his winsome and warm smile.

'Now, I don't think you two have met our Nancy before, have you?' said Kath, nodding at her daughter.

‘No,’ Douglas and Dorchadas both replied.

Kath looked at her daughter and said, ‘Nancy, there’s a love, go and put the kettle on, will you?' Then, looking at the visitors, she asked, 'Will it be coffee for you both?’

'Tea, please,' answered all three in unison.

'And coffee for me please, love,' said Kath. Nancy dutifully retired to the kitchen without saying a word. As usual, the sound of Country and Western music emanated from the kitchen. It appeared that Nancy shared her mother's musical tastes.

‘Sit yourselves down,’ said Kath, and the three men sat at the table. Douglas instinctively grabbed a serviette and placed it under the wobbly leg to steady the table.

'It's good to meet your daughter,' said Douglas.

‘Oh, aye,' replied Kath, attempting to reignite her vape. ‘You'll be meeting the other one soon as well. Brí is planning to come over.'

‘Over?’ said Douglas.

‘Aye,’ responded Kath. ‘Over from the States. Years ago, she met an American boy who was working in a pub in Limerick, and he took her back home with him and married her. How long ago would you say that was now, Kev?'

‘Oh, over twenty years ago now, Ma, I should say. She left soon after I came out of jail. I'm so glad that she’s coming over. It will be good to see her again.’

Kath leaned forward to Douglas and grasped his arm. ‘Nancy,’ she said in a low voice and glancing at the kitchen door. ‘She’s, you know…’ She pushed up her bottom lip and nodded.

‘Ma, she’s fine,’ said Kevin. ‘Just a bit shy, Doug.’

‘Don’t be put off by her unfriendliness, that’s all I'm saying, Doug,’ said Kath. She had to raise her voice as the music being played in the kitchen had grown noticeably louder. Kath called to the kitchen, 'You best turn Willy Nelson off, love, much as I love the man. It would help to hear ourselves think in here.'

'All right,' came the voice from the kitchen, and the song of the Country singer came to an abrupt halt.

'My two sisters sure saved my life when I was inside,' said Kevin to Douglas and Dorchadas. 'Brí was single in those days, and they both lived in Limerick at the time. They would travel up to Newry of a Friday night and stop with my da's brother, God rest his soul.'

'He was a good man, sure he was,' added Kath, as she finally managed to get some life out of her vape.

'And then they would come and visit me in the Maze on the Saturday. They would do it every month, they did. As I say, it saved my life. And you, Ma,' he added looking at Kath. 'It was harder for you with my da being ill, but you would often come as well.'

'But sorry to say, I've not been so close to my girls,' said Kath, drawing from her vape then lowering her eyes. 'It's a long story, Doug,' she said, patting Doug's arm. Looking up at him, she added, 'And you've heard enough of my woes, you surely have, you poor soul.'

Nancy entered the room backwards to part the fly curtain, then turned and lowered a tray of mugs on the table, spilling a couple of them. 'Drinks,' she said.

'You not joining us?' asked Kath, looking up at her daughter.

'Going out,' said Nancy and promptly walked to the door and left.

'Well, I look forward to getting to know the girl,' said Dorchadas.

'Aye, but that could take a lifetime, Dorch, if you know what I mean,' said Kevin. He grasped his mug from the tray and, looking at his mother, he said, 'Ma - Doug and Dorch know you are not well, and you need to tell them what's up.'

Kath slowly took her mug of coffee from the tray and placed it on the table in front of her. She breathed in slowly and looked up at Douglas and Dorchadas. She cleared her throat and said, 'Dear God,' she said smiling. 'What a lot we have gone through these past few weeks, haven't we? What with the car smash; the visit to that holy place that changed our lives; and now I've got myself ill.'

Kath took a sip of her coffee and said, 'Started smoking when I was a youngster and, as you all know, I only gave it up a few weeks back. So, it's not going to surprise you to hear that I have the cancer.'

'Oh, Kath, I'm so sorry,' said Douglas.

'Aye, lad, I know you are and this is the worst of it. I could cope with the darn thing if it was just me carrying it. But I know it's going to affect all of you one way or another, and that's what I don't like. The distress I'm causing others.' She sighed.

'So have you had the results of the test yet, Ma?' asked Kevin.

'I have son' said Kath nodding. 'The Chiropodist phoned me yesterday.'

'That would be the *Oncologist*, I think Ma,' said Kevin.

'That's the one,' said Kath. 'She phoned yesterday. It's why I sent you the text, Doug. Didn't quite feel up to seeing anyone yesterday.'

'And what did she say?' asked Kevin, leaning forward gripping his mug.

'It's bad son. There's no point in beating about the bush, so I will give it to you straight. The cancer's not just in the lungs, but has got into all kinds of places it has no right to get to.' She looked serious yet calm as she added, 'You all deserve to know the truth, so I'll tell it to you straight: I am dying. It's terminal.'

'Oh, God, no,' said Kevin and came and knelt beside his mother gripping her tightly. To Douglas, Kevin looked like a little boy as he tried to hide himself in her embrace. Kath stroked his back and added, 'Now it's not an exact science, so they tell me, so don't go digging my grave just yet. Come on, son,' she said, and Kevin got up and returned to his seat.

Douglas was very unsure of what to say but decided to try and be practical. 'So, what happens next, Kath? Will there be chemo? Radio? Can they do surgery? What are they suggesting?'

Kath took a long sip from her coffee and said, 'You know, Nancy makes surprisingly good coffee. You should have tried it. Much better than the stuff Peter makes. Anyway, to answer your question, Doug. There will be no treatment.'

'No treatment, Ma?' said Kevin, wiping his reddened eyes hard. "But...'

'No treatment, son,' said Kath firmly. 'I don't want to go down that road. I'm too far gone. Yes, they might be able to win me a few more weeks, but I'd have to go to hell and back to get those. And why should I fight for a few more weeks of life? I'm at peace now. Dorch, has Doug had a chance to fill you in on what happened to us at that deep memory place after Doug took us headlong down the hill in that motor of his?'

'Aye, that he has, Kath,' said Dorchadas.

'Well then, you'll know we were all touched with the glory there. I'll never for the life of me be able to explain where we were or what happened, but all I know is that my heart was changed so much that I am now truly at peace. Even with this news. I'm prepared. A little scared, of course. But prepared. Honest to God, that's the truth.'

'But Ma,' said Kevin reaching across the table and grasping her plump hands, 'We need you here with us. We don't want to lose you, God knows we don't.'

'I know, son. I know. But we now know that death is not the end, don't we? I can't believe it's me, Kathleen Griffin saying all this pious stuff, but I am as certain now about the afterlife as I am that I am sat here in my home talking to you three. We're all heading somewhere, and it's not all coming to a sudden halt at death's door. There's plenty beyond it, Kev. Plenty.' As Kath said this she smiled and Douglas thought she looked quite radiant. It was hard to believe she was terminally ill.

Dorchadas also reached over and grasped her hand and said, 'Well, Kath, I want you to know that I am going to be around here for a while.'

'No sudden disappearing just when we need you, Dorch?' said Kath and laughed a laugh that turned into a wheezing cough.

'No sudden disappearing, Kath,' said Dorchadas, squeezing her hand. 'And no-one knows how long any life is going to be apart from the One who has given the life in the first place.'

'Not even angels?' said Douglas, looking at Dorchadas and raising an eyebrow.

'Especially not angels, Douglas,' said Dorchadas, looking at his friend with a downturned smile.

'Well,' said Kath. 'Now that I have that piece of news out of the way, I'd like to make one or two plans.'

'Oh aye?' said Kevin, looking suspicious. 'Just what do you have in mind, Mother?'

'Well, first of all there's a bit of work to be done with your two sisters, Kev. You'll know all about this, of course. But Doug and Dorch, I'm sorry to confess, but me and my girls have not always seen eye to eye and there's a bit of mending to do.'

‘Well, Nancy has come down from Limerick to stay with you, which is a great thing, Mammy,’ said Kevin. 'Does she know what you've told us?'

'Yes, she does, son. She was here when I got the call and we had a wee walk by the sea and had a good talk. You know, we are getting on surprisingly well.'

'That's good to hear,' said Kevin.

‘And Brí,’ added Kath. ‘She called last night just when I'd got myself into bed. She's coming all the way from Philadelphia, would you believe? Should be with us in a week or two.’

‘is she coming on her own, do you know?’ asked Kevin.

‘Well, to be honest, I’m not sure who she’s with at the moment, Kev. It’s hard to keep a track. She’s been married twice. Or is it three times now?’

‘I don’t think she married the jockey, Ma,’ added Kevin.

‘Good thing, by all accounts,’ said Kath. ‘Who is she with now, then?’

'Ah… I don't think she's told you about this one, Ma, has she?' said Kevin. There was caution in his tone of voice.

'Oh aye?' said Kath looking hard at her son. 'Come on, tell me - she with a drug dealer? A guy in the porn business? You can tell me. It's hard to shock me these days, Kevin. You know that.'

'I know that, Ma,' said Kevin. 'Well, she is going to call you and tell you about it. But the fact is, she's not with a man at the moment.'

'Oh?' said Kath, reaching for a coffee mug.

'No,' said Kevin. 'She's with a woman.'

Kath was about to sip from her cup, then paused and placed the cup back on the table. The room was quiet for a few moments, then Kath looked up at Kevin and said, 'I'm so glad she's finally been brave enough to own it.'

'What do you mean, Ma?' said Kevin.

'Well, didn't you see it?' said Kath, and picked up her mug again and took a sip of her coffee. 'I saw it a long time ago. You know, that she preferred the women. I did wonder if that was the reason for all her struggles with the men. I believe they call it bilateral when you like both the men and the women'

Douglas was on the point of helping her with the correct term, when Kevin said, 'You never said anything about that, Ma. I thought you'd be shocked, I did.'

'Och, no,' said Kath, shaking her head. 'Well it's her business, isn't it? I mean, she's a grown woman of 44 years now. It's no shock to me, Kev. Might be a problem for the Pope, but not for me.'

'She was mighty worried about what you'd think, Mother,' said Kevin, leaning back in his chair and looking relieved. He was concerned that this might have been a hard bit of news for his mother to receive on top of the cancer.

'Well, why should she be worried about telling me? I am her mother, so I am,' responded Kath.

'Indeed,' said Kevin.

'Well, I don't think you can blame the girl for being worried,' said Dorchadas, who had been listening intently to the conversation. 'There's been many a grown-up child who, when they come out, have been worried sick about what their parents might say. I know your world is changing, but there are still many fears around this subject. And there's many a parent who's turned on their child because of it. I can understand the girl's caution.'

'Aye, there is indeed, Dorch,' said Kath turning to Dorch. 'And to be honest, Brí and I have… Well, you know. We've had fights in the past.'

'That's the truth,' said Kevin with conviction.

'So, what about you, angels?' said Kath, deflecting the attention from her relationship with her daughter for a moment. 'You got any lesbian angels up there?'

Dorchadas smiled and looked down at the wooden table and scratched at an old, hardened piece of cake icing for a while. He then looked up and said, 'The world of angels, Kath. I sometimes think it is so similar to the world of humans, and other times it seems so different. So, angels don't get together in the way humans do. No marrying, no sex, no children. That's the gift for humans. But it doesn't mean we are not fond of each other, because Love made us.'

'I always meant to ask, Dorch,' responded Kath. 'Do you get male and female angels then?'

'I think the simple answer to that one, Kath, is "yes and no",' replied Dorchadas. 'You could say they are male and female, but not as you know it.'

'Oh my, that's all too complicated for my little brain,' said Kath and sighed.

'No, Kath, I love your brain and the way it works,' said Dorchadas. 'It's nothing to do with the size of brain. It's to do with the world you inhabit and what's become familiar to you. But angels love the people of this world, and they are familiar with all that delights them and all that hurts them. So, they know all about the gay thing. They don't fuss themselves with all the arguments about it, though. They are always looking at the heart. They are particularly sensitive to human hurt, and in the whole area of sexuality, there has been a great deal of hurt. So, they just want to know how they can bring the healing.'

Douglas had been quiet during the conversation, as he was remembering very similar discussions with Saoirse. How she would have loved to have been here. And now she was with the angels, she would understand all this in a way he couldn't. 'Yes, there has been much hurt in this area, Dorch,' he said. 'And we must make Brí very welcome when she comes.'

'Aye, that we must,' said Kath. And then, opening her eyes wide, she said, 'Now, I have some very good news to tell you all.'

'Oh aye,' said Kevin, with a note of caution in his voice.

'Yes, son. And I hope you will all think it is good news. Can you guess what it is?'

Dorchadas smiled at her. She winked at him and said, 'You've guessed, Dorch, haven't you?'

'I have, Kath,' said Dorchadas, his smile broadening.

'I have no idea,' said Douglas, longing to discover the piece of good news.

'I can't guess,' added Kevin.

'Well, just a few days ago, when I was up in Adare, Peter proposed to me.' As she said this, she laughed in delight, and though the laughter produced a coughing fit, it did not disturb the look of pleasure on her face.

'Well, the saints be praised, Ma!' said Kevin and got up again from his seat and bent down and gave his mother a kiss on her cheek. 'Congratulations!'

'Thanks, son,' she said holding his cheek to hers for a few moments.

'Wonderful news, Kath,' said Dorchadas.

Douglas also added his congratulations, but was also conscious of the poignancy of the situation. Kath marrying her childhood sweetheart, yet only to enjoy no more than a few precious weeks together.

Kevin sat back at the table and asked, 'But Ma, forgive me being practical for a moment. It takes a while to prepare a wedding. I mean, it can take several months, and...'

'I know, son. We've thought about that. We may not have the time to plan a formal wedding. To be honest, we don't really need one. I mean, you don't want to see this fat old lady dressed in white and lace, struggling her way up an aisle, do you? No, we're not planning that sort of thing. So this is where you come in, Doug,' she said, looking at Douglas.

'I come in?' said Douglas, sitting up and raising his eyebrows. 'How?'

'Well, son. Now, you can say "no" to this as it may be awkward for you. But we thought we'd ask all the same. We don't want to get formally married, because we really need it to be soon, and to get the thing done properly and legally takes too long. So, we just thought it would be special to get some of us together and... Well, would you do something like marrying us, only not official, if you get my meaning?' She started to struggle for words and added. 'I mean, we're not asking you to do the priest thing. But, we thought if you could just say some prayers and make it something like a wedding. Well, then in the few weeks we have, we would see ourselves as married, and I'd like to think God would too. I get the feeling He'd be happy with that.'

Douglas was quite taken aback. He felt such a strong emotion rising up in him that he could hardly speak. Kath added, 'You don't need to reply now, son. I know you'll have to think about it. But I hope to God that it's not the kind of thing where you have to go getting permission from that lady bishop of yours. And by the way, I did think of asking Father Pat as well, but it would put him in an awful dilemma. I mean, between you and me, the man would marry us tomorrow as he doesn't take too much account of all that church shenanigans. But I really don't want to make life hard for him, I sure don't. I'm hoping he'll come all the same.'

It was now Douglas' turn to reach across the table and grasp Kath's hand and he said, 'Kath, I would be completely honoured to do it. Thank you so much for asking. Just say the date and time and I'll be there.'

"Och, son, you are too good to me, you surely are,' said Kath, her eyes filling up. 'But listen, I don't want any of your marriage preparation courses and all that stuff about the birds and the bees, if you get my meaning. It's a wee bit late for all of that!' She wheezed again, and all the table laughed with her.

As they laughed, the door to the café opened and an Australian voice asked, 'You open?'

'Och, yes, come in and I'll get you a coffee,' said Kath, rising from the table. Dorchadas, Douglas and Kevin supped the last of their drinks and made their way out of the café.

As they walked back, Douglas asked Kevin, 'So what's the story about your sisters, then?'

'Ah, well that could take us the rest of the day, Doug. But the brief version is that Nancy, whom you met, is on the spectrum as they say. Though she was never officially diagnosed as such. That explains her... well, I think you saw.'

'Yes, I get the picture,' said Douglas. 'But no doubt a heart of gold.'

'Aye, that's for sure,' said Kevin. 'But it's been hard for her to get the work. People don't understand her. Sadly, a good heart is not enough for some people. She's lived in Limerick for a long time as she's got friends there, but I think with Mother as she is, Nancy will be moving here now.'

'And Brí?' enquired Dorchadas.

Kevin chuckled. 'Yes, well Bríana was beautiful, wild and free. She took her father's death very badly and then got hooked up with lots of people that did her no good. But I think the love she has now found with her woman, may well settle her. I hope so. Anyway, if you gents will excuse me, I have to be getting back to the garage. See you at the Good Friday service tomorrow?'

'Yes,' Dorchadas and Douglas replied.

'I'll walk with you to St.Raphael's' said Dorchadas to Douglas. 'Kath's taken the news well, hasn't she?' he added.

'Yes, really well,' said Douglas. 'We've got a tough few weeks ahead of us, though, Dorch.'

'Aye, we have,' said Dorchadas. 'And you've got your friends coming over soon, have you not?'

'Yes, I have,' said Douglas. 'They'll be here next month. Mavis and Alice from Sheffield, and Daisy and Franklin from the US. I'm looking forward to you meeting them, Dorch.'

'It will be very good to meet them,' said Dorchadas. As he strolled back to the Presbytery, he thought about the name *Alice*. He remembered being sent to an Alice once in France. It was one of the pieces of work for which Gabriel had particularly commended him. When he reached the door of the presbytery he spent some moments brushing his feet on the mat. 'Could it be?' he asked himself as he worked at a particularly stubborn piece of mud on his boot. 'I wonder,' he said, as he placed the key in the lock and entered the house.

CHAPTER 5

It was Alice's last night in her home town of Bideford and she was in her bedroom packing her case. Generally, it had been a good few days with her mother and they had managed not to annoy each other too much, apart from the argument about the bike ride to Morwenstow. She paused her packing as she reflected on that beautiful, breezy bike ride and the afternoon she had spent on the headland. It had done her so much good. She would be sorry to leave her beloved West Country, but she needed to get back to Sheffield for her interview. She put down the jumper she was folding and went over to the window and opened it, welcoming the cool, Spring air. She closed her eyes and breathed in. Her nose was always quick to report that the tide was low. That unique, muddy reek of the estuarine river at low tide.

For millennia the River Torridge had snaked its way through the town. She once even tried to wade across it at low tide, but when the water got to her shoulders she turned back. She always wished she had persevered, as her friends did. As they splashed and swam their way to the other side, they turned to Alice and mocked her for her cowardice. And yet she knew it wasn't cowardice that stopped her. It was the threat of another rebuke from her mother. It wasn't so much the smack on the bottom that hurt, it was the look on her father's face. It was as if he was taking the hurt for her. Such vivid memories.

She opened her eyes. How often, as a child, she would kneel on her bed and gaze out of this window. She could see the Long Bridge from the window. She would often count all twenty-four of the arches, each of a different size. Most of all, she loved coming to the window in the early evening to watch the starlings. Sometimes a great murmuration would swirl over the town, and she would shout downstairs to her father, who would rush upstairs to sit beside her and together they would marvel at the glorious dark shape-shifting cloud of winged life, before it dispersed and the birds gathered under the arches to roost for the night.

'You all packed, then?' said her mother as she came into the bedroom.

'I am,' said Alice, closing the window.

'I don't know why you can't stay a few more days with your old mother. You know I need you here, Alice,' said her mother, as she sat on the bed.

'No, you don't, Mum,' said Alice, sitting down next to her.

'I do,' said her mother, inching a little further away from her daughter and looking out of the window. 'You know my heart's not been good. And my leg, Alice. It's been really playing up these past few days. You've seen the way I limp now, haven't you?'

'Mum, you are not even seventy yet. You are perfectly fit. You've had your heart checked and there's nothing wrong with it. And we went to the doctor about your leg, and she is convinced that you've pulled a muscle. That's all it is.'

'It's a bloody sight worse than a pulled muscle, Alice. It's hell trying to get up and down these hills. No, you mark my words. There's something going on in this leg that's not right. Not right at all.'

Alice sighed, for she knew there was nothing she could do to reassure her mother. 'Mum, you know I have to go back tomorrow. I've got the interview on Friday.'

Her mother sighed. 'Well, it's not right that they are interviewing you on Good Friday. When I was your age, everywhere was shut on Good Friday out of respect. Things were done properly in those days.' She furrowed her brow and sighed a long sigh. 'I suppose if you get the job, that's you up in Sheffield permanently then. Living with that sister-in-law of mine for a good many years, I dare say.'

'You like Mavis, Mum,' said Alice, drawing a lock of her unruly hair away from her glasses.

'She's all right,' said her mother. 'Your father and Mavis were so close, weren't they?'

'Yes,' agreed Alice. 'There can't have been many brothers and sisters as close as they were.'

'Hit her hard when your father died.' Alice noticed the way her mother pulled her cardigan tighter around her. There was always some little act of comfort whenever she mentioned her bereavement.

'Hit us all hard, Mum,' said Alice, and took her mother's hand.

'It did, love,' said her mother. 'Long time ago now, though.' She exhaled sharply and pursed her lips. 'Anyway, what I really came up to say is that supper is in ten minutes. Bit earlier because I want *Midsomer Murders* tonight. I'm not missing it this time.'

'I know you love it, Mum. I'll be down in time.'

Alice never cared much for murder mysteries, so after supper she came back up to her room and, for a time, browsed the bookshelf that was stuffed with books, many of which had been there since her childhood. There was one she loved - a children's book on Egypt - and she pulled it off the shelf. She put on her pyjamas and curled up on her bed and opened it. It was years since she had looked at it. Perhaps it was the pictures of the vast pyramids and ancient temples that influenced her dream that night. But also into the mix, there were those frequent, intruding thoughts about the grieving English priest in Ireland. Or maybe it was the mysterious Spirit of God, so admired and loved by those early Celtic saints, that had a hand in her dream. Or was it her favourite, Morwenna, calling from the land beyond the horizon of death? Whatever it was that provoked the dream, it was one that felt full of significance. It was one of those that did not flee at first light. Nor was it one that was so obscure as to be hard to understand. No, it was a night-time dream that was as clear as day. And it was one that, far from fleeing with the dawn, pinned itself to the forefront of Alice's waking mind, so she could not avoid its presence, nor its clear message.

Alice could not say quite when the dream arrived during that night. But at some point, when the town was hushed and the starlings were safely tucked in under their arches and the reflection of the moon was rippling on the Torridge, Alice's mind slipped into the domain of dreams. Here was a world where her eyesight was strong and she could see with great clarity. It was an eyesight for use in the realm of the imagination. At first there were one or two dreams that were located back in Marseilles. Not the bad dreams that were once so troubling. But gentle dreams of drinking coffee in side streets and even one of Georges - sober yet restless, searching for something. They were coherent dreams, yet carried no weight.

Then there was the dream that carried considerable weight. She found herself in a night-time scene. It was dark - beautifully dark. The dark beloved of astronomers. Perhaps it was somewhere on Exmoor. The briny air that was coming in off the sea was mild. She felt it as a caress. Above her the stars and planets shone with an ecstatic brilliance. She had her telescope with her, and, peering through it, found her favourite Jupiter. She was delighted to see its four Galilean moons spinning around their planet. She saw them in such detail. As she admired these moons she felt a tap on her shoulder and, drawing her eye away from the spectacle in the sky, she saw a young woman standing next to her. She knew immediately that it was Morwenna, the girl who had come from Ireland on a leaf. Alice wept at the sight of her. She had yearned to meet her for so long. The two hugged one another like long-lost sisters. They spoke with one another for a long time, and danced together on the moor under the kindly light of the moon. It was a slow, lilting, dance. Alice knew they were telling each other stories of their lives through the dance movements.

As the dance slowed, Alice realised with glee that she was no longer on Earth, but was on one of the moons around Jupiter. She was sure it was Callisto, her favourite. Morwenna led her to a huge telescope that was mounted in the base of one of the many craters, and Alice peered through its lens which had been set to view her own planet, Earth. The scope scanned her world until it found a desert area, and there it focussed on the unmistakable shapes of the great Pyramids of Giza. As she was looking at this beautiful sight, Morwenna spoke to her. These were the only words of Morwenna that she remembered the next morning. She said, 'Alice, you must travel with him to this land. It is for healing and for destiny.' Alice then realised that both she and Morwenna were standing on an Egyptian street corner. Across the road from them there was a car, the front of which was badly damaged. There was a group of women standing beside it, looking dazed. She walked up to the car and peered inside and saw in the passenger seat a young, dark-haired woman who seemed to be fast asleep. When Alice saw the bright red blood oozing from the side of the head, she knew just who it was, and she felt a terrible sadness. She then left the dream and returned to a quiet sleep.

When a ray of sun stroked the blonde curls of her hair in the morning, waking her from sleep, the dream was still vivid in her mind. But it was not a sense of sadness that lay in her soul, but a strong sense of hope. And the words of Morwenna were resonating in her mind like a prophetic call from the deep. It was hard to concentrate on the conversation with her mother at breakfast, because the dream was still so loud. It remained with her on the train all the way to Sheffield, and in the taxi to her Aunt's home. It would not leave her and she knew it would stubbornly remain there until she did something about it.

*

It was Good Friday and Douglas was in his room reading through his journal. For him, and those who had been part of the Golgotha deep memory experience, this Good Friday held a significance and meaning that transcended anything they had experienced on previous Good Fridays over the years. At noon, he would be joining Dorchadas, Kath and Kevin at the three-hour vigil led by Father Pat. He was looking forward to it. He was sitting at his desk watching the April clouds skid swiftly over the harbour on their journey East.

His phone started to ring and he saw that Alice Fournier was calling him. She had not called him before and his first thought was that something had happened to Mavis, so he answered it quickly.'

'It's Alice,' said the West Country voice.

'Hello, Alice. Is all well?' asked Douglas.

'Yes, I think so,' said Alice with some vagueness. 'Should I only ring you when things aren't well?' she asked with a slight tone of mischief in her voice.

'No... of course,' said Douglas. 'It's just... Well, you've not called before, and I was worried that it might mean that Mavis wasn't well.'

'Oh, no,' said Alice, and he could tell she was smiling, 'No, my aunt is just fine. I'm just back from a few days in Bideford with my mum.'

'Oh, nice,' said Douglas, not entirely certain that being with her mother was a nice experience or not.

'Yes, not bad this time,' said Alice with candour.

'So, you must be phoning me about your trip here next month,' ventured Douglas.

'No. Wrong again, actually Douglas.'

Douglas could hear the smile broadening. He said, 'OK, so I guess it's the bishop who has come on her knees to Mavis begging her to persuade me to return.'

'Oh, you heard?' said Alice, and her smile migrated to a chuckle.

'Ah, sorry to disappoint her,' said Douglas. 'Well, thanks for telling me,' and he pretended to start signing off.

'No, I'm not phoning about any of that stuff, Douglas. Now, are you sitting down?'

'Yes, I am actually. I am even more intrigued now!' Douglas was curious indeed.

'I have a suggestion to put to you, Douglas. I know you will think me totally barmy now, but I shall say it anyway. I'd like to go to Cairo for a few days. And I'd like to go with you.'

Douglas was indeed completely taken aback. For a few moments he really did not know what to say and so he was silent for a few moments.

'You still there?'

'Yes, Alice. I am. I could have sworn you said you wanted to go with me to Cairo.'

'I did.'

Douglas now stood up and started walking around his room. 'Alice,' he said, trying to gather his mind into some coherence. 'It's a lovely idea...'

'Is Cairo lovely?' asked Alice.

Douglas sighed. He needed to be honest. 'Not to me, actually Alice. I'm not sure if I told you...'

'You did, Douglas. You told me about the shooting. It's why we need to go.' Her voice sounded calm, as if she had really reasoned this out carefully.

'Alice,' said Douglas, struggling. 'I am really not sure what to say. I feel much is resolved in me about my wife's death, but I am not sure I want to go anywhere that could dig up all that pain again. I'm feeling settled now. I know you are really kind, and...'

'No, it's not because I'm kind, Douglas,' she said. 'It's because I've been told we must do it.'

'Been told? By God?' Douglas felt he could ask Alice this question, because he instinctively felt that she was probably one of the few in this world who could really hear the voice of God quite clearly.

'Sort of,' said Alice. 'Actually, it was Morwenna,' answered Alice.

'Morwenna?' said Douglas, completely mystified. 'Don't think I know her.'

'No. She's a saint. She came to me in a dream.'

'Dorch will like this,' thought Douglas to himself.

'It's all right,' said Alice, who was starting to feel bad that she was disturbing her new friend. 'Maybe it was just a dream. It's just that it felt so... so real, if you know what I mean. I felt I had to at least check it out with you.'

Douglas stopped pacing his room and returned to his seat. He liked the way Alice was not making huge claims of divine authority about the dream. In fact, he was rather surprising himself at starting to take to the idea.'

'Um... When were you thinking of going, Alice?' he asked.

'Next week,' said Alice calmly.

'Next week!' said Douglas. 'So soon?'

'Why not. You got a passport?'

'Er, yes. But what about injections or visas and all that stuff.'

'Checked all that and its OK. Also checked flights. You'd need to come over here first and then there's a good deal going on a flight from Manchester Airport. I've also checked an Airbnb in Cairo. It's a fab one near the Pyramids. It's all right, Douglas. Two bedrooms! Just to assure you this is not a subtle trap to lure you into my bed.' She laughed.

'Most reassuring,' Douglas replied, also laughing. 'But I don't quite get the purpose of the trip.'

'Well, to be truthful, I'm not entirely sure. But the words I was given, Douglas were these: "It is for healing and for destiny."' As she said it, Douglas not only *heard* the words, but *felt* them.

'Alice, are you thinking we should go to... you know, the site of the accident.'

'Yes, Douglas. That is what I am thinking. How does that feel to you?'

'Very disturbing,' said Douglas, and he felt an old fear resurface in his chest. And yet he continued, 'But that does not mean it's wrong. Will you give me today to think about it? I'm going to the three-hour service soon and I can give it thought there.'

'Three hours in church?' said Alice, not disguising her shock at the thought.

'It's traditional on Good Friday. Sometime I'll tell you why it's so important to me this year.'

'Well, that's taken care of our conversation subject on the flight over, then,' said Alice. 'Look, it's not a big deal, this. If you don't think this is right, that's fine. I'll just put the dream down to the stress of being with my mother for five days.'

'Yes, I think I'd be having nightmares if I was with mine for that length of time,' said Douglas.

Alice chuckled. 'Anyway, it's nice to hear you. Oh, by the way, I've got an interview this afternoon.'

'Oh? What for?' enquired Douglas.

'I work voluntarily for this charity that does resources for the visually impaired?' She spoke her statement as a question.

'Oh yes, you did tell me that,' said Douglas.

'Well, they like what I do and they want to employ me to be their Development Manager. The job starts in the summer.'

'Wow. Sounds impressive.'

'Oh, it's very impressive, Douglas,' she said and giggled. 'Actually, it did surprise me when they asked me to apply. But there are several interviewees, so I don't know what my chances are. But perhaps you could have a word with Him, when you are in church this afternoon.'

'Yes, of course, Alice.'

'OK. Let me know what you think about Cairo. Love you,' said Alice.

'Thanks, Alice. I'll be back in touch soon.' The phone went dead, and Douglas carefully placed his phone on the desk and sat down. He ran his fingers through his thick yet greying hair.

He sighed a long sigh. 'Well, Romer,' he said to himself. 'Are you up for this? Are you up to seeing the very place where she was shot? Are you up to going on holiday with a woman you hardly know and facing all the wild speculations of your friends?' He carried on brushing his hands through his hair, releasing his sense of nervousness. 'And more to the point, Romer, are you prepared to acknowledge that you enjoyed the sound of her voice and you rather like the thought of a few days on your own with her?'

He brought his hands down on his desk with a thump. 'I don't know' he replied to himself. 'Back to my usual default these days: if in doubt, ask Dorchadas.' He smiled as he said it, for he was thinking about how next month Alice would get to meet Dorchadas when she came over with Mavis. He somehow sensed they would get on very well.

CHAPTER 6

Dorchadas, Douglas, Kath and Kevin settled in a pew for the three-hour Good Friday service. It was the first time they had sat together in the church since that fateful day in January, which saw them escaping from the church (not with dignity in Kath's case) and being involved in a high-speed car chase that ended in the pile-up and the extraordinary visit to the very place where the events of the original Good Friday took place. For each one of them, the service was a reminder of what they had experienced that day: Dorchadas was again back in the company of Gabriel hearing those comforting words of affirmation; Kath was with Mary Magdalene and Brigid of Kildare and felt afresh the gaze of Love, and in those moments she forgot her fears about her health and mortality; Kevin saw again the young woman with crimson on her hands, and felt the liberating power of forgiveness; and Douglas experienced a renewed conviction that his grief was being carried by the One on the cross, and it felt no longer like a suffocating shroud around his soul. And he felt afresh the hand of Saoirse lightly touch his shoulder. He sensed her beckoning him on into new life.

Father Pat led the service in his usual tender way and, though there were about fifty faithful souls in the church that afternoon, his attention was mostly drawn to his four dear friends, whose experience at Golgotha was one he would admire and envy all his days. He could not deny that envy was stronger than admiration. How he would so love to have even a tiny taste of their experience - it would so help those dark days when he, the priest who pastored the parish, had to confess the inner darkness that assailed his soul, and the frightening doubts that taunted him so fiercely. But at least on this Good Friday, after hearing the extraordinary testimony of his friends, he felt a new conviction about the meaning of the death of the young man from Galilee strung up on the wooden cross outside the city walls.

What was harder to believe was what happened next: the whole business of the resurrection. That is, the business of the tortured body of Christ springing back to life only two days after its death. Of course, officially he believed the creed. But in his heart, it was a very different matter. Why was resurrection so hard for him to believe? Why did he have to be such a doubting Thomas? Why could he not be a genuine beacon of hope on Easter morning, when the faithful would return to celebrate the triumphant rising from the grave of the man on the cross? Once again, he would do his best to proclaim the good news, even if his heart was never quite in it. But how would God look upon him on the day of judgement? What would he make of such a faithless heart? Such thoughts always came to trouble Pat's soul during the Good Friday three-hour vigil. It always made it an ordeal for him. Maybe that suffering of his soul was as good as penance. Maybe that would look good on his otherwise very mediocre record. He took some comfort from the thought.

In recent years, towards the end of the third hour of this annual service, his rather depressing train of thought would lead to consideration of his retirement. After the final reading, following which there was a twenty-minute silence, almost with comforting regularity, he would start rehearsing in his mind the letter to the bishop. He would be honest, of course. Thank God there was no scandal - no woman involved. Or no man for that matter. No, it would not shake or shock the establishment. Just a priest losing his way in old age. It happened and the bishop could sort it quite easily. His pension would be adequate - he had checked recently. Yes, maybe this was the year. It really was time to get the wretched letter done.

But then someone knocked a hymnbook off their pew that created an almighty crash that resounded around the silent church, waking all from their thoughts and a few from their slumbers. For Pat, it had the effect of shocking his soul out of its rather miserable thoughts in a way that quite took him aback. The sound was a hymnbook smacking against a cold, tiled floor, and yet to Pat, it reminded him of the sound of a wave crashing against the hull of a small boat. It was a sound that used to thrill him when he was a youngster in the days when his father would take him out to sea. His mind now led him out of the church to the thrilling surf of the sea. He was heading for an island and he knew exactly which island. It was an island he had not visited for nearly sixty years. Several times had his father taken him there as a child. A local fisherman bundled he and his father into the old creaking boat that smelt of fish and diesel and took them out to Illauntannig - the island of the great St.Seannach.

Father Pat was sitting at the front of the church, as still as a standing stone. His eyes were closed, but his imagination was now very open. Energised by his memories, his spirit was on the move. He remembered so clearly the exciting trip from mainland to island, then clambering over the side of the boat, often waist deep, into the waters of the island's bay. He recalled wading ashore against the pull of the waves and sprinting over the sand and the rocks, with his father calling and laughing behind him. Then up over the stones to explore the ancient ruins. His father would sometimes rest on the beach while Pat would run over the tufty grass and inspect the ancient dark-stoned ruins built by Seannach and his friends. And here - yes, here, in these hallowed ruins, with the squally, Atlantic breeze in his face, and the sound of the crying gulls in his ears, he felt touched by Life. Surely that was resurrection life! Something in his childish soul felt so utterly alive in this place. It was an aliveness of light alongside which any death would lose its power to darken. It was such a precious memory. Oh, to be a child again! But he grew up. And Easter faith died with his childhood.

There was a touch on his arm and he woke abruptly from his thoughts. It was the voice of Elsie saying, 'Father... It's time for the final hymn.' She assumed that the priest had nodded off and failed to be awoken by the clock chiming three. Pat rose quickly to his feet, announced the hymn and Oonagh, the organist, launched the congregation into their final song of worship. Throughout the hymn, Pat's mind was on the little island, and several in the congregation noticed the disconcerting sight of their parish priest breaking out into several of his swift smiles during the singing of a sober Good Friday hymn.

Pat greeted the quiet worshippers as they left church. Dorchadas and the others were among the last to leave the church, and as they emerged into the Spring sunshine, Pat grasped Dorchadas' arm and said, 'Now tell me, Dorch, what are you all doing on Easter Day?'

Dorchadas looked at the others and said, 'Well, I for one have no plans as it happens. What about all of you?'

'Well, Peter will be down,' said Kath. 'And Nancy and me will be getting the room ready for Brí. But apart from that, nothing's happening.' And Douglas and Kevin also acknowledged that they had no plans.

'Well, now,' said Pat, his bright eyes gleaming behind his spectacles. 'I have a plan. Would you drive with me to the other side of the peninsula because I have an island I want us to visit. I've got a friend there who can take us over in a boat, so long as it's not too rough. What say you? After mass. We could take a picnic, could we not?'

Everyone looked a little perplexed by the unusual look of childish excitement in the priest. 'Well, we will need more than one car,' said Douglas. 'And Elsie's nephew is bringing me a new motor tomorrow afternoon, so it would give me a chance to try it out.'

'Oh dear...' said Dorchadas and winked.

'She assures me that it will be perfectly sound, Dorch,' said Douglas. 'And, as far as I know, there is not likely to be any black ice on the road on Sunday.' Dorchadas chuckled.

'Kath?' said Pat. 'Can I take it that you, Peter and Nancy will all come?' Kath had not yet had a chance to inform Pat of her illness, and Kevin looked anxiously at her. But she was determined not to let the current cough and general pain in her ribs rob her of an adventure, so she quickly replied, 'Of course, Pat. I'm sure they'd love to join us. Why wouldn't they?'

'Then we have a plan!' said Pat.

'And Elsie,' said Kath. 'Don't forget Elsie - she'll be wanting to see the island, sure she will. She's not one to miss an island.'

'We'd better get a coach!' said Kevin.

'Grand, grand,' said Pat, rubbing his hands together in delight. 'Well, Kevin could we use your car? And yours, Douglas? Yes, that should be fine. Straight after mass, then. Straight after mass. That would be grand.'

'And the picnic?' said Kath, being typically practical. 'My sister...'

'Oh, no worries about that,' interrupted Pat. 'I'll be having a word with Mrs McGarrigle.'

'Ah well, no fear of any of us getting hungry then,' said Douglas.

'Grand, grand,' said Pat again. 'I'll be seeing you Sunday then,' and he sped off back to the Presbytery, still muttering 'Grand' to himself.

'Is the man all right in the head, Dorch?' asked Kath, looking up at Dorchadas. 'I mean, I'm no expert on this kind of thing, but you wouldn't normally expect to see priests all excited like that on a Good Friday, would you?'

'Well, yes, as far as I know, his head is fine, Kath' said Dorchadas. 'Though the man sure feels a little animated about something.' They all agreed that Pat was displaying unusual and slightly disturbing symptoms of excitement. But they also agreed that a fun trip to an island on Sunday afternoon was not an idea that should be turned down.

They were all about to part, when Douglas said, 'Dorch, Kev. Could we just grab a coffee? I have something I want to check with you both.'

'Sure thing,' said Kevin. 'I'm not working today, so have plenty of time. Come back to mine.' So, the three men made their way back to Kevin's home.

*

Kevin's house was a small former fisherman's cottage situated next to his garage. Both Dorchadas and Douglas had to stoop to enter the home that both of them had come to know well, as they often called in for a drink with him after he closed up his garage for the night. They entered the small kitchen and sat at the much-stained wooden kitchen table in the middle of the room. Kevin opened a door of the elderly Aga which released a welcome burst of heat into the room. He cleared the table of several engine parts, newspapers and a breakfast bowl and mug. He was pleased with the opportunity to talk with his friends about his mother's cancer and, as he prepared the coffee, he talked about how he had noticed the signs of her ill-health developing over recent weeks. Together they discussed the various options for alleviating pain and making life tolerable for her for as long as possible.

'But, Kev. How are you feeling about it all?' asked Dorchadas when Kevin passed him a steaming cup of coffee.

'Aye, well, Dorch, you know. I mean, I had hoped... But my ma was clear, was she not? The cancer's going to kill her and we have to accept it.' Kevin sat down at the end of the table.

'She was clear. Typically honest,' said Douglas reaching for the packet of digestive biscuits that Kevin had put on the table.

'Oh, aye. Always been honest has my mother,' said Kevin. 'But you know, lads, of course I am hurting desperately about the thought of losing her. But... Well, we have seen something, haven't we? We've seen beyond. I mean, it doesn't make the hurting any the easier, but we have the hope now, don't we?'

Dorchadas smiled and placed his hand on Kevin's arm. 'I can see that hope in you, Kevin. It's got lodged in your guts and it looks strong to me.'

Kevin sipped from his cup and leaned back in his seat and looked at Dorchadas. 'Dorch, I do see now that you are... you know, from the Other Side, so to speak. I mean, I'm not up on all this and haven't read my bible as much as I should have, but could you tell me, what happens after folks leave this world and pass over?'

Douglas thought back at the conversation with Grace that he had enjoyed just a few days back. Dorchadas looked down at his mug and pushed his bottom lip forward for a while. He then looked up at Kevin and said, 'Kevin, have you ever been homesick?'

'Yes,' said Kevin with conviction. 'Yes, I have, Dorch. When I was in the Maze, I was homesick something dreadful. Just the little things that we take so much for granted - how I longed for them.'

'What did homesickness feel like?' asked Dorchadas.

Kevin looked up at the ceiling for a while and said, 'Huge sadness. Pain - almost physical in my chest. Fear of forgetting the places and people I loved. Fear of beginning to think that the prison was my only world, and that this was it for life now. Fear that in that prison I would become a different person, not the free person I could be in my own home and in my home town, but a different man, tuned to the violent and sad world of prison.'

'So, let me get this right,' said Dorchadas, leaning forward at the table and cradling the warm mug in his hands. 'When you were in that prison, you longed for home. You began to worry that the prison would become too familiar - that after a while you would come to believe that it was the only world for you.'

'Aye, that sums it up well, Dorch,' said Kevin nodding.

'And you worried that once you believed that the prison was your only world, and you forgot about your home, you would be a different person.'

'Yes, that's the truth. I could become what the prison would make me. I would live a much smaller life.'

'And yet, Kevin, it was in prison that you found a freedom for your soul.'

'Well now that's the truth, Dorch. You are right there,' said Kevin agreeing.

'So, if I take that as a picture of this world,' said Dorchadas. 'You could say that this world is the equivalent of your life in prison. And yet your soul longs to be somewhere else where you know you can be truly yourself and fully free.'

'So you mean, here in this life we get homesick for heaven?' said Kevin, furrowing his brow and putting his hand behind his head.

'That's part of it, Kev,' said Dorchadas. 'But this world doesn't have to be a prison. I mean in your prison, Kev - well, that's where you got a taste for freedom in your spirit. So, you see, here on Earth, it is not a prison exactly. Not at all. But compared to what is to come, it is, shall we say, confined. And if you lived your life as if this world was all that there is, then you would live a confined life. It would be limited. And yet, all through the ages, the people of this world have caught the scent of their true home in heaven, and they are homesick for it. Longing for that home doesn't make this world worse. Quite the reverse actually.'

'So my mother... We need to pray that she catches the scent?' asked Kevin.

'I think she already has a good nose for it, if you ask me,' replied Dorchadas. 'But the fragrance will get stronger, the closer she gets.'

'Still not sure what everyone gets up to when they get there, though,' said Kevin, maintaining his frown.

'You won't be mending cars, that's for sure,' said Dorchadas with a smile. 'But you will be all that you were created to be, because you will be fully at home in the place. You will have no fears, Kev. You will only know love. Can you imagine how you would be if you feared nothing and knew you were utterly loved?'

The conversation about heaven and Kath's health continued for a while, and for most of the time Douglas was silent, which prompted Kevin to pat Douglas on the arm and say, 'So, Douglas, how come you're so quiet?'

'Oh, I love this conversation, Kev, 'said Douglas. 'And I must admit in recent weeks I have completely revised my view of heaven. No, I'm sorry to be quiet, but I'm a bit distracted by a phone call I had this morning.'

Kevin frowned and said, 'Oh aye? Not bad news, I hope?'

'No, not bad news. But rather strange news.'

'Strange?' said Dorchadas raising one of his bushy eyebrows.

'I have a friend in England called Alice,' started Douglas.

'Ah, I know' said Dorchadas. 'Your friend Mavis' niece.'

'That's the one, Dorch,' said Douglas. 'You met her briefly when she was over in the autumn, Kev.' Kevin nodded thoughtfully.

'Well, I hardly know the woman,' continued Douglas, 'but she phoned me this morning to tell me she had a dream last night and um... Well, in the dream a Celtic saint... I forget her name - a female saint - she told Alice that she and I were to hive off to Cairo, would you believe?'

'Cairo!' said Kevin with a start. 'That would have taken you by surprise, I'm sure, Doug.'

'Yes, it certainly did, Kev. Pretty weird isn't it? And she wants us to go next week. Well, of course, the first thing I thought of was my Saoirse who was killed there. And I'm far from sure I want to go and see the very street where she was shot. Which, I think is what Alice is thinking of.'

'What was the name of the saint, Doug. Can you remember?' asked Dorchadas.

'Mor-something?' said Douglas frowning and looking up.

'Would it be Morwenna?' asked Dorchadas.

'That's the one. I suppose you are the best of friends with her, Dorch?' said Douglas.

'No, as it happens, I never met the girl,' answered Dorchadas. 'But I do know of her. From Ireland she was, and did a grand job in the land you now call Cornwall. A much-admired lady by all accounts.'

'Hm...' said Douglas, looking thoughtful. 'Well, I don't doubt Alice at all. She's a very genuine person. She's partially sighted, as it happens, but has amazing sight in other ways. It's the kind of seeing that I have learned to trust.'

'Oh, I've met many of those,' said Dorchadas.

'So, Doug. Doesn't sound like a bad gig to me. Egypt would be a grand place to visit. So, what's the risk?' asked Kevin.

'Well the risk is, Kevin, that I'll be going on a wild goose chase over to Egypt, head off to the street where my Saoirse was shot, and all the peace I've finally gathered in recent weeks about her death will be shattered, and I will be back in that hell-hole of despair again. There's a fair bit to lose in this.' Douglas sighed and pursed his lips for a time and then added, 'And yet, I also sense there is a fair bit to gain.'

'Do you trust this Alice?' asked Dorchadas. He was feeling this was not the time to check out if this Alice was the same person as the Alice he once met in Marseilles. But if it was the same one, he knew Douglas could trust her.

'Actually, Dorch, I do,' said Douglas, surprising himself by the assurance in his voice.

'Then I think you have your answer, Doug. You've taken quite a few risks in the last weeks, and they've all done you good,' said Dorchadas.

'And Doug,' said Kevin, leaning forward to Douglas. 'Tell me. Is this Alice pretty?'

'I thought you might ask that, Kevin,' said Douglas. 'And to be honest, it is the first thing everyone will think. "Douglas has a new woman," they will all say. And before you know it, they will be planning my wedding. I'm still not ready for that.'

'Doug, son,' said Dorchadas, 'Are you really going to let that put you off? I mean, not doing something important for fear of what people might think, is hardly a good reason for not doing it, is it?'

'Well, it's put me off plenty of times in my life before now, Dorch,' said Douglas, who, until he had met Saoirse, had always been concerned about what people thought of him. 'But Saoirse helped me so much with that. I was far less afraid when I was with her.'

'It's one of the gifts she gave you, Doug,' said Dorchadas. 'And what do you think she would want?'

Douglas sat very still for a long time, staring at the table. He then blinked several times and looked up at his two friends who noticed the watery edges of his eyes. He said, 'At Golgotha - you know, when we were there - she spoke to me... I didn't say anything at Father Pat's because I wasn't ready to share it with anyone then. But I think I can tell you both. There's few people I trust as much as you two.' He looked up at each of his friends and the looks on their faces assured him of this trust. 'She said, "There is plenty of room in your heart for another, for He has expanded your heart more than you will ever understand. There is another. Do not be afraid. She is not far from you. I bless her." I remember all those words so clearly. It's like she gave me permission to.... you know, find someone else.'

'So did she say the girl's name was Alice?' asked Kevin.

Douglas smiled at him and said, 'I guess that would have made it simple, Kev. But no, she gave no names. But, I have to admit that when she said this, it was Alice who was in my mind.'

'Well then, son,' said Kevin smiling broadly, and he reached out and patted Douglas on the shoulder.

'These things are very tender,' said Dorchadas, noticing how vulnerable Douglas looked as he was sharing this news with his friends.

Kevin turned and looked at Dorchadas and said, 'So you been in love, then, Dorch?'

Dorchadas looked down at his empty coffee mug and both men noticed a look of great sadness on the face of their angel friend. Dorchadas looked up at Kevin and said, 'Yes, Kevin. Yes, I have, as it happens.' He looked back down at the table again and played with the handle of his mug for a few moments, then added, 'Only once. On one of my first visits to Earth as a human actually. Several centuries back from this one. I knew it wasn't possible. How could I open the heart of a woman to me, only to leave her when I was called away? I knew it was not possible for me to settle in this world, and so I could never rest my soul in another heart or allow that heart to settle in me. But I was sent here as fully human. And, as a human being, I did experience this kind of sweet love.'

Dorchadas paused for a few moments. Then, looking at Douglas said, 'You'll know these words, Doug: "Let me not to the marriage of true minds, Admit impediments..." I lived that sonnet of Shakespeare's for a time, I surely did.'

Douglas smiled and leaned forward towards Dorchadas and quoted the next line from the sonnet he also knew and loved, '"Love is not love Which alters when it alteration finds, Or bends with the remover to remove:"'

'"O no;"' Dorchadas continued, smiling at Douglas, '"it is an ever-fixed mark, That looks on tempests, and is never shaken;"' He shook his head with conviction as he spoke the lines. '"It is the star to every wandering bark, Whose worth's unknown, although his height be taken."'

'"Love's not Time's fool,"' said Douglas, fixing his eyes on Dorchadas, '"though rosy lips and cheeks Within his bending sickle's compass come;"' Douglas paused for a moment and then raised an eyebrow and asked, 'Were the lips and cheeks rosy, Dorch?'

'That they were, Doug. That they were indeed,' said Dorchadas wistfully. Then added, '"Love alters not with its brief hours and weeks, But bears it out even..."' Here Dorchadas' voice cracked, and he wiped his eyes briefly, then continued, '"But bears it out even to the edge of doom."'

'"If this be error and upon me proved,"' quoted Douglas.

And both men, said in unison, '"I never writ, nor no man ever loved."'

The room was quiet for a few moments, then Kevin said, 'Honest to God, I have no idea what you two are talking about, but there's no doubt in my mind that you've both had a strong taste of love in your lives. Sounds like it turned you into mindless eejits for a time!'

They all laughed, then Douglas said, 'It's Shakespeare, Kev. It's his sonnet number 116.'

'Dear God he wrote enough, didn't he?' said Kevin.

'That he certainly did,' said Douglas. 'And you, Kev. What about you? You been in love?'

'Ah well, Doug, I've not been lucky in that respect,' replied Kevin leaning back in his chair and folding his arms. 'There were plenty of girls in my earlier life, and I'm ashamed to say I did not treat them well. Not well at all. But there was one wee girl I really did love - and she had the rosy lips and cheeks your man Shakespeare speaks of, sure to God she had. So beautiful, she was. But she couldn't take the violent world I was in at the time, and I don't blame her. But I swear, lads, my heart broke in two the day we ended it. It was a terrible pain, it was. I so hope it wasn't hard for her, but she did love me and I fear she was as sore as I was. I often wondered what became of her. I hope she found a good man. She sure deserved one.' He sighed for a moment and unfolded his arms and continued. 'Then I was inside for those years and when I came out, I had such peace in my heart, and did not really yearn for a woman, if you get my meaning. But I guess now, hearing you two telling me yarns of your love life and quoting the bard at me, well... you got me thinking. Maybe there's girl for old Kevin yet.'

'Maybe there is,' said Douglas with conviction. 'And she'd be a lucky girl, too.'

'Aye, that she would indeed,' said Dorchadas.

'But she'd have to be very tolerant of my looks,' said Kevin. 'I mean, look at my broke nose, lack of teeth, scars and that. But then, Doug, it looks like God could be sending your way a girl whose eyesight is none too good to shield her from your looks, so perhaps there's hope for me, then!' All three of them laughed, then Kevin said, 'So, guys, to change the subject from our love lives for a moment. Father Pat's taking us off to St.Seannach's island on Sunday, would you believe?'

'Sounds fun,' said Douglas. He then rose from his chair and added, 'Listen, I'd better be on my way now. Looks like I might be needing to book a flight to Cairo.'

Dorchadas smiled his generous smile. He had no doubt in his mind that this was an excellent plan and that, for Douglas, this visit would mark both an ending and a beginning. Though, as he made his way back to the Presbytery, he did worry for his friend. How would he really be if they did visit the sight of the shooting of his Saoirse? Dorchadas had been sent to watch over this Englishman, and he was sure his work had not finished yet. But how could he look after him in Egypt? Unless... An idea formed in his angel mind.

In the midst of darkness
something new always springs to life
and sooner or later produces fruit.
On razed land
life breaks through,
stubbornly yet invincibly.

Pope Francis
Evangelii Gaudium

CHAPTER 7

Journal Holy Saturday evening

Kath definitely does have cancer and its terminal. Terrible shock for us all. Though she's amazing and taking it really well. Her experience at the deep memory Golgotha has affected her so powerfully that it is helping her face this. Met her daughter, Nancy. She's large, short hair and looks cross. She hardly said anything and was pretty brusque in her manner. There's another daughter too called Bríana who lives in America. Has recently come out as gay apparently after two failed marriages. She's coming over soon so I'll get to meet her too. Not sure Kath has got on that well with her.

Had a phone call yesterday morning before I went to the Three-hour service. It was from Alice. I was really pleased to hear her Devonian voice again. But she shocked me rigid by saying she had a vision which involved a Celtic saint telling her that she and I should head to Cairo next week!! Of all the many weird things I've done recently, this would certainly be one of the weirdest. Chatted to Dorch and Kev yesterday about it, and they think I should go for it. So I phoned her again today and sure enough we are on - I'm going over to the UK on Weds, and we fly out on Thurs for a few days. She's booked us an Airbnb overlooking the Pyramids. We'll do some tourist stuff (I always wanted to see the Pyramids), but also visit the place where the shooting happened. I got the exact location a long time ago and have often studied it on google earth. But it's going to be very disturbing to actually see the street where she was shot. She didn't die there but it was the place where her life effectively came to an end, and so it is a sacred spot. How will it affect me? Will it set off my grief again? Dear God please not. I'm really not sure about the plan, but I do trust Alice. I think. I'll get some flowers to lay there.

Also chatted to Kev and Dorch about love. I actually told them what Saoirse said to me at Golgotha. Felt ok to tell such good mates. They agreed it didn't point a big celestial arrow at Alice, but they said I must be open to new love. And I think I am now. Though feels very odd to think about loving another woman - can't quite get past it feeling disloyal. And yet, I do know I have her blessing. Dorch spoke about how he once fell in love with a woman in the early days of his becoming a human. Made me want to cry listening to him. He obviously loved this woman very much, but of course he couldn't develop a relationship. I saw such sadness in him. I sometimes think he has loved being a human more than he loved being an angel. And Kev also loved a girl once, but she couldn't cope with his violent life when he was in the IRA. Feels like he's rather closed that part of himself down now. Though I think I saw a flicker of hope in him.

And Kath wants me to do a blessing for her and Peter - a sort of marriage. Keeping it very informal so as not to offend any church rules. I feel SO honoured they should ask me. Not sure when it will be, but I'm afraid it may have to be soon as she is so poorly now. Probably after I get back from Cairo.

Jonny (Elsie's nephew) came over this morning from Cork to deliver a new car to replace the Fiesta which was a write-off after the accident. Came with his girlfriend who drove him back in a BMW, so they can't be doing too badly. Still so generous of him, though. The car he brought for me is a VW diesel and, as he put it, it's 'only been round the clock once.' Actually, Kev says it's not in bad condition though he slightly disturbed me by advising that I didn't take it on any long journeys. Again, Jonny wouldn't take any money for it - amazing kindness. But he clearly loves his Aunty Elsie. Actually, I discovered she isn't a real aunt - she used to baby sit for him years ago and she always considered him a nephew. Anyway, it means I now have wheels which is handy. And I will be using it tomorrow because Fr Pat wants to take us over the hill to an island on the other side of the peninsula. Seems to be a special place for him. Quite a few of us are going after the Easter mass and taking a picnic. Amazingly, the weather forecast is brilliant!

I'm feeling so much more content. If it wasn't for Kath's cancer, everything would be wonderful. Easter will mean so much this year. Golgotha was such an amazing experience and even at the foot of that cross with Him dying above me, I could feel resurrection life beginning. It's like by His dying, life exploded into this world. A new kind of life was released into this world. I feel it as a power even now as I write. And yet, I feel there is still so much to learn about the resurrection and death and heaven and all that. Perhaps that is what the coming weeks will bring?

Not long now before Frank and Daisy will be here. They're spending a week or so travelling in Ireland before coming to Dingle. The boys don't want to come, but they are bringing their 8 yr old niece with them. Didn't know they had one, but she belongs to Daisy's sister. Should be OK and Elsie says she can put an extra bed in their room. Be so good to see Frank again.

*

Easter morning blazed into life with a most wonderful sunrise over the Macgillycuddy's Reeks on the Iveragh Peninsula. All over Ireland, there were gatherings of the faithful who had risen for sunrise services. However, in Dingle, where the priest favoured a vigil the previous evening in preference to the sunrise service, few were awake to witness the glorious spectacle of the rising sun scattering the darkness from the streets, and causing the still waters of the bay to glisten and shimmer. However, some were awake. Dorchadas was on the beach with his arms raised to the warming rays of the emerging sun. Kath was sitting at the open bedroom window humming a much-loved tune from her childhood. Peter, who had arrived in Dingle the previous day, was listening to the morning birdsong as he sat on a wooden bench in the small garden of Kath's home. Elsie was berating herself in the kitchen as she prepared breakfast for her guests. And Father Pat was in his study managing his guilt with the aid of several cigarettes.

By his reckoning, any priest worth his salt would be out, whatever the weather, celebrating the sunrise on this most holy festival day. But no. Not the priest of Dingle. The usual darkness had descended on his soul and failed to be dispersed by the resurrection message that was at the core of his church's faith. And yet, the dark was not quite as dense as normal, and this year, he only needed three cigarettes to gain the equilibrium needed to face Easter Sunday. He could get through the service, he knew. He was professional. His homily was prepared. This year it was time for doubting Thomas to have his airing. Thomas was so useful. Such a helper to doubters like Pat. He could bring Thomas out on Easter Day and present him to his congregation. It was Thomas, more than anyone, who could provide validation for all those who found a body coming back to life just a step too far for a mortal mind to comprehend. Thomas had always been a good friend and ally to Pat, especially on Easter Sunday. No, as he stubbed out the last of the cigarettes, Pat felt the signs were good. He could get through another Easter service without anyone detecting that their priest was a fraud. Thank God, no-one had ever apprehended him at the door saying something like, 'But Father, do you *really* believe He rose from the grave?' Occasionally a child would ask a daring question, but that was quickly sorted by a kindly smile at the child and a laugh with the parents.

He inhaled the smoky atmosphere of his study, and opened the window a little, and thought about the visit to the island. Polishing his glasses hard he wondered what had possessed him to suggest this to his friends. For some crazy reason, he had planned for two carloads to head over the Connor Pass and sail off to St.Seannach's island. It was so unlike him to be so spontaneous. He had phoned his friend Colm, who, sure enough, for only a few euros, could take them over to the island. The tides were perfect for the afternoon visit and the weather was good. Mrs McGarrigle had prepared a splendid picnic. Pat actually felt a sense of excitement about it. It was spontaneous and not thought-through, yet somehow right. He had not been there since he was a boy, and it was boyish excitement that rose in him as the sun filtered its way through the smoke to shine upon him.

And to be on his special island with such good friends! How he thanked God for these friends. Most of them he felt he knew so well now. All except Nancy and Peter. But the others...Yes, he could honestly say he loved them. What he appreciated was the way they accepted him as Pat and did not allow his priesthood to be a barrier to real friendship. It was a friendship that was beginning to heal the deep loneliness that had so blighted his life. The wretched clerical collar and priest's robes had kept so many potential friends at arm’s length. His main method for tackling the loneliness was to berate himself for it, and to remind himself that he had given his life to God and therefore had died to personal needs including the need for affection and closeness in this world. By and large it had worked, apart from the times when the depression overwhelmed him. Then the method of relief more likely than not involved alcohol. But such times were mercifully few and far between now, especially now he had real friends.

He pulled the window shut and made his way to the kitchen to gather some breakfast. It was not long before he was donning his robes and making his way over to the church, ready to celebrate the Easter Eucharist.

*

With the tune of the final Easter hymn still ringing in their ears, Pat's group of island pilgrims made their way to the Presbytery to gather the picnic, the size of which looked considerable. Kevin and Douglas had parked their cars near to the Presbytery and the picnic baskets were duly loaded into the boots, along with a box containing cans of Murphy's Stout. Pat, Dorchadas and Nancy travelled with Douglas, while Kath and Peter went with Kevin, and soon the cars were making their way out of the busy streets of Dingle.

Slightly to Douglas' dismay, Dorchadas insisted on putting Nancy in the front seat. He was not sure why, but he felt awkward in her presence. It was not long before he realised there was good reason for this awkwardness. She was quiet for the first part of the journey, in contrast to Pat and Dorchadas in the back who were engaged in an animated conversation about Gaelic football. But as they left the town behind them and crawled up the hill behind some slow traffic, Nancy somewhat startled Douglas as she said, 'Mam says your wife's dead.'

'Er... yes, that's right, Nancy. I'm sorry to say she is,' said Douglas, glancing briefly at his passenger, who looked particularly large and ungainly in the seat that had been pushed forward to allow for Dorchadas' long legs.

'Shot, was she?' pursued Nancy, her eyes set fast on the road in front of her.

The bluntness of her question again startled Douglas, but he was quite strong enough to face such a direct question now and he answered, 'Yes, I'm afraid she was.'

'I don't agree with guns,' said Nancy and folded her arms, burping as she did so. 'Should never have been invented. They've made the world a very unhappy place.'

'I'm afraid they have,' replied Douglas. 'My wife, Saoirse, hated them and...'

Nancy did not allow Douglas to finish as she asked, 'You like living in Ireland?'

'Yes, I do, thanks,' replied Douglas, watching the road carefully as it narrowed towards the top of the pass.

Nancy was quiet for a while, then as the traffic ground to a halt at the top, awaiting the oncoming traffic, she said, 'My brother, Kev, used guns. He had to go to prison, he did. He's different now.'

'Yes,' said Douglas, not feeling fully sure of how to converse with his passenger. 'He says you were a great help to him when you visited him.'

'Aye, I was,' said Nancy. 'And Brí - she was in Ireland in those days. Miss her, I do,'

'She's coming over soon, I hear,' said Douglas as the traffic started to move again.

'She's gone lesbian,' said Nancy.

'You OK with that?' asked Douglas, now carefully negotiating the narrow road and being careful not to look too carefully at the drop on the left side of the road.

'Makes no odds to me,' said Nancy, then sighed a long sigh. 'Just miss her, that's all. She's the only one that's got me. I speak my mind I do. The way God made me, you see. You afraid of heights?'

'Not afraid really, but I would say I respect them,' said Douglas, still needing to drive carefully now past the slow oncoming traffic on the narrow road.

'Long way down there,' said Nancy looking out of her window. 'You drove Mam down a hill like that. She said you rolled the car over a few times.'

'Well, it was not exactly by my choice,' said Douglas, feeling a little defensive.

'Did her good,' said Nancy, opening her window and breathing in the fresh air.

'Well, I'm not sure the accident did her much good,' said Douglas. 'It was more...'

Again, he was not able to finish as Nancy said, 'Changed a lot she did after that. Told me she had a religious experience. Never been religious, has our Mammy. But she is now. Peter's religious too. I'm not against religion. Just not had much to do with it. Seems to cause a lot of bloody aggro though.'

Pat and Dorchadas had finished their animated discussion, and Douglas guessed they were now listening to the conversation going on in the front seat. He looked in the mirror and saw Pat smile at Nancy's comment. 'I heard that, Nancy,' said Pat, reaching forward and patting her on the shoulder. 'And I agree with you, lass.'

'I had a religious experience once,' said Nancy after a pause. The road had now widened and the traffic was speeding up. 'Met God in a field of cows, I did. It was November. Remember it clearly.'

All the passengers were intrigued. It was Dorchadas who asked her to say more. Nancy continued, 'Decided to walk across the field one day on my way home. Crossed the field often, but this time the cows got frisky and started running towards me. God, I was scared. Started running like hell. Tripped over, and landed in a big cow pat. Covered in cow shit, I was. Didn't get up, but just waited for the cows to trample me dead. Could feel the ground shaking as they got closer. Pissed myself 'cos I was so afraid. But then they all stopped.'

There was a long pause as they all waited for her to explain the reason for the cow's sudden halt in their charge. Eventually Douglas asked, 'Why did they stop, Nancy?'

'God told them to,' said Nancy, sniffing hard before wiping the back of her hand across her nose. She wound up her window as the car now increased its speed.

'How?' asked Douglas.

'He was there in the field, of course,' said Nancy, keeping her gaze on the road in front, yet in her mind visualising the scene she could never forget. 'I saw him. All in white and dazzling a bit. Nice to look at. He was big. About your size,' she said, thumbing over her shoulder in the direction of Dorchadas. 'He stepped between me and the cows, he did. Told them to stop charging, and they did.' She rummaged in her pocket for a few moments and pulled out a packet of sweets. 'Anyone for a mint?' she asked. Dorchadas reached forward and pulled a couple out and gave one to Pat. Nancy continued, 'The bit I liked was when he reached out his hand to me. My hand was all covered in cow shit, it was, and I thought "God won't like that". But he just took hold of my hand and pulled me up and gave me a hug. He got shit and piss all over his white robe.' She unwrapped her sweet and popped it in her mouth. 'You wouldn't think he'd like all that stuff, would you?'

'Who do you think it was, Nancy?' asked Douglas, glancing again at her.

'Angel, of course,' said Nancy. 'Didn't give his name.'

'Well, what happened then?' asked Pat.

'He disappeared,' said Nancy. 'I went home. Told Mam when I got back, but she didn't believe me and gave me a scolding for my dirty dress. Told my friends at school and they mocked me. So I stopped telling people.' She then smiled a rare smile and said, 'Felt I could tell you, though.'

Pat and Douglas were somewhat stunned by the story. Dorchadas leaned forward and, placing a warm hand on her shoulder, said, 'Lass, thank you for telling us. It's a precious story, it sure is. You know we believe you, don't you?'

Nancy chewed on her sweet, and for some time said nothing, but just nodded. After a while she ran her hand across her nose, sniffing loudly, and Douglas noticed her red cheeks glistening in the rays of the Easter day sunlight that blazed upon her.

CHAPTER 8

'There's Colm,' said Pat as Douglas steered them down the narrow road to the small quayside at Fahamore. As soon as Douglas parked the car, Pat got out and made straight towards a stocky man who was sitting on the quay. When he saw Pat, he got up, threw his cigarette into the sea, and greeted him with much laughter. Douglas waited by his car and then beckoned Kevin when he arrived with his carload. Douglas watched Peter helping Kath out of the car. He admired the tender way he was supporting her, which conveyed so clearly the love they had so recently rediscovered.

Colm then helped all the party aboard his small fishing boat. Pat, who made his way straight to the bow of the boat, beckoned Dorchadas and Douglas to join him. Peter carefully guided Kath to a seat near the centre of the boat. Elsie looked very uncertain as she clambered aboard, waving her arms wildly in an attempt to steady herself. Kevin and Nancy were last aboard, carrying the various picnic baskets with them.

Colm started the motor and soon they were chugging away from the small harbour and there, ahead of them, they could see the Magharee Islands. Colm was controlling the boat from inside a small cabin. For a moment, he stepped out of the cabin and called out, 'Over there - that's the great Kilshannig. Burial ground now, but in Seannach's time it was the harbour. Many saints of God have launched their boats from there and put out to their adventurings. Some came to these islands, like Seannach. Others had the divine restlessness, they did, and they journeyed to the ends of the world.'

'God bless the lot of them,' called Elsie, who harboured a soft spot for the saints of her land.

Douglas was not particularly interested in ancient history and saints, though he loved the sense of adventure Colm evoked in those few words. Pat was silent throughout the journey and simply gazed out to sea. He kept breathing in the briny air and savoured the familiar smells of fish, ropes and diesel fuel. He was a boy again, delighting in the thud and spray of the surf against the bows and the sound of the gulls above him.

Colm steered the boat toward the larger of the several islands, and it was not long before he was slowing the motor and skilfully navigating his craft towards a sandy bay. 'God knows you have to have sharp eyes for the rocks in this bay,' he said. When he reached just a couple of yards from the shore, he said, 'Now, this is where you get out. You'll need to get your shoes and socks off, you will.' And dutifully all on board pulled off their boots and socks and rolled up their trouser legs. Kevin was the first off the boat, and helped out his mother, sister and very anxious aunt. The others followed carrying the picnic baskets and they all managed to clamber ashore without getting too wet. 'I'll be back to collect you in a couple of hours, Father,' shouted Colm and revved his engine. Within moments his boat sped away as the others made for the rocks on the seashore, to don their socks and boots.

'Well, I don't know about the rest of you, but I am sure ready for some lunch,' said Kath, and she and Elsie set about unpacking the lunch. Whilst Kath marvelled at the magnificence of Mrs McGarrigle's provisions, Elsie commented that, in her view, there were some serious omissions and lamented the fact that there was insufficient butter on the scones. Meanwhile, the party made themselves as comfortable as possible on the rocks in the unusually warm April sunshine.

'The name of this island is Illauntannig,' said Pat, his mouth partly full of cheese and ham sandwich. 'Some call it "Old Man's Island".'

'So that's why you've come, Father' said Kath and wheezed a laugh.

Pat smiled warmly back at her, 'Aye, Kath,' he said, washing his sandwich down with a sip of his ale. 'But the last time I was here I was a wee lad. Don't suppose any of you can imagine that,' he said.

'I can,' said Nancy, who was holding in her mind the image of an eager-eyed, lanky and tousled-haired boy scurrying over the rocks.

'So can I,' said Peter, who was sitting close to Kath and looking up at the dark stone wall on the edge of the island. 'But Pat, can you tell us, please. What are these buildings here?'

'Ah, I can that, Peter,' said Pat, his eyes brightening. 'Your man Seannach came here around fifteen hundred years ago and decided this island would be a grand place for a Christian community. And so, this is where they lived and prayed.'

'Can't see there's much fun in that,' said Kath, munching a piece of pork pie. 'I mean, grand on a day like today, but when the wind gets excitable and comes off the Atlantic, it is something powerful. And can you imagine the winter here? You'd need more than that Aran jumper of yours, Pat. Dear God, that wind would freeze your... It would freeze you to death, Father.'

'Well done, sister,' said Elsie, commending her for watching her language.

'Well now, they were made of tougher stuff than us, I think, Kath,' said Pat. 'But you need to go and have a look at those ruins, Peter,' he said, responding to Peter's earlier question. 'There's so much that's interesting here. You have a cross, the beehive huts - and those stone huts gave them good shelter by the way, Kath. There are oratories, altars and the thick walls are magnificent. It's truly glorious,' said Pat, brushing the crumbs off his jumper. The Easter message proclaimed in church that morning may have failed to give resurrection life to Pat's soul but here, on this island, he was sensing a renewal. Was it just the childhood memories? Or was it something deeper? A kind of blessing rooted in the soil by Seannach and the others - some kind of spiritual radiation that reached through the arc of time even to the faithless heart of this wayward priest?

When the party had made a valiant attempt to finish Mrs McGarrigle's supply of sandwiches, pies, scones, apples and stout, Pat said, 'Well, I suggest we just wander the island for the next hour before Colm comes to collect us.'

'Grand idea,' said Kevin, 'But first, Pat, if you'll excuse me, I'm just going to lay my head on this rock for a few minutes. That Murphy's just needs a little settling, it does. Kath and Elsie agreed and set off looking for relatively comfortable places where they could lay their heads. But the others got up and clambered up from the beach on to the grassy mounds of the island. Nancy strode off to the other side of the island, while Peter, Douglas and Kevin walked over to inspect the ruins of the old monastery.

Dorchadas chose to walk with Pat. He was aware of a growing conviction that they were not here by chance. More accurately, he knew that Pat was not here by chance. He had been called here, and had heard the call. Dorchadas knew without doubt that his job now was to help his friend discover whatever treasure had been placed for him here.

'This way,' he said to Pat, as they approached the remains of one of the large beehive cells.

'How did you know?' said Pat.

'Sorry?' said Dorchadas, and paused for a moment.

'Why did you choose this cell, Dorch?' asked Pat, standing straight and brushing his hand through his thick hair. 'Did you know this was my favourite place when I came here as a kiddie?'

'I think I did, Pat,' said Dorchadas.

'There are times, Dorch,' said Pat, 'when I really do believe you are an angel of God, you know,' said Pat.

Dorchadas chuckled and said, 'Well, you won't be the first priest to go exploring with an angel. Come on, let's go in.' He stooped low to enter the cell. Pat followed behind him and, as he entered, he let out a cry of alarm, for standing there, near the far wall of the cell was a middle-aged man of short stature, with a tanned and bearded face, wearing what looked like a grey linen skirt, and a bright blue cheesecloth shirt.

'Dear God, I thought we were the only people on the island,' exclaimed Pat, and was somewhat confused, not knowing quite what to say. 'Forgive me... I hope we have not disturbed you, now?'

'Welcome, Patrick,' said the stranger and walked towards him.

Pat was now even more confused and looked at Dorchadas, 'Do we know him, Dorch? The man seems to know us.'

'To be fair,' said Dorchadas, 'I've not met the gentleman before, but I think I know who he is.'

The man came up to Dorchadas, and placed his hands together as if in prayer and bowed before Dorchadas and, in an accent that Pat guessed placed the man from somewhere in the Middle East, said, 'I believe you are Dorchadas. It is an honour to meet you.' He then turned to Pat and, making the same gesture of greeting, he said, 'So you are Patrick the priest. I have heard much about you, my friend. It is good to meet you.' He bowed again.

Pat was open-mouthed throughout the greeting and raising his thick eyebrows high on his forehead, he looked again Dorchadas.

'Come,' said the stranger. 'Let us sit here on these rocks,' and the three men settled themselves on some rocks inside the cell. The roof of the cell had collapsed centuries ago, so the warm sun now shone freely upon them.

'Forgive me,' said Pat, still in a state of confusion. 'But, honest to God, I have a fearful memory. You say we have met, and I have no reason to doubt you, now. But I regret I don't recall your name or quite where it was that we met.'

'Ah, we met this morning, Patrick,' said the man.

'Ah, you were in church, then?' said Pat with some uncertainty. He could not have missed a person dressed like this, surely?

'Can I suggest you put the poor man out of his misery,' said Dorchadas. 'Let me make a guess? Is your name Thomas, by any chance?'

'Ah, Dorchadas, you are as wise as they said you are,' said Thomas. Dorchadas felt surprised and very flattered by the compliment.

'Thomas?' enquired Pat. 'Thomas Who? Do I know your family?'

Dorchadas stepped in again. 'Thomas. You need to know that your man here is not used to these kinds of meetings, so let me explain to him.' Then, turning to Pat, he said, 'Pat, my friend, this is going to be hard for you to grasp. But you know how Douglas and the others made their way to Golgotha for the deep memory?'

'Y... yes,' said Pat, and shuffled nervously on his stone and adjusted his glasses.

'Well, this is similar,' said Dorchadas placing his large hand on the priest's arm. 'Try not to fight it or argue with it. I know what you can be like. Just hear what the man has to say, could you?'

'Dorch...' said Pat with some hesitation, and he pulled off his glasses and started to wipe them rigorously on the hem of his jumper. He lowered his head and his voice and said, 'Are you trying to tell me, Dorch, that this gentleman here is...'

'Yes,' said Thomas laughing. 'Yes, Patrick. I am Thomas. I think most of the world knows me as Doubting Thomas.'

Pat felt a coldness run down the length of him. He had stepped into something truly supernatural and he was feeling a great sense of disturbance. He put on his glasses. He was going to need to see clearly now. Putting aside his many questions and his not inconsiderable fears, he said, 'I am very pleased to meet you... Thomas.'

'And I you, Patrick,' said Thomas.

'So, it's true,' said Pat, now locating the origins of the clothes the man was wearing. 'You did make your way to India.'

'Oh, yes,' said Thomas. 'But, Patrick, don't believe all the stories. They are very fanciful.' He smiled broadly, revealing a couple of missing teeth. 'But that is not what you want to hear about today.'

'Don't I?' said Pat, still feeling very confused.

'Oh, no' replied Thomas. 'Because we need to talk about your sermon this morning.'

'Oh, dear God,' said Pat, now fearing there was going to be some kind of celestial sermon class, which, he was certain, would accord him with very low marks.

'I heard it and I loved it, Patrick,' said Thomas.

'You did?' said Pat, looking both shocked and pleased.

'I did.' said Thomas. 'You spoke very well about my struggle to believe something that was incredible. But, if I may say so, you were not so strong on my change of heart that day. May I tell you how it was?

'By all means,' said Pat, adjusting his position on his stone, and starting to relax a little.

'Following Jesus was wonderful,' said Thomas with a broad smile. He stretched out his legs before him and turned his face to the blue sky. 'We saw such things. Such beautiful things.' He paused for a few moments, then turned to look at Pat. 'You see, we were used to a world where the bullies always won, where power was in the hands of those who were corrupt and cruel, and where only a few were wealthy. The rest of us battled with poverty. Everything seemed loaded against us. And it was a world where we so often got sick. Our children died so easily. They were difficult days. And then this Galilean rabbi came along.'

He crossed his legs and continued, 'You know, He wasn't that special to look at. When I first met Him, I thought He was just another regular rabbi. He passed through my town once and there was great excitement because He healed a little boy who was dangerously sick. I managed to get to chat with Him and, straight away I realised He was not a regular rabbi at all. The other rabbis, though good men, they were - how shall I say? They were a bit high and mighty. But He was different. If anything, He made *you* feel higher and mightier. So, I decided to follow Him wherever He went. It was crazy - me, always a bit of a sceptic, following a holy man around Galilee.

'Then one day He got twelve of us together and told us that we were to be His special group. Disciples, we were. I could not believe He chose me to be one of them! But then, I think we all felt the same way. None of us were very suitable!' He laughed a high-pitched laugh that resonated around the ancient cell. Pat, who had been looking at him intently, looked down for a few moments as he recalled his days at Seminary. He also carried a sense of astonishment that God should call one such as he, from a poor and broken home with little education to boast of. He had never overcome his sense of being an inferior type of priest.

Thomas shifted his position on his stone and continued his story. 'Well, what I discovered was that this rabbi was a great walker. We walked miles and miles! I travelled further than I ever imagined I would. We even made it up to Caesarea Philippi. And always on those journeys, we saw so many wonders. I mean, it just became a regular thing to see lepers healed, and people who had been maddened by evil released. On a few occasions He even raised the dead!' Thomas looked up in excitement, but then his expression changed quickly as he added, 'Though I was always the one to ask "But were they *really* dead?" A bit of me just couldn't believe it.'

Thomas' countenance then became one of great sadness. 'Then it all seemed to go wrong. It all happened so fast. One minute we were celebrating the Passover meal with Him, and the next we were running for our lives while He was dying nailed to a Roman cross. That was a most terrible day.' Thomas looked down at the earth for a while and shook his head. He then looked back at Dorchadas and Pat and said, 'The day after we all gathered back together again and we were a miserable group. No-one knew what to say. Peter was completely silent. That was unheard of!' He smiled a limp smile.

'You see, we had not just lost a friend we loved so much, but we lost all that hope we had gathered: that there was at last a power in this world greater than all the evil powers that oppressed everyone so terribly. We had come to believe that His way of love really could change the world.' Dorchadas and Pat were both listening intently as Thomas continued. 'The others… They found comfort in being together. One or two of them tried to find some positive in it all, but I couldn't face that and I left them to it.

'Then, a couple of days after His death, I went for a long walk in the country and got back a bit late. Well, when I got back to the others, I was astonished. I had left a funeral wake, and I came back to a wild celebration! They all said that *He* had been to visit them. They said He was alive. Not just back from the dead, but had come *through* death and was more alive than ever. And they said what an ass I was to have missed it.' He kicked his feet in the grass for a moment then looked at Pat and said, 'You know my story well, Patrick, and I do come over as a fool, don't I?'

'Not at all,' said Pat with utter conviction. 'I really, really understand.'

Thomas smiled in appreciation and then continued his story. 'I'm not proud of myself and I won't make excuses. But there was a cold, lifeless little piece within me that I had not allowed Him to touch and change. It was a piece that refused to believe the impossible. Now, the others were full of belief, but old Thomas here was full of doubts. I felt such loneliness. It was a dreadful week after that. The others were so excited and delighted. They would often sing - even dance. I mean, these were my good friends, but I felt a stranger amongst them. I just couldn't believe what they had told me. I knew it was possible to hallucinate. I knew that even a group of people could long for something so much that they could all imagine it happening. I was convinced this what happened. I felt I was the only sane one amongst them. So I said that if He did turn up again and I was there, I would need clear proof that it was Him. I'd need to know it wasn't someone else pretending. I'd need to know it wasn't a ghost. I'd need to know we were not all hallucinating. I'd need to see the wounds made by the cross and, if I could actually touch those, then I could be certain it was Him.' Thomas tapped his hands as he said this and frowned. 'I knew we all had to be completely honest - there was no point in pretending to believe when we didn't. So each day went by and it got worse and worse. The day that you call Thursday came and we all remembered the meal we had with Him the week before. And then Friday - a week after the terrible Friday. It all came back to me - me standing at the back of the crowd watching the trial...Not doing anything to help Him.' Thomas shook his head and said nothing for a while.

'You know, there was a bit of me that really did hope my friends were right,' he said, looking up for a few moments at the sky. 'I loved the thought of His conquering death. But such a hope seemed impossible. And then, the chilling thought came to my mind, that if my friends *were* right and He really was risen from the dead, then what would He think of me - the only one of the group *not* to believe?' Thomas sighed for a few moments as he relived this haunting memory. A group of seagulls squawked overhead, circled the cell for a while, and then flew off. Thomas watched them and then continued his story. 'On that Saturday - the Sabbath - they all celebrated and I couldn't bear to be with them again. I thought that if He really had risen from death, then He would probably come and see them again on the Sabbath. But when I got back that evening, they said He had not been. Strange wasn't it? That He should appear one day and then just not come back. It didn't seem to bother any of the others, though. But it made me all the more convinced that they had dreamed the whole thing up.

'So, the first day of the week came around again and I was back with them all. Actually, they were quite kind to me and, though I now felt so different from the others, it was still nice to see them. And on this occasion, I was having a chat with Matthew about something or other, when Joanna started tugging at my sleeve. As she did so, the room grew very quiet. Joanna was smiling and was pointing to the edge of the room. And there He was. And yet the door was locked! At first, I thought I had fallen asleep and was in a dream, but as He walked towards me, I knew it was no dream. It was dreadfully real. You can't imagine how disturbing it is to see someone who was so obviously dead one day, walking towards you just a few days later.

'Everyone there could see He was heading for me. I could feel my whole body shaking. I wanted to hide, but I knew I could not hide from Him. As He moved towards me I felt such a sense of shame and failure. I could hear myself, in that very room the week before, telling the others that they were wrong and that there was no way a man could raise himself up from the grave. And yet here was this man moving through the group of friends towards His unbelieving disciple. He looked just like He had looked when we walked with Him for those wonderful years before all this. But He also looked somehow different. I fell to my knees as He got nearer and lowered my head. I knew how dreadfully disappointed He must have been with me. I had let Him down when He died, and now I had let Him down when He had risen. In the years before, He had told us several times that He would rise from the dead, but I had failed to believe Him. My friends had told me they had seen Him, but I doubted their word. I felt totally and utterly useless and I was fully expecting for Him to speak to me like He used to speak to some of the Pharisees. He was surely angry with me. I was ready to be told to flee the room, the land, and maybe even the life that God had given me on this Earth.'

At this point, Thomas got up and moved so he could be closer to Pat. He spoke almost in a whisper as he said, 'He came and stood right in front of me. As close as I am to you now, Patrick. His robes smelled so clean - almost fragrant. I was looking down and looked at His sandaled feet. He stood still, but His toes were moving, like those of an excited child. And then I heard His voice. It sounded so familiar and so wonderful. He told me to stand up. Joanna helped me get to my feet. I was about the same height as Him and I faced Him, but still could not look Him in the eye. He then took my hand and invited me to place it into His very wounds! Can you imagine it, Patrick?' Thomas was still speaking quietly. Pat was frowning with concentration, and slowly removed his spectacles. He was listening intently to a story that was so familiar, and yet one he felt he was hearing for the first time, and it was touching the very roots of his soul.

'Imagine being asked to touch the wounds that had caused His death,' said Thomas. 'Just a week before I had told the others that I would only be convinced He had risen if I could touch His wounds. And now here He was, inviting me to do the very thing I requested. So, I knew that He had heard me. He must have been in the room when I was talking with them. I realised then that He knew everything. I could not hide from Him. I could not pretend. I could not make excuses.'

Thomas shook his head for a while, and then reached out and grasped Pat's hand that was clasping his spectacles. 'And here is the truth, Patrick. He did not admonish me; he did not make an example of me to the others. He did not tell me that faithless men like me deserved eternal damnation. No, He was holding my hand like this, Patrick. I knew then that, even if I carried on doubting for the rest of my days, He would still be my friend. Finally, I stopped looking down, and I looked into His face. The last time I had seen this face was from a distance. It was disfigured, with blood all over it. It was a face of agony. This was the same face, and yet it was a face full of incredible peace. As I looked at Him, I knew He had forgiven me. There was no doubting any more. I did not need to touch His wounds. I could see that this dearest preacher and healer really was a God, whose life was so powerful and wonderful that no death in this world would be a match for it.'

Thomas then grasped the spectacles that were clutched in Pat's hand. He lifted them up to the sky to look through them, and then, lowering them, he started to wipe them on His bright shirt. He smiled and said, 'I guess my eyesight was healed. I could see things that I was blind to see before. Because that's really what faith is, my friend. It is simply learning to use our eyes differently. And in those moments, when He was standing before me in that room, with all my friends standing around, I was like a new born baby opening his eyes for the first time and seeing the world of wonders into which he has been born. I looked at the One who had opened my eyes with His love, and I started to worship Him. For the rest of my days He would be my God and I would tell every soul I met about Him.' He handed Pat's glasses back to him, and Pat slowly placed them back before his closed eyes and sat down.

A light breeze scuttled around the ancient walls of the cell, ruffling Thomas' shirt. Pat had listened with great intent and struggled to find words to match his feelings. Thomas then knelt down in front of Pat, who was rather horrified that this hallowed saint, after whom a myriad of churches in Christendom had been named, should kneel before him, and he attempted to dissuade him. But Thomas did not budge, and, looking Pat in the eye, he took his hands and said, 'I have been sent to you, Patrick, because He has looked on your heart and He knows it is good. True faith can only be born in a heart of love. And He has seen how you have loved your God and you have loved His people. I have come to water the seeds of faith that have been there, ever since you first felt the presence of His soul when your father walked with you on this very island in the days of your childhood. Such seeds never die, my friend.'

Pat studied the face of the man kneeling in front of him. He knew it was a face he would never forget. He knew he would never understand what was happening to him in this little cell on his favourite island, but whatever magic had caused the great St.Thomas of old to make his way through the passageway of deep memory to this struggling priest, he knew it was a magic that was doing its work. The etched lines of the Mediterranean face creased into a smile. The brown eyes glistened, and the grip of the hands tightened. Pat knew Thomas was imparting something to him. It was something to do with courage. And it was something to do with stepping out of a safe, well-ordered, predictable world, into one of wild and delightful impossibilities. His first attempt to speak was hesitant and inaudible. It would not do. He needed to take a risk. So, he stood and, using his rich, clear, baritone voice, he said, 'I am Patrick, and I will follow my sweet suffering and risen Christ to the end of my days.' Thomas also stood and the two men, separated only by history, clung to each other, while Dorchadas closed his eyes and turned his face to the beams of the Spring sunshine.

*

Father Pat and Dorchadas emerged through the low gateway of the cell out into the open ground and found the others gathered back at the beach in readiness for the boat ride home. They heard Kevin's voice call out, 'There they are!' and all in the group turned to the two men making their way down from the ruins.

'Where in God's holy name have you two been?' asked Elsie, as they arrived at the beach.

'We were up there in the beehive cell, Elsie,' said Dorchadas. 'Did you not see us?' Several of the group said they had been through the ruins but had not seen them, but they all agreed that they must simply have missed each other. As they watched Colm's boat bouncing on the waters towards them, they spoke to each other of how much they loved their time on the island and agreed it was a blessed place. It was only Douglas who noticed that there was something different about Pat. As they watched Colm navigating the boat carefully towards the shore, he said to Pat, 'I can see why you have loved this island, Pat.'

Pat threw several of his rapid smiles and replied, 'And now I love it even more.'

'You know, I did look in that cell several times,' said Douglas. 'But I never saw you and Dorch there.'

'Och, these places are like that, aren't they?' said Pat, removing his glasses again and wiping them on his jumper. Something about the way Pat gave his reply made Douglas a little suspicious. He was getting to know well the mysterious ways of Dorchadas. But he also knew that Father Pat was a private man, and he had no desire to intrude on that privacy. But as he clambered into the boat, he was aware of a sense that something very holy had happened on the island and he could not escape the thought that the priest from Dingle had been at the epicentre of it.

As they rode back bumping over the waves, Nancy suddenly cried out, 'Over there!' They followed her arm stretching out to the West and, to their great delight, they saw a school of dolphins leaping through the waves towards them.

'Some say they catch sight of the saints around that island,' called Colm as he slowed the engine. 'And every time they sees one, they go chasing after them for a blessing.' He chuckled and added, 'Such legends, eh?'

Pat glanced at Dorchadas, then back to the leaping dolphins who were moving closer to the boat, and said, 'Well, it is Easter Sunday, Colm, and that's a fine day for miracles by my reckoning. So maybe the dolphins did see a saint of old today.'

'Well maybe they did, Father,' said Colm. 'Maybe they did.' For a time, the dolphins raced alongside the boat before veering off back out to sea. Colm then steered the boat towards the mainland. It was a boat that carried a group of tired but contented friends. And as they approached the quayside, Douglas said quietly to Dorchadas, 'And now I have to prepare for the next adventure.'

'Indeed, son,' said Dorchadas. 'From the wild seas to the desert sands. That's quite an adventure I should say,' and he placed an arm around Douglas' shoulder.

'I don't suppose you've got any appointments over there next week, have you?' asked Douglas.

'There's been no call, yet Doug,' replied Dorchadas. 'But in this world, you never know, do you?'

'You never do,' said Douglas. The boat docked at the quay and everyone clambered ashore. As Douglas stepped on to the firm ground of the Fahamore quay, he heard the sound of Father Pat behind him, humming the refrain of an Easter hymn.

CHAPTER 9

A couple of days after the Easter boat trip, Douglas was packing his case for his foray to Cairo when there was a knock at the door and in walked an animated Elsie. 'Douglas, darling,' she said, rubbing some moisturising lotion firmly into her hands. 'I hope you don't mind me disturbing you now, but I thought you'd like to hear that our Brí has arrived from America. Kath called me just now.'

'That's good news, Elsie,' said Douglas placing a shirt carefully in his case. 'I do look forward to meeting her.' He then paused and added, 'If you've got a moment, Elsie, can you tell me a bit about Kath's girls. She's told me very little about them.'

'Ah, yes…' said Elsie, now working the lotion into the tips of her fingers. 'Well, I do have a few moments as it happens, but then I must get Room 3 finished for some guests from Japan who are arriving this afternoon.' She walked over to the window and settled herself on the creaking chair next to the desk. Douglas cleared a space on his bed and sat on it.

'So,' said Elsie, neatly crossing her legs and folding her gleaming hands on her lap, 'Kath and her Kevin had the three children. Kevin is the eldest, as you know. He was a nice wee lad, but his father was fearful strict with him. Too strict in my opinion. Well something or other got into the lad when he hit the teenage years and, as you know, he got himself tied up with the life of violence and all that stuff that I don't like to think about. Thank Joseph, Mary and all the saints he came to his senses when he was inside that prison and then became the lovely lad he is now. But Douglas,' she said turning to Douglas and looking hard at him through her gleaming cat-eye glasses. 'He could sure could do with a good woman, don't you think? Perhaps you could help him in that department, son?'

'I'm not sure that's really my expertise, Elsie,' said Douglas.

'No, well. It's not mine either, as you know only too well,' said Elsie shaking her head. 'Anyhow, that besides, let's think about Brí, who is the two years younger than her brother. Bríana is her full name, but we have always called her Brí. Well, she came out with a head of bright red hair and a temper that would frighten even the demons of Hades. My God, Douglas, she was a terror when she was in a mood, she surely was. You could hear her crying from one end of the town to the other.' Elsie laughed for a few moments, then added, 'But she was also a lovely girl, she was. Oh, I was so fond of her. And so was her da. Kevin senior *adored* her.' Elsie stressed the word, squeezing her hands together. 'She grew into such a beautiful little girl and her da was so proud of her. He would take her round town showing her off to his friends, and buying her ribbons for her hair and toys and that. To be honest, he spoilt the child terrible, he did. She was the light of his life. And, you know, she never vented her anger on him - it was always at her mother or at her brother or sister. But he couldn't do a thing wrong in her eyes.'

'So how did Kath feel about that?' asked Douglas.

'Well, son,' replied Elsie, 'I think you've already guessed that Kath was none too impressed with the favour her husband was showing to her daughter. Once or twice I did try to broach the subject with Kevin senior. You know, just trying to point out to him that Kath might feel just a wee bit jealous. But oh, my, he didn't like that. You see, he was a good man was Kevin, but, like his daughter, he could also be an angry man. And, I regret to say,' said Elsie, lowering her head and her voice, 'there were times when he was just a bit too fond of the liquor. Especially when the fishing was bad. But he never laid a hand on any of them, let me make clear. But his anger was frightening, and I think Kath was frightened by it, if the truth be told.'

'So, how did Kath and Brí get on?' asked Douglas, intrigued by the new things he was learning about this family.

'Well, how do you think, Douglas?' said Elsie, now sitting up straight, animated by the memories. 'Poor Kath was ever so jealous of her. I mean, when Brí got into her teens, my God, she was a beauty: long, beautiful red hair; great boobs; slim waist; the sweetest smile. She had everything. Drove the boys of the town mad, she did. Then, of course, Kath was scared that history was going to repeat itself and that Brí would go and get herself pregnant. So, she became over-protective and if there was so much as a suggestion of a boyfriend, then Kath came on her like a ton of bricks. Well during this time, I got close to Brí and she would come and confide in me. I knew that she was sleeping with most of the boys in town by now - well, slight exaggeration.' She chuckled for a few moments. 'There were a few boys, though. Thank God for the contraception, that's all I can say. Oh, but don't you go telling the Father I said that,' she added quickly, pointing a finger at Douglas.

She paused, inspecting the scarlet nail varnish on her forefinger for a moment, then continued. 'Then Kevin senior became sick. It was just after his son was let out of prison. To be honest, the man's body was shot to pieces. Sea fishing is not an easy life, and he was not a strong man. Then one January he got a terrible chill after he had been out at sea on a rough night, and it turned to pneumonia. Well, sure to God, he'd given his lungs a hard time with his smoking. And the rest of his constitution had been hit hard by the alcohol. By early March, his body had had enough and he left us, God rest his soul.' She rapidly crossed herself and then, looking down, said, 'Very sad it was. Kath took it really well, I thought. In some ways, she was probably a little bit relieved. But Brí - oh, my God!' Elsie raised her eyes and hands to the ceiling before slapping them back down on her lap and adding, 'She was distraught, she was. She clung to me at the graveside - not her mother, note - and she sobbed and she wailed like a woman possessed. I had never seen such wretched soul in all my life. Well, I'm sorry to say she blamed her mother for her da's death. That wasn't fair at all, poor Kath. But I think Brí honestly believed that it was Kath that drove the man to the drink and smoke and put all the stress on him. Brí went off to America soon after that and she and her mother didn't talk to each other for a long time.' Elsie brushed the top of the desk for a moment with her hand and looked out of the window, then said, 'Truth be told, I really missed the lass. She was like a daughter to me. I was fearful fond of her, I was.' She turned and looked back to Douglas with dampened eyes and said, 'Never had my own, you see.'

'I'm sorry, Elsie,' Douglas said, noticing her vulnerability. 'I can see she has meant a great deal to you.'

'Aye, she has that, son.' She then sighed for a moment and continued, 'Then, of course, she had those broken marriages, poor girl.'

'What happened to those?' asked Douglas.

'Ah well, the first man was an American lad that she had met when she was working for a newspaper in Limerick. She met him in a pub. I think her da quite liked him actually, but I didn't feel he was at all suitable. But he was handsome and funny. They both went off to the States not long after we'd buried her father and they quickly married. None of us went to the wedding. Then, sad to say, he started treating her badly. Well, I guess he was none too fond of her moods and her temper, but in my book, there is no excuse for violence in a marriage.'

'Oh, dear, I am sorry,' said Douglas.

'Aye,' said Elsie, looking back at her finger nails again. 'I had hoped she would come back to Ireland when the marriage broke up, but it wasn't long before she was in another relationship, this time with a man who was twenty years older than her, would you believe? She actually brought him back here a couple of times for holidays, and, to be honest with you, I quite liked the man. He was very wealthy, Douglas. Oh, my God - Gucci clothes and Rolex watches and all that. Brí came back very well dressed, she did. But, clearly the lass wasn't happy because, after about five years, he found out that she had been having at least two affairs and, as you can imagine, he was none too pleased with her. So, that was the end of that.' Elsie sighed again and, looking at the ceiling for a moment, she shook her head. 'Poor soul - she really was searching for love, wasn't she?' Douglas was impressed and touched by the devotion Elsie had for her niece.

'One of the affairs,' she continued, 'was with a jockey. She was always fond of the horses and loved the races, so it didn't surprise me when she phoned and told me about the man. He was Irish and, again, I hoped that might bring her back to her homeland. But no, that didn't last long either.' She paused for a while and glanced back out of the window. She leaned forward to gain a better view and said, 'There's Mrs McGarrigle getting the groceries for the Presbytery. My God, what's she got in those bags? That's a big cabbage, that is. It's too big - there'll be no flavour in it. And she's not good with her cabbage. Ah well, let's hope she manages not too bad a dinner for the Father.'

'I think he eats very well most nights, Elsie, if what I have sampled is anything to go by,' said Douglas.

'Yes, but she puts too much salt in the food,' said Elsie frowning.

Returning to the subject of Brí, Douglas asked, 'Elsie, I assume you know about Brí's latest love?'

Elsie turned back from the window and smiled a broad smile. 'Oh yes, I have, Douglas. She phoned and told me all about it. Has Kevin told you?'

'Yes, he has. Just a little.'

'Well, I suggest you ask Brí about it when she comes,' said Elsie. 'But, you know, I've always been quite broad-minded when it comes to these sorts of things. I mean, we've all moved on a lot over the years, haven't we?' Douglas could think of several people he knew who had most definitely not "moved on". He saw a charity in Elsie that he admired. 'It wasn't working out for Brí with the men,' said Elsie. 'And I guess she realised that she was... you know. And once she had decided that it was really the women she preferred, then I suppose that could make sense of things not working out with the men. I get the feeling she will be very happy with this lady. I do hope so, poor love.'

They were both quiet for a few moments, and then Douglas asked, 'And what about Nancy?' I got to know her a bit on the journey to the island on Sunday,'

'Ah, Nancy, yes,' said Elsie, adjusting her position in the chair causing it to creak noisily. 'My God, Douglas, this chair needs some oil, don't you think? I'll speak to Kevin about it. But Nancy, now - the youngest of the three. Well, let me tell you, Douglas, Nancy and Brí could not be more different. Where Brí was beautiful, Nancy was plain. Where Brí was outgoing and sociable, Nancy was private and withdrawn; Where Brí had a raging temper, Nancy just smouldered. Where Brí was at the top of the class (when she worked, that is), poor Nancy was usually at the bottom. Poor lass, life has been tough for her, it sure has.'

'What did her parents feel about her?' asked Douglas.

'She was not an easy child to have in the house, Douglas,' said Elsie frowning. 'I mean, you never knew what she was thinking. It was obvious that her father was a bit ashamed of her and, I'm sorry to say, he rather ignored her.'

'And Kath?'

'Well, she has loved the girl, she surely has. But she has had to work hard with her daughter, if you know what I mean.' Elsie leaned forward and spoke in a confidential tone. 'Kath once told me about her birth. She said that when the babe came out, she noticed the cord was tangled around the neck. Though nothing was said at the time, Kath thinks the baby was lacking the oxygen for a wee while and that... you know... had its effect.'

Douglas was frowning. In his pastoral work he had once come across someone with intellectual disabilities due to problems at birth and he did recognise some similarities with Nancy. 'Was nothing ever formally identified as a problem?' he asked.

'Kevin wouldn't allow it,' said Elsie. 'Kath felt there was something wrong, but he hated the idea of having a child with any kind of disability and he wouldn't allow any investigation.'

'Poor Kath. And poor Nancy,' said Douglas.

'I know,' said Elsie. 'The family have never really liked to talk about it. But, you know, once you get behind that rather gruff exterior, there is a sweetheart in there. Her brother adores her and would cross the world for her. He adores both his sisters actually. They were so good to him when he was inside.'

'Yes, I've heard,' said Douglas.

'Now listen,' said Elsie checking her watch and abruptly rising to her feet. 'I must be getting that room ready. I find the Japanese are very particular about cleanliness, and, to be fair, it's a quality I admire. But it makes for extra work. And my knee, God bless it, would choose today to play up.'

'Of course,' said Douglas, rising from the bed. 'I know the room will be spotless after you have worked on it. And thanks, Elsie, for filling me in on the family.'

'Oh, not at all, Douglas,' replied Elsie making for the door. 'As I've said before, you're one of the family now, so you might as well get to know these girls.' She turned when she got to the door. 'Why not call in this afternoon? I'm sure Brí would love to meet you.'

'Good idea,' said Douglas. 'I will.' But Elsie failed to hear or respond as her mind was now firmly set on getting the better of Room 3 before her guests arrived.

*

When Douglas arrived at the café in the afternoon, the door was ajar and yet the *closed* sign had been posted on the door. He could hear the sounds of voices inside so, as he entered, he called out, 'Anyone at home?'

A cloud of cinnamon smoke from Kath's vape greeted him as he entered the room where a group of people were gathered around the table.

'Oh, come on in, Douglas, son,' called Kath through the smoke. 'So glad you've called. Come and meet Bríana' she said. 'She got in late last night, she did.'

A rose-cheeked, elegant and vivacious lady stood up and said, 'Oh, I've heard so much about you, Douglas. It is so good to meet you,' and she made her way to Douglas and kissed him firmly on both cheeks. As he inhaled her heady perfume and felt the softness of her undulant hair, he realised why she had turned the heads of many men through her years. She took him by the hand and led him to the table, where he sat in a vacant seat next to her.

Peter stood up and, reaching across the table, he grasped Douglas by the hand and said, 'Douglas, it is good to see you. May I go and fetch you a cup of tea? In fact, I think we might all be ready for another brew, don't you think, Kath?'

'Aye, that we are, Peter, darling. God bless you,' said Kath, and wrestled with her cough for a while. Douglas was aware that both daughters watched her with furrowed brows. Peter made his way to the kitchen. 'Och, this cinnamon and pomegranate doesn't really suit me, you know,' she said when she had breath for speaking. Kath was sitting at the end of the table, with Peter and Nancy on her left, and Brí on her right. Douglas noticed that, though Brí was sitting next to her mother, there was some distance between them.

'Don't you think my mother has done well, giving up the ciggies?' said Brí to Douglas. He noticed that her hair was a fascinating mix of reds and auburns. Brí did not miss his glance to her hair and, patting it, she said, 'Still my own colour, you know,' and smiled a beguiling smile.

'I'm sorry,' said Douglas, embarrassed that he had been caught out admiring her hair.

'No, no,' said Brí, and clasped Douglas' hand briefly in affectionate reassurance.

'Mine's going grey,' ventured Nancy, pulling a strand of the straight hair that fell over her ear.

'Aye, but it's a beautiful grey, Nancy, love,' said Brí. Douglas noticed the hint of American influence on Brí's native Irish accent.

Kath was wincing in some discomfort and said, 'Nancy, love, would you fetch me the pills, now. It's almost three o'clock and I think I'm due them.' Nancy immediately rose from the table, accidentally knocking the chair noisily as she did so.

'Gets that clumsiness from her mother, she does,' said Kath as she watched her daughter make for the kitchen. 'And, Douglas, don't you go telling my Brí about my antics at the Memorial Mass, will you now?' she said. Her smile was quickly checked by a dart of pain.

'Nancy, can you find them?' called a concerned Brí to the kitchen. Nancy soon returned through the fly curtain with a couple of pills and a glass of water.

Kath gratefully received the pills and soon knocked them back. 'These are my miracle pills, they are, Doug,' she said grimacing as she swallowed them. 'I don't know what they pack in them but, sure to God, they do wonders for the pain, they do.'

'I'm sorry, Kath,' said Douglas, frowning. 'Has the pain got worse then?' he asked.

'Aye, just a little in the last day or two,' she replied.

'Oh, Mother,' said Brí, her brows furrowing over her clear, blue-green eyes.

'It's easing,' said Kath. 'Don't think I'll be dying on you all today,' she said, 'So don't you go contacting Jim Tarney just yet.'

'Is that your doctor, Ma?' asked Brí.

'No, he's the undertaker, lass,' said Kath. 'Makes beautiful coffins, he does. Good, strong Irish oak. Built to last.'

'Oh, Mother!' said Brí.

At that moment, Peter entered the room carrying a tray laden with tea, cups and one of Kath's cakes and he placed it carefully on the table. 'We're on to the undertaker already, Peter,' said Kath, reaching out for the cake knife.

'Oh, so you'll be leaving us this afternoon will you, Kath?' said Peter, settling himself at the table. After squeezing Kath's hand, he starting to pour the tea.

Brí received her cup from Peter and, looking at Douglas, said, 'I've got so much to catch up on, you know. It's been too long. I think you know I've lived in America for nearly twenty years now. Mostly in Virginia, but now in Pennsylvania.' She took a sip of tea and sighed in contentment and said, 'Oh, there's nothing like a cup of proper Irish tea.'

'Aye, you missed that more than your family, love,' said Kath.

'I did, Ma,' said Brí smiling. She glanced at her mother who was not smiling, but rather concentrated on cutting her cake. Brí looked back at Douglas and said, 'My Mam has said she's told you a bit about us all, so you know we've had some ups and downs over the years.' She turned to look at her mother who remained focussed on the cake-cutting. 'Haven't we, Mammy?'

'I don't think we need to trouble poor Douglas with our family disputes,' said Kath, shovelling slices of cake on to plates and handing them out.

'Mammy and Brí used to fight,' said Nancy, as she lunged into her slice of cake.

'Nancy!' protested Brí, tightening her lips and delivering a fierce look to her sister.

'No family is perfect,' said Kath. Douglas noticed how awkward she looked. She forked a large portion of cake into her mouth and chewed hard on it.

'Certainly not ours, that's for sure,' said Brí.

'Well, I for one, have never met a perfect family,' said Peter, seeking to calm an increasingly tense atmosphere. 'Have you, Douglas?'

'No,' said Douglas. He felt one of his Vicarish bland reassurances coming on, so opted to say nothing instead.

For a few moments there was an awkward silence in the room. Kath, still with her mouth partly full glanced briefly at Brí and said, 'Well, it took me getting close to death's doorpost to bring you here.'

Brí had not embarked on her slice of cake, but had been poking at it with her fork. She looked at her mother and said, 'Well, I can go home tomorrow if that's what you want.'

'No, lass,' said Kath shaking her head. 'I'm sorry, I shouldn't have said that.' She looked up at Douglas and said, 'Douglas, darling. I'm sorry to bring you into all of this. We're not proud of it, are we, lass?' she continued, glancing at Brí who was clutching her cup of tea. 'It's all in the past.'

'Hm,' muttered Brí, and drank slowly from the cup.

'Kath, love,' said Peter, taking her hand. 'We are on tender ground here for the both of you. Yes, Brí has come here because she got the news of your cancer. We know you two have not had the best of relationships.'

'Hm' said Brí again, and took another large slurp of tea.

'But,' continued Peter, 'she's here now.' Glancing across to Brí, he said, 'Can I suggest you take a day or two to settle in to each other's company again?'

'The man's been in the psychic therapy trade, you see, love,' said Kath, smiling briefly at Peter. 'So he knows a thing or two about all of this stuff.'

'You're right, Peter,' said Brí, before Peter had a chance to give a more accurate explanation of his trade. 'I've not come over to fight. Maybe, Mammy, we just need to do a bit of getting to know each other again.'

'Maybe, lass,' said Kath, taking a slow sip of her tea. The pain in her chest was easing, but it was now an emotional pain from the past that was disturbing her. But she also felt something of the power of her Golgotha experience lapping at the jagged edge of this relationship with her daughter. She looked at Brí and said, 'Yes, I'm sorry, love,' and reached out her plump hand to her daughter's and squeezed it lightly. She breathed in deeply, and, looking at Douglas, said, 'Now, Doug. Peter and I have been talking. We hear you are off to Egypt soon...'

'Egypt?' cried Brí, her countenance brightening.

'Bloody Pharaoh. Got what he deserved,' said Nancy, and downed the remains of her tea.

'Er, yes,' said Douglas to Brí, not knowing quite how to respond to Nancy's interjection. 'Just for a few day's holiday. Cairo. Going with a friend.' Then turning to Kath, he said, 'I'm leaving for England tomorrow and we fly out to Egypt on Thursday.'

'That's grand, son,' said Kath. 'It will do you a power of good, it will. All them pyramids and temples and the like. We don't have any of them kind of things over here. They wouldn't suit us.'

'Plagues of frogs and flies,' interrupted Nancy.

'Now, when will you be returning to Dingle, then?' asked Kath, ignoring Nancy.

'Oh, I'll be back here in Dingle by Tuesday. We are just going for the weekend,' replied Douglas.

'That's grand,' said Kath. Then, taking Peter's hand she said, 'Douglas, son, we'd like to do the marriage before I get too... you know, uncomfortable. Would you be up to doing something for us on the Thursday of next week?'

'Of course, Kath,' said Douglas, feeling some anxiety as he was far from sure when he would have time to prepare the service.

'Can I be a bridesmaid, Mam?' asked Nancy. A portion of the cake icing was edging her upper lip that now quivered as it awaited a response.

'Oh, Nancy, love, it's not going to be that kind of wedding. But, sure to God, I want my two girls close to me. So, you be there, wearing your best frock.'

Nancy smiled an endearing smile and said, 'I won't let you down, Mam.'

'No, you won't, lass,' said Kath.

'Neither will I,' said Brí and briefly touched her mother's hand and was taken aback by its coldness. For the first time, and certainly not the last, she felt a stab of grief at the thought of losing the mother with whom she had known such a strained relationship through the years.

Kath looked at her eldest daughter and said, 'Thanks for coming, love. I'm glad you're here. I truly am.' She then turned to the others and said, 'Now, who's for more of the tea? You made a grand pot today, Peter, I will say.'

'Not for me, thanks Kath,' said Douglas rising from the table. 'I really need to go and get ready for my holiday.'

With that, all at the table except Nancy rose to their feet and, after receiving hugs and good wishes, Douglas left the café to prepare for the forthcoming foray into the land of the Pharaohs, and the land where his beloved Saoirse received the fatal bullet that closed her vibrant eyes for the final time.

CHAPTER 10

It was unusual these days for Alice to feel nervous, but after she had been to the toilet for the third time that morning, she had to acknowledge that there was an agitation in her soul. Her aunt Mavis had been a great help. She had spoken with one of the wardens of the church - a man called Brian - and arranged for him not only to put up Douglas for the night, but also to drive them to the airport. Alice was sitting on the staircase and watching the front door, waiting for their arrival.

'Brian's just phoned,' called Mavis from the kitchen. 'They'll be hear in ten minutes. Are you ready?'

'Yes,' said Alice. 'I'm waiting in the hall, Aunt,'

'Got your passport?'

'Yes.'

'Your currency?'

'Yes.'

'Your glasses?'

Alice smiled, 'Oh, do you think I'll need those?' she asked.

Mavis came hurrying through from the kitchen, 'Of course, you will need...' but then saw her niece sitting on the stairs with her glasses planted firmly on her nose, smiling a mischievous smile.

'Oh, you...' said Mavis. 'So... You looking forward to your adventure?' she asked, untying a garish purple apron.

Alice remained sitting on the stairs with her chin resting on the palm of her hand. 'Mmm' she said.

'You don't sound too convinced,' said Mavis, folding up the apron into a tidy bundle.

'Oh, I'm convinced we should be going, Aunt. But… It feels a bit awkward, doesn't it? I mean. it really looks like we are going on a date, doesn't it?'

'Well, I'm not going to intrude into your personal life, my love,' said Mavis. 'But why don't you just go to enjoy yourself and not worry too much about all of that, now?'

'Yes, Aunt. As ever, you are my wise companion,' and Alice stood up and embraced her aunt.

'Oh, now get away with you,' said Mavis and was about to say something else when the doorbell rang.

Mavis opened the door and standing there was Brian, her driver to the airport. 'Your chariot awaiteth,' he said, his angular mouth stretching into an awkward smile. He took Alice's case and bundled it into the boot of his car. Meanwhile Douglas had got out of the car and made straight for Mavis giving her a warm hug before moving to Alice giving her a brief kiss on the cheek.

'You coming to whisk me off for a weekend in Egypt then?' she said, looking amused.

He smiled at her, then said, 'Congratulations on the job. So, you are the new Development Manager?'

'That I am, Reverend,' she said. 'Starting in the summer.'

She was about to say more when Brian called, 'Come on, and in you get. Kate says there's a hell of a hold up in Glossop.'

'Who does?' asked Douglas as he climbed into the passenger seat after Alice had chosen to sit in the back.

'Kate the satnav,' said Brian, starting up the car. Thus, they left a waving Mavis and made their way out of Sheffield on to the glorious Snake Pass. For a time, Alice listened to the men's conversation in the front of the car, with Douglas catching up on bits of news from his old parish. At one point she heard Brian say, 'You know, Doug, I'm the soul of discretion, don't you?

Won't say a word about this to anyone in the church.' Although she felt grateful for the discretion, she couldn't help but feel that such a reassurance was an indication that Brian deemed this trip to have something distinctly immoral about it.

She turned and gazed out at the glorious moorland and felt again that disturbing nervousness. What was at the root of this fear? She decided that, in part, it was a worry that she might have got all this terribly wrong and she would be leading this admirable man back into the dark valleys of grief that he had only so recently vacated. And yet, and yet, she trusted the dream. These dreams had never been wrong before. She had learned to trust them utterly. No, she actually felt confident that he would not suffer on this trip. So, what was it that was bothering her?

The car journey now took them through the Snake Woodland, and shafts of sunshine flickered through the firs and across her face. No, the fear was not for him, it was for her. For the first time since Georges, she was feeling drawn into love again. There was no point in denying it. She *did* feel attracted to Douglas. But was she really ready to risk again, after all the hurt from last time?

'Been to Egypt before?' shouted Brian from the front seat, peering into his rear-view mirror at Alice.

'No,' replied Alice. 'First time.'

'Nope. Neither have I,' shouted Brian again. 'Been on a camel once, though. At a zoo. Only just managed to stay on the thing. I think they have lots in Egypt. They say you can visit the pyramids on a camel.'

'Oh, OK,' said Alice, somehow feeling very disinclined to enter into conversation with Brian, and he soon returned to a conversation with Douglas about the benefits of camel transport on desert terrains.

As it happened, the congestion in Glossop had cleared before they got there, so they made the airport with time to spare. Douglas and Alice thanked Brian and entered the restless transition world of the airport.

*

As the plane soared into the sky clearing a foggy Manchester, Douglas closed his eyes, and his mind took him back to that January day when, through some kind of out-of-body experience, he was taken to a place which held the story of Golgotha in deep memory. And there he entered a remembrance of the terrible and great story of a man who claimed to be God who loved this world to death. He heard again the sound of thunder that rumbled from the dark, glowering clouds above him. And once again he saw the wounded eyes that gazed so searchingly yet lovingly into his soul. The memory of those eyes was never far from him these days. Every time he recalled them, it was as if he was actually witnessing them viewing him from a place just out of reach of normal sight.

The plane hit a pocket of turbulence that disturbed his thoughts for a moment, but it soon settled and he was quickly back in that valley again. The memory was vivid. The sense of the weight of grief, that had been like an oppressive shroud, slipping from him. Such a sense of freedom. And the hand on his shoulder. *Her* hand on his shoulder. And her word, freeing him. That's why he was here, now twenty thousand feet above the English midlands, speeding towards the Middle East.

And on his right, peering out of the window with only one working eye, was Alice Fournier, a woman he hardly knew, but who somehow had convinced him to travel with her to the land where his Saoirse had met her fate. He knew, through an instinct that he was fast learning to trust, that Saoirse was blessing this trip, and blessing this friendship. And already this woman next to him felt like a good friend. She was in her mid-forties, just a few years younger than him, and yet she only looked mid-thirties to Douglas. Her head was framed by the bright light of the window. He could see the attractive hints of grey scattered among the blond curls. She leaned back in her seat and patting Douglas on the arm she smiled like a child and said, 'Look!' He leaned across her. 'The clouds...' she said, as he scrutinised the scene beyond the window. Not far below them lay a blanket of undulating cloud. 'I was imagining that if I jumped out of the plane, and landed on it, I would be bouncing on the softest duvet ever.'

As Douglas eased himself back into his seat, he became aware of just how close he was to her and a sensation he had not experienced for several years touched him. Was it sexual? Was it spiritual? It was hard to say. Somehow a mixture of both, but he was aware that he would gladly have laid his head on this shoulder. But she was not long out of an abusive and broken marriage. He hated the thought of causing any hurt. They were both tender. He turned to her and said, 'Actually, Alice. I'm very glad you didn't try and see if that duvet was as comfortable as you supposed.'

'Oh, you never jumped out of a plane, then?' she asked, raising an eyebrow over her hazel eye. As Douglas looked at her he noticed an intriguing and somewhat beguiling corona of dark grey surrounding the hazel.

'No, as a matter of fact I haven't,' he answered. 'Have you, Alice?'

'Yes,' she said, with a gentle nod. 'When I was first married, Georges gave me a birthday treat of a parachute jump.' She looked back out at the clouds again.

'Did you enjoy it?' asked Douglas, envious of her experience.

'Once I managed to persuade myself to jump out of the plane, I did,' she said, still gazing out of the window at the soft cloud beneath them. 'The parachute opened almost immediately and once it did, the fear left me. I was being held by the wind. I floated down through thin wisps of cloud. As I got nearer to earth, I was met by the warm air of Provence and the fragrance of lavender. It was special, Douglas.' She looked back at Douglas for a few moments. 'It was so special. They were the good days.' She smiled briefly, then returned her gaze to the skies.

Both were quiet for a few moments, then Douglas said, 'I'm sorry Alice that they had to be followed by bad days.'

She turned from the window and looked back to Douglas and said, 'Everyone has the bad days. But let's make some good days now, shall we?' She placed her slim hand over Douglas' and held it there for a few moments.

*

'Look!' said Alice, opening the blinds of their Airbnb apartment. Douglas walked across the room and stood next to her. He could find no words as he beheld the sight of two vast Pyramids, lit by the evening sun, and rising from the desert sands in extraordinary magnificence. They opened the glass doors and stood on the spacious balcony in the mild evening air.

'I had no idea we would see these so clearly from our apartment,' he said.

'Well, they are big!' she said, chuckling. 'They'd be hard to miss.'

Douglas smiled his downturned smile and said, 'That they would, Alice.' Together they gazed in wonder and admiration at the ancient spectacle and remained in silence for several minutes. Then Douglas turned to Alice and said, 'Alice, are you OK if we go to the street where the shooting took place tomorrow morning? I'd like to do that before we see the sights.'

'Yes, Douglas. Of course,' she said, settling herself into a chair on the balcony. 'Are you going to be OK about this?'

'I think so,' said Douglas, lifting his eyebrows for a few moments. 'I know it's right to come. But I can't deny, I'm feeling a bit anxious.' He sat in the other seat on the balcony and watched the lights of the setting sun playing on the rooftops around them. 'It does feel weird - coming to the very place of the shooting. I've had much healing, but I can also feel the sadness. Saoirse meant everything to me. Poor girl...' He slowly shook his head and looked out across the rooftops to the desert scene beyond him, and the vast pyramids rising from the sand.

'Yes, I know she did,' said Alice softly and noticed the mix of emotions playing across the face of her friend. They were both quiet for a moment as the sun edged its way to the sandy horizon.

'Do you know exactly where... you know. Where it all happened?' asked Alice.

'Oh yes,' replied Douglas, releasing his eyes from the horizon, and his thoughts from his sorrows. 'I got all the details from the police some time ago. I spent hours actually, poring over Google Earth and locating the exact spot and trying to imagine it all.' He went back into the apartment and searched for a few moments in his back pack and pulled out a ragged-looking map. He returned to the balcony and said, 'Got hold of this last year.' He placed it on the small balcony table. 'Look.' Both Alice and

Douglas inspected the road map of Cairo and in particular the crossing of two streets that had been marked on the map by a large red circle and a cross. 'That's where it is,' said Douglas tapping the marked area.

'The local taxi drivers should find the place easily from this,' said Alice, removing her glasses temporarily to clean them.

'Or we could get a camel,' suggested Douglas who kept a serious face for a few moments, then laughed.

'Well, funny you should say that,' said Alice, polishing her glasses carefully on her scarf. 'Because on Saturday I have booked us two camels for a trip to the pyramids, so you might want to get some practice in.'

'You have?' said Douglas surprised and delighted.

'I thought you'd look very British on a camel somehow. The new T E Lawrence.'

'Yes, I will do my best to commend the Empire,' said Douglas. They both laughed and Douglas turned and looked again with admiration at the Pyramids. 'This was a good idea, Alice,' he said nodding his head.

'Not my idea, Douglas,' said Alice, rising from her chair, 'Morwenna's. Anyway, I'm going to my room to unpack, then I suggest we find a restaurant for a meal.'

'Good plan. I could do with a good pie, chips and mushy peas.'

'What?' cried Alice

Douglas pointed at her and laughed. 'All right then, couscous it is,' he said. Both Alice and Douglas surprised themselves by how relaxed they each felt, and the evening meal that consisted neither of chips nor couscous was one they both enjoyed greatly. It was a good start to their brief holiday that was to hold surprises for both of them.

CHAPTER 11

It was the sound of the muezzin from the nearby mosque that woke Douglas. He climbed out of bed and went to the balcony window and watched the dawn break over the great Pyramids of Giza, whose peaks were glowing crimson as the sun made its glimmering way into the morning sky. Alice who was clearly more owl than lark, slept her way through the prayer call and only emerged from her room after Douglas had showered and dressed and was enjoying a coffee on the balcony. For a time, she came and sat with him, clasping her cup of tea.

'There's a book of ancient Egyptian poetry in my room,' she said, frowning at Douglas due to the brightness of the morning sun.

'Really?' said Douglas eagerly. 'You fluent in hieroglyphics?'

'Of course,' said Alice. 'Part of my Physics degree.'

Douglas chuckled, then asked, 'Did you like their poetry?'

'I did,' said Alice, taking a swig of her tea. 'They didn't seem to mind dying,' she said.

'Well, I suppose when you spend most of your life seeing a monster of a pyramid being erected as your tombstone, you can't altogether ignore it,' replied Douglas.

'Good point,' said Alice nodding. Her hair almost looked electrified in the brilliance of the desert sun. 'There was one I really liked. Apparently, it appears on a tomb next to a blind man playing a harp.' She closed her eyes and turned her face to the sun, and then quoted some lines that she had read:

> 'Rejoice and let thy heart forget the day when they shall lay thee to rest.

Cast all sorrow behind thee,
and bethink thee of joy
until there come that day of reaching port in the land
that loveth silence.
Follow thy desire as long as thou livest,
put myrrh on thy head, clothe thee in fine linen.
Set singing and music before thy face.
Increase yet more the delights which thou has,
and let not thy heart now faint.'

'It's beautiful, Alice,' said Douglas and she looked at him and smiled. 'You learned it by heart so quickly?' he asked.

'It happens when I find words that I love,' said Alice. 'And I love the thought of heaven as the "port in the land that loveth silence."'

Douglas nodded. Neither spoke for a time and the only sound was that of the hum of the city traffic. He looked at Alice and asked, 'Do you think that heaven will be a land that loves silence, Alice?'

Alice furrowed her brow and raised her hand for a few moments to shield her eyes from the sun. 'Aren't you supposed to know those sorts of things?'

'Hm, well. I don't remember them teaching us that at college,' he said and smiled.

Still shielding her eyes from the bright sun, Alice looked out at the glowing peaks of the great Pyramids and said, 'I don't think it would be a silence of absence. Far from it. But I think of it as a world where no more need be said. Real silence is when you reach that point when you no longer feel the need to fill space. It is the silence of knowing someone so well, that you don't feel awkward with the silence. It is the silence of contentment, like a silence after a beautiful concert or a glorious sunset or love-making. It is when any words would be an intrusion. Then you can finally just be, without having to say anything.' She turned and looked at Douglas. Her smile was full of such kindness. 'That's the kind of silence I like,' she said. 'Don't you?'

'Yes,' said Douglas. 'If I'm honest, I think it's the kind of silence I tried to avoid through much my life. But not now. I like the thought of that kind of silence, Alice.'

And so they sat in silence for some time watching the light change on the great triangular, stepped sides of the pyramids ahead of them. It was Alice who broke the silence as she said, 'Let's go out for breakfast.'

'Alice, that is an excellent idea,' replied Douglas. 'Especially as we don't actually have anything in for breakfast!'

*

They found a small café just a couple of streets away and enjoyed a breakfast of fruit, cake and coffee at a pavement table. Just as Douglas was draining the last of his very strong coffee, he looked down the busy street ahead of him and saw a tall figure walking towards them. 'What the...?' he said, placing his cup firmly on the table and staring in front of him.

'What is it?' asked Alice, looking first at Douglas and then in the direction of his gaze. She also saw the figure making his way towards them and said, 'It can't be...'

'What?' said Douglas, now utterly puzzled not only by the identity of the person making their way towards them, but also by the fact that Alice seemed to know him as well.

'I know this man,' said Alice and started to wave to him.

'What?' said Douglas. 'You know him?'

'Not a man, I think,' said Alice still looking at the figure who was now only a few paces from them.

'Dorch - what on earth are you doing here?' cried Douglas, leaping to his feet so fast that he knocked his chair over.

'Well now, Doug. Fancy seeing you here!' said Dorchadas laughing. 'And Alice,' he said, approaching the woman slowly rising from the breakfast table. 'We meet again.'

Alice was as surprised as Douglas was to see Dorchadas and she was struggling to speak, only managing a quiet 'Hello, Dorchadas.'

'Well, you better sort out your chair before people are tripping over it, Doug,' said Dorchadas, as he reached their table. 'And yes, as you are about to ask. Make mine an Americano, if they serve such a thing here.'

Alice gathered another seat from a nearby table, then called the waiter and ordered three coffees. There followed a rush of questions, mostly from Douglas, and little by little they established how they all knew each other. Douglas was initially shocked to discover that Alice had already met Dorchadas and hadn't told him, but as the conversation wore on his sense of shock changed to one more of comfort. And it was particularly comforting to discover that Alice had no trouble at all in believing that Dorchadas was an angel visiting earth in human form.

'But Dorch, you've got to tell us,' said Douglas, as the steaming cups of fresh coffee arrived. 'How did you get here? I mean, you weren't on our plane - we'd have noticed.'

'No, Doug - I wasn't on your plane,' said Dorchadas smiling broadly.

'Douglas,' said Alice. 'Dorchadas travels - you know that. The more important question is, *why* have you joined us, Dorchadas?' She raised an eyebrow as she looked searchingly at Dorchadas, and Douglas noticed that, unusually for Dorchadas, he looked a little shy.

'Well now, Alice. That is a good question, and the honest answer is that I'm not fully sure myself. I mean...' he hesitated for a few moments and took a sip of his coffee. 'I don't want to get in your way at all.'

'It's all right, Dorchadas,' said Alice with her characteristic directness. 'We are not on a date. And there's nothing happening that would shock an angel.'

'No, no. Quite,' said Dorchadas, still betraying a slight awkwardness. It was Douglas' turn to smile broadly at Dorch now and he winked at his friend when Dorchadas glanced up at him. 'No, I'm here because I was sent here,' said Dorchadas. 'And I'll be here for as long as I'm needed, which I think will only be for this morning's work.'

'And do you know what the "work" is this morning, Dorch?' asked Douglas, who was sipping a cup of coffee that was even stronger than the first.

'I think so, Doug. I believe we are off to see the scene of...the, er...'

'Yes,' said Alice, helping out Dorchadas who did not know quite how to define the place where Saoirse was shot. 'That's where we are going.'

'Do you know where it is, Dorch?' asked Douglas.

'No, I'm hoping you know that,' said Dorchadas.

'I do,' said Douglas smiling at the angel. 'They don't know everything, Alice,' he said.

'No, that we certainly don't,' said Dorchadas, draining his cup. 'Just as well we don't, if you ask me.'

'And another thing that angels are not brilliant at,' said Douglas standing up and picking up his light jacket from the back of the chair, 'and that is fashion sense. Dorch, I've only ever seen you in that thick jumper, but this shirt you are wearing...' He reached out and pulled at the sleeve of the ill-fitting and garish coloured shirt.

'Alice,' said Dorchadas, 'I'm afraid my friend Douglas here doesn't recognise real style when he sees it.'

Both Alice and Douglas laughed and then Douglas said, 'Right. Let's hope they have loos here, which I'll need after all that strong coffee, then let's be on our way.' Douglas made his way into the café to search for the toilets.

'Is he going to be all right, love?' asked Dorchadas.

'I'm not sure,' said Alice thoughtfully. 'I'm just hoping so. I believe it's the right thing to do.'

'Oh, so do I,' said Dorchadas. 'It's so good to see you again, lass.'

'And you, Dorchadas,' said Alice, and added. 'I'll never forget those meetings. They...'

'I know,' said Dorchadas, reaching over and grasping her hand. 'I'll certainly never forget them either.'

*

It was not long before they were clambering into a rickety taxi with Douglas managing to explain to the driver where they needed to go with much pointing of the map. The driver was clearly puzzled as to why a group of tourists should be wanting to go to a very obscure part of the great city of Cairo, but nonetheless he was happy to take them. He first drove them to a flower vendor where Douglas collected some bright gladioli. Then the driver sped along some main roads before turning into a part of the city that seemed to be a maze of backstreets. All three passengers peered out of their windows as the driver skilfully drove the taxi down the narrow streets that were just wide enough for two cars. He carefully avoided all kinds of obstacles such as fridges, fruit stalls and tables and chairs, not to mention the steady stream of pedestrians and cyclists making their way down the streets. He passed oncoming cars with great dexterity, and once or twice more impatient drivers behind him would accelerate and overtake their vehicle with a great sounding of horns and revving of engines. The buildings rose high on either side of the streets. Some upper rooms had small balconies decorated with plants and occasionally between the houses hung washing lines with an array of clothes drying in the morning air.

'Would this be a main route from the airport if you wanted to travel east out of the city?' asked Douglas to the driver as he thought of Saoirse's last journey when her friend Lolly drove them to her hometown.

'This is the main route,' replied the taxi driver,' for those who know the city well. It avoids the main roads which get jammed with traffic. Traffic is terrible in Cairo. Terrible!' To the alarm of the passengers, the driver raised his hands in the air, returning them to the steering wheel just in time to avoid a street vendor. 'But these roads usually good.' Then he abruptly stopped the car and reached for Douglas' map. 'Yes, here,' he said, stabbing his finger on the marked part of Douglas' map. 'You get out here. Thank you.'

They disembarked on to the street into a flurry of children demanding baksheesh and Douglas paid the driver. Once they had dismissed the children, Douglas pulled from his back pocket a photo of a street corner and raised it up, quickly matching it to the scene opposite them. The high buildings gave welcome shade as the sun was getting warmer. The street was wider at this point and contained a mix of domestic houses and small shops, some of which had sand-covered awnings over their entrances. The three spent a few moments standing on the narrow and broken pavement surveying the scene.

'Yes, this is the place,' said Douglas quietly.

It was Dorchadas who noticed some notches in the wall. 'Looks to me like this was made by a vehicle,' said Dorchadas, and both Douglas and Alice looked closer to inspect it.

'Yes, I think this is where Lolly, the driver, lost control of the car and hit the wall,' said Douglas.

'So this is where it happened,' said Alice, and slowly covered her mouth with her hand as she all too vividly imagined the scene.

Douglas reached out his hand and felt the stone, rubbing his hand over the gash marks many times. It was hard at first to believe he was in the very place that the dreadful shooting took place. He could see it all so clearly: Lolly driving carefully down the street, with Saoirse in the passenger seat beside her, eagerly looking out from the car, admiring the ramshackle buildings either side of the street. Who knows what her last thoughts or words were, but maybe she commented on the dangerous driving of the car that overtook them on the narrow street. Was the smashing of the windscreen by the hail of bullets the last thing on earth that her beautiful eyes beheld? Lolly also saw the windscreen spray wildly in front of her and felt the pain of the bullet lodging in her shoulder. He saw her wrestling the car to a halt, crashing it into this very wall. He saw the dazed passengers clambering out of the car, then noticing the horrifying sight of Saoirse slumped in the front with blood oozing from her head. As Douglas ran his hand over the wounded wall, he felt the familiar wound of grief in his soul. And yet, despite the proximity to the very place of the shooting, he did not feel overwhelmed by emotion. It was a sure sign that so much had been mended within him. A few weeks back, a visit to this street would have added to his pain. But he had a clear sense that today, by contacting this place of trauma, he was experiencing yet another healing - a further stage forward on the road of grief.

Dorchadas and Alice said nothing as they stood with their friend at this sad crime scene. After studying the wall for a while, Douglas then laid his flowers at the side of the road. He then said, 'Alice, could you say the lines from that poem again. Just the first couple, about the land that loveth silence?'

'Of course,' said Alice. A motor scooter raced past and she waited for its high-pitched roar to soften in the distance. She then breathed in and closing her eyes recited for the second time that day,

> 'Rejoice and let thy heart forget the day when they shall lay thee to rest.
> Cast all sorrow behind thee,
> and bethink thee of joy
> until there come that day of reaching port in the land that loveth silence.'

'My, there's both beauty and wisdom in them words,' said Dorchadas. He then looked at Douglas and said, 'How is it, son?'

'I've done much casting of sorrow behind me, Dorch, as you know. But there will always be a little that will never leave my heart, and it is a precious part of the sorrow and it is one I can hold without it breaking me. So, it is good to be here. I feel something of a completion. I have come to the place where it happened, and in a funny way, I can now say I was there with her. If you see what I mean.'

'I do see what you mean,' said Alice.

Dorchadas was about to say something when a man came up to him and said, 'Excuse me, which of you is Mr Douglas?'

'I am,' said Douglas, surprised to have someone asking for him in this obscure place.

'Ah,' said the stranger bowing to him. He was a man younger than Douglas. He was of medium height, dark-haired with a short beard, and spoke with a Middle Eastern accent. Douglas felt he had a remarkably kind and trustworthy face, and he felt quite comfortable in being recognised by him.

'Have we met?' asked Douglas.

'I think.... This way, please. Come.' He beckoned them down the street a short way and led them in to a small courtyard. Two of the walls of the courtyard were decorated with a vine that was coming into leaf. There was also a lemon verbena plant which filled the place with its fragrance. Pots of geraniums both on the ground and on the windowsills added vivid colour to the scene. Under the overhanging vine, there stood a rickety table and the stranger beckoned the visitors to sit on the shaded, ancient-looking iron chairs around it. 'You like Coca Cola, please?' he asked them all, again bowing and pressing the palms of his hands together.

'That would be perfect,' said Dorchadas. Alice and Douglas nodded.

As the man left the group for a moment, disappearing into a room off the courtyard, Douglas looked at Dorchadas raising his eyebrows at him. 'Have you met him before, Dorch?'

'No, I haven't, son,' said Dorchadas.

'Any ideas who he might be?' he asked.

'I think I know,' said Alice.

'I need to explain, Alice,' said Douglas leaning towards her, 'Dorchadas has this way of introducing us to people, who, well...'

'You don't need to explain, Douglas,' said Alice. 'You see when Dorchadas helped me in France that time, he introduced me to a couple of people from the past. It made perfect sense to me that they should visit my time.'

'Oh, I see,' said Douglas, still a little disquieted by the fact that she and Dorchadas had met previously. 'Well, it took me quite a while to get used to it,' he added.

'Look, the gentleman's on his way back to us, so let's ask him shall we?' said Dorchadas. The man came back out into the courtyard with a tray of Coke bottles and an assortment of glasses and set them down on the table.

'My friends and I would be very interested to know your name,' said Dorchadas as the man pulled up a chair and sat on it.

'Ah, forgive me,' said the man. 'I should have told you at the beginning. My name is Joseph.'

Douglas glanced at Alice and she nodded. She had guessed right. So, this was another Bible character somehow emerging into the present time. But Douglas was still uncertain as to which Joseph this was. He checked his clothing and there was no sign of a multi-coloured dream coat. But before he could speculate further, Joseph continued. 'So, you are Mr Douglas,' he said, looking at Douglas. Then turning to Alice he said, 'And your name please, Madam?'

'Alice' she said.

'Ah yes. A beautiful name, if I may say so.' And turning to Dorchadas he said, 'So you are Dorchadas. I have heard about you, but we have not met.'

'No, lad. But it truly is an honour to meet you,' said Dorchadas.

'Oh, no, no. None of that, please. I am just a man who was called to serve his God. And it was not difficult, because he gave me a most beautiful wife to care for.'

It was now dawning on Douglas that this particular Joseph was the one married to Mary and who was given the task of being the earthly father of the Messiah. But this was no haloed Joseph of Christmas cards and cribs. Here was a man of the earth who looked as human as any, with calloused hands, smelling of perspiration and currently swigging back a glass of coke.

'But, if you don't mind my asking,' said Douglas, 'What brings you here to speak with us?'

'Ah yes,' said Joseph, again nodding deferentially. 'Well, Mr Douglas and Miss Alice, it is so good to meet you and thank you for spending time with me today in this courtyard filled with the fragrance of Spring. I have been called here to tell you just a little piece of my story. But let me say, Mr Douglas, that...' Here Joseph paused and looked so sad that Douglas felt concerned for him. Joseph continued, 'I know of your dear and precious wife. I know of the terrible fate that befell her on this very street. There is a great wound in the soul of this street now. You must know that the local people tried so hard to help her. There was great love for her. This is one of the things I have to tell you, Mr Douglas. She was not alone. There were her friends in the car of course. But there were also the people from the street. There were many arms who held her that day, and many tears shed for her. The people here will always remember her, and honour her greatly. They call her their Irish friend in Paradise and often pray for her.'

Douglas felt a momentary unwelcome return to the grief as he heard this, but he also felt a great sense of comfort. He had hated the fact that she was so far from home when she was shot, and yet he was hearing from Joseph that she was surrounded by love. Though the hatred of one man robbed her of her life, the love of many had held her as she slipped into her unconscious world that led to her departure from this world a few days later. 'Thank you, Joseph,' he said. 'That is very comforting.'

'Ah yes,' said Joseph. He shuffled the position of his glass and bottle on the table for a few moments, and then continued. 'So, my friend. My story. My wife, Mary, and I were given this most beautiful son. Oh, it was a greatly awesome thing to be entrusted with this child, but we were always given strength for this task. Well, news of the birth of our son, Jesus, came to the ears of Herod. He was not a good man and, while humble shepherds and foreigners from the East were delighted at the birth of the Messiah to our world, for Herod, our child was nothing but bad news. And one of your friends, Dorchadas,' he said, patting Dorchadas' arm and nodding at him, 'appeared to me in a dream and told us to flee the country, otherwise Herod would kill our little one. And so, we left that night and travelled the long, long journey here to Egypt.'

'Why Egypt?' asked Alice, pouring some of the coke carefully into her glass.

'That is what we were told, Miss Alice. Some things are well beyond my reason. I am a simple man. I am a carpenter - not a scribe or a rabbi. The messenger from God made it clear that we had to come to this land of the Pharaohs. The prophets spoke about it, and the wise men of God tell us about why the Messiah had to come down to Egypt. But for me, it made sense because some of my relatives lived here. And also, here we were a long way from Herod. We were sure some of his men would have tracked us down if we had remained in Judea. I had never left my country before, and, if I'm honest with you, I was very scared.' He frowned and looked down for a few moments, and then looking at Alice he said, 'It is a terrible thing to leave your country, Miss Alice. I can't describe how it feels. It is so frightening to step out of your land into a world that is so very different. The journey was terrible. Poor Mary. My, she was a courageous woman.' He shook his head in appreciation, then turning back to Alice he asked, 'Miss Alice, do you have children?'

'No, I don't have children,' said Alice and Douglas noticed the sorrow in her eyes.

'No, no...' said Joseph. 'Well, it is a wonderful gift to be given a child. But to have to carry that child with your few possessions away from your home town, away from your family, away from the country you love, fearful of the people who hate you and would kill you if they found you. It is a terrible thing.' He shook his head for a few moments, then looked up at Douglas and said, 'Why do people allow hatred to enter their hearts, Mr Douglas?'

Douglas was taken aback by such a searching question. It was not a comfortable question for him, because it was hatred that had stolen his precious Saoirse from him. And yet, he had been to Golgotha in that extraordinary vision back in January. This child that Joseph was speaking off, grew up and was hated so much that he was pinned to a wooden cross. Yet there he challenged the powers of hatred head on and triumphed. The memory was strong in Douglas. He looked at Joseph and said, 'I don't know why people allow hatred to enter their hearts, Joseph. But I do know that the child you so wonderfully protected on that journey and in this land, grew up and conquered the powers of hatred through the power of His love, and He has changed the hearts of millions since. Including mine.'

Joseph smiled and nodded his head. He gathered his scarf around his neck and thought for a few moments. 'Yes, I know now how my son lived and died.' He smiled warmly at Douglas and said, 'Yes, I know of that power. Well, returning to my story of our escape to Egypt. We settled here, even though we never really felt at home, and we missed our families so much. But we slowly got used to the food and learned the language. I did my carpentry and Mary taught not just our son, but other children in the neighbourhood.' He then leaned forward to Douglas and said in a quiet voice, 'You see, it was destiny. We had to be here. My son had to live the life of the refugee. It has been the fate of so many of His beloved children. He often spoke of his experience of exile here when He was growing up. He knew He was called to help the children find their true homeland. He knew it was His destiny. Do you understand destiny, Mr Douglas?'

'I'm not sure I do understand it,' said Douglas with candour. 'But I do sort of believe in it.'

'What is your destiny, Mr Douglas?' said Joseph. He now grasped Douglas by the hand and held it firmly. 'What are you going to do with your story of pain? You were taken out of the land of your beloved into a wild exile of terrible grief. But since then, you have found a pathway to a new home, and I see you are settling. But you still have the seeds of that pain. They must be planted in the good soil, Mr Douglas. Today, here in Egypt, you are planting the seeds in the good soil of your new-found faith. The soil of your old faith would never nurture these seeds. But this new soil is perfect for such seeds. Plant them Mr Douglas, and in time you will see the seedlings, and you will be delighted. And soon the seedlings will become plants that rise up and give shade and fruit to many. This is the way of my son, Mr Douglas.'

Douglas felt moved not only by what Joseph was saying, but by way he was saying it. All the time Joseph was leaning towards Douglas, and the creases on his forehead looked to Douglas like a child's drawing of waves, and the waves shifted with every word. Douglas was also frowning as he asked, 'But what is the plant, Joseph?'

'Ah, Mr Douglas, you must wait and see,' said Joseph. The waves calmed and the eyes beneath them brightened. 'But I think you should listen to what moves you in this land. Listen to what stirs in your heart. Listen to what ignites your mind, Mr Douglas.' Joseph reached out and placed his hand on Douglas' arm and said, 'I know you were meant to hear my story. In time, I think you will start to *feel* my story. You see, I have only told you a tiny amount of my story. But let it settle in. It is one of the seeds. Give it time to spring to life. Mine is a story of a family being forced to flee their homeland because of hatred, and to settle in a land that felt far from home. Is this not a tragedy that happens in your world, Mr Douglas? Was your dear wife not attacked in the land where your Lord came as a child refugee? Mr Douglas, you did not come here to remember the past. You came here to discover your future.'

Joseph then looked at Alice and said, 'Miss Alice, it has been a great delight to meet you.' He paused for a few moments, and then added. 'And Miss Alice, if I may... You are here, of course, for a reason. But I think you know that, don't you?'

'I... I think so,' said Alice, lowering her eyes and betraying a coy smile.

'And Dorchadas,' said Joseph. 'You have said very little, my friend.'

'Most unusual,' said Douglas, glancing at Dorchadas.

'But I am so pleased to have met you,' continued Joseph. He frowned for a few moments as he studied Dorchadas and then said, 'I know... it will not be long, my friend. I know there is great grief and great joy. But do not be afraid.'

'Thank you, Joseph,' said Dorchadas, and both Alice and Douglas noticed his look of vulnerability.

For a few moments the group sat in silence together. Similar thoughts were going through the minds of Douglas and Alice. It was a realisation that, somewhat to their surprise, this brief trip to Egypt was not just about attending to a piece of Douglas' grief journey, but was actually about catching a glimpse of the future. Douglas was just about to speak, when there he heard the voice of someone calling from the courtyard entrance. A small, elderly woman, dressed in black approached the group slowly and, as she got a little closer, bowed and said, 'Excuse me. Is one of you the husband of our Irish friend in Paradise?'

Douglas rose slowly from his seat, looked briefly at Joseph, and then back to the lady, and said, 'Yes. Yes, that is me.'

The lady smiled the smile of one discovering a long-lost friend, and approaching Douglas, she said 'Ah, that is good. That is *so* good.' She took hold of his hands and pulled them to her cheek and looking up at him with moistened eyes said, 'It is a great honour that you are here and it is an answer to our prayers. Please, would you come tonight to a meal at our house. Many neighbours from the street wish to meet with you. We who live here come from different nations, but we most speak the English. Forgive us, please. It is poor English, but we try....' She paused again and looked at the others at the table and added. 'And of course, your friends must come. Please...' She spread out her hands to the others.

'We would be delighted,' said Alice.

'Of course,' said Dorchadas, who was now also standing.

'Then we meet this night just before sundown. Come to this courtyard, and we will lead you to our home.' She then bowed to all of them saying, 'As-salamu alaykum,' and made her way out back on to the street. But before she disappeared, she called, 'There is a taxi here for you. We have arranged. This same taxi will bring you back here tonight. As-salamu alaykum.'

'Wa ʿalaykumu s-salām,' said Dorchadas, bowing to her as she left them.

'You fluent in Arabic, Dorch?' said Douglas, chuckling and gathering his jacket from the back of the chair. He then looked around and said, 'Where's Joseph?'

Dorchadas pursed his lips, then said, 'Doug, he's done his work. Though I should liked to have bid the fellow a good-bye, all the same. I liked the guy.'

'Our taxi,' said Alice pointing to the car that was sounding its horn in the street, and they all made their way to the waiting vehicle.

They encouraged Dorchadas to travel in the front due to his height, and Alice and Douglas climbed into the back. The taxi, that bore bold testimony of its many encounters with walls, vehicles and other solid objects, sputtered into life, then accelerated down the street. None of them spoke much on the journey. Alice spent the time gazing out of the window at the animated streets. But her mind was not on the streets. It was on her dream. So Morwenna was right. Already on their first full day in Cairo there were signs of healing and signs of destiny. 'It's good that we came here,' she shouted over the roar of the engine to no-one in particular. Douglas reached out and clasped her hand and said, 'You have good dreams, Alice.' He left his hand there for the rest of the journey back to their apartment. And Alice was content to have her hand held by his. Yes, it was good to be here.

CHAPTER 12

As Douglas, Dorchadas and Alice were being transported to their evening meal in Cairo, Kathleen Griffin was shutting up her Dingle café after a busy Friday afternoon. It was a great relief to bolt the door, and she made her way through the café area to the small living room at the back of the house, where she slumped down into her favourite and much-worn armchair. She grasped her vape, but quickly thought better of it. It never comforted her like the nicotine used to. A cup of tea would be grand, but she had no energy to go and make it. Peter would be in soon and he would bring her the tea and then go to cook the evening meal. What a godsend he was. Someone in her life with whom there were absolutely no complications. If only, if only... How would life had been, if they had been allowed to stay together all those years ago? 'Ah, come on Kathleen, you old misery,' she said out loud. 'Give thanks for what you do have, for God's sake, and don't mope about what you've missed.' But the pain in her chest made it hard to keep positive.

Her eyes closed and, as they did so often nowadays, her mind was immediately back at the bleak yet radiant scene she had visited just three months ago. At the edge of sleep, her mind led her back to the deep memory of Golgotha and she felt again the gaze of love caressing her soul. Again, Mary Magdalene came to her and comforted her. And Brigid - her beloved friend Brigid. She was just starting to hear again her words when she was brought back to this world with the sound of the back door scraping against the flagstones and Peter's voice calling out, 'I'm home, Kathleen. I picked up some beautiful mackerel from your man at the fish shop. They were caught fresh this morning. Let me get them in the fridge, then I'll be putting on the kettle.'

'You're a star, Peter,' called Kath. It was not long before she heard the welcome sound of the kettle.

'You shut up shop for the day?' he called.

'Aye, that I have, love. All done for the day now, the saints be praised.'

'Well, let me go and bless the porcelain, then I'll come and bring you a pot of tea.' She heard him make his way upstairs and closed her eyes again, this time falling into a dreamless sleep. She was awoken by Peter entering the room with a tray of tea and cake.'

'Oh, sorry to wake you, love,' he said, placing the tray on the table beside her. 'Here, let me turn on a few lights as the sun is settling itself now.' After turning on the lights and pouring the tea, he sat down in the chair next to Kath's. 'So, my beloved fiancée, how is it today?'

Kath chuckled and said, 'Sounds funny, doesn't it. A pair of old codgers like us!'

'Speak for yourself,' said Peter, tidying his long hair and gathering it afresh in the ponytail at the back of his head.

'Peter, love,' said Kath, leaning towards him from her chair and grasping his arm. 'Tell me honestly. How are you feeling about me dying and that? I mean, it can't be easy for you, now. You finally get to meet me again after all these years, discover you still like me, and the moment we get together again, I go and die on you. It's not exactly friendly, is it?'

Peter placed his hand on hers and started stroking it. 'I remember it all so clearly, Kath. You were such a sweet young thing. So full of laughter and light. I couldn't believe that God could create someone as pretty and vibrant as you. And I was angry with Him.' He pointed to the ceiling as he said this.

'You were angry with Him because you thought I was pretty?' Kath asked, raising her eyebrows.

'Of course, I was. I mean He had called me to a be a priest and to live a life of celibacy and then he sends you across my path.'

'Aye,' said Kath, smiling broadly. 'Well, that celibacy bit didn't last too long, did it now?'

For a moment Peter looked down, 'I know, Kath. I know.' He continued to look down, pausing for some time before he said, 'You know, I loved God so much and I loved you so much. It was a terrible conflict. I suppose that in the weeks we had together, my love for you was the stronger. I had to do much work in my soul after it all and, do you know, in time, I came to believe that God did not reject me for what happened and I discovered his tender love. I'll never really understand the rights and wrongs of it all, Kath. All I know is that in those precious days that you and I had together, I found a quality of love that I never thought was possible.'

'We had something very special, pet,' said Kath. 'Very special. I didn't know that kind of love with my Kevin, I'm sorry to say.' She picked at the arm of her sofa with her right hand for a time, while Peter continued to hold her left. She then looked up at Peter and said, 'I never stopped being in love with you, Peter. But you had a good marriage, and I am so glad you did. I love hearing you talk about your Marilyn. She sounds a sweetheart. And I wanted you to be happy after all you had gone through.'

'Yes, that is true, Kath,' said Peter nodding. 'But, all the same, I think it is a good thing I never saw you during my years of being married to Marilyn. I think... well, let's just say it was a good thing.'

'I know, love. I know,' said Kath and squeezed his hand. 'But we are here now, and we haven't got long. And you are going to lose another wife. You're getting careless, Peter!'

He smiled at her, but she could also see the pain in his watery eyes. 'But Kath, I will go through the rest of my life having had these precious weeks with you. I can't begin to tell you what a difference that makes to me. Something in me feels healed now. When it is my turn to be called to the other side, I will feel that I go with a sense of completion. I will rest in peace, Kath. I surely will.'

'Aye, but you will have both me and Marilyn welcoming you at the other side,' said Kath, chuckling. 'That'll test you!'

'Well, now, Kath, let's jump that fence when we reach it, shall we,' said Peter, very unsure how that particular conundrum would be resolved.

'Aye, we will. And there are plenty of fences to jump first,' said Kath, reaching for her tea cup.

'And you've got the biggest fence of them all,' said Peter, clasping her hand more firmly.

Kath swallowed most of her mug of tea before she replied. She was about to speak, when an involuntary burp stalled her, causing them both to laugh like schoolchildren. 'Yes, well,' she said, composing herself. 'I would have been really scared about this before my moments at that Golgotha place. But I'll now tell you something that I've not told anyone else. But before I do, could you cut me a piece of that cake there, Peter. Just a small slice to keep me going. It's one of my favourites, it is.'

Peter sprang to action, cutting the cake and passing her the plate. She took a couple of bites and expressed appreciation, and then continued. 'You see, Peter, you remember my love for your girl, Brigid of Kildare.'

'Oh, I do, Kath. We used to love telling each other stories about her, didn't we just?'

'That we did. Well, I told you that in this thing called the deep memory, you get allowed to see people from different times and that. Well, I was allowed to meet with your girl, Brigid, would you believe?'

'What? You met with the great Brigid of Kildare?' asked Peter with raised eyebrows.

'Aye, that I did,' said Kath confidently. 'And, if the truth be told, she didn't look in the least bit like I expected. I thought she'd be a shining and brilliant creature that I couldn't get anywhere near for sheer saintliness. But the truth is, she looked pretty much as normal as any of the girls you might meet strolling down the quay here in Dingle. She had a fair bit of dirt on her, to be truthful, like she had just been scrubbing the floor. But that didn't bother me at all. I far preferred her like that than as we see her on those statues: all prim and proper, like. She had a cheeky smile, she did. To me, she looked like she was one who could get herself into a fair bit of trouble. Anyways, she and I had a little natter. To be fair, I felt like a little girl again talking to her, because I always used to chat to her - you know, in my girlie imagination. Well, as we were talking, she told me things.'

'Things?' said Peter, his curiosity rising all the time.

Kath lowered her voice, as if to avoid being overheard. 'Aye. Things, Peter. Things about me. Now bear in mind this was three months ago, before I knew about the cancer. Well, she said, and I can pretty much remember her exact words...' Kath leaned forward and closed her eyes to aid her memory. 'She said, "Kathleen, your heart is now healed, but your body is wounded. Rejoice in the healing of your heart, and do not fear the infirmity of your body. All the days to come will be filled with light." Then she raised her arm, and it was clear she was holding something in her clenched hand. She asked me to open my hand which I did. "Here take this," she said. Well, you can imagine, Peter, I was curious to know what was in her palm, I surely was. She opened her hand, and I felt something drop into mine. Well, this is a bit hard to explain, but when I looked at my hand, I could see there was nothing in it. And yet I knew I was holding something. More to the point, I knew exactly what it was that I was clutching in my hand. And, to be sure now, it wasn't nearly as heavy as I expected it to be.'

Here Kath took another bite of her cake and munched at it for a few moments. Peter assumed she would soon reveal to him what exactly this gift from Brigid was, but it was becoming clear that Kath would not declare it without a prompt, so he said, 'Please, Kath. What was it?'

'Oh, sorry, love,' said Kath, wiping crumbs from her mouth. 'I guess it's not clear to you, even though it was to me. No, the thing she dropped in my hand was death.'

'Death?' said Peter, opening his mouth and sitting back in his chair.

'Aye. Death,' said Kath, popping the final piece of cake into her mouth and wiping her hands together to clear them of crumbs.

'Well, that doesn't sound like much of a gift to me, if I'm honest,' said Peter.

'Oh, doesn't it?' said Kath genuinely surprised by Peter's response. She brushed more crumbs from her skirt and said, 'Ah well. You see, I had always been that scared of death that I could never talk about it. When my Kevin became ill, I wouldn't let anyone speak of it. The girls and Kevin got that cross with me about it, but I never let them say that the poor man was dying. And afterwards, they were never allowed to use words like 'died' or 'dead'. Foolish, I know, but I couldn't bear to hear the word in the house. It scared me stiff. And do you know why, Peter?'

'No, I don't know,' said Peter, his furrowed frown betraying his concentration and curiosity.

'Is there more tea in the pot, love?' Kath asked. Peter refilled her cup with the tea, milk and sugar and when he had done, she took the cup and looked at Peter and said, 'Because of our little one, Peter. You know, the miscarriage.'

'Oh, dear Jesus, Kath,' said Peter, his eyes filling with water. 'You mean...'

'Aye, Peter, love. I mean our little girl. I'm so sorry I lost her...' Kath was aware of the familiar, wrenching grief that was threatening her composure. 'But let me finish what I'm trying to tell you.'

'Of course, Kath,' said Peter, who also was aware of the strength of his feeling to this reference to their child, lost through miscarriage when only a few months old and in the time when he was forbidden to see Kath. It was a grief he had never managed to reconcile in his own soul.

'Well, Peter love, the thing is this. When Brigid placed death in my hand, I knew that at last, I could take hold of it and not be frightened by it. I grasped it firmly like this.' She clenched her fist to demonstrate. 'I was holding it, and it was no longer holding me. Do you get my meaning?'

Peter, still frowning and looking intently at her through his round-rimmed glasses, nodded as Kath continued. Slowly unclasping her hand, she said, 'Then your lass, Brigid, says to me, "Open it, Kathleen," and I did.' Kath opened her hand wide and held it out in front of her. 'And I knew, Peter, that, then and there, I had let go of a whole pile of rotten old fear and grief that had been clogging up my life for donkey's years.' She paused for a few moments, lowering her hand, then added, 'I know, love. You with all your psycho stuff spend hours working on this kind of thing with your clients and I should probably have gone to one like you years ago to sort myself out. But the thing is, in that moment with Brigid, it all happened. I have no doubt at all. How you explain it, God only knows. But I was set free from my fear of death. And Peter, love, I was free of the fear my own death. That's quite something, don't you think?' Kath looked at Peter to check his response.

'Why, it certainly is,' said Peter, his face still betraying his surprise and wonder at what Kath had shared with him. 'You are right, Kath. Some people work in psychotherapy with this material for months and years. But it doesn't matter *how* it happens. For you it *has* happened, and that's what's important.'

'Aye it is, Peter,' said Kath, smiling with relief that Peter had understood her. 'So, you see, I can talk about my own passing now without flinching. It's happening, and I'm not being scared by it. In fact, I have a few moments of being a wee bit excited, if I'm honest. If you'd been in that place where I was with the sweet lass, Brigid, well, I think you'd have seen without any doubt that death doesn't have to have the last word. Dear God, no. There's a whole new story beyond it all. Quite some story, Peter. Oh, and Brigid told me another thing. She said that the Mary who had been nice to me by the Cross - the one that I thought had once been a slapper, but Father Pat said we couldn't be sure about that. Well, Brigid said that this Mary would be there to help me over when the time came. I took great comfort from that. A nicer girl to help you over the threshold, you couldn't ask for. But hark at me - old, cynical, godless Kath talking in this way!' She started chuckling. 'Quite a miracle it is, Peter! You'll have to be calling me Saint Kathleen of Dingle now, you will!' Peter laughed with her and stroked her arm.

They were both quiet for a while, and sipped the remains of their tea in silence. Peter was very familiar with silence, and Kath was growing to trust it. But it was Peter who ended the silence and asked, 'Kath, dear. May I return to the subject of our little one?'

'Of course, pet,' said Kath. 'I'd like to talk about it.'

Peter shuffled in his seat for a few moments and clasped his hands together. 'I never liked to ask... but did she have any kind of funeral?'

Kath looked down at some resilient crumbs that still clung to her skirt and methodically swept them to the floor. She then looked up at Peter with watery eyes and said, 'My mother took care of all of that. And not very well, I'm sorry to say. I... I've not wanted to tell you this, Peter. But the baby was very tiny. Though there was no life in the wee thing, she was so beautiful, and I wanted time with her. I would have given her a beautiful burial, you can be sure of that. But my mammy was so determined to keep the story of our child a secret from the family and the town, that she took on herself to do the cremation. It was the darkest moment for me, that surely was. That's a wound which won't find healing in this life.'

'Dearest Kath,' said Peter, who could see the agonised and beautiful teenager so clearly in his mind's eye. 'I wish I had been there for you. I am so sorry.' Tears held no shame for the man who had given most of his life to helping others to own the complex and varied aspects of their humanity, and he leaned over and leaned his damp cheek on Kath's shoulder.

After another time of quiet, Kath asked, 'How old would she be now, Peter?'

Peter sat up and turned his reddened eyes to the ceiling for a few moments and answered, 'Forty-seven, Kath.' Turning his eyes to Kath he added, 'And if she looked anything like her mother, she would have been a beauty.'

Kath tapped his arm and said, 'Och now, you don't need to flatter an old woman, sure you don't'

'But there is something I'd like to do,' said Peter. 'If you felt up to it, Kath. Would you mind if we asked Father Pat if he would take a Requiem for her? What do you think? I'd understand...'

'Now that is a grand idea, Peter,' interrupted Kath, sitting forward in her chair. 'Nothing fancy. Just a few official words by him would bring us a whole heap of peace, would it not?'

'That it would, Kath. That it would,' said Peter, smiling. 'And you know what he will ask us, don't you?'

'What is that, Peter?'

'He'll ask us for her name, don't you think?'

'Aye, that he will Peter. For certain he will. Did you ever give her a name by any chance?'

'No, I didn't,' said Peter. 'I never knew if it was a boy or a girl, you see. Only when we met up again recently and we talked about it briefly, did I discover. Though I did have my suspicion.'

'That she was a wee girl?'

'That she was a wee girl, Kath. Yes, I did,' said Peter nodding gently. 'But, knowing you, Kathleen, I expect you gave her a name long ago.'

Kath smiled at him, 'That I did, Peter. But I want you to be happy with it.'

'So...?' said Peter, raising his eyebrows.

'So, straight away I got to calling her Róisín. As you know, the name means *rose,* and, to me, she has always been a beautiful rose.'

'It's a perfect name for her, Kath,' said Peter clasping her hand firmly. 'And she has had forty-seven years of her mother calling her Róisín, so I see no reason to confuse the girl by changing it now.'

'Thank you, love,' said Kathleen and leaned forward and kissed him. 'Dear God, you have been a strength to me in these days, Peter, you surely have. I'm so glad I came and found you.'

'And I've never been so glad to be found,' said Peter. 'Now listen, why don't I go and phone Father Pat and see if he would do the service for us soon.'

'That's a grand idea, Peter,' said Kath. 'But, Peter, love, could I ask one thing. I don't want a fussy service, as I said, and I'd really not want it done in a stuffy old church. Do you know where I'd love to do it?'

'Tell me where, Kath,' said Peter, raising his eyebrows in expectation.

'I want to go up high, Peter. I don't know why, but I want to go up high where there is a grand view and the wind is bold and the air pure. What do you think, love?'

'I think that would be exactly right, Kath,' said Peter. 'We could drive up the Connor, park the car and walk a few steps up towards your Mount Brandon.'

'That's perfect, Peter. I know our Róisín would love that,' said Kath, who sensed a strong and unusual fount of joy in her heart. She was almost having to contain a laughter that was welling up in her.

'May I check one important practicality,' said Peter. 'Do the girls and Kevin know about Róisín?'

'Oh aye,' said Kath. 'I didn't keep any of that story from them. They don't know her name, but they knew she was a girl.'

'Very good,' said Peter. 'Then I guess they will want to be with us.'

'That they will, Peter,' said Kath starting to move out of her seat. 'That they will. So, let's speak to them at supper as they'll all be here. Then you can get on to the priest after that. He'll be having his tea now and we don't want to disturb him devouring one of Mrs McGarrigle's specials.'

As Kath and Peter made their way out to the kitchen, they were both aware of a deep sense of contentment. For Kath, there was now only one serious matter in her life that felt very unresolved. It was the matter of her daughter, Bríana. There was still uncomfortable distance between them. Somehow, the gap felt like a huge crevasse. Could there really be any way of bridging the gap, even healing it, before Kath left this world? The old Kath would have been very doubtful about this. But this new Kath, the post-Golgotha Kath, whose soul was now suffused with a new verve, was able to own that there could be hope for even this damaged relationship.

As Peter set to work on the mackerels, she peeled the potatoes and, much to her amazement, found herself praying for her daughter. Not with words of great eloquence, but more with a wordless, silent yearning. She paused for a few moments and looked out through the kitchen window at the crimson clouds of the evening sky and whispered, 'What a very long way you have travelled, Kathleen Griffin. What a long, long way.' Peter, preparing the fish nearby, heard every word of the whisper and slowly nodded in agreement.

CHAPTER 13

Alice was feeling remarkably content as she was packing her case. There was no doubt that it had been a wonderful and successful weekend. Not in the least what she was expecting, for it had been full of very unexpected surprises. But each day felt somehow golden. And there was no denying that she and the English priest were getting on remarkably well.

They would soon be going out for an evening meal, but she had a bit of time, so she drew up a chair to her desk and got out her notebook. This was the notebook of her letters to Martha. It was volume 14 of her collection. Martha was a companion she invented in childhood and, during teenage years, she took to writing to her rather than speaking to her. Although Martha never replied to any of Alice's letters, she had a way of giving a very helpful response just by being there. Alice would scrawl away in her illegible writing, and she always knew exactly how Martha was responding, as if she was glancing over her shoulder and making helpful comments as she wrote. So, it was time for her to write to her friend, for she had not corresponded for quite a while, and Martha would definitely need to hear about this weekend. The sun was slowly setting on the warm city beyond her window, as she fished out her much-chewed pen and began to write.

Martha 19 April

Hello Martha. It's me again. Apologies for not writing for a while. Well, believe it or not, I am in Cairo. So, when I last wrote, I told you about Morwenna telling me to come out here with Douglas Romer, the English priest who lives in Ireland. Well, to be fair, I've already told you quite a bit about him. Anyway, we got here on Thursday evening and we're staying at a cool Airbnb. You can see the pyramids from the balcony! Friday was extraordinary. We were having breakfast when, who should turn up, but the angel called Dorchadas. You remember me writing about him a few years ago when I was going through that tough time in Marseilles. Well, it turns out he's been doing work in Ireland recently and is now a good friend of Douglas. Some coincidence, eh?

I told you that the main reason for coming was to visit the site where Douglas' wife was shot. We were both a bit nervous about this, so we were very pleased that Dorch was willing to come with us. Douglas knew exactly where the place was - he's quite a thorough researcher. The taxi dropped us off in a slightly dodgy part of the city, so we were even more grateful for Dorch's company. Not many would pick a fight with someone of his height. Straight away Dorch found some scratch marks on a wall and he and Doug were pretty certain this was the exact spot of the shooting, and where the car careered into the wall. Douglas went straight over and I watched him brushing his hand lovingly over the scratched area. It was so sweet and sad. I started to feel guilty - encouraging him to come here and have to feel the pain of it again. But I didn't need to worry. I got closer to him so I could focus more clearly on his face, and I then realised that he looked OK. He said it was really helpful being there. I was relieved! But then a guy turned up. You remember, Martha, me telling you about those two "meetings" I had in Marseilles. Well, this was another "meeting". This time it turned out to be Joseph, the husband of Mary. Of course, they'd been down here after the Herod thing. I really liked the guy. Somehow more humble than I imagined him. Quite handsome too, actually. We had a coke with him in a beautiful courtyard. Amazing fragrance of verbena. Could also smell fresh bread from nearby bakery - heaven!

We had a long chat with Joseph and it was becoming clear why we had to come here. Morwenna had said 'for healing and for destiny.' The healing was already happening for Douglas by visiting the place of the shooting. The destiny bit was becoming clear as Joseph spoke. Douglas was really gripped by this. I could see there was a stirring in him to do with refugees. Before Joseph left (he sort of vanished) he looked at me and said 'And Miss Alice, if I may... You are here, of course, for a reason. But I think you know that, don't you?' I felt pretty embarrassed to be honest, Martha. Although I couldn't see Joseph's face very clearly, I felt what he was saying. Something about the way he said it made me pretty sure he was referring to me and Douglas. I felt awkward, because the last thing I want is to put Douglas under any pressure. But he didn't guess this was about him. He did ask me about it again yesterday, but I was evasive. I don't want him to think he's in some kind of trap. He's too decent for that.

Me, Douglas and Dorchadas had a light lunch together. I love talking to Dorchadas. I asked him about all the people he's met and we heard lots of fascinating stories. Gave me a chance to tell Doug a bit about how Dorchadas helped me in Marseilles. They also told me a meeting they had with a lady called Svetlana in Dingle. Apparently, she's the woman at the well in the gospel stories. Didn't know the story very well, but she sounded brilliant. Made me feel quite a bit better about being a divorcee.

Doug has just popped his head round the door and says we should be leaving for dinner soon as it's getting late. But, Martha, I must tell you that we had a brilliant supper on Friday night. We went to this little house on the same street where the shooting was. Great mix of people there - most of them refugees from Sudan, Iraq, Ethiopia, Eritrea, Palestine. Those are the ones I remember. Amazing how good their English is. They were beautiful people, full of kindness. Douglas loved hearing about the care they took of Saoirse, his wife, when she was so badly injured. Most of them were living here at the time. Some of them were Christians and some Muslims, but they all seemed to get on so well together. They even prayed for us before we left. Definitely one of the most special evenings ever.

Then on Saturday we made it to the great Pyramids. And yes, on camels!! Found out I was a pretty good camel rider. Douglas not so good! Great pictures. But what a wonderful place - those mighty and great pyramids rising up out of the desert. I know in a way they are not brilliant. Built by the sweat of slaves and to the glory of narcissistic kings. But somehow the magnificence of them and the fact they have survived so many years is inspiring. Then I persuaded Douglas to go on a day trip to Karnak today. We got up really early to get the plane and just got back now. My, how we loved that temple. Phew! We had such a great time. Such wonders. What a place Egypt is. But the people are restless. Not a place I'd want to live, and in some ways, I'm looking forward to going home.

Anyway, must get changed. Oh, and I know you'll be asking, Martha. Yes, I like Douglas very much. Why didn't I fall for someone like him years ago? I'll admit to you, Martha, but to no-one else, that I am starting to love him very much. I adore being with him. But does he love me? I don't think so yet. But let's see, Martha. Let's see. Thanks for being here.

*

Unbeknown to Alice, Douglas was also engaged in a similar activity in the room next door. There was no Martha in his world, but he did like to keep a journal.

Journal 19 April. Cairo

I'm coming to the end of an extraordinary weekend in Cairo with Alice Fournier. The main purpose of the trip was to visit the sight of the shooting. The first major surprise was old Dorch turning up on our first morning! Couldn't believe it. But it was great having him with us. Turns out that he and Alice already met a few years ago in Marseilles!! Actually, find it rather comforting. Anyway, he joined us for the visit to the place where Saoirse was shot. Very strange to actually be at the very place where the terrible event took place. Saw the scarred wall where the car crashed. Even paint marks of the car on the stone. Alice recited a beautiful ancient Egyptian poem. I wondered if the old grief would overwhelm me again, but it didn't. Instead, there was a strong sense that this was another piece of the grief work achieved. I felt that at last I was in some way 'with' her in the place where her conscious self left this world. That terrible sense that I should have been with her in that moment has haunted me so long. But that finally left me. It was a true healing.

But then there was another of Dorch's 'meetings'. This time with Joseph. We had a drink with him in a courtyard just off the street, and he told us of his journey with Mary and Jesus to Egypt to escape the murderous threats of Herod. I was captivated by his story and felt something rise up in me as he was talking. I wasn't quite sure what to call it, but I then realised it was this thing called *destiny* that keeps emerging these days. He said, 'Mr Douglas, you did not come here to remember the past. You came here to discover your future.' Something to do with refugees stirred in me. It is a world I know absolutely nothing about. But in the evening, we were invited to a dinner party by some people who live on that street. Turns out most of them are refugees from lots of different countries. Such a mix of people and former professions. I was absolutely gripped by their stories and felt such a surge of anger at the causes of their having to flee from their homeland. And I felt such a love and compassion for them. Had lots of chats with Alice over the weekend about this, and she certainly thinks there could be signs here about my future work here on Earth. I'm pretty sure I won't go back to being a Vicar, but I do want to remain a priest. But I think my priestliness is going to be lived out in a very different way. I know all this goes back to Golgotha where He died. Something about His death released a new vitality in me. More accurately, a new calling in me to give life to others. It's like a power of resurrection was released in the very place of His death. I'm not sure I understand it all, but Alice says it makes perfect sense. I do like the way she thinks. She sees things differently from me, but I like what she sees.

Such a beautiful thing at that dinner on Friday night: three of the ladies there told me how they had been at the scene of the accident. One of them rested Saoirse's head in her lap while they waited for the ambulance. Another fetched water to bathe her head and to try and staunch the wound. The other sang an Arabic song of healing over her. She sang it to us at the meal. It was so beautiful it made me cry. Not the usual tears of grief, but more of gratitude. I knew - I really did know - that Saoirse would have heard this song and it would have comforted her so much. So even though I couldn't be with her, others were there to care for her. And they said that when the paramedics arrived, one of them made the sign of the cross over her before they took her into the ambulance. I find that so comforting.

Dorch left us after that meal and said he was heading back to Dingle. So Alice and I explored Cairo and the pyramids on Saturday and we took an extravagant guided excursion to the great Karnak temple today. Wow, they are brilliant places. What I love about Alice is that she has such a capacity for wonder. At times she was not able to see things clearly, so I would need to explain to her about bits of hieroglyphics on walls and that kind of thing. But though she couldn't see clearly with her eyes, she was seeing such things with her heart. I've never been filled with wonder in the way that she has, but being with her I'm learning. What a dear thing wonder is. Wasn't it Carlyle who said, 'worship is transcendent wonder'? Well, for the first time for many months I felt like worshipping today in that glorious hypostyle hall at Karnak with the sun beaming on us through the great pillars.

It's getting late and we need to go and find some dinner. It's been nice being with Alice. Very nice.

*

That evening Alice and Douglas ate in a small restaurant only a short walk from where they were staying. They sat under a sprawling vine and drank Egyptian wine till late in the evening. Even though they had been up so early, they were not tired. They were sustained by the surge of excitement of the weekend's events, and talked animatedly until the owner of the restaurant, with great apology, insisted on closing up. He also insisted that one of his waiters walk with the couple back to their apartment, to ensure their safety. They spent the last moments of their day on their balcony, gazing upwards at the canopy of a myriad brilliant stars above them and they stayed there until the tiredness finally overcame them. When their heads eventually did touch their pillows, they were asleep within seconds and their dreams were suffused with an array of glorious images inspired by their travels of the last few days. And though neither remembered it in the morning, each dreamed of the other, and the dreams were radiant and tender.

CHAPTER 14

While Alice and Douglas were admiring the ancient ruins of the great Temple at Karnak in the warmth of the Egyptian sun, Kath was firmly clasping the arm of her daughter, Nancy, in the face of an Atlantic gale. They were on their way to the church. 'You'll need to hold tight to your skirts in this storm, Nancy,' she cried as they made their way cautiously down the slippery pavement of Green Street to the parish church. Somewhat to her surprise, this church had become a safe sanctuary to the once pagan Kathleen. In recent times she was inclined to make her way there every day. She would pause at the door and dip her stout fingers in the cool water of the stoup, sometimes even making the sign of the cross over herself before entering the spacious and quiet interior. There she would shuffle to one of the side pews and settle there for a time and chat to the God who was becoming a good friend. Before leaving, she would light a votive candle and head off back up the hill to her café and her day's duties of baking cakes and serving drinks to her steady stream of customers.

But today was Sunday. The café was closed and she and Nancy were on their way to Mass. Father Pat was greeting his flock at the door and, when he saw his friends approaching, he waved his hand at them and said, 'Welcome, Kath. Welcome, Nancy. Come in out of that cold wind, now. You'll soon be warm in here,' and sure enough the church was warm and hospitable.

As they settled into their pew, Kath said to Nancy in a hoarse whisper, 'Nancy, love, you're going to have to guide me through this book. I can't make head nor tail of it, to be truthful. I mean Father Pat whistles his way through it at some speed, and, by the time I've spotted what it is he's reading out to us, he's cantered several pages ahead of me.'

'Yes, Mammy,' said Nancy dutifully. Though she was not much wiser about the mysteries of the Catholic Missal than Kath, and as the service progressed, neither of them ever succeeded in finding the correct page. But that didn't stop Kath from thoroughly enjoying the service. Father Pat preached and the congregation were taken aback by the fact that this sermon had much more of a spring in its step than anything they had heard before from their priest. Most of his sermons left them either close to dormancy, or in a state of mild perplexity. But this sermon on the visitation of Christ to his apostle Thomas was full of life and sparkle, not to say ebullient faith. As the wind rattled the rafters of the church, there was a sense of a new breath of air breezing into the church. At one point in his sermon, Pat even told the congregation a joke. Such a thing was unheard of, and the congregation was so surprised by the event that no-one had quite the confidence to laugh. No-one, that is, except Kath, who let out a mighty guffaw, which quickly turned into a coughing fit that provoked Nancy to beat her mother severely on the back, and sent a member of the congregation scuttling off to the kitchen for a glass of water. Pat, grinning wildly, removed his spectacles and thanked Kath for appreciating the joke, then soldiered on, quite unfazed by this most rare of phenomena - someone displaying emotion in a Sunday service.

After Mass, the congregation started to file their way out of the building, but Nancy told her mother she wanted to study the ceramic stations of the cross decorating the grey stone walls of the church. Only a few months previously, the same images had caught Douglas' eye. So she and her mother made their way to the first one, and Nancy looked on it with awe. 'I like these, Mammy,' she said, and moved on to the next one.

After the first two or three, Kath sat in one of the pews and said, 'You have a good look as many as you like, love. But if you don't mind, I won't traipse round them all with you. I'll rest my legs here.'

‘Right,' said Nancy, and continued her exploration. At each picture she paused and raised her hand and gently stroked the contours of the figures. Kath noticed that she stalled by one picture in particular, so she rose from her pew and went over to be with her daughter.

'What is it, love?' she asked as she observed her daughter's cheeks glistening with fresh tears. The ceramic picture was entitled 'Christ is crucified' and depicted a sorrowful and lightly-haloed Christ inclining his head toward the blue-robed figure of Mary standing beside him. She in turn was bending her head towards her son. Her hands were held up before her as if in blessing for her son. 'Does this make you sad, lass?' said Kath.

'Aye, it does, Mammy,' said Nancy sniffing. 'That lady in blue. Is that his mammy?'

'That it is, Nancy,' said Kath, now vividly recalling the scene she had witnessed not many weeks before. This picture was nothing like the scene she had seen, yet it held the same feeling.

'Who is that?' asked Nancy, referring to a figure in green standing on the other side of the cross.

'I've no idea, love,' said Kath.

Before either could say anything else, the resonant yet gentle voice of Father Pat, who was now standing behind them, said, 'That, Nancy, is the apostle John. A fine young man, he was. And when Our Lord was dying there, He asked your man, John, to take care of His mother.'

'Well, that's a fine thing,' said Kath.

'Aye, a fine thing indeed, Kath,' said Pat.

Nancy once again reached up her hand and stroked the figure of Mary. She turned and looked at the priest with her reddened eyes and asked 'Was she a kind lady, Father?'

'Oh, she was a kind lady, and that's the truth, Nancy,' said Pat, offering his brief and generous smile, and lightly patted Nancy's shoulder.

'Like my Mammy,' said Nancy.

'Oh, now...' said Kath.

'Yes,' said Pat, butting into Kath's protest. 'She was kind like your mother.'

'Must have been hard for her, then,' said Nancy, turning back to the picture.

'I believe it was, lass,' said Pat. 'I believe it was. But she was a courageous lady.'

Nancy turned around to Pat again and said, 'I've not been a mammy.'

'No, lass,' said Pat, his brow furrowing above his glasses.

'Wouldn't have been a good one,' said Nancy.

'I think you would have been a wonderful mother, Nancy,' said Pat.

Nancy smiled coyly and then turned back to the picture again. She reached up and gently stroked the face of Christ. 'Sad, isn't it?' she said, as another rivulet of water made its way down her ruddy cheek.

'Yes, it is, lass,' said Pat. 'It is perhaps the saddest thing ever. But it is not the end of the story, Nancy. In many ways, it was just the beginning.'

Nancy turned around to Pat again and wiping her face with the back of her hand and sniffing hard, she said, 'That's good.' Then, looking at Kath, said, 'Time for lunch, Mam, isn't it?'

Kath, who had been watching and listening intently, said, 'Aye, Nancy. It is, love.'

As they all walked slowly back to the door of the church, Pat asked Kath 'Tell me, Kath, how is Bríana doing?'

Kath was about to reply when Nancy said, 'She's cross. Cross with Mammy. And she's a lesbian now. She told me last night she likes having sex with another woman. Says it's better than with a man.'

Even Pat, who was familiar with straight-talking people in his confessional, was somewhat taken aback by the directness of Nancy's statement. But before he could speak, Kath said, 'Oh, Nancy, love. The Father doesn't want to hear about all of that.' She grasped her daughter's arm and said, 'Come on, now.'

'Well now, Kath,' said Pat as they stepped outside into the wind that was showing signs of abating. 'I don't know your Brí well, and I'd love to get to know her a bit. So, I was going to ask if you would all like to come down for a cup of tea at the Presbytery this afternoon?'

Nancy immediately asked, 'Will there be cake?' to which Pat replied that there would, and Kath said she would speak to Brí and give Pat a call to let him know.

'Grand, grand,' said Pat. 'Hope to see you, later.' He made his way up the path to the Presbytery. The story of Kath's damaged relationship with Bríana was well-known in the community, and Pat felt a responsibility (or was it a calling?) to do something to help it to mend.

Kath and Nancy walked slowly back up the hill. Kath paused for a moment to catch her breath and said to Nancy, 'You know, love. Your sister doesn't necessarily want the whole of the town of Dingle knowing about her sex life, interesting though it might be. So, do you think you could keep that conversation with her just a wee bit private?'

'All right, Mam,' said Nancy, and the two women continued their journey home in silence. When they got back they were greeted by a delicious fragrance, as Brí had spent the morning making a vegetable soup, and soon Mother and daughters were enjoying generous supplies of soup and buttered soda bread. Over lunch, Brí agreed that she would like to have tea at the Presbytery, so Kath phoned Pat and said they would all be there for tea soon after three.

*

Father Pat ushered Kath and her daughters into his lounge. Brí smiled at the assortment of idiosyncratic furnishings and pictures. She was glad she was wearing her thick jumper as the lounge was distinctly cool. However, Pat soon fetched a basket of turf and set to work making a fire. 'Mid-April, but still cold, isn't it?' he said, as he lit the paper beneath his carefully-built stack of fuel. He stood up and said, 'Now, do settle yourselves down and I'll bring in the tea.'

'And cake,' added Nancy

'And cake, indeed,' assured Pat. 'One of Mrs McGarrigle's best, Nancy.'

Brí sat in the chair by the fire. 'Make yourself comfortable, love,' said Kath. 'It's usually where I sit, but don't you worry yourself.' Brí didn't miss the note of irritation in her mother's voice. Pat returned with the tea and some slices of a sponge cake. Nancy reached for the plate and helped herself. She was the only one to eat cake, but the others gratefully received their mugs of tea.

Brí watched the dishevelled priest awkwardly pour the tea. There was something about his manner that made her feel she could trust the man. Up until now, she was distinctly wary of clergy. But this one seemed different. She sensed that his presence in this room provided a secure foundation for a very difficult conversation that was long overdue. When she flew over the Atlantic a few nights previously, she came to a difficult decision: that before her mother died, they must talk about the rift that existed between them. It had been there for so many years that it was hard to imagine life without it. Yet Brí knew that if she did not at least try and do her bit to shift it, she would carry a sense of guilt for the rest of her days. Things had to be said before her mother died, even though the saying of them carried considerable risk.

She looked at the woman who was sitting on the other side of the fire from her, slurping from her mug of tea and chatting to the priest about the weather. This was the woman who had birthed her into this world, yet from whom she had become estranged even in the early years of her life. At first it was the green veil of jealousy that separated them, as it became very apparent that her father delighted more in his daughter than he did in his wife. Then a further veil of resentment arrived when Brí became convinced that it was her mother who had driven her father to drink and ill health and resultant untimely death. This was the mother whom she could never look in the eye, for fear that such a connection could release an uncontrollable flood of anger. And yet this was the mother whose eyes now looked somehow so different. Several times in the last twenty-four hours Brí had dared to let her eyes rest on her mother's for just a few moments. Even in those few moments, she could see that these were eyes that no longer carried jealousy or accusation. Some new quality had transformed them. Maybe it was the immanence of death? Maybe it was the effect of the road accident in January. Her mother had referred to some kind of religious vision following it. She had not told Brí the details of it, but Brí could see that whatever it was, a surgery had taken place in her mother's heart as a result of it. So, if her mother had really changed so much, maybe there was hope of some kind of reconciliation. That is, if Brí could do her part and forgive. But could she?

'And how's life for you now, Brí, over there in the States?' She was so lost in her thoughts, she failed to hear the question.

But she did hear her mother saying, 'Brí, love. Father Pat is speaking to you.'

Father Pat repeated his question and Brí took a sip of her tea and replied, 'Oh, thank you. Yes. Life's good for me at the moment.'

'And which State are you living in?' he asked, raising his eyebrows above the thick frame of his glasses.

'Pennsylvania now,' replied Brí. 'I live just on the outskirts of Punxsutawney.'

'Groundhog Day,' said Nancy. 'Bill Murray and Andie MacDowell.'

'Ah, indeed,' said Pat, throwing Nancy one of his rapid smiles. 'And what is your work there?' he asked, looking back to Brí.

'I've got a job working at some stables,' said Brí. 'I have always adored the horses...'

'I like the horses,' said Nancy, as she reached for another slice of cake. 'Prefer them to cows, I do.'

'And I found this job,' continued Brí, ignoring her sister. 'There's a farm near where I live that offers horseback riding on the nearby trails. They have a lot of horses. Such beautiful creatures. And they needed help tending the horses and wanted someone to be a guide on the trails. I've been there a few years now. It's a great job and pays surprisingly well as it happens.' She took a sip of her tea. She was happy to tell the priest about her work, but there was another subject of conversation that was pressing up from somewhere deep within her. She looked at her mother who was saying something to Nancy about the *Groundhog Day* movie. She knew this was the moment to embark on the subject they had both avoided for so many years. So, butting into her mother's conversation with Nancy, she said to Pat in a loud voice, 'Father, my mother's dying, as you know.'

'Aye, lass,' said Pat, placing his mug carefully on the table beside him. 'And we are all fearfully sorry about that.' Kath put down her tea mug and looked hard at her daughter. She sensed danger and she started picking at her thumb nail.

'I know, I know,' said Brí. 'And thanks be to God she has you and all her friends here. But...' She took another sip from her mug and returned it to the heavily-stained table next to her. She did not know quite where to start. She just knew something needed to be said. She glanced over to her mother and then lowered her eyes. 'It's a long time since my daddy died,' she said in a quiet voice.

'It sure is,' said Kath. 'God rest his soul.' Her fingers calmed a little.

'I regret I never got to meet him,' said Pat. 'But I hear he was a great man.'

Brí nodded and said, 'Yes, he was and I absolutely adored him.' She knew she was on shaky ground. She was well aware that both her mother and sister did not feel loved by her father in the way that she was. 'Mam,' she said, looking over to Kath who was now clasping her hands on her lap and was staring hard into the fire. 'I've been thinking a lot in recent days about this.' She looked nervously at both her mother and sister, took a long intake of breath, then continued. 'Mammy, I want us to part as friends. I...' She paused and sighed, then continued, 'My Daddy... I don't know what got into me after he died. Grief does strange things, it does. But I'm not wanting to make excuses. Let me just say it straight. I... I blamed you for his death, and, Mammy, I'm so sorry that I did.' The emotion was swirling around in her, yet was not overwhelming her, and her voice remained calm and her eyes dry. 'I had no right to do that, Mammy. I see that now. It was a terrible thing to think. Honest to God, I'm sorry. I truly am.'

Kath was still looking hard at the burning turf on the fire and she appeared to be chewing at something. She was being less successful than her daughter at containing her emotions. This was a sore nerve indeed, and she was not sure she had the energy to attend to it. But Brí had drawn attention to this nerve, and she knew she was right to do so. Her lip was trembling for a while as she looked over to her daughter and, for the first time, she allowed herself to see the beauty that was so evidently in her. Her jealousy in years gone by had prevented her from seeing the beauty, even though she knew it existed. But now, something enabled her to finally see straight. There was a new light and things looked different in it. 'Bríana, love...' she said, looking across the glowing fire at her daughter. 'I know you felt that. I know you did. And maybe you're right. Maybe I did drive your poor father to the drink.'

'No, no!' protested Brí.

'Let me say my piece,' said Kath, holding up her hand. 'I wasn't good to your father when he needed me. I know that now. And the truth is, darling, that I was jealous of you. It's a simple as that. He adored you, and you had every right to grieve as deeply as you did when he passed from us. I...' She paused and, for a few moments, looked back into the fire. She then looked up, not at her daughter, but at her priest. 'Father Pat, he never loved me like Peter loved me and I always yearned for that love. There was a wee girl in me craving for that love, and my Kevin couldn't give it me. Not his fault. You can't make someone love you. But, you see, the problem for me was that he could give it to my Bríana. And to see the love in my house, but not given to me... Well, that caused my bitterness, I'm sorry to say.' She paused for a few moments and then looked back to Brí. 'But Brí, darling, something happened to me a few weeks back that changed things in me. Something got straightened up inside of me. All that old bitterness... Well, so much of it has gone now. Do you know, love, I'm sitting here staring at you, and do you know what I see? I see a beautiful, sweet and kind woman. A woman any mother would be proud of.' She struggled again with the wealth of feelings that were swirling within her, but she composed herself and said, 'Maybe, finally, I now see you as your da used to see you. I think we can mend, lass, don't you?'

Brí had never heard her mother speak in this way before. She was so much more open. All those old knee-jerk defences had gone. And she was actually apologising. After all these years. And here they were, having just the kind of conversation she hoped they might have, but feared they never could. She felt something shift inside her - it was like a piece of machinery that had always grated, now finally fell into its correct place. The friction had gone. Something felt smooth. She looked at her mother and did not know what to say. But at last the woman who was sitting opposite her looked like a mother she could trust. A mother in whose arms she could rest. She got up from her chair and moved to her mother's side. She knelt beside her and kissed her on the cheek, then laid her head on her mother's shoulder and stared at the glowing fire in the hearth.

At first Kath was taken aback by the sudden closeness and intimacy of her daughter. But as she began to stroke the copper-red hair of the woman who was her daughter, she felt a surge of genuine affection. She said, 'I never thought this day would come, darling. I thought I'd done too much damage.'

Brí lifted her head and said, 'Well, Mammy. Miracles do happen, don't they?'

Father Pat looked on in admiration. He felt a pain in his heart, and rubbed his chest for a few moments. His heart always reacted to scenes such as this. He knew humanity well, and knew that the healing of damaged relationships such as Brí and Kath had known did not come easily. He had seen far too many go unhealed. So yes, he could not think of a more suitable word than 'miracle' for what he had witnessed.

Brí stood up and returned to her seat. Nancy, whose mouth showed evidence of her enjoyment of the slices of cake, looked at Brí and said, 'You got a bit of snot on your nose.' Brí quickly pulled a tissue from her sleeve and wiped her nose. Nancy added, 'I told the priest that you're with a woman now. Told him you were happy with her.'

'And you don't need to say any more about that, Nancy,' said Kath, keen to intercept any further details that Nancy might have felt obliged to share at that moment.

Brí chucked. She was very familiar with the ways of her sister. She looked at Pat and said, 'Yes, Father. Nancy is right, I am living with a woman now. We are in a relationship. I'm sorry, I know that's against your religion.'

Pat smiled and removed his spectacles to give them their usual futile polish on his jumper. 'Ah, well now, Brí, all that is a matter for the church authorities and theologians. I'm afraid I'm just a simple parish priest. It's not for me to pry into your personal life. My job is to teach people to find God in this world, and to help them discover that he is a wonderful God who is infinitely kind. Once you have found Him, you then chat to Him about the things to do with your personal life. I gave up trying to act like God for people long ago now. I found it was far too exhausting.'

Brí and Kath both laughed, and Kath said, 'I'm not so sure, Pat. I think if God ever needed someone to stand in for him at any time, I reckon you'd be as good as any for the job.'

They all laughed as Pat protested. Nancy then said, 'Any more cake?'

'No, no, Nancy,' said Kath, starting to ease herself out of her seat. 'You've had quite enough, pet. We need to be on our way now.' Pat helped her out of the seat and the two sisters made their way out of the room. Pat held Kath back for a few moments.

'Kath, love,' he said. 'About the requiem. Peter called me and I'm happy with all the plans. I believe we agreed two o'clock tomorrow at the top of the Pass.'

'That we have, Pat,' said Kath. 'It's so good of you.' Pat noticed how much Kath was leaning on his arm. There was no doubt now that this new member of his congregation was losing her physical strength. But there was also no doubt that another kind of strength was growing in her. Kath then said, 'Oh, Pat, you will bring Dorch with you, won't you, now. He was in the café yesterday and I told him about our wee requiem. I'd really like him to be there.'

'Of course, Kath,' reassured the priest. 'We'll travel together and meet you up there.'

'That's grand,' said Kath and they joined her daughters at the front door where Kath said, 'So we will all see you tomorrow then, Pat. And thanks a million for the tea and... for helping us with our conversation.'

'It's my pleasure,' said Pat.

He was more delighted than he felt he should have been when Brí leaned forward and planted a kiss on his cheek and then hugged him, holding him tight for a few moments. 'Thank you, Father,' she said as she held him. 'You have helped us so much. I'm truly grateful.' The softness of her hair against his poorly-shaved face, the hint of a delicate fragrance, and the tone of her warm, husky voice triggered an old longing. After he said farewell to the three women and closed the door, he touched the place on his cheek where the kiss had landed. He removed his glasses and wiped them furiously on his jumper. Why did such things still make him want to weep? He berated himself and made straight for his study and set about impatiently searching for his packet of cigarettes, which he knew was hiding somewhere among the pile of books and papers on his desk. When he finally found the packet, he pulled out a cigarette and lit it.

He sank into his creaking chair, and leaned back, inhaling the reassuring smoke deep into his lungs. For some moments, his mind led him back to the days of his calling and, more specifically, to the cost of his calling. He was never able to put the memories out of his mind of the beautiful acquaintance that he had known for such a short and yet such a wonderful time not long before his ordination. He recalled again the dearest smile, the dimpled cheeks, the auburn hair, the tender voice, the warm hand. And he recalled the last, agonised, desperate embrace followed by the days of relentless, lonely tears, always shed in private. Tears that even now, after all these years, would surface at such moments as these. 'You silly eejit of a priest,' he said to himself and, after taking one last inhalation, he stubbed out his cigarette and set about preparing for his evening service.

CHAPTER 15

On Monday morning it was cool in Cairo by Egyptian standards, but warm for Alice and Douglas who were enjoying a final breakfast on the apartment balcony. They watched the changing light of the rising sun play on the sides of the grand pyramids and both were content to enjoy long moments of silence in between snippets of conversation. Then Douglas said, 'So, Mrs Fournier. In a few months you will be beginning your new work as the Development Manager?'

'I certainly will be,' said Alice, adjusting her sunglasses and adopting a posture to give the impression of a competent and authoritative manager.

'They are lucky to have you, Alice. I think you will be excellent at the job,' said Douglas.

'Well, to be fair, you don't really know that, do you? I mean, you haven't seen me at work or really know anything about what the work involves.' Her slight smile betrayed the fact that there was a note of teasing in her response.

'I know,' said Douglas, lowering his head. 'I can still be a bit Vicarish, can't I?'

Alice laughed. Her laugh always made Douglas want to join in her laughter. It was truly infectious. He felt it was always a kind and safe laugh. She then said, 'And back to Ireland tomorrow for you.'

'Yes, Alice,' said Douglas, sipping his coffee and turning his gaze from the pyramids to his new friend who was smiling at him. 'Yes, and I'm looking forward to it. It really does feel like my home now.'

'I think it is,' said Alice, squinting her eyes as the sun now shone brightly on her. 'It suits you perfectly. And I'm so looking forward to when Aunt Mavis and I come and visit you next month.'

Douglas smiled warmly and said, 'I'm really looking forward to that, Alice.' Her hair was now bathed in the rays of the sun, and Douglas once again noticed and admired the interesting mix of blonds and greys. He was also amused at the way her hair had obviously received no attention yet this day and seemed quite content to be its own glorious, crazy self.

'You said you've got other friends coming? From the States, I think?' said Alice attempting to draw one of the many stray locks into some kind of order.

'Yes,' said Douglas, who still felt a bit awkward that he had somehow managed to double book the visit of two sets of friends. 'I'm sorry, Alice, I'd rather...'

'No, no,' said Alice. 'Don't worry about it. You've told me a bit about them, and I look forward to meeting them.' The feeling was genuine for Alice, though she could not deny that she felt a little disappointment at not having more time alone with this increasingly interesting friend.

'Actually,' said Douglas, stirring his coffee. 'They are really good friends of mine. Frank is an Anglican priest and was in the next-door parish to me. He was an incredibly good friend to me when Saoirse died. He took her service. He's a big guy. You can tell he played American football. But he has such a soft heart. I leaned on him a lot in those terrible weeks after she died. Then they decided to move back to the States and I've missed them so much since then. His wife's called Daisy. She's a special person too.'

'Did you say she'd been ill?' enquired Alice.

'Oh, yes, she had been. Seriously ill with cancer. But he phoned me some weeks back now and said she'd had healing prayer at a church they went to. Apparently, she's much better.'

Alice smiled and leaned forward and clutched Douglas' hand and said, 'That's wonderful Douglas. It's curious, isn't it? God makes some people better, but others... Well, you know, your friend Kath. And your wife. There are miracles and tragedies all around us, and you never really know which one will come your way.' She released his hand and sat back. She removed her sunglasses and, closing her eyes, bathed her face in the sunshine.

'And you, Alice,' said Douglas. 'Your eyes. Did you ever ask God to heal them?'

'Yes,' said Alice, still facing the sun with her eyelids closed. 'Oh yes, we had quite a few chats about all of that. Quite a few.' She chuckled for a few moments and Douglas could see it was not a cynical chuckle but one of contentment. It was the natural response of someone who somehow or other had managed to wrestle with a disturbing mystery and arrive at a place of not just peace but joy. He looked at his friend with her eyes closed and her wild hair catching the morning light and felt he was in the company of one who had somehow managed to tread the thorny pathways of human suffering and emerge with that rare quality of genuine wisdom. He had seen several signs of it over the weekend. She really was good company.

She opened her eyes and said, 'You've been staring at me Reverend Romer. You spotting some sins in here?' she tapped her head and her eyes smiled.

'Quite the opposite,' said Douglas.

She replaced her sunglasses and took a sip of coffee, then said, 'So, you got the wedding service for your friends all prepared?'

'Oh, thanks for reminding me,' said Douglas, leaning back in his chair and exhaling loudly. 'I've not even thought about it. And it's happening on Thursday.'

'Well,' said Alice, leaning on the table towards him, 'My advice is, don't prepare too much. Just think of Kath and... Oh, what was his name?'

'Peter'

'Yes, Kath and Peter. Just spend time thinking about them. Let them wander around in your heart for a little while. Then words will come. But don't go all Vicary on them!'

'I know, I know, Alice,' said Douglas, pulling himself back up in his chair. 'You are getting to know me well. Do I often speak like a Vicar?'

Alice took off her sunglass and smiled a beguiling smile then said, 'I really don't know many Vicars. But, Douglas, I see you becoming more and more yourself each day. And is it a bad thing to speak like a Vicar anyway?'

'Well it is if you are playing to a role and not being your true self.'

'Hm...' said Alice, pulling her lips in for a moment. She turned her head to one side and said, 'I really don't think you will be a Vicar again, Douglas. Joseph and those fabulous people at supper were steering you on to a new path, weren't they?'

'They were, Alice. They were,' said Douglas and drained his coffee mug.

'Well, listen,' Alice said, grasping the last piece of her croissant. 'I need to go and get showered and packed if we are to get to the airport on time.' The couple were soon packed and on their way to the airport and it was not long before they were flying high over the Mediterranean on their way home.

*

The sun also shone brightly in Dingle that morning, though the air was a good deal cooler than the air of Cairo. Father Pat was in his study foraging in various books for suitable prayers and rites for the laying to rest of a miscarried child. He was by no means a novice at this, but he had not actually taken such a service when there had been a long space of time between the event and the rite. He admired Peter and Kath greatly. He had never known Peter in the days when they were both new priests in this part of Ireland, but he had heard of the scandal that had resulted in the humiliating defrocking. He remembered clearly thinking 'there but for the grace of God...' Whether it was through the grace of God or the sheer fear of disgrace but, one way or another, he had managed to hold to his vow of celibacy throughout his long career as a priest. And now... Well, he was well past the time when women were tempted to tempt the local priest. But all this meant he felt deep sympathy for Peter. He could see he was a man of great integrity who had recovered well from the trauma of his broken vows, broken love and broken reputation. And it was clear that he had such love for Kath as she did for him. He was glad Douglas would be taking their wedding in a few days. But today was a day of dealing with one last piece of their shared history, and Pat wanted to serve them well.

'We should leave soon after one-thirty, I guess,' said Dorchadas who entered the study holding a tea towel.

'Oh, good man yourself, Dorch,' responded Pat. Have you done all that washing up, now?'

'Aye, I have, Pat,' said Dorchadas who never minded the fact that, despite Mrs McGarrigle's carefully worked out rota, it was nearly always Dorchadas who ended up washing and drying the dishes.

'Well, now,' said Pat, closing one of his prayer books. 'I'm so glad you'll be with us, Dorch. Tell me...' Pat was struggling a little and said, 'Could you sit yourself down for a few moments,

Dorch?' Dorchadas cleared a large pile of papers from the chair by the window and sat on it, folding the tea towel and laying it neatly on his lap. Pat placed his elbows on his desk, and rested his head on his hands for a few moments. Then, frowning deeply, he looked up at Dorch through his thick lenses and said, 'Dorch, assuming you are one of God's angels, then you are qualified to know much more than I do about these things. So what happens in heaven to the wee souls that die way before their time and never take a step into this world?'

Dorchadas looked more sorrowful than Pat had seen him in a long time. After a few moments, he looked at Pat and said, 'It's never right that a life should leave this world so soon, Pat. And every life that's conceived deserves to live a full and long life in this world. Now, remember I was only an angel, so I had no say in any of these things. I just noticed things. But whenever one such soul came into Paradise, we all felt the sadness. It was like there was a stream of sorrow trailing behind the precious souls, and we could all feel it. But you see, Pat, Paradise is the place that can hold all of this. It is different to Earth. In Paradise pain is held, you see. It is held in such an intensity of love, that the pain is soon transformed. The wee child is so full of innocence that she or he is very quickly drawn into the whirlpool of delighting love. And so there is healing.'

Pat studied Dorchadas hard for a few moments, and then asked. 'But, if you don't mind me pressing you on this, Dorch, does the child not feel any sense of sorrow at being separated from the parents, or indeed the life they should have lived on this Earth?'

'As I say, Pat,' said Dorchadas, 'I was just an angel. I don't know the answers to many things. I just know what I saw. I saw sorrow in those kiddies, but a sorrow held in the Great Love is a very different thing from the way sorrows are held in this world. You see, He notices every tear. And yes, there are tears actually in Paradise, but they are beloved tears so they are very different. I've shed a few of them myself, as it happens.'

'So, Kath and Peter's child, Dorch,' said Pat, doing his usual routine of polishing his glasses. 'They called her Róisín. So, what do you think, dear friend. Will Róisín know what's going on when we are up on that hill giving the lass her requiem.?'

'Oh, I believe so, Pat,' said Dorchadas, nodding his head. 'She'll know about it all right. And she'll be very pleased.'

'Well, that's grand, Dorch,' said Pat. 'That's grand. Is there any kind of prayer that is the best for this kind of thing?' Pat started to open one of his books.

'Yes, Pat,' said Dorchadas. 'There is. And it is the prayer from the heart.'

'Ah, well,' said Pat. 'In that case I might as well put this lot back in the bookshelf again, where they belong.' He stood up carrying several books and made his way to his well-stocked bookshelf, returning the books.

'Good plan, Pat,' said Dorchadas, rising from his chair. 'I'll see you at one-thirty.'

*

Kevin was the driver for the short trip up to the crest of the Connor Pass. Peter sat with him in the front and Kath and her two daughters sat in the back, with Brí making some complaints about the lack of room. The April sun continued to shine on the family as Kevin drove them out of the town and up the winding road to the agreed meeting point with Dorchadas and Pat. Sure enough, as they turned into the car park, the tall figure of Dorchadas was there to greet them, enthusiastically guiding them into a parking space next to Pat's car. Pat, whose black cassock was fluttering in the wind, was standing next to it.

Peter helped Kath climb out of the car and he noticed her breathing heavily. 'Peter love,' she said wincing as she attempted to stand upright. 'I'm not going to be able to walk too far up the hill today. But help me get clear of the car park, would you?'

'We all will, Mammy,' said Brí who had overheard her mother. And sure enough, during the slow climb up the path from the car park, each one took a turn in supporting Kath to a point in the hill that Kath decided was the right one.

Kevin had carried with him a camping chair and opened it for his mother. 'Sit yourself down here, Ma,' he said and Kath gratefully lowered herself into the chair.

'My God, son, it's beautiful isn't it?' said Kath as she surveyed the scene before them. Mount Brandon rose to its peak to their left, and ahead of them, in multiple shades of greens and browns lay the gentle hills and valleys that Kath had grown to love so much over her years. She pointed to one of the lakes below them. 'Do you know, we used to skinny dip in those waters. My God, those waters were cold, son. But we had a hell of a laugh, all the same.'

'I'm sure those waters are never warm, mother,' said Kevin. 'To be fair, it's not that warm here on this dry land today.'

'No, that's the truth,' said Pat, coming closer to the seated Kath. 'We don't want you getting cold, Kath, so let's get going on the prayers, shall we?'

'Aye, Pat, that would be good,' said Kath. Then looking over to Peter, she called, 'Peter, love, get yourself over here will you. I need you close for this one.'

'Of course, Kath,' said Peter who had been spellbound by the beauty of the scene stretching before him. He made his way over and started to kneel on the grass next to Kath's chair.

'No need to kneel,' said Nancy, who had also carried a garden chair with her. She opened it and Peter gratefully pulled it up next to Kath's, and they grasped each other's hands and both looked to their friend and priest.

'So, now my dear friends,' said Pat, with his dark hair being tousled by the wind. 'We have come together to honour a sweet life that was conceived in such simple and private love.'

Peter and Kath looked at each other. This was a story that had been so wrapped in guilt, shame and rejection for both of them over most of their lives. But the dark of that time had slipped away in recent days, and all they were left with now was a sense of gratitude for the life that was a tangible sign and result of their delight in each other. For a few precious weeks they could love the innocent life that was their flesh and blood. For Kevin, Brí and Nancy there was a sense of freedom that they could talk so openly about their lost older sister. At last, they too could allow their hearts to reach over the divide of death and truly love her.

Pat then looked at the group and said, 'Let's now imagine the little one. She is beloved by her family here, and she is beloved in the uplands of Paradise. The life of this world left her many years ago now, but her soul has never died.' He then pulled an old bible from his cassock pocket and, after fumbling for a time to find the right pages, he read to the group a psalm and also a reading from the Gospels. He then said, 'I'll now lead a prayer that should have been said many years ago and would have been if Peter and Kath had been kindly treated. But, as Dorch often reminds us, time in heaven is a very different matter to time here, so the delay of this prayer is no problem. So now let us commend this dear soul of Róisín to her maker.' He then raised his hands to the skies and said a traditional prayer that he had adapted and made his own many years ago:

> 'Go forth from this world, dear precious Róisín
> In the name of God the almighty Father who created you.
> In the name of Jesus Christ, who suffered death for you.
> In the name of the Holy Spirit who gave you life.
> In communion with the blessed saints,
> and aided by angels and archangels,
> May your portion this day be in peace
> and your dwelling the heavenly Jerusalem.'

For a time, Pat stood on that hillside with his arms raised high above his head which was lifted to the heavens. His robes flapped wildly around him. Only Kevin saw the moisture in the priest's eyes. Kath and Peter were clutching at each other. Brí had an arm around her sister. Dorchadas was standing a few paces away from the group and he was gazing at something that was further up the hill. 'Dear Lord...' he said. He turned to the group and called, 'Kath, Peter, look!' He pointed up the hill and all followed the direction of his arm.

'Well, by all the saints of heaven...' said Kath.

'You're not far wrong, Kath. I think it's one of them,' said Dorchadas.

'Is it...?' said Peter, placing his hand over his forehead to shade his eyes from the bright sun.

'Dorchadas?' said Brí.

'It's her,' said Nancy. 'It's our sister. She's dancing. She's free.'

Dorchadas turned to Nancy and said, 'Aye, lass. It's her. It's your Róisín.'

Kath pulled herself up from her seat and Peter joined her. They both instinctively waved to the figure of a young woman who was ahead of them, up the hill. She was wearing a flowing dress of sky blue and emerald green and she was dancing a vibrant, swirling dance. The colours in her dress seemed to fly off in rainbow rays as she spun around on the hillside.

'My, my...' said Pat. 'I've never seen anything so alive, honest to God I haven't.'

'It's our sister, all right,' said Kevin. He turned to Dorchadas, 'Is she... Is she allowed to come here to see us, Dorch? Could we speak with her?'

Dorchadas turned to Kevin and said, 'She could choose to, Kevin, but I doubt if she will. Father Pat here has just freed her and she'll be wanting to enjoy her Paradise now. But don't for one moment think that means she doesn't love you all. Quite the opposite.'

'Oh, I understand,' said Kath, whose tears were now flowing freely. 'But Dorch, can she see us? Does she know we love her?'

'Oh yes, Kath. You can be sure of that,' said Dorchadas. 'She knows she's loved, all right.' They were all spellbound as they watched the dance for a while. Dorchadas then looked to Pat and said, 'It's time, Pat.'

'I know, Dorch. I know.' The priest stepped forward a few steps in the direction of the dancing girl, who was now not just dancing, but doing cartwheels on the grass. When she saw the priest, she paused in her dancing, and all the group could make out the features of her face. Afterwards they all agreed her smile was one that they would never forget. It was a smile that penetrated to the deepest recesses of their hearts and they knew from that moment that something of Heaven was planted in their souls that day, that no work of Earth could ever dislodge.

Pat raised his hand high above his head, and Róisín did the same. Together they both slowly made the sign of the cross and by the time Pat was touching his left shoulder at the end of the gesture, the figure of Róisín was gone. Pat was shaking as he walked unsteadily back to Dorchadas. 'Dear God,' he said, 'I have seen things in recent days that I never imagined possible.'

'Aye, you have that, old friend,' said Dorchadas. He then added, 'But you know, Pat. Just because you haven't seen them in the past, it doesn't mean they were never there. The eyes of your heart were not in focus. But I think they are now.'

'That they must be, Dorch,' said Pat. 'But why now, Dorch?'

'That's not a question that needs an answer, Pat,' said Dorchadas. 'Come on, we need to get Kath back into the warm.'

'Aye, that we certainly must,' he said, and he set about guiding the group back to the cars. Soon the cars were filled and they were on their way back to the sun-tinged town of Dingle.

As they drove down the hill, Nancy nudged her mother and said, 'Mammy?'

'What is it, love?' said Kath.

'Did she come out of heaven into our world? Or did we step from our world into heaven?'

'Oh, Nancy love, I'm hardly qualified to know the answer to that,' replied Kath.

'Well, as far as I'm concerned,' said Brí, 'I feel I visited a wee bit of heaven today, I surely did.'

'Aye, me too,' said Kath.

They were all quiet for a while, until Nancy said again, 'Mammy.'

'Yes, love,' replied Kath.

Nancy grasped her mother's hand and said, 'You'll be all right, you know. You'll be all right. We know that now, don't we?'

'Yes, love,' said Kath almost in a whisper. Yes, she did feel she would be all right. Death did not look nearly as fearsome as it once had looked to her. And yet still, the days ahead were not ones she looked forward to. She was given courage and hope today without a doubt. But would it be enough to see her through her final days of her time in this world? And what about the final part of the journey? The final crossing. 'Well, you silly old fool,' she thought to herself. 'If Róisín can do it, so can you.' And with that thought she closed her eyes and dozed peacefully for the rest of the journey home.

We may be sure that none of our acts of love will be lost,
nor any of our acts of sincere concern for others.
No single act of love for God will be lost,
no generous effort is meaningless,
no painful endurance is wasted.
All of these encircle our world
like a vital force.

Pope Francis
Evangelii Gaudium

CHAPTER 16

Rosa Parks Chatterbury always struggled to marshal her luxuriant black hair into pigtails, but today she was really quite pleased with the result as she studied her image in the mirror. At eight years and five months old she believed herself to be an expert at platting hair. She used to plat her Aunt Daisy's hair, until the chemotherapy stole it all. But it was growing back again now so the day would come when they could sit side by side again at the mirror and plat away to their hearts' content.

She had always loved her Aunt Daisy. She never had rows with her Aunt like she did with her mother, but her friends assured her that all daughters argued with their mothers. Aunts were easier than mothers, because there was just that extra bit of breathing space in the relationship. And there was Uncle Frank. Huge Uncle Frank. Huge, but so gentle. He was the kindest man she knew. She had not seen her own father for over two years now. Her mother used to take her to the penitentiary to visit him, but she hated the place. And to be honest, she really did not want to see him. Not after that terrible day when he hurt them both. But that was long ago. And now that Frank and Daisy were back in Santa Maria after their time in England, she was in their home pretty much every day.

'Rosa,' came her mother's voice from downstairs.

'Yes, Mom,' called Rosa, adjusting her pigtails for one last time.

'Time you were going, baby.'

'I know. Down in a minute,' replied Rosa. It was Wednesday and she always had dinner at Aunt Daisy and Uncle Frank's on a Wednesday. That was followed by their 'home church' as they called it. Her Mom never came to churchy things, but Rosa had loved church from the moment she first remembered coming in to Uncle Frank's church a couple of years ago when he returned to Santa Maria and became the Rector of the church. Aunt Daisy led her in on a Sunday morning with her two cousins and she was spellbound by the size and beauty of the place. She had never seen such a high ceiling, which she imagined must have been close to heaven. And there were flowers everywhere. Aunt Daisy let her wander around the church building for a while as they were early for the service, and she marvelled at the colour in the windows, the beautiful carved wooden table at the end of the church that she later discovered was called an altar. But then she came to the best place of all. In the corner of the church, standing in a garden of flowers and flickering candles was the most beautiful of women. She stood tall and slim and dressed in a blue robe. She was cradling a little boy. Both mother and child were dark-skinned - not quite like her, but not far from it. Both the woman and her son were gazing out into the church, and they looked like they were about to burst into either song or laughter. Rosa was never quite sure which, but yet she knew also, that if she were to tell this beautiful lady the story of her home, she would burst into tears.

Rosa recalled how she stood in front of that statue for a while, and then heard the gentle voice of Aunt Daisy saying, 'That's Mary, the mother of our Lord Jesus. Our town is named after her - Santa Maria.' Rosa knew a little bit about the Christmas story, but she never realised that this Mary was such a nice lady and was the kind of person who could be a good friend. She knew immediately that her Aunt Daisy and Mary the mother of our Lord were the two people in the world who would always understand Rosa. She had never felt so safe, and from that day onwards this church was one of her favourite places. What she liked to do more than anything else was to go and light a candle and place it at the foot of the woman who loved her.

'Rosa...' came the voice again from the hallway. Rosa grabbed her bag and ran down the stairs.

'Bye Mom,' she cried as she skipped out of the house into a warm Spring evening for the short journey down the road to her Uncle and Aunt's home. As she walked down the sidewalk - always avoiding the cracks between the paving stones, of course - she had an unwelcome memory of the time, not that long ago, when around this time last year she arrived at the house and everyone was in tears. She remembered her Aunt Daisy gathering her in her arms and telling her that she had a serious illness. She tried to push the memory out of her head, but it was not an easy one to dislodge. She remembered feeling so frightened. But over the weeks she kind of got used to it and her Aunt Daisy didn't seem too bad, except she lost all her gorgeous hair. And then there was the miracle. Just before Christmas, she and Uncle Frank went to this meeting in a church up the coast and her Aunt Daisy got the healing as she lay flat out on the church floor. Rosa was sure her friend, Mary, had a hand in it. Rosa smiled as she remembered the evening not long before Christmas, when she went round and they told her all about it. She laughed out loud as she remembered her Uncle Frank telling how he actually sang with Aunt Daisy while she received her. Everyone knew Uncle Frank could not sing to save his life. In fact, though he said he was now good at it, she was not convinced when he gave her a sample of his new-found gift.

But now there was the exciting trip to Ireland to look forward to. She skipped on the sidewalk excitedly as she thought of this adventure that was now only twelve days away. She ran up the steps to her Uncle and Aunt's porch and pushed her way through the screen door and entered the kitchen where Daisy was preparing the supper.

'Hi, sweetheart,' said Daisy, putting down the pan she was washing. She quickly dried her hands and knelt down to give her niece a warm embrace. 'How was school?' she asked, rising from the floor and returning to her duties at the sink.

'OK,' said Rosa, throwing her bag on to a sofa in the nearby lounge. 'What's for supper?'

'Roast dragon, pickled newts and peppered cow dung!' called Frank as he arrived at the bottom of the staircase. He laughed his usual generous laugh and picked up Rosa and swirled her around. 'I know exactly what you're going to say next,' he said going over to the fridge.

'No, you don't,' said Rosa, pouting her lips.

'All right, I'll whisper it to Aunt Daisy, then we'll see.' He went to Daisy and whispered into her ear which precipitated a smile. He poured a glass of fresh orange and gave it to Rosa who was quiet for a while, determined not to be guessed by her Uncle. Everyone in the kitchen was quiet for a few moments, but Rosa could not stay quiet for long.

'Twelve days to go!' she finally erupted, unable to stay quiet any longer.

Both Frank and Daisy roared with delight as Frank had clearly guessed right. Twelve days until they travelled to Ireland. They all laughed. 'To give a serious answer to your question,' said Frank opening the lid of a pot on the stove, 'I've made us an Irish stew to prepare us for our trip.'

Rosa screwed up her nose. She was far from convinced this was a meal she would like. But as they settled at the table and she nervously took a first bite of the meal, she had to concede that it was not as bad as she feared. In fact, when mixed with a lot of mashed potato, it was really quite acceptable. Both the boys were out with friends overnight, so it was just the three of them that evening to host the home meeting. Once it turned seven o'clock, various people arrived at the home. Rosa always enjoyed the mix of old and young, black and white, rich and poor. Each and every one clearly felt at home in the group. It was Daisy's turn to lead and she had prepped Rosa to read a bible passage which Rosa did and received many accolades for the excellence of her diction. Much of the following discussion was above Rosa's head, but she always loved being there.

Towards the end of the evening, old Mrs McCarthy, the one-time terror of the church, asked, 'Reverend Frank, can you tell us a bit about your trip to Ireland.'

'That I certainly can, Mrs McCarthy,' said Frank beaming at her. It was the smile that was a strong influence in transforming her from being a prickly and cantankerous member of the church, into someone a good deal warmer and kinder. 'We were going to go straight down south, but we thought, "What the heck. Let's check out their capital city first." So, we fly into Dublin and take a look at that great city for a few days. Then we head over to Galway...'

'The boys of the NYPD choir were singing Galway Bay...' chimed up Chuck, always a fount of knowledge about anything musical.

'Indeed,' said Frank, smiling broadly at Chuck. 'But I don't think we'll hear no Christmas bells ringing out there in April, Chuck!' Everyone laughed and Frank continued, 'So, a few days exploring the west coast, before we head down to a little town in the South West called Dingle. Don't suppose no-one's ever heard of it?' There was a shaking of heads all round, except Rosa who put up her hand.'

'Yes, Rosa?' said Frank to her niece.

'The *National Geographic Traveler* has described the Dingle peninsula as "the most beautiful place on earth,"' she started, edging further forward on the sofa. 'It is bounded on three sides by the sea. It has a landscape of...'. She paused for a few moments looking at the ceiling, then continued, 'A landscape of rugged rocky outcrops and cliffs, soft hills and mountains and coastal lowlands. The main town is the beautiful and quaint town of Dingle itself, with its rich variety of pubs and shops.' When she finished, she clasped her hands together around her knees and looked at the group with sparkling eyes. She loved memorising things.

'Well, if that's the case,' said Mrs McCarthy, 'I want to come too!'

'But you have friends there, have you?' asked Greta, an elderly member of the group whom Rosa loved.

'I sure have,' said Frank. 'You guys remember I worked in the UK for a few years. And I told some of you that the Rector, who worked in the parish next to me, was a guy called Douglas.'

'I know the one,' said Chuck. 'The poor guy, who lost his young wife tragically.'

'That's the one, Chuck,' said Frank. 'Well, he has left that parish and now lives in Dingle. And we are going to visit him and the friends he has made there.'

'How is the poor man?' asked Mrs McCarthy.

'Douglas is doing just fine, ma'am,' said Frank. 'He sure was cut up about losing his beautiful wife, Saoirse. A man couldn't love a wife more than he did. He was in a desperate state after she died and I thought the poor guy was completely gone. But just recently he's had a healing. And it sounds like it has been a mighty healing of a wounded heart.'

Rosa had heard her Uncle talk about this Douglas and the more he told her of him, the more she liked the sound of him. She felt such sorrow at the thought of the death of his wife. In fact, she had to stop herself thinking about it, because it made her cry. So she was very pleased to hear that this friend of her Uncle's had found a healing for his sorrowing soul.

By the time her Uncle hoisted her on to his back for the walk back to her house, she felt sleepy but happy.

As they reached her home, she clambered off his back and said, 'Tomorrow it will only be eleven days.'

'Rosa, honey, we are going to have just such a great time,' said her Uncle.

'Uncle Frank?' said Rosa looking up at his large black face that was now lit by the lamp of her porch.

'Yes, honey?'

'Will Saint Mary be in Ireland?'

'Of course, she will, Rosa. They love her there. And from what I understand, she loves being there too.'

'Then we will be all right,' said Rosa and pushed her way through her door into her home.

'That we will, honey,' said Frank. He was so glad that Daisy suggested that little Rosa should join them on their trip. He had no doubts that she would feel quite at home in the land that Douglas had come to love so much. And as he walked slowly back to his home, pausing once or twice to admire the starry sky above him, he found himself praying. Not for Rosa. Not even for Daisy. But for himself. A prayer for something for which he could not quite find the words. But he knew that he too was in need of healing. Seeing Rosa at her tender age reminded him of his turn of passing through those junior years. It was around that time he learned that cruel people could treat you badly just because your skin had a different colour. Even at a young age he had learned strategies for managing it. But it was still hard thinking back. He kicked a stone off the sidewalk as he continued walking along. The memories would so easily invade his happy moments. Memories of insults, jibes and ostracization. And then, in his later teens, the arrests and police cells. Douglas said he found Ireland to be a place of healing. Maybe there might be something for him also in this land that they called *The Emerald Isle.* Maybe there might be a greening for the parts of his soul that had wintered for too long.

CHAPTER 17

Peter O'Callaghan made his way carefully down the narrow staircase into the room that served as Kath's Coffee Shop. There were still some embers in the fire, and he stoked it up and threw on a briquette of turf before going into the kitchen to fetch himself a whiskey. He returned to the fire which had cheerfully blazed back into life, and he turned out the light so that he could enjoy the room lit only by the flickering flames from the fire. Kath had settled well this evening and was not in too much pain. In fact, she had been a good deal better these last couple of days since they had witnessed the remarkable vision of their daughter dancing on the mountainside.

He pulled up the Windsor armchair and sat quietly for some time, taking tiny sips from his glass. He pulled off his spectacles placing them carefully in his shirt pocket. He found himself pondering the strange twists and turns his life had taken. He recalled his compelling call to become a priest when he was only a child. How clearly he could remember that fiery longing to be a bright flame of God to spread the good news of His glorious love for all people, especially those broken and battered by the trials of this world. He loved his training at seminary, and his few years of being a parish priest felt deeply fulfilling. And then that young Kathleen came into his life and he was led into those days of extraordinary light in the discovery of such deep human love. But he was also led into the darkness of that love's terrible conflict with his precious calling. He had never realised his heart was capable of such love. Only in meeting Kathleen did he discover this. Had he known this earlier, almost certainly he would never have taken the step into celibacy. He would have known that he was not strong enough for it.

The briquette shifted in the fire. Peter sighed. He was replaying such familiar scenes in his mind. He was remembering how he was on the verge of announcing his resignation when he and Kath were discovered in bed by his sour-faced aunt. And then all hell broke loose. That's how it really felt to him. He felt the terrible, cold, loveless power of hell break into the little sanctuary of their love, and everything was shattered. But he survived and he found the Society of Friends. In these Quaker meetings he found such solace and healing in the silence, and the people were so understanding. And one of these Friends was Marilyn, the girl from the Highlands of Scotland who, in time became his wife. And what a devoted and sweet wife she was. The marriage did not have the passion that he had known with Kathleen, but it had stability, kindness and companionship. And there was Cormac and Lizzie both now with their families in New Zealand. How he wished they all lived nearer, especially in those dark and lonely days after Marilyn was taken from him by the MS against which she had fought so bravely for much of her life.

And then, all of a sudden, Kathleen came knocking on his door after all these years. Despite being a woman in her sixties and bearing very little physical resemblance to the teenager who had stolen his heart, he saw straight away and so clearly the soul of the young woman he had adored. There was no question in his mind. They were to spend their final years on this earth together. But then the shattering news. Such final years were not to be years, but merely days. For all the confident words he gave to Kath and others, he couldn't deny the voice within him which asked how God could lead him to rediscover the love of his life, only to take her away again.

The flame in the fire dimmed. For some time, he let the watery evidence of his love flow unhindered down his cheeks. He took another sip from his glass and turned his thoughts to tomorrow - the day Douglas would take a wedding ceremony for him and Kathleen. It was fitting that Douglas should take this service. He was a man who had known the bitter pains of grief and Peter felt confident that he could manage well the bitter-sweet mix of emotions that tomorrow would inevitably bring. As he thought about his betrothal to Kathleen, his sorrow was soon replaced with a much lighter feeling. Yes, he couldn't deny it - he felt a sense of joy. He always felt he had rather lacked joy in his life. Seldom had he properly laughed, except recently when he had been with Kath. She had the ability to make him laugh from the pit of his stomach. He smiled as he thought of her and the joy she had brought him in recent weeks. They may only have a few weeks, possibly days. But why should they not fully enjoy these precious days together. Why should the future dominate the present? He raised his glass and said out loud, 'To my beloved Kathleen' and drank the remaining whiskey and, after securing the fireguard, he made his way to bed.

*

As Peter was climbing the staircase to bed, a few streets away in St.Raphael's Guest House, Douglas was wide awake. He was sitting on his bed and working hard on his phone. He had just sent a long WhatsApp message to Alice to let her know he had got back to Dingle safely. Only it turned out to be more than a brief message because he couldn't help but write quite a bit about their time in Cairo and how much he had enjoyed it. He couldn't quite bring himself to say how much he had enjoyed it with *her*, but he suspected that the length of the message would have conveyed that. And he really had enjoyed the weekend. It had been spectacular. Although it was such a flying visit, he had fallen in love with Egypt. They both had, and vowed one day to return to do a proper exploration of the country. But it was not just a new land he had discovered, but a new calling. He couldn't get out of his mind the meeting with Joseph and the subsequent evening meal with the wonderful and hospitable group of refugees. Every story he had heard that evening had lodged firm in his mind, and he kept on recalling each one, imaging their frightening escapes and desperate journeys and their deep longings for a new and safe homeland. He felt fired and quickened in his soul and he had already contacted various refugee agencies and charities to gain more information.

But once he had finished the message, thoughts of Egypt slipped from his mind, for there was a more urgent matter to attend to. Tomorrow he was taking an informal marriage service for Kath and Peter and he had done absolutely nothing as yet to prepare for it. He had scribbled some notes at Cairo airport. He smiled as he remembered his futile attempts. He would write something down in a notebook and read it out to Alice, but they were in such a light-hearted mood that all of his attempts simply evoked hysterical laughter from them both. He had stopped last night at his friend Brian's home, but that was no use as Brian insisted in plying him with alcohol all evening and he was in no fit state to put together a service. He tried again at Birmingham Airport this morning, but he had no inspiration whatsoever.

He got up from the bed and walked over to his desk. It was getting late and no inspiration was coming. He flicked open a few books he had brought with him and jotted down some prayers he had found but somehow, they were leaving him cold. Then he remembered his conversation with Alice. She had driven him to the airport, and just before they parted she reassured him about the wedding. He could hear her speaking to him in her soft Devonian accent: 'Douglas, they don't want anything fancy. Forget all your posh books. Just be yourself and let them be themselves. Just turn up and see what happens.' Turn up and see what happens? Douglas had never been a 'turn up and see what happens' kind of priest. He was always very nicely prepared. But the truth was that he had left that persona behind a while ago now. Maybe Alice was right. It felt risky. Horribly risky. He so wanted to do a good job for Kath. He sat down at the desk and rested his head in his hands. A silence filled the room. A warm silence. A silence of assurance. A silence of presence. A silence that carried a very clear unspoken yet felt message: 'just turn up and see what happens.'

'So that's what I will do,' said Douglas and made his way to bed. By the time a long reply message from Alice appeared on his phone, Douglas was fast asleep.

*

News of Kath and Peter's wedding had gone swiftly around the town and had caught the attention of Oonagh Kelly who was not only the elderly landlady of *The Angel's Rest* but also served as the church organist. As soon as she had heard of Kath's wedding, there was no question in her mind: the event had to be held in the function room of her pub. She marched straight up to Kath's café and, as soon as she saw Kath who was seated at one of the tables enjoying a cup of tea, she said, 'Oh for God's sake, lass, you'll be having your wedding in the function room, you will. I'll get it all prepared for you, now. Just let me know how many are coming.'

Kath and Oonagh had been good friends for many years, and Kath said, 'You're a darling Oonagh. We'd love to come to *The Angel's Rest* for our wedding.' She then added, raising her voice and speaking in the direction of the kitchen, 'Wouldn't we, Peter?'

'That we would, Kath,' came a voice from somewhere near the coffee machine.

'To be honest with you, Kath,' added Oonagh, 'it will make a change to use it for a wedding rather than a wake.'

'Aye,' said Kath.' Well, the truth is Oonagh, love, the family will be needing it for a wake before too long.'

'Why now?' said Oonagh, sitting down on a chair next to Kath. 'Whose dying on us?' Thus it was that Kath had to break the news of her illness to yet another friend.

'But listen, Oonagh,' said Kath, as Oonagh was drying her eyes and smudging her rather extravagant makeup, 'I don't want any mourning at my wedding, do you hear? We're going to have a grand party, is that clear?'

'Oh, absolutely,' said Oonagh.

'So how about twelve noon next Thursday?' asked Kath.

'That will be perfect, Kath,' said Oonagh grasping her friend's hand.

Oonagh found herself sniffing a fair bit on the Thursday morning as she prepared the buffet for the wedding. She was doing her best to not let the news of Kath's terminal illness spoil the day, but she couldn't quite get the sense of tragedy out of her mind. However, when Kevin arrived to help with the bunting and balloons, she soon cheered up. The function room had not seen a paintbrush for a couple of generations and Kevin noticed a fair number of maintenance jobs that needed attention. Nonetheless, by the time they had both worked on decorating the room, it looked suitably festive and Kevin knew his mother would be pleased with it.

About half an hour before the service, a rather nervous Douglas arrived.

'You need a little something to steady those nerves, Doug?' asked Kevin.

'I think I'm all right, Kev, thanks,' lied Douglas, as he could well have used something to steady him. But he knew he would need a clear mind for the task before him.

'So, how long will be the service, Doug?' asked Kevin as he folded some paper napkins.

Douglas had no opportunity to answer as Pat and Dorchadas both entered the lounge. Pat was looking his usual dishevelled self, but Dorchadas had managed to find something resembling a suit, though the trousers were clearly far too short for his legs. He was also sporting a 70's garish tie that he had dug out of Pat's wardrobe. Both Douglas and Kevin could not contain their laughter at the surprising sight. Dorchadas joined their laughter but did however protest that he anticipated being the best dressed person in the room. Pat approached Douglas and said, 'So Douglas, I'll be interested to see how you conduct this ceremony. I understand you won't be using an Anglican rite?'

'No, Pat' answered Douglas. 'I'd get into trouble if I did. You know... the rules and that.'

Pat smiled a brief smile, 'Oh, aye. Don't I know all about the rules? Thanks be to God, Kath and Peter just wanted something simple. They don't need anything fancy.'

'It's very unorthodox though, isn't it Pat?' said Douglas. 'I mean, they are not going to be legally married. I'm not doing any of that stuff.'

'Oh, don't be bothering about legal, Douglas,' said Pat, reassuring his friend. 'They just want their love for each other blessed. They want to be married in the sight of God, and as far as I'm concerned, God is here and wants to bless them.' He then lowered his voice and drew closer to Douglas. 'You know, Doug, Kath is looking much weaker, don't you think? I'm not sure she's got too long for this world.'

Douglas nodded. 'I know, Pat. I know. But that is for us to worry about tomorrow. Today we celebrate.'

'That we do,' said Pat, throwing one of his bright smiles and slapping his large hand on Douglas' back. At that point Brí and

Nancy arrived. Nancy was wearing a patterned pink dress which did little to help her figure. By contrast, Brí was showing off her figure in a very contemporary, bottle-green dress, high heels and a cream scarf around her neck. She carried a slim black Gucci handbag over her shoulder. She also exuded a strong fragrance of an exotic perfume. While Nancy stood awkwardly by the door, clasping her hands in front of her, Brí greeted and kissed everyone in the room. Dorchadas moved over to Nancy and said, 'So Nancy, love. How do you feel about your Mammy getting married today?'

'It's nice,' said Nancy and, unusually for her, she smiled a broad and winsome smile. 'I want her to be happy before she dies. I like seeing her happy.'

'Aye, we all do that, lass,' said Dorchadas.

The door opened again, and Elsie arrived walking backwards and carrying a large tray of home-made and elaborately decorated cupcakes. 'She didn't want a wedding cake,' she called out as she turned carefully and moved towards the table, 'But she did say I could do some of the cupcakes, and so that's what I have done. Can I put them here, Oonagh?'

'Aye, that you can, Elsie,' said Oonagh as she wiped down the bar. 'Will anyone be wanting a Guinness?' But all in the room agreed they would wait until after the ceremony.

Dorchadas moved over to Douglas and, placing a hand on his back, said, 'So Doug, did you enjoy the rest of your trip in Egypt?'

'We did, Dorch,' said Douglas. 'Fancy you knowing Alice?' he said. He did not get an opportunity for a private conversation with Dorchadas in Cairo.

'I know, son,' said Dorchadas. 'When you had mentioned Alice before, I'd never connected her with the Alice I'd met in France. That's quite a coincidence, don't you think? But a nice coincidence. But you know, Doug. When I first met the girl, I was so impressed by her. And when I saw her again in Cairo, there was no doubt her strong spirit was shining bright. But have no fear, Doug. I'm not going to pry or ask any questions. I just want you to know that I think the girl is grand. That's all.'

'Thanks, Dorch,' said Douglas and squeezed his friend's arm. He then frowned for a moment and said, 'But Dorch, I really need your help.' He lowered his voice, and drew Dorchadas a few steps back from the others. 'I've tried to prepare something for this wedding, but I've not been able to find anything that has helped me. Every prayer and blessing I looked at just didn't seem right. I've tried writing something, but that didn't work. I can't do anything that looks like the proper Anglican service, because that would get me into legal problems. So, what do I do, Dorch?'

Dorchadas gave Douglas one of his amused, down-turned smiles and said, 'You really have changed, Reverend Romer, haven't you?'

'Well such a change does not exactly help me at this moment,' protested Douglas.

'Doug, tell me,' said Dorchadas. 'What have you been told?'

'Told? By whom?'

'Doug. What have you been told?' persisted Dorchadas.

Douglas looked at the dark eyes that were peering into his and said, 'I've been told to turn up and see what happens.'

'Ah, I thought so,' said Dorchadas. 'So, what's the problem with that?'

'There are plenty of problems with that,' said Douglas.

But before he could say more, he heard Brí's voice cry out, 'They're here!' and the door opened and in walked Peter and next to him, holding tight to his arm was Kath. Peter was wearing a navy-blue three-piece suit, with a silk tie decorated with an array of scarlet roses. Kath was wearing a knee-length, floral patterned dress with a smart burgundy jacket on which was pinned a corsage of red and white rose buds. Everyone went quiet at the sight of her, for no-one in Dingle had ever seen her dressed as elegantly as this.

'Well, it's not just our Bríana who can make an impression with the smart clothes, you know,' she protested, which precipitated much delighted laughter. Everyone made their way to greet the couple, and several other local friends arrived, most of whom made their way straight to the bar. After a while Kevin came over to Douglas and said, 'Well, Doug I think everyone is here, so we can make a start. Shall I call them to order?'

'Er, yes,' said Douglas, now regretting his decision not to receive help from the bar. Oonagh had arranged for a couple of relatively comfortable seats for Kath and Peter, who now settled themselves on them. Kevin clapped his hands and made a few awkward welcoming remarks before handing over to Douglas.

Douglas stepped towards the couple as the room fell silent. Kath looked up at him and said, 'Before you get going, son, would you let me say a few words?'

'Of course, Kath,' said Douglas, grateful that the public discovery of his lack of preparation had been deferred for a few more moments.

'Well, son,' she said, looking up at Douglas. 'I expect you have prepared some lovely words for this occasion, but I was awake in the night thinking.'

'Always a dangerous thing, mother,' chimed in Kevin and several laughed.

'Well, son, it was a good thing,' responded Kath. 'I've talked with Peter this morning and we are both agreed about this. We would just like to say a few words to each other - vows if you like - and then, anyone else might want to say something. Then you, Douglas, love, could just say a wee prayer for us.' She looked at Father Pat and added, 'And you too, Father Pat, if it didn't get you into any kind of trouble with the church.'

Pat smiled and removed his glasses for the polishing routine. Douglas felt highly relieved and said, 'That would be excellent, Kath. So, do you both want to say what you want to say now?'

Kath squeezed Peter's hand, and he looked up at the group through his round-rimmed spectacles that glistened as they reflected the ceiling lights. He cleared his throat and looked back at Kath briefly, then back to the group who were now closely gathered around the couple. 'Yes, well. Thanks a million everyone for coming, and it is so good to welcome friends and family. So here we are. Kathleen and I, in the evening of our lives, rediscovering each other.' He looked back at Kath and reached out and briefly stroked her cheek. 'This is the girl I fell for many years ago now. As you all know that got us both into a fair bit of trouble. But we came through. We both had to go our separate ways and found wonderful life partners and had our beautiful children, and thank God for all we have been given. But we both know, that the love we had for each other never left our hearts. So when this girl breezed back into my life again, I felt... Well...' He looked at Kath and kissed her lightly on her cheek.

'And so, this is my promise to you, my Kathleen,' he continued. 'I, Peter, take you Kathleen to be my beloved and precious wife. I will be devoted to you for every day that we spend on this earth together. My heart is now yours. In the presence of God and our beloved family and friends present here today, I make my solemn vow to be your loyal husband, and to love you with all my heart for all the days God grants us in this lovely world of His.'

The room fell silent as Kath's plump face flushed. She coughed for a few moments, and Elsie stepped closer to rub her back. Kath looked at Peter, then up at the group gathered around her. 'Dear God, I'm not one for making speeches,' she said.

'Oh, I'm not so sure about that, mother,' said Kevin and everyone chuckled.

'Get away with you, son,' said Kath, then continued. 'Peter's right. When I first met Peter…' She paused and leaned back studying Peter and added, 'You know, Peter you've lost none of your fine looks, sure you haven't. But I'm still not sure about the ponytail.' She frowned and tugged briefly at it, then smiled and continued. 'But, honest to God, when I first got to know Peter, I didn't know such love was possible. I have never felt so alive. But, as you all know, that all came to a rather sticky end. And I agree with you, Peter,' she patted him on his arm. 'We have been blessed. I had my Kevin and my three precious kiddies, and I have had a good life. But you are right. My love for you never left my heart. And my, it was so wonderful to discover you again after all these years. And… shocking as it is for some of you to hear me saying it - I believe the good Lord in heaven has brought us together again.' She looked up at her friends propped up at the bar. 'I know, I know, your old friend Kath's got religion in her final days. But don't you worry, I shan't be bashing you over the head with my bible.'

The group at the bar ventured some ripe comments and there was more laughter. Kath cleared her throat again and said, 'Now, I'm not wanting to fill the room with gloom and tears, but you all know that I've got the cancer and its wreaking havoc with my lungs and with most of my vital organs by the feel of it, and so my days in this world have been cut short.'

'Don't want you to die today, Mammy,' said Nancy.

'No, lass,' said Kath, turning around to her daughter. 'No, I've no intention of leaving you all today. For one thing, I'm not wanting to miss the fine lunch Oonagh's prepared.'

Nancy sniffed, and then said, 'Can we start eating it now?'

'No, love,' said Kath, 'I just need to see a few more words, and then you can all get going on that fine spread. So, where was I?'

She paused for a few moments, then looked back at Peter. 'So, Peter, sweetheart. I'm sorry our days have been cut short. But don't you agree, to have just have these few precious days is better than nothing?'

'Aye,' said Peter. 'It surely is.'

'So, "get on with it, Kathleen" I hear you all thinking,' continued Kath who shifted her position in her chair so she could look straight at Peter, who was sitting up and clasping Kath's hands. Kath said, 'I Kathleen, take you Peter to be my wife...'. There was an uproar of laugher in the pub, especially from the bar. Brí leaned forward to her mother and said, 'You coming out in sympathy with me now, mother?'

Kath was laughing as much as the others, and then steadied herself. 'Oh, God forgive me my foolishness,' she said. 'I blame the pills. Let's try again.... I Kathleen, take you, Peter to be my *husband.*' She emphasised the word which was greeted with sounds of appreciation from the group. She looked at Peter, still clutching firmly at his hands. 'I will have and hold you, darling, to the end of my days. I'm not a lot of use to you now, but the love that's still flaming in my heart now, I give to you...' She paused and for a few moments looked up at the ceiling. She then continued, 'I had other things lined up to say, but, I'm sorry, they have all completely gone from my old brain now. But I think the Almighty has got the measure of what I'm stumbling to say, don't you think?'

Peter was gazing at Kath in delight and said, 'Aye, I am sure he has Kath,' and he leaned forward and kissed her.

Douglas looked on with amazement. He had never witnessed such chaotic vows in a wedding ceremony, and yet he was also very aware that he had seldom seen such pure love between two people. It radiated from Peter and Kathleen and he was in no doubt that Kath was right - God Almighty was delighted at the coming together of these two lives. Douglas reached towards them and placed his left hand over their clasped hands, and then placed his right hand lightly on Kath's head. He beckoned Pat towards him, and Pat laid his hand on Peter's head. Douglas then closed his eyes and waited for words - words he knew would never be adequate for the task. But he also felt a delightful freedom. In this place, and in this company of people, he felt safe. He felt absolutely no need to impress anyone.

And so he said, 'My lovely friend, Kath. What a road you have travelled in your life. You suffered your deepest wound when your heart was most alive in love. Yet you have carried that wound with such courage through your life. And in recent days you have found a healing in your soul. And you have found your love. You have found Peter and now take shelter in his heart. And Peter. You have given your life as a priest and a healer of souls. And you have found the one to whom you have always been devoted. And so I ask for the blessing of Christ on the marriage of these true minds and true hearts. May peace be yours now and always, Amen.'

All around instinctively joined in the Amen, and Elsie crossed herself, sniffed and said, 'Those are fine words, Douglas. God bless you, son.'

Douglas looked at Pat whose face was crumpled in a deep frown of concentration. As his large hand rested on Peter's head of grey, he lifted up his closed eyes and said, 'Kathleen and Peter. Your friends and family are witnesses to your vows. You are now man and wife in the sight of God. So now may the God of every season send his blessing upon you both. May the vitality of the Spring now Easter up in your souls. May you know a bountiful Summer of love and joy. May you know a rich Autumn harvest of generosity and kindness. And when the cold Winter threatens to darken your hearts, may eternal light give you radiant hope. And may the blessing of God the Father, God the Son, and God the Holy Spirit be upon you.'

All in the room crossed themselves and, for a few moments, there was silence in the room. Then Nancy pushed her way forward and placed her hands on Kath and Peter and said, 'God, will you bless them. God, will you let my Mammy live a bit longer, please. We don't want her going just yet, because we love her, you see.' She sniffed hard before she finished, saying. 'Thanks very much, God. Amen.'

With Nancy alluding to Kath's terminal state, there was a sense of awkwardness in the room. Brí then stepped forward and said, 'Bless you, Nancy, love.' She brushed her auburn hair from her eyes and looked round the room. 'Nancy's right, of course. We're all aware that our Mammy is not well. And I agree with your prayer, Nance. Please God may we have a good many more days of our Mammy here on earth with us.' She then leaned forward and kissed her mother and said, 'But today we celebrate. Let's not talk of death and dying today, but of love and life. Let's crack open the bottles and celebrate two wonderful people who we'll all love always.'

'Well done, Sis,' called out Kevin, and started an applause that went on for several minutes, with people taking it in turns to greet the seated couple.

As people made their way to the bar, Kath beckoned Douglas over to her and said, 'Douglas. I'm so sorry, son. I know you will have had some holy Scripture and great prayers and blessings prepared for us. I hope you don't mind that you never got to use them.'

Douglas chuckled and replied. 'Actually, Kath, I didn't. You, more than anyone, have taught me to let go of my old formal, well-prepared and well-behaved ways.'

'Is that so?' said Kath, now pulling herself out of her chair. 'Well, then maybe you won't turn out like that Venerable Cecil Oakenham after all?' and she wheezed out one of her long laughs and made her way to the bar. 'Oonagh, a couple of pints for me and my husband, if you please. And one for our Douglas here.' Oonagh had already prepared several glasses of Guinness on the counter, and moved three towards Kath. Despite the various pains that were afflicting her body, Kath had never felt so content in her soul, and her smile radiated throughout the room infecting all who were present with a mirth and laughter that lasted long into the afternoon.

The story of the unusual and very unorthodox marriage ceremony in the function room of *The Angel's Rest* soon spread throughout the town, and, although it was greeted with one or two disapproving frowns and sour faces, there was no denying the mood of happiness and cheer that resounded in the town in the days that followed. As they settled for the night that evening, Kath said to Peter, 'You know, Peter, Father Pat said to me that he thought there was a good deal more light in love than there is darkness in death. And tonight, I'm inclined to be agreeing with him.'

Peter looked at his bride and said, 'Aye, Kath. I would certainly be agreeing with him about that.' And in the weeks to come, it was those words from his new wife that would give Peter great strength to face the inevitable valley of grief that was coming his way.

CHAPTER 18

The couple of weeks following Kath and Peter's wedding were wet and very windy on the Dingle Peninsula, yet each day the hours of daylight grew longer and, when the sun did make an appearance, it came out bright and warm. Kevin had invited Douglas to assist him in his garage, and Douglas was enjoying learning some basic motor maintenance from his friend. In the evenings he continued his research into the complex world of refugees and asylum-seekers, and it had also become his habit to give Alice an evening call.

On this particular Thursday evening he had agreed to join Dorchadas and Kevin at *The Angel's Rest* for an evening meal. Though they served a very limited menu, it was without doubt Douglas' favourite place for meeting with his friends. When he arrived, Dorchadas was already propping up the bar and when he saw Douglas, he called out, 'Ah, Douglas - the usual?'

'That would be great, please Dorch,' replied Douglas and made his way to a table.

'Will it be the fish and chips or steak pie and mash?' called Dorchadas from the bar as Douglas settled at the table. 'Kevin's already told me he wants the fish.'

'Same for me,' said Douglas.

Soon Dorchadas was manoeuvring his tall frame into the cramped seat and, placing two glasses of Guinness on the table, said, 'Sláinte, Douglas, my old friend.'

'Sláinte, Dorch,' said Douglas and both men sipped at the cream-tipped ale. Looking thoughtful, he then said, 'I was just thinking, Dorch, of the time I first walked in here six months ago and met you.'

A couple of musicians were tuning up in the corner. 'Feels like a lot longer than six months, doesn't it, Doug,' said Dorchadas, placing his glass carefully on the table in front of him.

'It feels like a life-time, Dorch,' said Douglas, looking up at the ceiling for a few moments. 'Do you remember you introduced me to old Jacob by the River Nile.'

'That was a good meeting, Doug, was it not?'

'It certainly was, Dorch. Scared the life out of me in some respects. The last thing I was expecting was to step from an Irish bar into the Old Testament and meet one of the old Patriarchs!'

Dorchadas chuckled at the memory and said, 'He was a nice old bloke, though, wasn't he?'

Douglas reached over and grasped Dorchadas' arm briefly. 'Thank you, Dorch,' he said. 'Thank you so much. You'll never know...'

'No, no,' protested Dorchadas, his bushy eyebrows twitching over his dark eyes. 'No, there's no need to thank me, Doug. I've just been doing... you know.' He shrugged his shoulders.

'You're looking sad, Dorch,' said Douglas. The musicians started on a well-loved song, much to the delight of the small group sitting by them.

'Aye. I am a wee bit melancholy this evening if I'm honest, Doug,' said Dorchadas looking down at his beer. 'It's my old weakness - the one that got me into trouble in the Garden when I couldn't bear to see the pain He was in. You know all about that story now, Doug.' He looked up at Douglas and smiled briefly before continuing, 'Seeing sorrow just upsets this eejit of an angel. I don't know... I've been among you humans for long enough now. But I can never get used to the sorrows of your world. Strange, when you think about it. I was sent to this world as a human because I couldn't bear to see His burning sorrow in the garden, and what happens? I get to see close-up a whole load of human sorrow. And not only that, but I get to see it with human eyes and feel it with a human heart. I've found that a lot harder, Doug, I sure have.' His rugged face creased deeply as he frowned. 'When I was first sent here, I didn't realise how much I would *feel* the sorrows. I mean, don't get me wrong, angels aren't without feelings. It's just that living here as a human, you get to feel a good deal more.'

Dorchadas paused for a few moments and took a slow sip from his Guinness. 'For example, Doug. When you first told me about Saoirse. I went back to my room at Father Pat's and I wept buckets, I did. I didn't want to weep in front of you. You had enough problems and you didn't need to be mopping up the tears of a banjaxed angel. But I felt your grief so keenly, I did.' He looked up at Douglas, and his dark eyes were glistening, 'Even now, Doug, it still makes me so sad. I mean, when we were there on that street in Cairo. Dear heaven, Doug. You were so brave, you were. There we were in the very place were your dear lass was ripped from this beautiful world, and you were so... You were remarkable, Doug. Remarkable.'

Douglas looked down at his drink for a few moments. 'Thanks, Dorch. I didn't feel remarkable at all. I *did* feel the horror of it all again. Only for a moment, though. So I wasn't being heroic because the stronger feeling in me was a strong sense of healing. I knew something was cured within me. I was moving on.'

'Oh, aye, I could see that,' said Dorchadas, his eyes brightening. 'And listen, Doug, I've no wish to drag you back into all that grief. I'm really just confessing the state of my own heart. During my days here on earth, back and forth through the centuries, I've seen so much heartache and I think the truth is, Doug, I've probably had enough.'

Douglas looked up at Dorchadas and said, 'Enough?'

'Well,' said Dorchadas, 'I've already told you that my days of doing this work will soon come to an end and I'm just struggling with such a great mix of feelings. I mean, on the one hand, I'm desperate not to leave this world - especially this beautiful land, because I've grown to love it so much. But I'm also desperate to leave, because I don't think I can carry any more of the sadness. I told you, Doug, about my meeting with Gabriel, when we all visited that dear and desperate Calvary place. Well, he was far more complementary than I expected, as I told you. But he did have one wee criticism, and that was that I had got too involved in the lives I was trying to help. Don't get me wrong, Doug. Gabriel is a fine and compassionate Archangel. I suspect he would have been just as bad as me at getting involved. But he did say I was... you know... just a bit too much involved. That's all.'

'You're tired, Dorch, aren't you?' said Douglas to his friend.

'Aye, that I am, Doug,' said Dorchadas, with the hint of a smile. 'But, Doug, let me tell you this. Of all the work I've done during my time as a human, this job with you has been the best.' Douglas felt quite unworthy of this sentiment, and wanted to protest, but before he could, Dorchadas put up his hand and said, 'It's not for you to worry about or comment on, Doug. It's my feeling, that's all. I know this is my last job of work as a human and I just want you to know that it has been the best. And it's been the best, because, of all the humans I have met in this world, you are the one who has helped me the most. You were the only one that was allowed to come with me to Gethsemane for my great healing. And I've only been to Golgotha once, and that was with you. I can't thank you, enough, Doug. I couldn't have been to those places and found my healing and restoration without you.' Dorchadas looked at Douglas with his warm, dark and moist eyes and said, 'Truly, Doug. Thank you. Your friendship has meant everything to me.'

Douglas sat very still and looked hard at his angel friend. He knew there was no point in protesting. He had to admit that, though he felt an abject failure as a Vicar and priest, he could not deny that in the weakest and most vulnerable moments of his life, he had somehow been a source of great strength to an angel of God. Such a thought needed no critique nor commentary. Only the grasp of a hand. And, as it turned out, there was no opportunity for comment, for at that moment, Kevin arrived and joined them at the table.

Soon the fish and chips and a further supply of Guinness arrived. Another couple of musicians turned up, one carrying a large accordion, and joined the group in the corner. As the accordion started up, Douglas asked Kevin. 'How is your mother doing this evening, Kev?"

Kevin was just about to cut into his fish, then paused at the question. He looked up first at Douglas and then at Dorchadas and said, 'You know, I've seen plenty of death and dying in this world. Far too much, if the truth be told. I've seen some people die with bitterness and fury, effing and blinding their way into the dark. And I've seen others just meekly surrendering to death, letting their life slip away like oil from a cracked jar. My da was one of those - he just, sort of, gave up and drifted out of this world. But my mother is different. She's not fighting, cussing and swearing, like she sure would have done not that long ago. But nether is she just slipping from us. She's doing it like I've never seen it done. She's very weak in her body now, and sometimes in a lot of pain. But she's mighty strong and vibrant in her soul. I asked her where she gets such strength from and she said it was given her at Golgotha and it has never left her. It's like the death she witnessed there is transforming her own death. She's more coming alive than dying. I tell you, lads, I have never seen anything like it. So, to answer your question, Doug: my Ma is physically very weak tonight. We've brought her bed downstairs.' Kevin shook his head from side to side and smiled as he continued, 'But when I left to come here, she was sat up in bed, enjoying craic with Peter, who was in his chair by the fire. Do you know, she even sings a bit now, would you believe?'

All three friends chuckled, then the conversation turned to less weighty matters for a time. The music group were playing some energetic jigs and reels to the delight of those at their end of the pub. Then, as Douglas was downing the last of his chips, Kevin said, 'So, Doug, are you going to fill us in a bit on your visitors that are going to be descending on our town in the coming days?'

'Of course,' said Douglas, placing his knife and fork carefully on his plate, and wiping his mouth with his napkin. 'Well, tomorrow, two good friends from England arrive - Mavis and Alice.'

'Oh, aye,' said Kevin. 'Well it was great to meet them last time they were here. You were away that time, Dorch, I think?'

'Yes, I was,' answered Dorchadas.

'Well, you missed a treat, Dorch. They were very nice ladies,' said Kevin.

'So I hear,' said Dorchadas. Douglas and Dorchadas had decided, out of respect for Alice, that they would not tell anyone of Dorchadas' previous meetings with her. Dorchadas was also keeping quiet about his recent meeting with Douglas and Alice in Cairo. This was Douglas's story, not his.

Kevin took a sip from his glass and then, looking at Douglas closely said, 'But I think, Doug, your woman, Alice, has become a good friend now, has she not?'

'Ye...es,' said Douglas, looking cautious, 'But as I said before, Kevin, I'm keen that people don't go leaping to unhelpful conclusions about my relationship with Alice.'

'No, rest assured, Doug,' said Kevin, struggling to gather the last of his peas on to his fork, 'I won't embarrass you. Well, not too much anyway.'

'It will be grand to meet her, Doug,' chimed in Dorchadas. 'And to meet Mavis as well. I understand she has been a wonderful friend to you. But you have also got other friends coming too?'

'Yes, I have,' said Douglas, feeling the need to loosen his belt after his substantial portion of chips. 'I've got friends coming over from California.'

'Aye, you have mentioned the priest guy, who was a good friend of yours when he worked in England,' said Kevin.

'That's right, Kev. Well remembered. Yes, Franklin was the Vicar of a neighbouring parish and Daisy is his wife. They have two older boys who are not coming over with them. But they are bringing their niece, Rosa, with them. She's around eight years old, I think.'

'Ah, the wee girl will love Dingle, she will,' said Kevin. 'We must take her out to see if we can find the dolphins. What did you say her name is?'

'Well, her full name is Rosa Parks Chatterbury,' said Douglas. 'She is the daughter of Daisy's sister. Sadly, Rosa's father turned to drugs and alcohol and hurt them badly.'

'That's sad,' said Kevin.

'So, why was she called Rosa Parks?' asked Dorchadas.

'I thought you might ask that, Dorch,' said Douglas taking a sip from his nearly empty glass. 'Well, her Grandma - that would be her mother's mother, and therefore also Daisy's mother, if you follow me - was very involved in the Civil Rights movement. She was, so Daisy tells me, a very feisty teenager and she got to meet Martin Luther King. And she also met the famous Rosa Parks.'

'Well, your man Luther King I know, but who's Rosa Parks when she's at home?' asked Kevin.

'Ah she was a splendid lass, Kevin,' said Dorchadas, running his thumb up and down the cool side of his glass. 'You look her up sometime. She was a black lady who stood her ground one day against a crowd of white men who wanted to humiliate her because of the colour of her skin. Some say she was the one who got the whole Civil Rights movement started.'

'Don't tell me you've met her, Dorch,' said Douglas smiling.

'No, Doug. No, I never had that privilege,' said Dorchadas. 'But if I could choose who I could have met in this world, I think she would have been well up on the list. But if I can't meet her, then I reckon it will be as good to meet her namesake.'

'Yes,' said Douglas. 'I've no idea what little Rosa is like, but if she is anything like her Aunt Daisy, then she'll be lovely.'

'That's grand,' said Kevin. 'And when will they be here?'

'They'll be here on Sunday. And they'll all be here for around two weeks or so. Elsie has got rooms for them and for Mavis and Alice.'

'It will be great to meet them, Doug,' said Kevin. 'And I hope they all have a grand holiday here. I'm only sorry that they are coming when my Mammy is so ill. I do hope that doesn't spoil their holiday in any way, or your time with them.'

'There's no need to worry, Kev. I'm sure it will all work out. And please be assured, just because I've got friends staying, I'm very much here for your mother. They'll be out and about visiting places.'

'Sure thing,' said Kevin, who then could not resist turning around to the music group and joining in their rendition of the *Wild Mountain Heather*, a song that never failed to bring a lump to his throat.

*

When Douglas arrived back at his room, he could hear Elsie in her kitchen and he called out a 'Good Night' to her. As he was about to climb the stairs, she came out of the kitchen wiping her hands on a tea towel.

'The rooms are all nice and ready, Douglas,' she said.

Douglas noticed that her eyes were red and he came back into the hallway. 'Thanks so much, Elsie. I know they will love it here. But... are you all right?'

'Oh, I'm all right, son,' she said, looking down and wiping her hands vigorously on the tea towel.

'Elsie, you are not, are you?' said Douglas.

Elsie stopped her hand-drying and looked up at Douglas with bloodshot eyes and said, "I've been to see my sister, Douglas.' She shook her head and looked back down at the hall floor for a few moments before turning back to look at Douglas. 'I've only ever had one sister, Douglas. I know we often snap at each other, but, as God's my witness, she's the finest, dearest...' She was unable to finish as the emotion got the better of her. Douglas stepped forward and drew her to himself. She buried her head in his chest and sobbed for several minutes. Such emotion and such closeness to emotion would, at one time for Douglas, have been impossible to manage. But here in this dimly-lit hall with this dear friend racked with grief, he surprised himself that he felt no awkwardness nor embarrassment. Elsie had become to him a much-loved Aunt, and he wanted to do all he could to help her through these desperately sad days.

After a few moments Elsie became still. She drew great strength from the calm and assured arms of her English friend. She stepped back, now using the tea towel to dry her eyes. She looked up at him and said, 'Thank you, son.' She turned towards the kitchen, then looked back and said, 'They will like their rooms, I'm sure they will. I've put a nice bed up for the wee girl.'

'Yes, I know they will all be very happy here, Elsie,' said Douglas. 'You sleep well.'

'The saints and angels give you good rest, son,' said Elsie, and made her way back to her kitchen.

Just before Douglas climbed into bed, he spotted his Journal on his desk. He had intended to write in it for many days now, but somehow never got around to it. But now he decided just to pen a few thoughts before the end of the day.

Journal 7 May

I'm living in curious days now. On the one hand, I'm loving life again. The weather has been awful these last couple of weeks, but the rain hasn't dampened my spirit at all. Amazing for me! A new strength is in me. Perhaps I could even say joy. Joy was something I only ever knew with my Saoirse, but recently I've been able to get there without her help. The Egypt experience has lit me up and I feel this drive - maybe a call - to do something in the world of refugees. Don't know what yet, but I think it will become clear. And I've been loving working with Kevin down at his garage. I'm finally starting to understand the workings of a car. I've also been seeing a bit of Bríana, Kath's daughter. She's really good fun. Rather reminds me of Saoirse at times - similar sense of humour. I've had some great chats with her. She's told me about all her broken relationships. Such sad stories, some of them. But Carol, the woman she is with now, is clearly doing wonders for her. They are very deeply in love. She thought that because I was a Vicar I would judge her for it. Sad really. She and Kath have had a bad relationship over the years, but there has been a wonderful reconciliation. Seeing them together now, you would never know they were so much at odds with each other. And then there is Nancy, her sister. She really makes me laugh. She is such an honest person - she has no censorship button, so she just says what she thinks. And actually, what she thinks is always so right. I think she is teaching us all to be more honest.

But despite all the joy I've been feeling, we are also living with this terrible sadness. Dear, lovely Kath is getting very frail now. The wretched cancer is advancing fast. She's had to close the café. Poor Elsie was desperately upset when I came in this evening. Peter is brilliant and they are so much in love. I did their 'wedding'. Never has there been such a random wedding service, and yet of all the weddings I have taken over the years, this one somehow felt the most special and most genuine. Their love for each other has an extraordinary quality about it. Can I say a heavenly quality? I think so. But the harsh fact is she is dying. And it looks like she may well leave us when all my friends are here. Not brilliant timing. If I'd known, I'd never invited them all at this time.

And tomorrow Alice arrives with Mavis. I'm feeling a bit nervous about it. I like Alice so much, but… But what? It's such a big leap, that's all. Not sure what to say about it. But I will love being with her again, and it will be great for her to get to know my Irish friends. And on Sunday the Americans arrive. It will be SO nice to see Frank again. I got a text to tell me that they had a great time in Dublin and are now enjoying Galway despite the gales.

Nice meal with Dorch and Kev this evening. Dorch is amazing. Said such nice things about me. But it really does sound like his days on this earth are also coming to an end. I don't think I can bear the thought of both him and Kath leaving us. Please

God…. But this is the deal: life and death, joy and sorrow, light and dark. None of them are ever far from us.

*

Some miles away from St.Raphael's Guest House, across the blustery Irish Sea and in a small upstairs room of a house in Sheffield, someone else was writing in their equivalent to a journal. Alice was packed and ready for her next adventure in Ireland, and she decided it was time to write a note to Martha.

Letter to Martha   7 May

Hi there, Martha. It's been an exciting evening. A very clear sky tonight and I've been having a long look at Venus through my telescope. She's a waning crescent now, but very bright. Hope you can see her, Martha, wherever you are this evening. Anyway, this is just to report that tomorrow me and Aunt Mavis head back to Ireland. Our second trip there. We're going for just over two weeks. Aunt Mavis has been quite tetchy today because she gets very nervous going away from home and she doesn't like flying. But I know once we are there she'll love it. She got on very well with Elsie last time and she's looking forward to seeing her again.

So I know what you want to know about. It's about Douglas, isn't it? Well, we've been in touch every day since Cairo so I guess he does quite like me. I'm really looking forward to seeing him again, but I'm not sure how much time we'll have together. For a start he's got a good friend there called Kath. She's fab. She runs the café and I had quite a few chats with her when I was there in the autumn. Sadly, Kath's very ill and from what Douglas told me last night, it looks like she could die any day now. And then on Sunday some American friends of his arrive. At first, I thought sod's law that we should all end up visiting Douglas at the same time. But maybe Someone has a Hand in the planning? Dorchadas will be there which will be great. Life always seems safer when he's around. Anyway, it's getting late and I ought to get some sleep as we are up early in the morning. I'm just going to have one more peek at Venus and then sleep. Bye for now.

CHAPTER 19

Rosa was having the time of her life. They were enjoying a wonderful holiday. They arrived in Dublin on Monday and spent a couple of days in the city. Actually, she felt just a bit disappointed with the city. It was too noisy for her liking, though she loved the children's museum, especially the puppet room. But then they went to Galway and she loved this town much more than Dublin. They stayed in a small hotel that smelt of toast and had creaky staircases and sash windows that were hard to open.

The best day so far was Friday, when they drove up to Connemara and caught a small plane over to the island of Inis Moir. She recalled the flight so vividly. She had never been in such a small plane. Uncle Frank sat in the front with the pilot and she sat behind, next to Aunt Daisy. There were four other passengers who sat behind them. The runway was made of grass! When the plane took to the air she whooped with delight, which made everyone laugh. She looked down at the sea below them with little boats bobbing on the surface, and then the plane swooped over the island and she saw hundreds of little fields bordered by stone walls. It was a bright, breezy sunny day and they spent the whole day on the island, visiting some very ancient churches. Rosa felt they were filled with love and light and spent a long time running and dancing among the ruins. It was most definitely one of the happiest days of her life.

And now they had left Galway and were driving south to a place called Dingle. She was sitting in the back of the hire car. Aunt Daisy was driving and Uncle Frank was fast asleep and snoring. When there was a particularly loud snore, her aunt looked in the mirror and winked, which made Rosa smile. 'Aunt Daisy,' she called to the front seat.

'Yes, honey. What is it?' said her aunt, looking briefly in the rear-view mirror.

'Will there be fairies in Dingle?' asked Rosa.

'Not that I know of,' replied her Aunt. 'Why? Have you heard there are?'

'No,' said Rosa looking a little disappointed. 'Just that it sounds like the kind of place that would have fairies.'

'Well, there have been lots of saints there, I believe,' said Daisy.

'Oh?' said Rosa. Saints sounded a good deal more boring than fairies. Apart, that is from her favourite Saint Mary.

At that moment Frank woke up and said in a child's voice, 'Are we there yet?'

'About 40 minutes according to the GPS,' said Daisy.

Frank turned around and smiled a broad smile at his niece. 'You OK back there?' he asked.

'I am,' said Rosa. 'You been snoring, Uncle Frank.'

'Hm. That's what you think,' said Frank. 'So, who are we going to meet today?' he asked raising his eyebrows.

Rosa breathed in and looked up at the car roof for a few moments and then said, 'Douglas, who was a Rector with you in England. Mavis and…' She paused for a few moments, frowning.

'Alice,' said Frank, helping out her niece.

'Alice,' said Rosa, smiling back at her uncle. 'Elsie, who runs the hotel we are staying at. Her sister Kath, who is ill. Kath's husband Peter, who is a Shaker…'

'Well, to be exact, it's *Quaker*,' said Frank.

Rosa frowned. 'I don't know what a Quaker is, Uncle Frank, but I hope it means he's nice.'

'Oh, he'll be nice, baby,' said Frank. 'Anyone else?'

'Yes,' said Rosa confidently, 'A man called Dor...' she paused for a few moments and closed her eyes. She then opened them and said, 'A man called Dor*cha*das.' She placed great emphasis on the soft *ch* to impress her Uncle.

'Very impressive, Rosa,' said Frank. 'You been taking Gaelic lessons?'

Rosa giggled, then looked serious as she said, 'But who is Dorchadas, Uncle Frank?'

Frank shifted his position in his seat a little and then said, 'I don't rightly know the answer to that, Rosa. But Douglas tells me that he is very tall.'

'Taller than you?'

'Well, so Douglas says.'

'My!' said Rosa with her eyes opening wide.

'And Douglas says he is a very special friend,' said Frank.

'Is he a wizard - like Merlin?' asked Rosa hopefully.

Frank and Daisy both laughed, and Daisy said, 'Whatever makes you think that, darling?'

'I dunno,' said Rosa, sitting back in her seat and looking back out of the window. 'Just sounds like he is, I suppose.'

'Well, Rosa honey, you will just have to ask him when you meet him,' said Frank.

'OK' said Rosa, and gazed out at the hills and the white, woolly clouds above their crests. She was pretty sure this Dorchadas was a wizard. But she acknowledged that even really good grown-ups like her Uncle and Aunt still struggled to believe important things like this, and she just had to make allowances.

*

Meanwhile, back in Dingle, Mavis and Alice had arrived just in time for a very ample lunch that Elsie had prepared for them. The early start and lavish lunch were enough to send Mavis straight up to her bed and she was soon off to sleep. Alice and Douglas helped Elsie clear up and were then sent out of the kitchen as Elsie wanted to prepare tea for the next group of guests to arrive. She had decided to make them some of her special recipe scones, and she was very pleased with the progress they were making in her oven. Douglas and Alice were next door in the dining room.

'Frank's just texted and they should be here in about ten minutes,' said Douglas.

Alice looked across the table at him and smiled warmly. 'I really like it here, Douglas,' she said.

'Does this coastland remind you of Morwington?' asked Douglas.

Alice threw back her head in laughter and said, 'Mor*wenstow*! How many times do I have to tell you?'

Douglas laughed with her. 'Sorry. Mor-wen-stow,' he said with great deliberation.

'To answer your question,' said Alice, 'yes and no.'

'A typically helpful answer, Alice,' said Douglas.

'Well,' said Alice, 'I mean "yes", in that this coastline does remind me a little of the coastline of north Cornwall. But "no", in that there is nowhere on earth like Morwington.' Both of them laughed again.

Elsie came through the door and said, 'Well, you two are surely having a merry time there. Now tell me, Douglas, have you heard from your friends yet? Are they nearly here?'

'Yes, Elsie,' said Douglas. 'They are only a few minutes away.'

'Well, that will be perfect timing, then,' said Elsie. 'When they get in, I can show them their room, and then they can come down for a nice cup of tea and that will be perfect timing for my scones.' She hustled off back to the kitchen.

'You've made such great friends here,' said Alice.

Douglas was about to respond when the doorbell sounded which brought a cry from the kitchen of 'Oh, Joseph and Mary! I've still got my blessed apron on!'

'Do you want me to go, Elsie?' called Douglas standing up.

'No, no. You're all right, Douglas,' said Elsie as she sped down the hall to the door, throwing her apron over the back of a chair and then patting her hair as she quickly glanced in the hall mirror.

Douglas and Alice made their way to the hallway, and sure enough, as Elsie opened the door, there stood the large and impressive figure of Franklin Oberman who, on seeing Elsie, said, 'So you must be the beautiful Elsie O'Connell.'

'Och, now, get away with you,' said Elsie, clearly delighted. After Frank had given her a bear hug which robbed her of most of her breath, she said, 'Come along inside, will you? I'll show you to your room. We'll do all the paperwork with passports and what have you later.'

Frank introduced Elsie to Daisy and Rosa and they made their way into the narrow hallway. Douglas and Alice emerged into the hallway from the dining room. ' Yo! You the man! How are you, dude?' hollered Frank when he saw Douglas. The two friends laughed as they hugged each other tight before there were further introductions and agreements about meeting in five minutes for tea in the dining room. Elsie took them upstairs, grateful at their delight in their room, then returned to the kitchen. Alice joined her to help with the tea.

'My, that Franklin is some powerful man,' said Elsie to Douglas, as she entered the dining room carrying a large pot of tea. Alice was following close behind with the warm and fragrant scones.

'He is certainly a large man, Elsie, but I assure you he is a gentle giant.'

'Well, that is good and reassuring to hear, Douglas,' said Elsie. 'The breath's only just returning to me now, I must say.'

'And did you see the little girl?' said Alice. 'She looks a darling.'

'I think they are all very special,' said Douglas, who was feeling so delighted to have his good friends from America here in Ireland.

It wasn't long before they were all sitting round the table enjoying cups of tea and sampling Elsie's scones and jam.

'These are the most delicious scones ever,' declared Daisy, and all agreed.

'And Alice, where is your Aunt?' enquired Frank. 'I hear you came over here with her.'

'Well now,' said Elsie, looking slightly embarrassed. 'I'm afraid I might be responsible for her absence from this tea party. You see, I offered her a can of the Guinness with her lunch. She declared that she had never had a glass of it before now.'

'I have never seen her touch a drop of alcohol before now, Elsie!' said Alice smiling and raising her eyebrows.

'Is that so?' said Elsie raising her eyebrows. 'Well, that very much surprises me, Alice, because the truth is she took to the drink like a duck to the water, she did. She wasn't shy about taking a second can. I did notice she was a little unsteady on her feet as she made her way up the stairs. Well, never mind. She'll be having nice dreams now.' She then looked across to Daisy and said, 'The Guinness gives you fine dreams, it does, Daisy. Will you be having another scone, darling?'

'No, I couldn't manage another, thank you, Elsie,' said Daisy.

'I'm just thinking, I should have brought you a coffee,' she said to Daisy looking at her t-shirt which read *This girl runs on coffee and Jesus*.

'Or you could have brought me Jesus,' said the smiling Daisy, to which everyone chuckled.

'Well, I'm not sure that's my department,' said Elsie coyly. 'I do go to church, though.'

This provoked Rosa to ask, 'Uncle Frank, can we see the church? Is Mary there?'

Daisy looked at Elsie and said, 'Rosa loves the statues of Mary. Do you have one in your church.'

'Oh yes, darling,' said Elsie to Rosa. 'Our church is dedicated to the very lady. And he is there all right. I polished her up last week. She's looking very nice. You must go and see her.'

'Is she wearing blue?' asked Rosa.

'That she is, sweetheart,' replied Elsie. She was about to continue but was interrupted by a rapping on the window.

'Oh!' cried a wide-eyed Rosa, jumping to her feet. 'It's the wizard!'

CHAPTER 20

Elsie opened the front door and greeted Dorchadas, Kevin and Brí, who had all heard news of the new guests arriving at St.Raphael's and were keen to meet them. Elsie ushered them into the dining room and as Dorchadas stooped through the doorway, Rosa bounded up to him, stretching out her hand and said to him, 'I'm Rosa, and I have been looking forward to meeting you, Dorchadas.'

Dorchadas chuckled with delight and kneeling down on the floor next to her said, 'Well, I have just been longing to meet you, Rosa. Tell me now, have you come here all the way from the far-off land of California?'

'I have,' said Rosa, studying very carefully the kindly creases on the face of the wizard.

'So did you come all this way on the back of a flying horse? Or did you use a moonbeam?'

Dorchadas and Rosa continued to have their conversation on the floor near the doorway, while the rest of the group introduced each other, and Elsie hurried out to the kitchen to make more tea. They settled at a couple of the dining tables. Frank sat with Douglas and Alice and was delighted to tell them about his first experience of Ireland. Daisy sat with Kevin and Brí and said to them, 'I am so sorry to hear about your poor mother. How is she doing?'

'Oh, it's kind of you to ask,' said Brí. 'To be honest she is very poorly just now.'

'Aye,' added Kevin. Daisy noticed the sorrow in his eyes. 'We don't think she has too long for this world now. Maybe a few weeks, if that.'

'Though to be fair,' added Brí, 'She does have her bright days. And she sure doesn't want to lock herself away from everyone. She very much hopes you'll visit her.'

'Of course, we will,' said Daisy. 'Just let us know when would be convenient.'

'Och, just drop in any time,' said Brí. 'If she's not up to seeing people, Peter will let you know. Peter's her new husband.'

'Oh, yes. Douglas has told us about the wedding,' said Daisy with a bright smile.

'Has she told you about the picnic?' The question came from Elsie who was passing round the scones and had overheard the conversation about her sister.

'A picnic?' asked Brí, raising high her eyebrows.

'Aye,' said Elsie, placing the plate of scones on the table. 'She's got it into her head that she wants a picnic on Ascension Day. She so enjoyed the Easter Day picnic on St.Seannach's isle and fancied having another on Ascension Day.'

Kevin, looking concerned, said, 'I'm not sure she'll be in any state to be going out for a picnic on Ascension Day, Aunty Else. I mean, she's not going out of the house at all now. And Ascension Day is ten days' time. You know…'

'Well, son,' said Elsie. 'You try telling your mother it's a bad idea. I tried, but to no avail. You know what she's like. No, she wants this picnic, and that's that.'

'Who said picnic?' called the loud voice of Frank, who overheard their conversation. 'I love picnics!' The room now became just the one conversation, apart from Dorchadas and Rosa, who were still sitting on the floor discussing various theories about unicorns.

'Oh, we are just talking about my mother,' said Kevin explaining. 'We all know she is very ill at the moment, but Aunty

Else here tells us that she has got it into her head that she wants a picnic on Ascension Day.'

'That's a beautiful idea,' said Alice.

'Aye,' said Brí. 'Beautiful, but not exactly practical. In fact, to be truthful, we don't even know if she will be with us on Ascension Day.'

'Well,' said Elsie. 'Argue with her all you want, but I know my sister. She's already phoned Father Pat.'

'Father Pat?' said Kevin.

'Oh, aye,' responded Elsie. 'She thought he could do some Ascension Prayers or some such. I didn't quite catch all of what she was saying, to be truthful.'

Douglas was listening to the conversation with interest. 'I think,' he said, 'If Kath wants a picnic on Ascension Day, then we must all do what we can to make it happen. And if she's too ill on the day, then so be it. But it will give her a lot of pleasure looking forward to it.'

'Those are wise words, as ever, Douglas,' said Elsie. 'You sure do know my sister well.'

'Elsie,' added Douglas. 'Do you know if this is a picnic just for the family, or...?'

'Oh, no,' interrupted Elsie. 'No, she wants you all there. She told me clearly. She said "All the family, and all of Douglas' friends. And Father Pat. So a big crowd of us. I've already thought about the sandwiches.'

'Oh, Aunty Else,' said Kevin, 'that's a lot of sandwiches. I'm sure we could ask Mrs McGarrigle...'

'I'll be doing the sandwiches,' said Elsie firmly and all in the room were in no doubt that she would be doing the sandwiches for the picnic, not Mrs McGarrigle.

'Aunt Daisy,' called the voice of Rosa from the floor. 'Uncle Dorchadas says there are dolphins in the bay. Can we go and see them? Please?'

'Well, sure we can, honey,' said Daisy.

'Tomorrow?' pleaded Daisy. 'Please, Uncle Frank?' She came over to Frank and sat on his lap. All in the room could see that Frank was not one who could resist easily the appeal of his little niece.

'Yes,' said Frank. 'Tomorrow.' He then looked up and said, 'So who knows how to find dolphins?'

And so, the conversation continued with plans for the coming week, which included a boat trip on Monday to see if they could find some dolphins.

*

Douglas had seldom enjoyed a week so much. He was delighted with how his friends got on so well with each other. Nancy joined Frank, Daisy and Rosa for a very successful boat trip on Monday to see dolphins, and they were all delighted when, several times, the dolphins leaped out of the water to greet those in the boat. Rosa was convinced that one of them kept smiling at her. Elsie and Mavis spent much time together and made daily visits to *The Angel's Rest.* Mavis was a true convert to Guinness, though she insisted on sticking only to the one pint. Frank and Kevin quickly made friends.

Frank found Kevin a very safe person to talk to, and much to his surprise, found himself one morning, sitting in Kevin's kitchen, telling him stories of his childhood which included sad stories of humiliations and racial abuse. He told Kevin of the frightening nights spent in police cells. In turn, Kevin told him of the long, lonely days in the Maze, and also of his friendship with a fellow inmate who told him all about Francis of Assisi, and who opened his eyes to the presence of a God of kindness. Something about Kevin's powerful listening and compassionate understanding of this nagging wound from his past brought great solace to Frank.

Everyone wanted to be with Dorchadas, who was much enjoying the time he spent with Douglas' friends. Rosa would not budge from her conviction that Dorchadas was a wizard. It was on the Saturday of that week that he took Rosa down to a café on the harbour for a hot chocolate. It was during that conversation that Rosa somewhat reluctantly agreed that Dorchadas could be an angel rather than a wizard. An angel was almost as good. As they left the café they saw a girl, older than Rosa, waving to them from the quay. Dorchadas called over to her, 'Well now, lass. What brings you here?'

Rosa and Dorchadas crossed over to the quay and Dorchadas said, 'Rosa, meet a friend of mine. Her name is Grace.'

'Hi Grace,' said Rosa. 'I'm Rosa.'

'I know,' said Grace.

'Are you an angel, too?' asked Rosa, squinting up at the girl as the sun was shining behind her.

'No, not really,' said Grace.

'You look like one,' said Rosa, which made Dorchadas chuckle.

'Dorchadas,' said Grace. 'How is Kath doing?'

'Not good,' said Dorchadas. 'What do you know, lass?'

'She needs to go on the picnic, Dorchadas. But I think you know that, don't you?'

'Aye,' said Dorchadas. 'I do.'

'Do you know where the picnic needs to be?' asked Grace, swishing her long hair back from her face.

'No. Tell me,' said Dorchadas, looking down at the young girl, waiting for the information he knew he needed.

'Reask,' said the girl.

'Ah,' said Dorchadas, scratching his beard. 'Yes, that would make sense, that would.'

'What's Reask?' asked Rosa.

Dorchadas looked down at his little friend and said, 'It's a wonderful place, Rosa. Not far from here. The hills surround it like the arms of God. It feels a very safe place. There you will find lots of dark stone walls and they are the remains of the buildings that once formed a monastery some fifteen hundred years ago.'

'What's a monastery, Uncle Dorchadas?' asked Rosa.

'Ah, Rosa, love. It's how the Christians lived in them days. They loved each other, they did, and loved to live together in a community - you know - a great big family. They called the community a monastery. And to be honest with you, Rosa, I've never researched that word. But all I know is that the monasteries of them days, which were full of men, women and children, not to say a fair few cattle, sheep and pigs as well, were great bright flames of love and hope in this land.'

'They weren't perfect, Dorchadas,' said Grace frowning.

'Aye, I know that, lass,' said Dorchadas, smiling.

'You visited them, Dorch?' asked Grace.

'Aye, that I have,' said Dorch. 'Not Reask. I never visited there when it was alive. But other ones like it. And you are right. There was a fair bit of bickering and that. But they were nice places, they were. So much laughter and song. And lots of sadness as well. But always bright, sparkling faith.'

'Can we form a monastery, Uncle Dorchadas?' asked Rosa.

'Well now, who should we invite into this monastery then, Rosa?' said Dorchadas.

'You and all of Douglas' friends,' said Rosa.

Grace laughed and, nodding her head, she said, 'Yes, Rosa. You are getting the idea! Well, nice to meet you. I'll be on my way.'

'Yes, great to see you, Grace,' said Rosa.

Grace turned to go, but paused and said, 'Oh, by the way. I hear you saw the dolphins and one was smiling at you.'

'Oh, we did! And one did keep smiling at me,' said Rosa.

Grace smiled her wide smile. 'Good one!' she said. 'He said he enjoyed seeing you.' And with that, she ran off, her long hair flowing behind her, and leaving Rosa looking up at the smiling Dorchadas with a very puzzled expression on her face.

*

Kath's Coffee Shop was now shut to visitors. Locals would pass by, glancing at the notice that had been carefully written by Peter, then walk on quickly, shaking their heads with sorrow. Inside the house, Peter, Brí and Nancy continued their support of Kath who had her good days and bad. As Dorchadas and Rosa were chatting to Grace at the quay, Kath was having a relatively good day. She was sitting in her chair by the fire drinking her coffee. It was proving to be a better day and the pain was nicely under control. Nancy had just finished her hoovering of the upstairs rooms and came and sat down with her mother. She opened her box of cigarettes, but then thought better of it and put it to one side.

'Nancy, love,' said Kath, 'Would you do one thing for me?'

'Yes, Mam,' said Nancy.

'Would you mind not asking me every day if this is going to be my dying day. I'm finding it a bit off-putting, if I'm honest.'

'OK,' said Nancy. 'I just like to know.'

'I know you do, lass,' said Kath. She looked across to her daughter who reached out for her box of cigarettes again and clasped it. 'You'll be all right,' said Kath. 'You know you will, love.'

'I'll miss you, Mammy,' said Nancy, looking down to the floor and turning the cigarette box over in her hands.

'Nancy, love,' said Kath. 'Look at me.' Nancy looked at her mother. 'We all have to die. It's not nice because most of us enjoy the life here on earth that we've been given, despite all its woes. And we don't like being separated from the people we love. But it has to happen. And when it does, it's sad. But it's not the end of things, darling. You know that. God knows, I was more atheist than any of you, but I've changed all that now. I've no doubt at all that there is a world beyond this one. And Nancy, it's a beautiful one. So don't you go worrying about me. I shall be enjoying myself. I know you will feel just a bit lonely for a time. But you'll be all right, love. I promise you will. Kevin will be here and he'll keep an eye on you. We all heal. It's the way we've been made.'

'How do you know, Mammy?' said Nancy.

'How do I know what, love?' asked Kath.

'How do you know it's beautiful?' Nancy placed the cigarette box back on the side table again.

'Because, Nancy, I've been given a glimpse of it. And a glimpse was all I needed to give me hope.'

'Can I get a glimpse one day?' asked Nancy.

'I don't see why not, love,' said Kath.

'OK,' said Nancy. 'I'll ask Him for one.'

'Good plan,' said Kath. 'Now, it is time for our lunch. The others will be back soon.'

And sure enough, just as Kath spoke, the others walked through the door carrying groceries and supplies for the coming days.

After lunch, and after her afternoon rest, Kath was sitting back in her seat reading, when there was a knock at the door. Peter answered it, and standing at the door was Daisy. She, Frank and Rosa had visited earlier in the week, but it was on a day when Kath was not feeling so bright. Today, however, she was feeling brighter and glad of the chance to chat with Daisy.

'Sit yourself down by the fire, love,' said Kath. Although it was quite a mild day, Kath now needed the fire burning all the time, and Peter made sure it was well fuelled with logs and briquettes. 'It's good of you to call. Are you enjoying your holiday?'

'Oh, sure. We are just loving it,' said Daisy. 'What a beautiful land.' Peter went to the kitchen to make a pot of tea. Daisy told Kath of the various visits and adventures they had enjoyed in recent days.'

'The weather's not been great for you, I'm afraid,' said Peter as he returned with the tea.

'Oh, that's no problem,' said Daisy. We don't get enough rain where we live, so we are just loving it!'

'It's hard to imagine loving the rain like that, eh, Peter?' said Kath chuckling.

Peter passed around the mugs of tea and then pulled a seat up from one of the tables and sat on it. 'Douglas tells us that you have also been very ill not so long ago,' he said.

'Why, yes,' said Daisy sipping at her tea. 'I was dying, for sure. It was cancer.'

'Well, it's nice to meet a fellow sufferer,' said Kath. 'But how come you are looking so bright now, lass? Have you managed to kick the cancer out of your body then?'

'Well, Franklin took me to a healing service just up the coast from us and…' Daisy paused for a few moments, then continued. 'Don't ask me to explain this, but someone said prayers for me and I just got better.'

Peter was looking at her intently and asked cautiously, 'Do you mean… You were miraculously healed?'

Daisy nodded. 'Well I guess so. I mean, I really don't get all this. Frank and I have never had anything to do with those big healing meetings. We don't go for that kind of thing. But the fact is, after that prayer, I got better. Maybe I'm in remission and the cancer will return one day. I don't know. But for the moment, I'm doing just great.'

Peter was frowning and looking hard at her. 'So, Daisy,' he said, still frowning deeply, 'Did you ask God to cure you?'

'Well,' said Daisy, 'I never liked those "name it and claim it" kind of healing shows. But there was a kind of little girl in me that felt that I should ask God for the one thing I really was hankering for. I wanted my healing, I sure did. So yes, I guess I did ask Him for it. Don't you think that's right?'

'Oh, yes, of course,' said Peter, releasing his frown. 'I think I'm just not sure of my ground when it comes to asking God for something so...Well, something so big.'

Kath smiled and said, 'Daisy, love, I'm so delighted for you. You're a young lass by my reckoning, and if I were God, I'd want to give you many more years in this world. I'm glad He healed you, I sure am.'

Daisy gripped her mug tightly and then looked across at Kath, her large dark eyes brimming with water and said, 'Oh, Kath. That is so generous of you. I was anxious about telling you, to be truthful. I just...'

'Oh, no, no...' said Kath waving her hand. 'Sure to God, nothing in this world makes much sense does it? I know what you're thinking. You're worried about the fact that our God has put you right, but is letting me die, is that it?'

'Well, I guess so,' said Daisy, rubbing her eyes dry.

'Look, lass,' said Kath. 'We've been given the one life to live. I've made a hell of a mess of mine at times, but I've also had many good days. Especially of late. But I've learned that it is not up to us to say how many days we should live on this Earth. Our job is to live the ones we have been given well. I don't know what you found, but I've found that doing a bit of dying is not a bad way of learning how to live.'

'Oh, yes,' said Daisy. 'I did discover that. But I also discovered something else so precious.'

'So what was that, Daisy?' asked Peter, who was listening intently to the conversation.

'Well, when we went to the healing service and they prayed for me, I had something like - well, I guess you would call it a vision.'

'Oh, aye? I've also had one of them,' said Kath. 'But tell me about yours, love.'

'Well, when they prayed for me, I found myself lying on the floor, and that's when I got the vision. I really believed I was dying and I was no longer afraid. It was OK.' Daisy nodded, warmed by the memory. She looked briefly at both Kath and Peter and then, looking at the burning fire, she continued, 'There was the most beautiful singing coming from somewhere. I got that feeling like you got when you were a child on a summer's day and you felt a burst of pure joy in your heart.' She tapped her heart and smiled a radiant smile. 'Well, I felt that joy even though I believed I was dying. It was incredible, because, before that, I was terrified of dying. So, I was full of this joy and then I saw Him.'

'You mean "Him",' said Kath pointing upwards.

'Yes,' said Daisy, still smiling. 'He was nothing like I was expecting, actually. It's really hard to explain, but He was the nicest, closest, kindest friend you could imagine. But He was also... blazing light - total power - utter holiness.' She shook her head, then said, 'I'll never be able to explain it, but I remember it so vividly. And all I knew then was that I wanted to be where He was, and I begged to go with Him. But He just said, "Not yet. Your time is not yet." And when He said that, I woke up on the church floor.

'Fetch me a tissue, would you, love,' said Kath to Peter who got up and found the box of tissues and passed it to her. 'That sure is a beautiful story, Daisy, love. Thank you for telling it to me. You're a darling, you surely are.'

'It certainly is a beautiful story, Daisy,' said Peter, who was clutching a tissue, as his eyes were also glistening. 'Your story will sure help us a lot.'

'Kath,' said Daisy.

'What is it, darling?' said Kath, then blew her nose noisily.

'You said you had a vision,' said Daisy. 'Are you able to tell me about yours?'

'Peter, love. We are going to need more tea,' said Kath. Peter gathered up the mugs and departed to the kitchen, and while he made a fresh pot, Kath told Daisy all about her visit to Golgotha, her meeting with Mary Magdalene and her time at the foot of the cross.'

'And there was another thing, lass,' she said to Daisy as Peter brought in fresh mugs of tea. 'I met another lady there. I know it's hard to believe, but I met the great Brigid of Kildare who all Irish people love, but I loved especially when I was a wee girl.'

'How wonderful,' said Daisy, then thanked Peter as he passed her the tea.

'Well it *was* wonderful, Daisy,' said Kath. 'But I will tell you this, which I have only told to Peter.' She leaned forward and spoke in a softer voice. 'This Brigid told me a few things in this vision. She told me about my sickness.'

'Oh, my!' said Daisy. 'So, it didn't come as a surprise when you heard you had cancer.'

'No, not at all,' said Kath. 'It was kind of her to prepare me, don't you think?'

'It was,' said Daisy, taking a sip from the fresh tea.

'But she also said something a bit strange,' said Kath, frowning. She said, "You have seen the day of the Great Death." Well, I sure had. I'd seen the poor lad on the cross dying, with the blood flowing from his broken veins. I'd seen the Great Death, all right. But then she smiled at me - a sweet smile it was - and she said, "You will also see the Great Beginning". To be fair, Daisy, I'm none too sure what she meant by that.'

'Well,' said Daisy, 'Maybe you don't need to understand it. But it sounds like it will be a wonderful thing to see.'

'Aye, that it does, darling,' said Kath. 'That it does.' The three chatted for a little while, then Daisy could see that Kath was growing tired, so she prepared to leave.

'Daisy, love,' said Kath reaching out her hand, 'It sure has been good to meet you. I feel we have a lot in common, you and I.'

'I have loved meeting you, Kath,' said Daisy and went over to Kath and embraced her. As she left the house and made her way back to St.Raphael's in warm April sunshine, she felt a curious mixture of sorrow and joy. She felt sorrowful at the thought of Kath's dying, but the sharing of the stories of their visions felt very enlivening. Always, whenever she told her story of her vision, she felt re-connected to the extraordinary surge of life and joy that she had experienced then. Kath's vision was quite different to hers, and yet it had a similar quality. And the promise of the Great Beginning intrigued her. As she strolled through the streets of Dingle, she became increasingly aware of an instinct that it would not just be Kath who would witness this Great Beginning. She hoped - no, she dared to believe - that she would be one of those who would also catch sight of such a glorious thing.

*

While Daisy was sipping tea with Kath and Peter, Douglas and Alice were on the Great Blasket Island. Kevin had arranged for a friend of his to take them there in his boat at the beginning of the day. Thus, they had been enjoying a breezy stroll around the island, a brief paddle in a very cold sea, and a cheese roll on the beach. Despite a cold wind, the sun had been shining most of the day and they were now sitting on the grass with their backs against a sheltering stone wall of one of the many ruined homes that once belonged to the islanders who lived here. There were no islanders now, and indeed Alice and Douglas were two of the very few visitors to the island on this day.

It had been a good week, but a busy one and Alice had been a little frustrated that there had been no time with Douglas on his own. But this day she could have him all to herself and she felt a deep sense of contentment.

'How are you feeling, Douglas?' she asked as they both gazed out to the heaving ocean.

'Happy,' said Douglas.

They were both quiet for a while, then Alice removed her sunglasses and looked at Douglas and said, 'How are you feeling about us?'

Douglas continued to gaze out to sea for a while, then he looked back at Alice. The light wind was ruffling her soft hair, which she frequently needed to brush from her eyes. As she pulled a lock of hair behind her ear, Douglas noticed her hazel eyes looking searchingly at his, and he saw a vulnerability that he had not noticed before. He became aware of the risk she was taking, daring to get close to a man again. He reached out his hand and grasped hers, not for the first time that day, but she was aware that this grasp felt truer and stronger. She looked at the clasped hands as he replied to her question, saying, 'I feel happy about us, Alice. I feel very happy. How about you?'

She looked back at Douglas, who watched the moisture gathering in her eyes. He thought she looked more beautiful than ever. She frowned in the brightness of the April sunlight. He felt a sense of dread emerging, for her face seemed to suggest that she was about to tell him that she was *not* happy with this friendship. But his fears were unfounded. Her frown quickly dispersed and slowly the corners of her mouth turned into a winsome smile and warm tears fell down her lightly freckled cheeks. 'I feel good about us, Douglas,' she said nodding, and leaned towards him kissing him on his cheek. He released his hand from hers, and put his arm around her drawing her tight to himself.

Together they gazed out on the glistening sea, each admiring and enjoying the strength of the other, and both daring to believe something that, not so long ago, neither imagined was possible.

Christ's resurrection is not an event of the past;
it contains a vital power
which has permeated this world.
Where all seems to be dead,
signs of the resurrection
suddenly spring up.
It is an irresistible force.

Pope Francis
Evangelii Gaudium

CHAPTER 21

Letter to Martha 20 May

Hello Martha. It's Alice here again. Well, I've been in Ireland almost two weeks and have had an absolutely fab time. Wow, what a country. Such beautiful lights here, especially over the sea. The people are brilliant. I haven't laughed so much in years.

So here's who I've met: There's Kath. She's the one who's really seriously ill with cancer. Douglas has taken me to see her a few times now, though once she slept through our visit. She looks very weak in body, but she's so alive in her soul. You'd be amazed, Martha. How can someone who is dying be so alive? Her husband's called Peter. He's a beautiful, quiet and gentle soul with a really cool silver pony tail and blue eyes with adorable blond eyelashes. Douglas did a kind of marriage service for him and Kath just a few weeks ago. They were childhood sweethearts when he was a priest. Yes, it's a long story. But they are so sweet with each other. Feels like they have been together for years and years. Kath has three children. There's Brí or Bríana. She's got hair to die for - such a beautiful auburn colour. You can tell that she can be fiery at times and I feel just a bit nervous of her. But I like her very much. She lives in the States and lives with a female partner and they are hoping to marry soon. Her sister, Nancy is totally different. She's pretty blunt and says what she thinks. She's hilarious actually. I feel very fond of her. And there's their brother, Kevin. Douglas says he was once in the IRA and in prison. At first sight he's a bit intimidating - looks a real bruiser. But he's got such a soft heart and his blue eyes shine so bright under his dark eyebrows. Then Kath has a sister, Elsie who runs the Guest House here. She's a scream. Often complains about the weather and her various ailments and has a slightly weird dress sense and pitch-black hair (not her real colour, surely?) But she looks after us so well and I love her. When the family are together they all talk together in their Irish accents and I can hardly follow what they are saying. And sometime they slip into Gaelic. Can't understand any of it, of course. But it sounds such a beautiful language. Took me an age to get hold of French, so don't think I'll ever learn Gaelic.

Then there's Father Pat. He's gorgeous. He always looks like he's lost something and keeps removing his glasses to polish them. His big woolly jumper really needs a wash. His trousers are too short for him and his shins are bright white. Don't suppose his legs have ever seen the sun. He's the priest of the local church. Some people don't like him because apparently, he's a bit radical. For one thing, he turns a blind eye at us Protestants (or "Proddies" as Kevin calls us) taking Communion. But he's such an honest guy. Told me about his depression, and how it lifted from him at Easter. Something special happened to him, he said, when they all went off to spend the day on some island. This is the thing about Ireland, Martha. People go to these places which are full of old ruins, and things seem to happen to them. There's something magical here. Well, Pat would say it's the Holy Spirit. He's become very keen on the Holy Spirit, he says.

So that's Douglas' Irish friends. Then there's the Americans who arrived just after us. There's Frank who's massive. He used to play American football and told me he was the Offensive Tackle, which sounds impressive. But he's the classic gentle giant. Douglas told me he was a brilliant help to him when Saoirse died. Douglas also told me that Frank and Daisy have given him some money to help him this year. They're really generous. Daisy is a sweetheart. Now here's the thing, Martha. Daisy was dying of cancer only a few months ago. Well, she's not now! She's been through chemo and all that and showed me pictures of herself with no hair. But she got healed by God at a meeting. An amazing story. I thought it would be really awkward with her being gloriously healed, and poor Kath dying here. But she and Kath have had loads of chats and it doesn't fuss Kath at all. Kath really is amazing. And Daisy has brought their eight-year-old niece, Rosa with them. She is so cute. I want to take her home with me. She was named after the famous Rosa Parks. Douglas, Brí and I went out for a long walk with them all yesterday. Frank told us such sad stories of terrible prejudice against him as he was growing up. I can't imagine how painful it must be to be hated just because of the colour of your skin. But little Rosa is going to be a politician, I'm sure. Well, a politician who believes in magic, that is!

Aunt Mavis is also enjoying herself and has made friends with everyone. Elsie has introduced her to lots of the locals here. I'm sure she's addicted to Guinness now. And of course, there is our beloved Dorchadas. He went off somewhere for a few days. Apparently, he does this quite often. But he was back yesterday and I had a good chat with him at the pub last night. He told me about some of the people he has met in his travels. I find no problem believing he's an angel. He tells people quite openly, but most think he's just a bit strange in the head. But nonetheless, everyone loves him.

And then of course there is Douglas. Now, Martha, you must keep this very secret, but I'm going to confess this to you and to no-one else: we've had our first kiss! It did take him two Guinness's and a whiskey to finally dismantle that British reserve, but we strolled on the quay after our evening at the pub (listening to brilliant music) and he just grabbed hold of me and kissed me so hard that I thought I was going to suffocate. But yes, Martha, I will confess to you that I did enjoy it. I enjoyed it very much. I think he found it a bit confusing, though, because the last woman he kissed was his lovely Saoirse. Must have been hard for him to remember that affection. But he says he's "adjusting" as he put it, and he also feels sure that Saoirse is happy with us being together. When he told me that, he started kissing me again, so let's hope he's right about that! You know, for a bit of an uptight guy, he's pretty passionate. The others are guessing now but are being very discrete about it. Apart from wonderful Nancy who over supper the other night asked us if we were having sex yet! I blushed crimson to the roots! Thank goodness her sister said something funny and changed the subject. The truth is we both look forward to that moment in our lives, but we are being tender with each other and Douglas has his principles. Actually, I love that about him. Well, I love everything about him really.

Sorry, Martha, I've rattled on too long tonight and I need to get to sleep. The thing is we've got a really big day tomorrow. It's Ascension Day and it's Kath's request that we all go off for a picnic together. Dorch knows the place where we are going - one of those places with ruins. I'm really worried about it, to be honest, because Kath is so weak now. The thought of her being outside all afternoon is scary. Though thankfully the forecast is beautiful for tomorrow. So, I'm just praying it will all go well and won't be too uncomfortable for poor Kath. So that's it, Martha. One day I must grow up and let go of you. I'm starting to talk to Douglas as openly as I talk to you. I was never able to talk to Georges like I talk to Douglas. We always agreed, didn't we, that when I reached a point in life when I was no longer lonely, you and I would part. I have a feeling, Martha, that it may not be long before you and I have to start thinking about that. But til then, I still need you. So goodnight and sleep well.

*

As the sun rose over the town of Dingle on the feast of the Ascension, Father Pat pulled himself out of his bed and opened the bedroom curtains and welcomed the morning sunlight. He had woken early with an almost explosive sense of excitement. He stepped on to the landing and from the next-door room he could hear the familiar sound of Dorchadas' snoring. Careful not to wake him, he made his way down to the kitchen to make his early morning cup of tea. As the kettle rumbled to its crescendo, he glanced at the empty ashtray on the windowsill. Lately he felt less need to reach for the cigarettes. Not that he had ever been a heavy smoker, but it was always something that comforted him - one of life's treats. A little gift allowed by the Lord to help calm his nerves and soothe his mind. But his nerves and his mind were virtually unrecognisable from their old selves, and neither required now the services of nicotine to soothe them. Several times he had opened the box of cigarettes, then simply thought better of it. Something so profound in him had changed on that extraordinary Easter day on St.Seannach's isle. Some beam of resurrection had permeated into his soul and body and he was loving its effect. Yes, there were the odd moments of relapse, but generally life was smoke-free and a great deal brighter.

He poured the boiling water into his mug and watched it immerse the tea bag. He prodded the bag with a teaspoon, removed it, then poured in the milk. He rubbed his chest, for he had awoken with that little pain that had its irritating habit of taking the gloss of these moments of happiness. As he gave it a good rub, he said, 'Ah, you poor old heart. What I have put you through.' This niggling pain was one of the things that kept telling him that he would soon need to think about retiring, a subject he had stubbornly tried to avoid. He made his way through the kitchen door out into the garden that was now bathed in warm sunlight. By the time he reached the bench by the recently mowed lawn, the pain had completely cleared along with all thoughts of retirement, so he could sit comfortably and peacefully on the bench. He raised his eyes to the glorious, cloudless sky. It wasn't even 6am, and yet the sun felt warm on his skin. His mind drifted back to Thomas. He chuckled to himself. 'Och, you old fool,' he said to himself out loud. 'You trying to tell me you actually met your man, Thomas, now? You must be softer in the head than I thought.'

He chuckled as his gaze wandered down to the ivy-strewn wall at the end of the garden. 'Aye, you cynical old priest,' he answered himself. 'Aye, indeed. I met the man alright. I met him on my island, and nothing you can say can make me doubt it.' Such was the conviction in his speech that no inner voice dared to contradict it. Yes, as far as he was concerned, he had met Thomas that Easter day on the island. He closed his eyes for a few moments and he could see clearly the glistening brown eyes of the saint and feel the firm grip of the tanned and weathered hand. 'I have come to water the seeds of faith,' Thomas had said to him. My, what a watering his seeds had received. He had never known such confident faith as he had in these past weeks. He had been given new eyes and at last he could see things which were once so hidden from him.

He crossed his pyjamaed leg and again spoke to himself. 'So, what are you going to preach about this morning, old man? What are you going to say about the Christ who rose up from this green earth to embrace his wild and wondrous heaven?'

He inhaled deeply and then answered himself. 'Oh, I don't know. I expect I'll ask them to imagine how it was for those men and women on the hillside who gazed up at the sandy souls of their Messiah's feet as He rose high into the wispy clouds above them. I'll ask, how come that little group didn't fold up in grief at the sight of Him disappearing from them. There can only be one answer, surely. And that is something to do with the pulling together of heaven and earth that day.'

'That's crazy talk,' he heard his cynical self reply. 'What do you think the folks in church will make of such words as that? Come on, you old fool. Give them something that's reasonable to believe.'

'Well, some may like it; some may not,' Pat answered. 'But wait till they get to singing. You try asking them what's reasonable as they fill their lungs with Spring air and then start flooding the church with the words of the Ascension hymn. Reasonableness has nothing to do with it, once you've lit that fire in the heart. Even old Oonagh lights up with this hymn and gets more life out of that old organ than anyone thought possible. We'll all be there in the church, as the rays of the sun blaze through the coloured glass, and we'll be singing as if we were with the choirs of Paradise:

'Alleluia! Not as orphans
are we left in sorrow now.
Alleluia! He is near us;
faith believes, nor questions how.
Though the cloud from sight received Him
when the forty days were o'er,
shall our hearts forget His promise,
"I am with you evermore"?'

Pat drained his tea and, as he stood up, he said, 'That's the whole point of it. Heaven's bursting out all over this lovely earth because of His journey in the silky skies that day. He only left them that day so He could get that much closer to all of us. I'd say that's good news, I surely would.' Just as he was about to return inside, a young seagull landed on the lawn near him and, throwing back its head, opened its beak and squawked a call that resonated throughout the waking town of Dingle. Pat paused and, looking at the gull, said, 'You've got the right idea, son. You sing until your dear heart breaks for the joy of it.' He made the sign of the cross over the bird and went back inside to prepare for the early service.

*

Elsie's day had not got off to a good start. Her leg had been playing up badly during the night, so when her alarm went off at 7am, she was in her deep sleep. She managed to knock both her clock and glass of water off her bedside table in her attempt to silence the clock, then succeeded in causing a small rip in her dressing gown as she pulled it down from its hook. This was not a good start, and this was a day that needed a good start.

However, she made her way downstairs without any further mishaps, fixed herself a cup of coffee, then returned to her room to make herself presentable for the day. After a short while, she was back down in the kitchen where she gathered together all the necessary supplies for the guests' breakfasts. She also assembled several loaves of sliced bread, an assortment of fillings, and an impressive selection of cakes, pies, biscuits and fruit. She heard Mavis making her way down to breakfast and checked her watch. Sure enough, it was 7.30am precisely. Mavis was always punctual for her breakfast. Soon the Americans made their way down for their breakfast, followed by Douglas. Then, last of all and still in her pyjamas and dressing gown, came a yawning Alice. There was such a buzz of conversation and laughter in the dining room, that Elsie did not hear at first the rapping at the front door, but eventually she did hear it and bustled through the hall to open it. Kevin, Brí and Nancy made their way in and were ushered straight into the kitchen. They were the picnic-making team for the Ascension Day lunch up at the monastery ruin.

Elsie then became the Commander-in-chief of a major operation of both supplying hot breakfasts to the guests as well as providing clear and firm oversight for a group of picnic-makers whom, it was soon apparent to Elsie, were not fully qualified for the task. The stress of the operation evoked even more colourful language than usual from Elsie, but nevertheless by mid-morning, the team were sitting at one of the dining room tables, admiring their work that was gathered in several large boxes. It was Mavis who had volunteered to make the coffees for them and she brought the steaming mugs through on a tray.

'Well, it's certainly a fine day for the picnic,' said Elsie, lifting her bad leg on to a chair and resting it.

'Aye, it certainly is that,' said Kevin. 'What time did we say we'd all gather there?'

'Well, Mam and Peter want to get up there for around twelve,' said Brí.

'Mam's not good, though,' said Nancy. 'Not sure she'll make it.'

'Oh, shush!' said Brí to her sister. 'She'll be fine. She's weak, I'll grant you that, Nancy. But she's very determined to get up there for the picnic.'

'I'm worried, though Brí, darling,' said Elsie, after taking a large sip from her mug. 'I mean, it's still cool, you know. It's going to do her no good at all. There'll be a breeze up there, there sure will.'

'Aunty Elsie, she'll be fine,' reassured Bríana. But as she looked down to sip her coffee, the frown on her face betrayed the concern that lay behind her assured words.

*

Earlier that morning, Brí had awoken and tiptoed downstairs. She crept through the living room so as to not to disturb her mother, but her attempts to be quiet were unnecessary as Kath was already awake. As Brí reached the kitchen door, the bedside light was switched on and Kath said, 'You're awake early this morning, Brí, darling.'

'Oh, Mammy,' said Brí, 'I'm sorry to wake you.'

'No, no. I was awake,' reassured Kath. 'But would you make us both a cup of coffee please. I'll just get myself to the jacks as my bladder's fit to burst, it is.'

Brí went into the kitchen and made two coffees, putting two teaspoons of sugar in her mother's mug. She then returned to Kath who was back, sitting up in her bed, still out of breath from the exertion from the journey to the toilet.

'Oh, Mammy,' said Brí passing her the mug. 'You don't look well this morning. Was it a bad night?'

'Aye, love,' said Kath, warming her hands around the hot drink. 'But don't go giving me that doleful look now. I have no intention of leaving you all today. I want my picnic, I do. This coffee will get me up and running nicely.'

Brí sat in the chair next to her mother's bed and sipped from her coffee for a few moments. She looked at Kath and said, 'Mammy...'

'Yes, love,' said Kath, adjusting her position a little in the bed.

'Mammy, I'm so pleased we are friends again,' said Brí, her eyes watering as she spoke.

Kath placed her mug carefully on the bedside table and reached out her hand to Brí who took it and held it gently. 'I'm also so pleased, lass,' she said. 'I was just a silly, jealous old fool and wasted far too many years in being a silly, jealous old fool.'

'Oh, Mam, don't go blaming yourself, now,' said Brí. She put her mug down so that she could use both her hands to clasp her mother's. 'I was just as guilty. But it's all water under the bridge now.'

'Aye, that it is, darling,' said Kath.

'But it's sad, Mammy,' said Brí, looking down at her mother's pale hand. 'I mean, just as we get to love each other properly, you are on your way to leaving this world.'

Kath used her free hand to search for a handkerchief under her pillow, and brought it to her eyes. It had been a very well-used handkerchief in recent days. 'I know, love,' she said. Her voice was not much more than a whisper now, but she spoke clearly nonetheless. 'But it's my time, and that's not something I should be fighting against. I'm at peace, Brí.'

Brí frowned and said, 'But Mammy, we don't want you leaving us just yet. Why should God want you up in his heaven now? I mean, what use are you going to be to God up there?'

'Oh,' said Kath smiling. 'In that world, being useful is not what it's about. No-one has to be useful in heaven. It's about *being*. Being fully alive. Being fully there. Being fully loved and loving fully. Won't that be special, Brí?'

'Special for you, Ma,' agreed Brí. 'But it's not that special for us when we're stood by your graveside arranging the flowers.'

'Oh, no, darling,' said Kath leaning forward. 'I know. You'll grieve and it will hurt, it sure will. But then you will start to heal. Honest, Brí. That's how He's made you. Just wait patiently, and you will heal. And then one day, many, many years from now, when you have had a wonderful life with that good woman of yours over in there in that groundhog city where you now live, your turn will come. And maybe you'll think of your old Ma at that time. And who knows? Perhaps I'll be allowed to come and help you step over the threshold. And then, Brí, love. Then, the fun will begin!' She wheezed a laugh.

Brí rubbed her mother's hand with her thumbs. She looked at her mother with her moistened eyes and whispered, 'Yes, Mammy. I'd like that. I'd like that very much.'

Kath adjusted her position again then said, 'And Brí, love. Once I've gone, you must make your way back to your home in the States. Don't hang around here too long. I know you will be worried for Nancy, but she's going to be all right. I'm sure of that. Our Kevin is here to care for her. I'm expecting her to move down to Dingle. No, you go on back home. You need to get on with your life and get back to your girl, Carol. She'll be needing you, she will.'

'Of course, Ma,' said Brí. 'And Peter? How will he be?'

'He will be sad, love,' said Kath, nodding her head slowly. 'I think he will be sad for the rest of his life. But, to be truthful, he has always been sad. Actually, it's a beautiful sadness. It's a sadness he can live with. Don't worry for him. He knows how to find his peace.'

Brí leaned forward and hugged her mother and both of them remained in a tight embrace for some time, until Brí leaned back and said, 'Well, I should be on my way soon. Nancy and I are helping Aunty Else to make the sandwiches for the picnic.'

'Oh, Holy Mother, you don't want to be late for that, you surely don't,' said Kath and chuckled her wheezy chuckle. 'You make some good sandwiches, darling. I'm looking forward to the picnic.'

'So am I, Mammy,' said Brí rising from her chair. 'So am I.'

*

Dorchadas had been woken up by the sound of Pat boiling the kettle in the kitchen, and he rose from his bed. His window was open. It always was, even on the coldest winter nights. His love for the air of this world meant he could never bear to sleep and dream without its influence. He stood by the window, pushing it fully open and looked out into the garden. He spied the figure of the parish priest in pyjamas and dressing gown, clasping a mug of tea and making its way to the garden bench. He felt a renewed surge of affection for this man, who had been such a good friend to him. This was the man who thought Dorchadas was a vagrant when he first met him. Typically, Pat had asked him in for a meal. Dorchadas remembered so clearly that first meal in Pat's kitchen. With the heavy scent of honeysuckle drifting in through the window, the two ate, drank and chatted until the church clock stroked midnight. Pat invited him to stay for the night, and he had been in this home ever since. Dorchadas looked down at this priest and friend, who seemed to be having a conversation with himself, and he whispered a brief prayer of thanks.

He drew his eyes away from the seated figure of his friend, and cast them over the unmown lawn to the tangle of buildings beyond the garden wall, and then out to the sea, sparkling in morning sunshine. Yes, he loved this land. He loved this town. He loved this people. And without doubt, he had loved them all too much. Far too much. Yes, he couldn't deny that there were some humans who lived very dark lives. Even religious humans, who should have known better, had often caused terrible suffering of their fellow humans. But, despite these sadnesses, Dorchadas still loved the humans with whom he had lived for a long time now, and he never ceased to be full of admiration at the qualities he found in so many of them. It was going to be so hard to say farewell to it all.

'Ah, well. Gabriel did say it was my weakness,' he said to himself as he put on his dressing gown. 'I guess I really have got too involved in their lives.' He pulled the cord tight around his waist and continued his musings, saying, 'But today's a new day. And it's Ascension Day.' He returned to his window for one more glance of the sea. He nodded his head for a few moments as he acknowledged that he was reaching a pivotal moment in time. The sun was indeed rising on a day that would be an auspicious day. It was one of those days that would stand taller than its neighbouring days. He watched a fishing boat chugging slowly towards the harbour after it's night's work, ploughing a furrow through the glassy surface of the calm waters. 'Dorchadas, old son,' said the angel. 'You always knew that it had to come one day. So, get yourself going, now.' He drew the window closed and made his way to the shower.

CHAPTER 22

Planning the travel arrangements to the site of the picnic was no easy task: Rosa insisted on travelling with Dorchadas; Peter would only take Kath in his car, as he was sure he would need to return her early from the picnic; Elsie was anxious to be in the same vehicle as her picnic and one that was driven smoothly. 'Just in case the worst should happen,' she said, aware of the delicate state of her two thickly-iced sponge cakes. So in the end, Peter drove Kath in his car; Kevin took his two sisters in his; Douglas took Elsie and Alice, with the picnic boxes carefully packed into the boot, and Alice and Mavis charged with nursing the cakes in the back seat. This car, Elsie assured the others, would be the last to arrive, as the cakes would not stand any fast cornering. Frank's hire-car carried Pat in the front seat, with Daisy, Rosa and the somewhat cramped figure of Dorchadas in the back.

The short journey from Dingle to Reask gave Rosa just enough time to fire her list of questions to Dorchadas and Father Pat about the ancient site. As Frank threaded the car through the narrow streets of the town, Rosa asked, 'So Uncle Dorchadas and Father Pat, can you tell me about this Ree-ass. Is it a magical place?'

'Well, now, Rosa' said Pat, turning around from the front seat and peering at Rosa through his thick spectacles, 'Its name is Reask or *An Riasc* in the Gaelic.'

'What does *An Riasc* mean, Father Pat?' asked Rosa, as she struggled to open a packet of fruit pastilles.

'Ah, that would mean 'the marsh', Rosa,' replied Pat. 'Though it can't have been too boggy, because they built some fine buildings in the place.'

'So how did it all get started, then?' asked Rosa, thrusting the bag of sweets forward to Pat, who carefully chose a dark red one and answered, 'Ah, well, to be truthful with you Rosa, darling, no-one really knows too much about the place. But it is thought that long, long ago...'

'How long?' asked Rosa with her mouth now full of a tangy orange pastille.

'Oh, probably about fifteen hundred years I'd say.'

'Wow! That's awesome,' declared the wide-eyed Rosa.

'A green one for me, sweetheart,' said Frank, reaching his hand behind him, and Rosa picked out a couple of green sweets and popped them into the waiting hand.

Dorchadas then chipped in, 'So I understand, and put me right, Pat, if I'm wrong, but they reckon just one or two of Christ's kindly followers settled in the place first of all to pray and bless the land.'

'That's how I understand it,' called Pat to the voice of Dorchadas behind his seat. As the car filled with the fragrance of sugary fruits, Pat continued, 'Rosa, after a while, a few others thought they'd like to come and join them. And before you knew it, there were a whole crowd of Christian people settling there and building a community.'

'Ah, they like community here, don't they, Uncle Frank?' said Rosa to her Uncle, recalling earlier conversations with her uncle.

'They sure do, honey,' said Frank, who was focussing hard on the road that was a good deal narrower than the roads he was used to.

'So, what will we see there, Father Pat?' asked Rosa, whose attempt at fishing a third sweet out of the bag was foiled by Daisy, who reported that it would not be long before Rosa would be eating her lunch.

Pat shifted his position so he could turn around and view the young questioner. 'You will see quite a bit, Rosa. Mostly old stones. But beautiful stones, if I may say so. And you'll see the foundations of a wee oratory. And of course, there's the beehive cells.'

'I love beehives!' called Rosa in excitement.

'Ah, Rosa, love,' said Dorchadas, 'Father Pat doesn't mean the actual beehive, now. It's just a term that's used for the houses that they used to build in them days. They look like the beehives. That's why people call them that. The real name for them is *clochán*.'

'Oh,' said Rosa with some sense of disappointment. 'I think I prefer "beehives".'

'And I do, too, Rosa,' said Pat.

'What are the other buildings?' asked Daisy.

'Oh, an assortment of buildings, Daisy,' answered Pat. 'There's the ruin of a small oratory, lots of low walls and a fair few grave stones and small standing stones with ancient writing on them. Very special, they are. It's a nice place, Daisy. Especially on a day like today. In fact, it will be glorious there, I have no doubt.'

'Will Kath be all right, Uncle Dorchadas?' asked Rosa looking up at the rugged face that was peering out of the window.

'Aye, love,' said Dorchadas, looking back to Rosa. 'Aye, of course. We're all going to be all right. More than all right, I should say.' He looked back out of the window again, and though reassured by Dorchadas, Rosa did not fail to notice the look in his eye. Was it sadness? Was it anxiety? Was it excitement? It was hard to tell. She still hadn't too much experience of angels.

As it happened, Dorchadas was completely right about Kath. Though in her body she felt very weak, and much of her upper body felt painful, yet in her soul she felt extraordinarily content.

She and Peter were the first to arrive at the ancient site, and she was pleased to see that there were no other visitors there. Peter had borrowed a wheel chair form a neighbour and, after parking the car, he helped Kath into the chair and trundled her through the gate and into the enclosure.

It was Peter's first visit to Reask, and Kath had only been a couple of times. Once through the entrance gate, they surveyed the scene. There was a sturdy, thick perimeter wall, and a wall running across the compound. All the walls were constructed of dark grey stones and were only a few feet tall as the roofs of the buildings had collapsed long ago. Despite being a ruin, the whole site looked to Peter and Kath homely and welcoming.

'Now, where would you want the picnic, Kath, love?' asked Peter.

Kath was quiet for a few moments then, pointing to the far side of the site, she said, 'I like the look of those wee circles over there, Peter. Do you think you can get me there?' He had to work hard to push her chair over the grass but eventually they came to the foundation stones of a couple of connected beehive cells. They passed through the opening and into the cell. The floor had been covered with grey shingle which made pushing the chair harder work for Peter.

'You poor soul, Peter,' said Kath. 'I'll be giving you a hernia pushing this thing, I surely will.' As they settled, they heard a shout from the gate, and Kath saw her sister issuing instructions to several people to ensure the picnic was safely conveyed to the spot where Peter and Kath had settled. Kath smiled as she heard her sister cry, 'Trust her to pick the furthest place from the car. Now Douglas, for God's sake, be steady with that tin, won't you? I don't want it ending up looking like those Eating Messes you get in restaurants nowadays.'

It was not long before all the cars had arrived and the passengers made their way through the gate to explore the ancient site. Rosa clambered on to one of the walls and ran the whole way around the ruin. Nancy soon followed her, though her ascent on to the wall took a little longer. Alice gripped Douglas' hand and led him straight to a decorated standing stone that was about the same height as her. The spiral designs carved by hands from an ancient time intrigued Alice. Douglas watched her carefully as she ran her finger along the contours of the stone for a while, the feel of her fingers providing information that her eye may have missed. Finally, she looked up at him and said, 'This is so special, Douglas. don't you think?'

'Yes,' said Douglas smiling, acknowledging that Alice was experiencing a dimension to this stone that was pretty much lost on him.

'What's this?' she asked, running her finger over a circular design at the top of the stone.

'Well, Alice,' replied Douglas drawing closer to the design, 'I'm no expert. You'll need to speak to Pat. But that looks to me like the design of a typical Celtic cross, where the top of the cross is often surrounded by a circle.'

'Why a circle?' asked Alice.

'I don't know, to be honest,' said Douglas, feeling rather out of his depth in this investigation. 'What does it say to you?'

Alice smiled and again ran her fingers round the circle. 'Oh, I like it, Douglas. I think the circle is the globe of this world, and the cross lies across it all. The cross is not just for a few religious types in one corner of the world. It's for everyone.'

'Well, Alice,' said Douglas, 'I should put that theory to the authorities.'

Alice replied, 'Oh, I don't think these things are for the authorities, are they? No, this is a beautiful and wild place. You don't want authorities tampering with a place like this. This is a place for breathing in.' She inhaled deeply and raised her face to the beams of the warm sun.

As Alice and Douglas were admiring the ancient stone, Frank and Daisy were also hand-in-hand and were taking a slow stroll around the buildings.

'You OK, honey?' enquired Daisy.

'Kinda,' replied Frank.

'Tell me,' said Daisy and stopped walking. Frank leant back against one of the ancient walls. 'Daisy, sweetheart, this is a great place. I really love it here,' he said, and stroked his hand over the dark stones. He paused for a few moments, then added, 'But there's something about this place, Daisy. It's opening something in me. Well, to be fair, that something has been cracking open since we first arrived here in Ireland.'

Daisy was frowning with concentration as she looked at her husband. 'Go on,' she said.

'You know, that guy Kevin is a great guy,' said Frank pointing over to the other side of the compound where Kevin was helping Brí, Elsie and Mavis sort out the picnic.

'He's got quite a story, hasn't he?' said Daisy.

'He sure has, sweetheart,' said Frank and smiled. 'But the guy's also a great listener. The other night I found myself telling him a whole heap about my life.'

'Aha?' said Daisy, still frowning.

'Yea, you know...' said Frank with an unusually vulnerable look. 'That stuff in my teens and twenties when I was always in trouble with the law.' He looked at Daisy who was nodding. 'Well, I guess not everything heals in us, does it? Just made me realise again that I was badly hurt in those days.'

Daisy took his hand in both of hers and stroked it. Frank looked up at the sky. 'God made us black, darling,' he said, continuing to gaze at the sky above him. He then looked back to Daisy and said, 'But it's not been easy, has it?'

'No, honey,' said Daisy, continuing to stroke the large, strong hand of her husband.

She was about to say something else but was interrupted by Rosa who was skipping along the wall towards them and, as she approached them, called out, 'Isn't this the most magical of places!'

Daisy and Frank both looked at her and smiled. 'It sure is, sweetheart,' said Frank. 'It sure is.'

Nancy was trudging along the wall not far behind Rosa and she called out to the Americans, 'What do you think of this place?'

'Magical,' said Daisy.

As Nancy arrived at the group, a little out of breath, she said, 'That's just what I was thinking.'

Nancy made a rather undignified attempt at clambering down from the wall with Frank doing his best to help her. As she was brushing down her corduroy skirt there was a large guffaw from a nearby clochán and they looked over to the figures of Dorchadas and Pat both rocking back in laughter.

'I love those guys,' said Daisy, instinctively laughing with them. 'Pat is such a great guy. He's just what a priest should be.'

'Hm,' said Frank, frowning briefly, then smiling.

'Dorchadas is an angel,' said Nancy.

'I hear some people really think that,' said Frank.

'I know that,' said Nancy.

'But he doesn't really look like an angel, Nancy,' said Daisy, trying not to sound critical.

'How do you know?' said Nancy.

Although Daisy had certainly had glimpses of Paradise, she had never actually seen an angel so she did not feel qualified to answer.

'I don't see no wings,' said Frank and chuckled.

'He doesn't need wings, does he?' said Nancy, and Frank stopped chuckling.

'He's an angel, for sure,' said Rosa. 'Come on,' she said. 'I'm getting hungry.' Together they walked over to the group that was gathering around Kath for the picnic.

'What's this angel thing?' asked Frank to Daisy.

'We're in Ireland, honey,' said Daisy, and she took her husband's hand and led him over to the picnic.

Elsie was relieved that the food for the picnic had arrived without any of the mishaps that had haunted her imagination during the past forty-eight hours. Kevin had provided a sturdy table that was securely placed in the centre of the gathering and on it was now arrayed a large selection of sandwiches, pies, cakes, crisps and fruit. Brí was responsible for the drinks, and on the shingle next to the table there stood tins of Murphy's and Guinness and bottles of fruit juice and water. Nancy had provided a bottle of Prosecco because, as she put it, 'the cork taking off from the bottle is like Jesus taking off at the Ascension.' Though Pat found this a dubious symbol of the Ascension, nonetheless he agreed that she could release the cork after the simple prayers he had prepared.

The sun beamed warm upon the little cell containing family and friends, who spread themselves either on the walls or on the shingle floor. No-one could resist regular glances towards Kath to check she was coping with the party. Generally, Kath was coping well and, though she felt very weak, she was not in pain. She was able to manage a sandwich and some cake, and she had enough energy to chat to the people around her. When Elsie and Mavis were convinced no more food was going to be eaten, they gathered up the remains and packed them away. Kath watched them carefully and, when she was sure they were done, she clapped her hands. The various conversations around the clochán stopped and everyone looked at Kath.

Though she could only speak in a hoarse whisper, all could hear her as the air was so still. 'I can't tell you what it means to me that you've all come up here with me today,' she said. Peter was leaning on the wall near her chair and leaned forward and reached for her hand. Brí was kneeling by the other side of the chair and leaned her head against her mother's arm. 'In a moment,' continued Kath, 'Father Pat here will lead us in a wee Ascension prayer. God bless you, Pat,' she said to the priest who was furiously cleaning his glasses. 'You've been a wonder to us in recent days. If anyone has still got a bottle or can in their hand, then here's to the best priest in Ireland.' Everyone raised their drinks in the direction of the embarrassed priest, who simply shook his head and rubbed his glasses even more vigorously.

'Now, I'm not going to get all morbid on you,' said Kath, 'but you all know I've not long to go.' She put her hand up before anyone could protest. 'No, no,' she said. 'Just let me say my piece, then you can have your go at me.' There were some smiles and chuckles. 'I just want you all to know that when the day comes for my passing, that I go in peace.' She adjusted her position for a moment, then continued. 'Now, I'm not going to pretend that I'm not a little sad about leaving you all.' Brí's face coloured, as she gripped her mother's arm tighter. 'This is the hard thing about dying,' continued Kath. 'Feels like I'm leaving the party early somehow. But leave I must, and I'm not going to fight it.

But I shall miss you all, surely to God I will. Even you dear folks from America. I've only just got to know you and I already love you, I do.' Rosa came over and sat in front of Kath, leaning against her leg. Kath smiled at her and looked around at the group. 'Look at you all,' she said, 'Each and every one of you is so precious. And what you have given me in my life! No words...' She felt the emotion rise and she checked herself. Peter rubbed her arm gently.

'And I shall miss all this,' Kath continued, raising her eyes to the sunlit country around her. 'Look at its beauty,' she said. 'Is there anywhere else on earth as lovely as this? Those of us who have lived here all our lives... Elsie, love, haven't we been blessed?'

'Sure to God, we have, Kath,' said Elsie, just managing to speak over her emotion.

'Well, soon I have to let go of this handsome land. No more for me the scent of peat and heather, nor the sound of the wind on the hills, making the grass to sing to us. Nor the sight of the gulls having their fun in the blue of the sky. No, I'll have to let go of all these dear sights and sounds.' She sighed, then continued, 'And I let go of all the years I've lived on this earth. I've lived some of my days well, and some badly, but I hand them all back to the God who gave them to me in the first place. He'll sort them out, I know that now. And last of all, I'll be saying good bye to this old body of mine, which is far stouter than it should be. But, despite the way I've treated it, it's served me well through my years. I won't go on. I didn't intend to make a big speech. So, Father Pat. Come on now, give us your Ascension prayer, and then Nancy love, you can let that cork fly. Then, Peter, you'd best be getting this old wife of yours back home, so she can rest in her bed.'

All in the group were working hard to check the wealth of feelings they were experiencing. Pat felt the usual pain in his chest when his emotions ran high, and he instinctively rubbed it, and as he did so, he said, 'Dear, wonderful Kath. I've got a pain in my heart, sure to God I have. We are going to miss you so much.' He no longer felt ashamed of tears these days, and so he allowed them to flow down his weathered cheeks as he took out his little notebook where he had written out some prayers. He threw a brief and wounded smile out to the group, then said, 'Today is a special day, indeed. Well now, Nancy. Have you got the Prosecco at the ready, love?'

'Ready,' said Nancy. Kevin helped her untie the metal band from its neck and having done so, Nancy held tight to the cork in readiness for her cue.

'Well, this is Ascension Day,' said Pat. 'What a great day to choose for a picnic. So, let me...'

But Pat was unable to continue, because he was interrupted by Alice. 'What is that?' she cried, both in wonder and alarm. Though she had the poorest eyesight in the group, she nonetheless was the one who spotted a curious phenomenon in the sky. She had stood up and was looking out over to the sea and stretching her hand out towards a shape in the sky. Others followed the line of her pointing finger and saw what at first looked like a flock of amber-coloured birds coming in from the ocean. However, as it got closer, it was clear it was not a flock of birds.

'It's a weird cloud,' said Daisy. 'But it's kinda orange. Do you get orange clouds in Ireland?'

'Well, I've never seen a cloud like that,' said Kevin, his mouth dropping open at the sight. 'It's... It's...' but he had no words to describe what he was observing. Most of the group were standing now, gazing at the marvel in the sky.

'It's a cloud made of shimmering gold!' cried Rosa. 'And it's coming our way. Look!'

'I've never seen the like of it in all my life,' said Mavis who had grasped hold of Alice. 'It looks like it's got electricity running through it. It looks dangerous to me, Alice. We'd best be careful.'

'It's totally, totally beautiful,' said Alice, quite ignoring her aunt's anxious warning.

'Rosa, honey, come here,' said Daisy. Rosa came over to her aunt, who grasped her tightly.

'What is this thing, Dorch?' said Douglas, who was standing next to Dorchadas.

'Oh, I know what this is, Doug,' said Dorchadas, his eyes fixed on the golden cloud that had now arrived directly above the group, irradiating everyone and the ancient ruins of Reask in an ethereal light. 'I know this well, Douglas. It's not something to be afraid of. It's...' He was about to say something else when there was a loud explosion near him, which caused everyone to jump.

'God! Sorry!' said Nancy, who had inadvertently released the Prosecco cork. The cork flew right up to the cloud, causing a spray of sparks where it met the surface of the vibrant, luminous phenomenon. Nancy, gripping the spouting bottle with one hand, pointed to the cloud with her other. 'I know what that is,' she said, her voice quivering as she spoke. 'It's called Shekinah. That cloud's made of glory, it is.' She turned to her mother, now glowing in the light of the cloud, and called out, 'It's made of glory, Mammy.'

'That it is, lass,' said Dorchadas, who had now dropped to his knees. And before anyone could say anything else, the cloud descended on to the ancient clochán, enfolding all of them in a soft mist of golden glory.

CHAPTER 23

The Irish family

'By all the saints, where in God's good earth are we?' The voice was Elsie's, but at first not everyone could make each other out because the air was so thick with the swirling golden mist.

'Is that you, Elsie?' called Kath's husky voice.

'That it is, sister,' replied Elsie.

'I'm here, too,' came Brí's voice. 'But it's hard to see through this stuff. What is it?'

'Shekinah. I told you,' said the voice of Nancy.

'Well, smart-ass,' said Brí, 'if you know so much about it, how do we find our way out of it?'

'It seems we have left Reask somehow,' said the calm voice of Peter.

'Oh, thank God, Peter,' said Kath hearing his voice. 'I'm so glad you are here with us.'

'It's clearing,' said the voice of Kevin and, as he spoke, the mist thinned and each could see other shadowy shapes that became figures of those they recognised.

'Looks like the six of us have been transported somewhere,' said Kevin, who was familiar with the curious dynamics of a world influenced by his friend, Dorchadas.

'What do you mean, Kev?' asked Brí, who walked over to her brother and grasped his hand for reassurance. 'What do you mean, "transported"? We're not in a sci-fi movie, you know.'

'Not a movie,' said Nancy, who was still holding her open bottle of Prosecco. 'This world is more real, isn't it Kev?'

'Aye, Nancy,' replied Kevin. 'You're not wrong there.'

'But where are the others?' said Elsie, tidying her hair and clothes, sensing that whatever place they had travelled to, she needed to be looking her best.

A light breeze dispersed the mist and soon they could all see clearly. Elsie was right, they were the only people in the place as far as they could see. They were standing on a sandy surface with some shrubs round about them. The atmosphere felt like that of a hot country. With the mist dispersed, the sun was shining warm upon them.

'This is so crazy,' said Brí. 'I must be in a dream. Or... O, God! Are we...?'

Kevin gripped his sister's hand tightly and said, 'No, Brí, love. We are all alive. We are very much alive. Your mam and I have been to a place a bit like this before. Don't try and argue with it. Just let it be. We'll be all right.'

Peter stepped a little ahead of the group, then turned around and said to them, 'Look over there,' he said. 'It's a cave, isn't it?'

'Not a cave,' said Nancy. 'That's a grave.'

'What?' said Brí, losing the brief moment of peace that Kevin's assurance had given her.

'Oh, holy mother of God, forgive me my sins,' said Elsie, falling to the ground on her knees and crossing herself.

'Oh, stop that nonsense, Elsie, darling,' said Kath. 'It's not that kind of a place. Now Nancy, love. You seem to have as good an idea as any of us about this. Where are we, now?'

'Ask her,' said Nancy, pointing to a lady walking towards them.

'Oh!' said Kath, and clapped her hands. Walking quickly towards the group was a woman dressed in a verdant green robe.

Kath, who had still been sitting in her wheelchair, rose and opened her arms to the woman who was a stranger to all but her. After the two women embraced, Kath said, 'Are we in the deep memory place again, Mary?'

'Yes, dear Kathleen, you are,' replied Mary.

'Mammy. Excuse me? But who is this?' asked Brí.

'Oh, Brí, love. Forgive me,' said Kath. 'I was just so pleased to see an old friend. So, everyone: this is my friend, Mary. Now it would take too long to explain how I know her, but take it from me, she's a fine lady and a wee while back, she was a great help to me.'

'Do you mean…' stuttered Peter. He knew the story of Kath and Kevin's visit to a place of deep memory where Kath had met Mary. 'Do you mean, you are Mary from Magdala?'

'Yes,' said the woman. 'That's what some people call me. Just "Mary" is fine.'

'Dear God!' said Elsie, working even harder on tidying her hair and straightening her clothes. 'Your ladyship. It is an honour and privilege to meet you,' and she curtsied as low as her knee would allow.

'Oh, Elsie,' said Kath. 'Stop all that kowtowing. She just wants to be a friend, for heaven's sake.'

Mary came forward to Elsie and said, 'So you are the sister of Kathleen,' and she grasped hold of Elsie and hugged her. Elsie stood looking dumbfounded with her hands hanging limply by her side.

She tentatively raised her arms to reciprocate the hug and said, 'But you're a saint, lass. You shouldn't be holding tight to a sinner like me…I'll tarnish your soul, I surely will.'

Mary clasped Elsie for a few more moments, then said, 'We are both saints, Elsie. Let's be saints and friends.'

Kath, who was still standing, but being supported by Peter, wheezed a chuckle and said, 'You'll get used to it, sister.'

Mary then stepped back and looked at Brí and Nancy and said, 'So you must be Kathleen's daughters,' and greeted the two women in turn and then greeted Kevin.

'And here's my Peter,' said Kath, proudly introducing Peter to Mary.

'Oh, Peter,' said Mary. 'I know you.'

Peter's eyes were full of moisture. 'Aye, Mary,' he said quietly.

'So when on earth did you two meet?' said Kath, surprised by this revelation.

'Kath, darling,' said Peter. 'Long, long ago, when I was so wounded after our sorrow, I made my way to the Friend's meeting house...'

'Oh, aye,' said Kath. 'Don't you go telling Mary here about my fatal visit to your Quakers, will you?'

Peter smiled, then continued, 'No, Kath. We'll pass over that one quickly! No, this was my first meeting. The room was so silent. It was Easter Sunday and someone read to me the story about Mary Magdalen, who was heartbroken after the terrible events on that first Good Friday, and how she came to the tomb in the early morning to bring her spices for the anointing, and then meeting with the risen Christ.' Peter looked over to Mary and smiled, then continued. 'That day, I listened carefully to the gospel reading that I knew so well. I'd preached about it during the days when I was a priest. But somehow on that day, in the deep stillness of that meeting room, I... Well, I seemed to actually *enter* the story. Was it a daydream? Did I fall asleep? Was it a vision? I don't know. But one way or another, I stepped into the story. And it looked just like...well, like *this*.' He swept his arm towards the scene before them. 'And I met Mary. I met *you*,' he said, looking at Mary. 'And we spoke and you told me about your meeting your risen Lord. And, well… something that was very broken healed in me that day.'

'Yes,' said Mary. 'I remember it well, Peter.'

'Well, well, Peter,' said Kath. 'You dark horse, you. I'm still learning things about you, I am.'

'Excuse me,' interrupted Brí. 'I am getting very lost here. I really need help.' She looked at Mary and said, 'So you are saying you are the famous Mary Magdalen of the Bible, and you can just step into people' imaginations whenever you like?'

'Not quite whenever I like, Bríana,' said Mary. She took a few steps towards Brí and looked at her. She reached up and stroked her freckled cheek. 'Dear Bríana,' she said. 'He wants you to know that all your questions are precious. Never stop asking your questions. But He also wants you to start opening your mind and heart to that which you thought was unthinkable and impossible. It will make life so much more beautiful for you.'

Brí frowned for a few moments, 'And just who is "He" when he's at home?'

'She means Christ, silly,' said Nancy, 'Who else?'

Brí frowned at her sister. She felt she was in one of her dreams where everyone else knows what is going on, but she doesn't have a clue. She also felt rather lonely. Everyone else suddenly seemed all pious. In this dream, or whatever it was, her agnosticism put her at a great disadvantage. Yes, this had to be one of those difficult dreams. Hopefully she would soon wake up. So, to avoid any further uncomfortable focus on herself, she simply nodded at Nancy and said, 'I see.'

Mary looked at Brí and said, 'You will see, Bríana. You just need to be like a child - that's all it takes. But now,' she said, turning back to the others. 'We need to go to the tomb.'

'Mary, love,' said Kath, wincing as she struggled back into her wheelchair. 'Is this the time then? I've already guessed this is why we've all come here.'

Mary swept back a lock of her long dark hair with her slender hand, and several in the group noticed a look of sorrow in her eyes. 'Are you ready for this, Kathleen?'

'Oh aye,' said Kath. 'I've been ready for some time now.'

'Since Brigid?' said Mary.

'Aye, love,' said Kath. 'She gave me the gift that's helping me now. I'd like to see that girl again. I guess I will be seeing her very soon now.'

'Whose Brigid?' asked Brí to Kevin as the group started to follow Mary.

'That would take some time to explain, Brí,' said her brother. 'I'll fill you in later.'

Mary led the way, followed by Kevin, who pushed Kath's wheelchair over the rough ground. Peter walked beside his wife. Elsie followed. She was sniffing hard. She still had little clue as to where they were, and did not like the sound of what was being said in the conversation between her sister and Mary. Brí and Nancy followed at the rear of the group. For a while none of them spoke as they made their way up a stony path to the cave ahead of them. Brí looked around and realised that, though the ground was dry and sandy, they were actually walking in a most delightful garden. There were lots of olive trees with their gnarled trunks and dark green leaves bold against the vivid blue sky. Much of the ground was covered in rough yet bright, verdant tufts of grass and, amongst the grass, was a myriad of flowers. In fact, the closer the group got to the cave, the brighter and denser the flowers seemed to be. And the birdsong also became more animated as they approached the cave. After a while, she paused and said, 'Will you listen to that, now? Listen to the gorgeous birdsong. Have any of you ever heard anything like it?'

The group stopped walking for a few moments. It had only been Brí who had been observing the world around them, as everyone else had been caught up in their own thoughts. But when they paused, they all marvelled at the beauty of the world in which they had found themselves.

'I assumed I was in a dream,' said Brí. 'I was longing to wake up. But now I'm seeing all of this, I never want to wake up ever again.'

'I think,' said Nancy, 'that I *have* just woken up. Brilliant, isn't it?' She realised she was still clutching her bottle of Prosecco, but she knew she had no need of it now, so she placed it on the ground.

'Them flowers have a beautiful scent,' said Elsie, sniffing the fragrant air. 'I've never smelt anything like it. Truly, I never have. It's a scent that makes me want to laugh and cry all at the same time.'

'Listen!' called Peter. 'What is that?'

'Is it a violin?' asked Kevin.

'Sure, it's an accordion isn't it?' said Kath raising her ear to the air.

'Sounds like a pipe to me,' said Nancy.

'Whatever it is,' said Brí, 'I have never heard anything so exquisite in all my life.'

'Tell us what it is, Mary, love,' said Kath looking up at Mary from her chair.

Mary smiled and said, 'You have not come to another world. This is your world. But this is your world fully awake and fully alive. This is how it was always meant to be. And this day that you are visiting is the day when He stepped from this tomb. It is the day when the morning stars sang together and all the angels shouted for joy. Just like it was always meant to be. Can you hear the laughter?' And sure enough, as they listened to the exquisite music, they could also hear, as if it were woven in to it, the sound of delighted laughter.

'So, this is the world of the Great Beginning,' said Kath, remembering the words spoken to her by Brigid. 'I could sure be at home in a world like this,' she added.

As she spoke, a light started to glow from the tomb. From the door something, that later they described as a creature of light, emerged. It had no specific form, as its shape was continually changing. In as much as it was like anything of this world, it was like a flowing stream. Peter later remarked that he felt like it was a creature that was flowing with everything that was good in this world. The music and laughter seemed to be coming from it.

As all Kath's family were admiring this fascinating creature, Mary walked to Kath's chair and, taking both her hands, she said, 'So, Kathleen, beloved soul. It's time.'

'Do we go in there?' asked Kath, nodding to the tomb.

'We do,' said Mary.

'And Brigid.' said Kath, grasping firmly to Mary's hands. 'Will my Brigid be in there. She said she would help me over.'

'Oh yes,' said Mary.

Kevin, Nancy and Brí all rushed to their mother and wept on her. None of them were able to find words other than 'I love you, Mammy.' Elsie also pressed herself to the little group and she also found it impossible to find any meaningful words, and was only able to offer her tears.

Eventually Kath pleaded with them, and in her whispering voice said, 'Come now, darlings. You must let me go, for its my time,' and with great reluctance they released her. Mary took her hand and started leading her to the tomb.

Peter, whose face was contorted with grief, ran forward and clasped Mary's arm and stammered out, 'Please, Ma'am. Please. Forgive me, but are we allowed to ask…? I mean… Here, of all places, surely, we could ask if, perhaps…?'

'Peter, love,' said Kath. 'We need to say our farewell. We'll only be apart for a time…' It was now Kath's turn to succumb to the emotion and she was unable to say more as the grief overwhelmed her.

'Who is making a request?' came a voice that was unearthly yet familiar, gentle yet majestic. Everyone turned and looked at the radiant creature at the mouth of the tomb.

'The request is from the man, Peter, the husband of Kathleen,' said Mary and lowered her head deferentially towards the creature.

'Then bring Kathleen,' said the creature. 'Bring Peter, the husband. And let Peter bring his request. It is a request from a heart of such great love, that it must be heard. Come.' The creature then formed into a shape that was as close as it came to human as it stretched out something that resembled an arm in the direction of Kath and Peter. Peter took one of Kath's arms and Mary took the other, and together they walked slowly in the direction of the tomb.

The rest of the family clung to each other as they watched Peter and Mary guiding the enfeebled figure of Kathleen to the entrance of the tomb. As they reached the tomb, Nancy spotted the figure of a young lady briefly emerge from the tomb. "Look!' she cried. 'It's our sister!' It was such a brief appearance that the others almost missed her, but they were in no doubt that their sister, Róisín had been there to help Kath over the threshold of this world to the next.

The creature of light then entered the tomb, with Kath and Peter following. Brí called out a strained, 'God bless you, Mammy,' but the sound of the sobs of the family was soon drowned by a roaring sound. It was the sound of a sea shore on a rough day. They could hear wave after wave breaking on a shore that they could not see.

Then the shimmering golden cloud descended upon them again and, for a moment, each one of the group was lost in a glorious, heady confusion of exquisite music, exotic fragrance, and the silky entwining of the cloud of gold around them. Each one felt something flow into their sharp pangs of grief. They felt drained of all that was sad, all that was harmful and all that was dark. The effect was so profoundly restful that they fell softly on to the sandy ground.

For a time, they existed in utter translucence before their humanity could bear it no longer. Then they succumbed to a dreamless sleep.

CHAPTER 24

The American Family

'It's snow!' called Rosa in excitement. Daisy was still holding tight to her niece and was glad she had done so, because for a few moments the golden cloud was so dense she could scarcely see even her hand as she raised it before her face. But now the cloud was clearing, and Daisy was right. Beneath their feet was the unmistakable and very disorientating sight of snow.

'Where are you all?' called the voice of Frank from the thinning mist.

'We're over here, honey,' called Daisy.

'What is going on?' said Frank as he emerged out of the mist and joined his family. 'And where are all the others?' he said, looking around.

'I think we're on our own here,' said Daisy. 'Wherever "here" is.'

'We're in a woodland,' said Rosa. She looked up and cried, 'Uncle Frank, look!' Frank looked up and saw the most enormous tree towering above him. Flecks of snow were falling from its branches.

'I know where this is,' said Frank in a hushed voice. 'Daisy, darling. We're in our most favourite place.'

'We can't be...' said Daisy, opening her eyes wide and lifting her eyes to the scene above her. The mist had now fully cleared and she saw that they were standing in a glorious snow-sprinkled forest. As the golden mist dispersed, a bright blue sky emerged beyond the tops of the trees and the dappled light of a winter sun flickered on them. 'We are, Frank!' said Daisy. 'We're in our favourite place!'

'Where is your favourite place?' asked Rosa, who had been gathering some snow into a ball, in preparation for building a snowman.

'Rosa, honey,' said Daisy. 'I don't know what's going on, but somehow or other we have stepped out of Ireland into the Giant Sequoia Forest on a beautiful winter's day.'

'But I'm not cold, Aunt Daisy,' said Rosa.

'No,' said Daisy, still gazing around her. 'No, that's so weird isn't it? It's perfectly warm.'

Frank was still gazing up at the huge heights of the glorious trees. He then looked back at Daisy with his watery eyes and said in a quiet voice, 'Daisy, darling. I think this is it. I think we must have stepped over. Whatever that great golden cloud was, it must have been poisonous. This must be...'

'Paradise?' said Rosa, looking up at her Uncle who, for the first time in her life, actually appeared to her quite small as he stood next to such a great tree.

'You are nearly right, Rosa' said a voice coming from behind them. They all turned around and saw a dark-skinned lady, with a winsome smile and bright eyes that shone behind her spectacles. Her long hair was neatly gathered in a bun, and she was wearing a smart green suit and a green beret to match.

'I know who you are!' cried Rosa and rushed towards her. The woman bent down and the two hugged each other.

Daisy and Frank simply looked at each other, their faces revealing their complete sense of bewilderment. When the long hug ended, Daisy, feeling protective of her niece called, 'Rosa, darling, come back here now.'

'Which Rosa are you calling?' said the gentle voice of the woman who was walking towards the couple, holding the hand of the young girl.

'Excuse me - are you also called Rosa?' said Frank to the woman.

She held out her hand and said, 'You don't recognise me, then?'

'No. Forgive me,' said Frank shaking her hand. 'Have you visited our church? I'm terrible at remembering people.' Daisy also shook her hand. She frowned as she struggled to recognise this person. Something certainly was familiar about this lady, but she could not quite place her.

'Aunt Daisy, don't you know who this is?' said the smiling Rosa to her Aunt.

'Are you...?' began Daisy.

'Yes,' said the woman, smiling broadly. 'I'm Rosa Parks. The lady on the bus.'

'I knew that,' said the young Rosa, her face alive with excitement. 'I knew straight away.'

'I'm sorry,' said Frank. 'It's just that we are having a very strange day at the moment, and I'm fairly sure I'm in the middle of a dream. But, forgive me again, but I thought you died in 2005.'

'Oh yes,' said the smiling Rosa Parks. 'Yes, that's right. I came Home that year. So you do know a bit about me then, Franklin'

'Why...' said Frank, still in a state of some shock, yet adjusting fast to the curious world in which he now found himself. 'Yes, we all know about you, of course.'

'You're such a hero of mine, Rosa Parks,' said the young Rosa. 'Let me see if I got this right.'

'Wait a moment, Rosa. I want to hear what you have to say. But look there's a picnic table just here. Let's sit down. And I prepared some coffee, fruit juice and cookies for you all.' Sure enough, just behind one of the great trees, there was a picnic table with benches, all covered in a light coating of snow. And on the table was a pot of steaming coffee, a jug of fruit juice, a plate of home-made chocolate cookies and a little bowl of fresh flowers.

As they sat at table, the young Rosa sat close to her namesake, and, after taking a bite of one of the cookies, she brushed her hair back, sat up straight as if she were answering a question in class, and said. 'Well, now. You were 92 years old when you died. So, you were much older than you look now.'

Rosa Parks chuckled and took one of the cookies.

'But the reason you are so famous is because you were very brave once,' said the girl. Daisy poured out some coffee from the flask into three mugs and passed them around.

'Well...' protested Rosa Parks, but said no more because the young Rosa would not let her.

'No, don't deny it, Rosa Parks,' she said. 'It was in those terrible days when black people like us could not ride on a certain section of the bus. You lived in a town called Mont...' She paused for a few moments and looked up. She then continued, 'Montgomery. And one day you got on that bus and you sat in the section for black people. Then, when the section of the bus that was for white people got full, the bus driver told you to give up your seat for a white man. And you said "No, Mister. I'm going to keep my ass on this seat and I ain't moving!" Here young Rosa mimed the scene, placing a bag on her knee, sitting upright and pursing her lips.

'Well, darling,' said Rosa Parks. 'You just about got the measure of it.'

'And,' continued the young Rosa, 'your action was so heroic that it got people going on something called the Civil Rights Movement. And me and Aunt Daisy and Uncle Frank are mighty glad you did all that stuff, because it means that we are free today.'

'Well, thank you, darling,' said the older Rosa. 'And I see you have similar fire in your belly, Rosa, as I did. And I know you were named after me because your Grandma and I were acquainted. And I believe that lady was your mother, Daisy?'

'Yes, that's right,' said Daisy, who was still in a state of awe at meeting the lady whose name was so well known in the home where she grew up.

'Well, I didn't know her well, Daisy, but I could see that she was a fine lady,' said Rosa. She then looked at Frank and said, 'But Franklin. It's not been an easy road for you, has it, darling?'

'Well,' said Frank, draining his mug of coffee. 'No, Rosa. It ain't been easy at times. But the work you started was awesome. It's just that some people... Well, they take a long time to lose their fear and their hatred.'

'You have scars on your soul, Franklin,' said Rosa, reaching her hand across the table and taking the large hand of Frank. 'But know this. Every wound you suffered is remembered and honoured. You have been just as heroic as me. And here is the thing, Franklin. You could have turned that hurt into bitterness and if you had, your life would have taken a whole different turn. But you are one of those who chose a road of forgiveness. That's what's heroic, Franklin.'

'My Uncle *is* a hero,' said the young Rosa, and she got off her bench and went around and hugged Frank.

Frank was unable to speak for a while and simply received the warmth of his niece's love. Then Rosa Parks said, 'Tell me, Franklin. What was the song that your Mama used to sing to you when you were feeling so sore?'

Frank looked at the hand that was holding his. He sniffed hard, then said, 'My Mama used to sing to me about the balm of Gilead.'

'I know,' said Rosa. She inhaled deeply, then looking to the trees above her she started singing

‘Sometimes I feel discouraged and think my work's in vain,
But then the Holy Spirit revives my soul again.
There is a balm in Gilead to make the wounded whole;
There is a balm in Gilead to heal the sin sick soul.’

Rosa had closed her eyes as she sang, and she swayed slightly to the lilt of the tune. Frank, Daisy and the young Rosa thought hers the most beautiful voice they had ever heard. It rose high into the snow-sprinkled trees and hushed the birds so that her voice was the only one heard in the forest. She opened her eyes and looked at Frank as she started the second verse. This time Daisy joined her and together they sang,

‘If you cannot preach like Peter, if you cannot pray like Paul,
You can tell the love of Jesus and say, "He died for all."
There is a balm in Gilead to make the wounded whole;
There is a balm in Gilead to heal the sin sick soul.’

'I ain't ever preached like Peter,' said Frank when the women had finished their verse. 'And I certainly ain't ever prayed like Saint Paul. But yes,' he said, nodding his head. 'Yes, I can tell the world that my Lord died for us all. Yes, I can talk about that.' He then breathed in and, as he had done only once before, he found an ability to sing beautifully and in tune. He started the last verse,

‘Don't ever feel discouraged, for Jesus is your friend;
And if you lack for knowledge, He'll never refuse to lend.’

Daisy and the two Rosa's joined him in the final chorus, and by the influence of the enchanted world in which they found themselves, they found harmonies as they sang,

‘There is a balm in Gilead to make the wounded whole;
There is a balm in Gilead to heal the sin sick soul.’

The tenderness and beauty of the song, sung by such true hearts, was inhaled by the great and ancient trees of the forest, and for a time the only sound was that of a light breeze rustling the long outstretched branches. Even that sound seemed to the group at the picnic table to be a sacred song. They all remained completely still for some time. Then, high above them, a tiny wren started her chirruping song. Soon a chickadee joined her. Then some warblers and flycatchers, and soon the whole forest had become a concert hall of birdsong. All at the table looked up and watched in delight at the birds swooping from great tree to great tree, scattering the humans below in soft snow.

'Is there anywhere as beautiful as this?' whispered Daisy.

Young Rosa, whose eyes were wide open in delight whispered, 'This is Paradise, Aunt Daisy. We are in Paradise.' She then turned to the lady sitting across the table from them. 'This is Paradise isn't it, Rosa Parks?'

'Rosa, darling,' she replied. 'The world you live in is a beautiful, beautiful world. But only those who truly open their eyes see what it's telling them. All the time your world is telling you about the beauty of Paradise. He has opened the door. He has made it possible. On that day when He strode out of that old, dark tomb, why, the whole of creation began to sing the song it had been aching to sing for a long, long while. He left musty, old death in that tomb, He did, Rosa. And He walked out into the sunlight and startled poor Mary and the other girls who had gone to the tomb. And He just carried on walking and, wherever He planted His feet, the ground cried out in excitement, it did! It had been groaning and moaning for a whole long time, waiting for this day. And the people who caught sight of Him - well, they just leaped like frogs from the lily leaf. They knew that sad old death had had its day and Life had got hold of us all. Yes, Rosa, Paradise got going that day. It was the day of the Great Beginning.'

'I like the Great Beginning,' said Daisy, who now remembered her conversation with Kath.

'Once he stepped from that tomb, all beginnings became possible, Daisy,' said Rosa. She then looked around at the forest and said, 'And what you see here today is pure beauty. But you don't have to die to get to see it. No, no. You just need to get a touch of that balm of Gilead plus a little salve of His precious Spirit for your eyes, so they get to see what they were always meant to see.'

The young Rosa, who still had her arm wrapped around her uncle's, had been listening intently to her namesake. But large tears started to leak from her deep eyes.

'What is it, hun?' said Rosa Parks.

'Mrs Rosa Parks,' said the child. 'What about my Mama and my Papa? They need a load of that balm from Gilead. Can I get some here and take it back with me?'

'Oh, Rosa, darling,' said Daisy, and got up from her end of the bench and came and sat with her niece.

'My, my,' said Rosa Parks. 'You have such love in your heart, child. Your Mama is a brave lady, even though she has been very hurt. But, listen. Even while we are having this little conversation here in this forest, she is knowing a few drops of that precious balm in her soul. You'll see, when you get back home.'

'Thank you,' whispered young Rosa.

'Now your Papa,' said Rosa Parks. She started to frown. 'He's got very lost, hasn't he? Well, Rosa, sweetheart, there is no place on Earth where the light that poured out from that tomb cannot reach. So never be without hope for your papa, Rosa. I think he may well find his way to the light. But none of us can force people there. We all make our own choices. Just keep love and hope strong in your heart, darling. And your prayers, Rosa. My, if only you knew what things changed because of your prayers, you would all pray a whole load more.'

Both Frank and Daisy felt a very familiar sense of guilt about their own prayer lives after this comment and looked down at the table. Frank then felt the hand of Rosa Parks on his. He looked up and saw her chuckling. She said, 'Oh, you do know how to feel bad about yourselves don't you? Don't you realise you were made to fly? We were all given wings. They may be fragile wings, but they work. So you both get going!' Her chuckle turned to laughter. Frank and Daisy both smiled at the sight of the lady opposite them creased in laughter.

'Mrs Parks,' said Daisy after the mirth had settled. 'Can you tell me, please. Why have we suddenly found ourselves here today? I mean, there we were in Ireland having a picnic with our friends, and then we are transported here in a cloud of golden mist.'

'Yes, darling,' said Rosa. 'I know, it's confusing ain't it? But, you see, you have all been gathered together for this time.'

'Is everyone else here, somewhere in the forest, then?' piped up young Rosa.

'No, no,' said Rosa Parks. 'No, not exactly in this forest. But you are all involved in the story of one who is dying. You have only known Kathleen for a few days, but even in those few days you have grown to love her and her family. You were called to the ancient place of faith because of death and because of life.'

'Has she died, then?' asked Rosa.

'Well, honey,' replied Rosa Parks. 'I'm not in charge of those things, and it's not for any of us to know when it's time for us to take the great journey Home. But, one way or another, all will be well. And now the time has come for me to leave you.'

She started to rise to her feet, and young Rosa leaped up from her bench and ran around the table and grasped hold of her. 'No,' she said. 'I'm not letting you go, Rosa Parks!'

Rosa Parks chuckled and said, 'No, child. You certainly are not! You and I will be close all your life. Granted, we will leave each other in one respect now. But you are made of the same stuff that I was. And I'm pleased to see that you got a good dose of stubbornness in you.'

'She certainly has that,' said Daisy, raising her eyebrows and looking hard at her niece.

'There's much work to be done, honey,' said Rosa Parks to the child. 'Enjoy the childhood God has given you. Don't grow up too fast. But let the passion grow in you. You, young Rosa Parks, have a destiny. And I think you will follow it. Bless you, sweet one.'

As she spoke the birdsong grew louder. No-one saw quite how Rosa Parks left the group, but Daisy, Frank and the young Rosa found themselves standing together beneath the great and glorious sequoias. The substance of the snow that was lightly falling on them seemed to change.

'It's kinda oily,' said Rosa. 'But it's not yucky.'

'No, sweetheart,' said Frank quietly. 'No, it sure ain't yucky. It's the balm. Smell that fragrance.' He raised his face to the sky and closed his eyes and repeated almost in a whisper, 'It's the balm. It's the healing balm... The balm that makes the wounded whole...'

The deepest calm any of them had ever known descended upon them and, though they were each standing with their faces to the sky, they fell into a slumber of utter tranquillity.

CHAPTER 25

The Devonian Family

'Alice! Alice, love, where are you? I can't see a thing in this fog.' Alice heard the panicky voice of her aunt somewhere to her left. She felt a little disappointed as she was rather enjoying the ethereal mist that had landed on the picnic party and wanted to spend some time on her own simply savouring its enchanting atmosphere.

But she could hear real fear in her aunt's voice, so she called out, 'I'm here, Aunt. This way.' After a little while, the anxious figure of Mavis materialised out of the mist.

'Oh, thank God!' cried Mavis, as she found her niece. 'I thought I'd lost you,' she said. 'In fact, I thought I'd lost everyone. I was completely on my own, Alice. And I was worried for you, what with your eyesight and that.'

'I'm fine, Aunt Mavis,' said Alice. 'To be honest with you, I'm rather enjoying this mist. It's beautiful, isn't it.'

'Oh, honestly Alice,' said Mavis shaking her head. 'I'll never understand you. Honest to God, I won't. But I'm relieved to find you, that I will say. So, what do we do?'

'I think we just wait for the mist to clear,' said Alice.

'Where are the others?' said Mavis. 'I have been calling for them, but heard nothing from anybody.' As she spoke, the golden mist started to clear and they started to see the green of the field in which they were standing. 'Where have all the stone walls gone?' said Mavis, now even more puzzled. Alice looked around her. She could see far more clearly than normal. This did not surprise her, as she sensed that they had somehow managed to step into a different realm. As the mist cleared, she began to recognise some familiar landmarks and she felt a flutter of excitement.

'Alice...' said Mavis, her voice trembling slightly. 'Alice, what on earth is going on. We are not where we were. We are definitely somewhere else.' As the mist continued to disperse, they heard the sound of seagulls and a distant breaking of waves on a seashore. 'Look!' said Mavis, stretching out her hand. 'We're near the edge of a cliff! We must be careful.'

'I know where we are,' said Alice calmly. 'Did you ever come here, Aunt Mavis?'

'Are w... we...' stammered Mavis, her eyes wide open. 'It feels a bit like the Devon coastland. Are we back there?'

'We are,' said the beaming Alice. 'We are not far from where you grew up. We are in Morwenstow.'

Mavis was frowning deeply and said, 'But how on earth did we get here, Alice. I don't remember doing any travelling. What's going on? This is not good for my nerves, Alice. It honestly isn't. I really think we need to be getting back to the others now.'

Alice put a strong arm around her aunt and said, 'Aunt Mavis, I really don't know how we got here. But you met Dorchadas, didn't you.'

'Yes...' said Mavis with some hesitation. 'A bit of a strange fellow, if you ask me. Nice enough in his own way, but there was something a bit odd about him, by my reckoning.'

'Well, Aunt,' said Alice. 'I know you will find this hard to believe, but he is actually an angel in the disguise of a human.

Mavis laughed and said, 'You always were a practical joker, Alice.'

Alice sighed and could see it was going to be hard to convince her very down-to-earth Aunt about this. 'Well, if you could just try and believe that for a moment, it might help you,' she said.

'So, the thing is, when he's around, strange things happen. So, I think, he has somehow arranged it for you and me to be transported here, because there is something we need to discover.'

'But what about the others?' said Mavis, still agitated. 'Where's Douglas? And Elsie. She and I were getting along very nicely. Where's she got to?'

'Just for a moment, forget about them all,' said Alice. She let go of her Aunt, and settled herself on the grass. 'Come on. Sit down here.'

'Oh no, the grass will be wet, Alice,' protested Mavis. 'It will do my arthritis no good. You know how it flares up if it gets the damp on it.'

'Aunt Mavis, the grass is completely dry,' said Alice. In fact, it was more than dry. It was almost velvety, and as Alice ran her hand over it, she felt a sense of delight in its texture. 'Honestly, Aunt. Do feel this. It's... It's not really like grass at all.' This time it was Alice's turn to be surprised. The scene they were in certainly looked like her beloved Morwenstow, and yet there was a difference. It was like it was a highly enhanced version of the land she loved.

Mavis, still looking suspicious, bent down and touched the grass with the tips of her fingers. 'My,' she said. 'I see what you mean. It is... Well, it's different isn't it.' Now, trusting Alice's judgement of the terrain, she sat down on the grass and said, 'Oh, Alice, love. It's gorgeous isn't it,' she said, running her hand over the grass. 'I've never felt anything like it my life. Well, perhaps I have. I'm thinking of that nice faux blanket you have on your bed. But I've not seen anything like it out of doors. Very strange.... But very nice, I must say. Perhaps we could get some for my garden. The lawn at home's in a shocking state after all the rain we've had.'

Alice stretched her legs out in front of her and lifted her face to the sun that was now shining warm on them. 'I can see perfectly here,' she said.

'What?' said Mavis, looking hard at her niece. 'You mean you can see through your bad eye?'

'Yes. Perfectly,' said Alice, brushing her bright, curling hair from her face. 'Look at the sea,' she said. 'It's *so* blue. Or is it blue? What colour would you call it, Aunt?'

'I'm really not sure, Alice,' said Mavis, staring out at the sea. She started to chuckle.

'What are you laughing about?' asked Alice, amused at the sound of her Aunt's laughter.

'Oh, I don't know, Alice,' said Mavis. 'But this is the kind of place where you just feel... You know... Just so happy. And yet. Not just happy. It's... Well, it's hard to explain.' She started chuckling again.

'I think I know,' said Alice. 'It's a happiness that isn't about forgetting the unhappiness. But it's a happiness that makes the unhappiness safe.'

'Yes, that's it, Alice,' said Mavis. 'Yes, that's very well put. You always have a way with words. Mine are always all of a jumble, they are. But I don't think that matters here, does it?' She was quiet for a few moments and then added, 'I'm feeling younger. I can't feel any of my usual aches and pains. Must be the Devon air. It always did me good.'

Alice now lay back on the grass and admired the flock of seagulls who flew overhead. Their cry was familiar, yet different. It was almost as if she could hear their voices. And they were beautiful, lilting voices even though they were seagull voices. 'What are they singing about?' she asked.

Mavis, who was now also sitting with her legs outstretched and her arms reaching behind her, looked up and listened. 'I can hear them, Alice,' she said. 'They *are* singing, you are right. I can hear the words, can't you? Something like, "How glorious the land that they have created.... we dance with the Three who have given us wings... How precious the Spirit... Her breath is our life..." Is that what you are hearing, Alice?'

'Yes, it is, Aunt,' said Alice in a dreamy voice. 'Yes, I hear those words and so much more. So much more...'. Mavis also lay back on the soft grass, and together they gazed at the sky as other birds flew overhead and joined in, filling the world with songs of delight.

They were not sure how long they lay there, revelling in the world in which they found themselves, but at some point, they were disturbed by a voice not far behind them, which said, 'May we join you?'

Both Alice and Mavis sat up with a start and looked behind them. Approaching them were two women. One was older, and walked with a slight stoop. The other was a young woman, who had her arm tucked into the arm of the older woman. Both women wore long robes which were various shades of brown, and both wore dark blue scarves over their heads, though pulled back somewhat so that the grey hair of the older, and the dark brown of the younger could be clearly seen.

'Yes, of course,' replied Alice. Both she and her aunt stood up. She thought the visitors looked most intriguing. Their accents, appearance and dress suggested they were foreign and reminded her a little of some of the refugees she and Douglas had met in Cairo. Mavis did her best to tidy herself up by brushing down her skirt and adjusting the jacket she was wearing.

'May we introduce ourselves?' said the younger of the two women. 'My name is Ruth, and this is my mother-in-law, Naomi.' Both women gave a slight bow.

'Pleased to meet you,' said Mavis. The song of the birds had done a grand job of settling Mavis' nerves and she was now so peaceful, that this arrival of two women from the Middle East felt remarkably normal.

'It is good to meet you,' said Alice, who shook their hands and introduced herself and her aunt to the visitors. As they sat on down on the soft grass, Alice asked, 'So where are you both from?'

Ruth removed the scarf from her head, and the sunshine revealed a rich chestnut colour in her hair. 'I come from a land called Moab,' she said. 'And my mother-in-law is from the town of Bethlehem in the land of Judah.'

'Oh, my,' said Mavis. 'You *have* come a long way.'

'Yes, we have both travelled far,' said Naomi.

'But you each come from a different country,' said Alice. 'So how did you meet?'

'Ah, now, that is a long story,' said Naomi, and her dark-skinned face creased into a warm smile as she looked at Ruth. She then turned and looked at Mavis. 'It starts with a famine. I was happily married with two sons and all was well until the famine. But hunger is a terrible thing. We were literally starving to death, so we had to leave our homeland and we travelled to the neighbouring land of Moab.'

'Oh, you poor souls,' said Mavis. 'I had to move from Devon to Sheffield, and that was bad enough. I can't imagine having to leave my country, though.'

'It was bad, Mavis,' said the elderly Naomi. 'But God was with us and we soon settled in our new place. However, then the next tragedy happened. My husband died.'

'Oh, no,' said Mavis. 'Oh, to suffer that and be in a strange land. You poor thing.' She reached out her hand and for a few moments placed it over Naomi's.

Naomi acknowledged Mavis' sympathy with a smile, and then continued her story. 'Well, that was hard, Mavis. But I had my sons and we started to heal. And in time both of them met lovely girls. One of them was this young lady.' Naomi nodded in the direction of Ruth who smiled at her mother-in-law.

'They were happy days, mother, were they not?' added Ruth.

'They were. They were indeed,' replied Naomi. 'Both my boys were married to beautiful women and they all looked after me. But then there was more tragedy to come. There was a terrible disease in the land and…' She looked down at the grass for a few moments, then looked up at Mavis and said, 'And both my boys died.'

'Oh, dear God, no,' said Mavis. 'Oh, that's terrible. And you, Ruth. You lost your young husband.' Ruth nodded. Alice was also listening to the story intently and frowning at the thought of such a weight of grief. She had not lost a husband through death, though the separation and the divorce from Georges felt like a painful bereavement. But she had known the agony of grief when her father was killed so suddenly all those years ago. Always, when she heard a story of grief, she remembered her father. The father, with whom she used to lie in the grass of Morwenstow and chat and giggle and play and tell stories. It did not take much for that cold shard of grief to penetrate her thin defences. Grief had a nasty habit of intruding into places even as beautiful as this.

As she was getting lost in these thoughts, she heard Ruth speaking with her soft voice, 'We were all beside ourselves in grief.' Alice looked up and saw that Ruth was looking at her as she spoke. 'We each had our own grief to bear. But because we loved each other, we also felt each other's hurt so keenly. We carried much pain in our hearts. It was a desperate time.'

'I'm so sorry,' said the compassionate Mavis again. 'I don't suppose you ever recovered from such a tragedy.'

'Ah, well dear Mavis,' said Naomi. 'The story did not finish there. In fact, one thing I learned from that time is that grief is never the end of the story. Grief is a terrible burden. But it also opens us in ways that nothing else can. And my eyes became open to the wonder of my daughters-in-law. Orpah, who was my other girl, and Ruth - they grieved so deeply, but do you know, our shared grief brought us so close together.'

'So, did you all stay living together?' asked Alice. She assumed that these two ladies were from a bible story, but her knowledge of the scriptures was not strong, and this story was new to her.

'Yes, we did for a time,' said Naomi, adjusting her position on the grass for a few moments. 'But, you know, I did miss my hometown. Like you, Mavis, I really did love my homeland and when I heard that the famine there was over, I yearned to go back to Bethlehem. So, the girls persuaded me to return home and off I went. I was all prepared to leave the girls, but this one here' - she pointed to Ruth - 'she wouldn't leave my side.'

Ruth smiled and said, 'She had become my mother. How could I leave her?' She reached over and tucked a stray lock of Naomi's hair into her head covering and kissed her.

Naomi smiled and briefly shook her head, then said, 'Such a foolish girl! Anyway, I couldn't persuade her to stay in her homeland, so the two of us came back to Bethlehem. And what happened there, young lady?' she asked, looking at Ruth.

'Yes, mother,' said Ruth smiling. 'I met a man. I never thought I'd meet a man in Bethlehem. And I never imagined a man from Judah would want to be seen with a woman from Moab. But the man was called Boaz and he was different from other men. God had touched his heart and he had no prejudices. He was full of kindness and...' She smiled a coy smile. 'And yes, we got married.'

'And they had a baby,' added Naomi. 'And a few generations on from that, came the great King David. And many generations on from that, a young child was born - again in Bethlehem. And He is the one who was put to a cruel death.'

'But broke out of his tomb,' said Ruth, her face alive with joy. 'And death and grief finally lost their terrible, dark power.'

'Just a minute, please,' said Mavis. 'My mind's a simple one, I'm sorry to say. But here you two are talking to us, but you are talking about great, great, great, grandsons, but... you are still alive. And you are suggesting one of those grandsons was the famous babe born in Bethlehem?'

'Aunt Mavis,' said Alice, cupping her hand over her aunt's. 'We are in a different land here. There is no time in this place. Think of it as walking into a fairy tale. Only it's a fairy tale that is truer than any world we normally live in. And it is so alive, that it makes our world seem only half-awake. Isn't that so?' she asked, looking at the two visitors.

'That is so, Alice,' said Ruth. 'This is the world of deep memory. It is the place where memories are so alive, that you can live in them. But it is not just memory. It is imagination. It is the place where you can see, not just what has been, but what is to come. And it is the place where you not only glimpse your future, but you can take hold of a bit of it and live with it in the present.'

'I'm not sure I'm following all this,' said Mavis. 'But I must admit, I do like it here. And I am enjoying meeting you two ladies, even though I feel very sad to hear your stories of loss.'

Naomi smiled and said, 'Mavis, tell us about your loss.'

Mavis looked a little startled at being asked such a personal thing. And yet, the company felt safe. Before now, she had only really told Douglas and Saoirse about her loss. They were the only people who seemed to understand. And Alice, of course. So, trusting the present company, she said, 'Oh, there's not much to say really. I was a very lucky lady. I met my Bert in the little town called Bideford where I lived. Not far from here... I mean. Well, to be honest I'm not sure where "here" is just at the minute. Anyhow, I met my Bert, who came with his family on holiday. I was serving in a bakery at the time, and he would come in for a Cornish pasty every day. Well, we fell head over heels in love with each other, we did. And - long story short - he married me and whisked me off to his home town of Sheffield, where I've lived ever since.

'Then one sad day - oh, it seems only like yesterday.' She sighed and frowned. 'After forty-three years of a very happy marriage, he left this world. That's when I got to know our Vicar - or the man who used to be our Vicar, I should say. He's called Douglas, and he went and visited my Bert in hospital and, well, I don't know quite what he did but, one way or another, he not only gave my Bert peace of mind and heart, but he also helped me a great deal. And despite going through hell at that time, I did actually get to know God and quite liked what I saw of Him. Found He wasn't quite the cold and angry God I thought Him to be. I still got things to say to Him, mind you. I mean, my Bert had almost reached his six score and ten, but not my brother, Cliff. Cliff was Alice's father. He was such a good man, he was, and he left this world far too soon. He was only a young man. His wife - Alice's mum - has never recovered. And poor Alice... Well. That's what I need to speak to God about. Why he takes such a good soul as our Cliff, and leaves others in this world who are wicked people.'

Alice was listening to her aunt relating the story that she knew so well. She couldn't deny, that she also harboured similar questions in her own soul. How she would have loved her father to have lived the years that her Uncle Bert was given. Her grief completely knocked her off course. She always felt that she would never have married Georges had her father been alive. She married young because she was missing her father so much. Besides, he would have seen though Georges long before she did. She had missed her father every day since his sad and violent death on that roadside all those years ago. Both Alice and Mavis were now looking down at the ground, lost in their memories of grief.

'Thank you, Mavis,' said Naomi. Mavis and Alice both looked up and noticed that both Naomi and Ruth had been weeping.

'Oh, I'm sorry, love,' said Mavis. 'I didn't mean to upset you both.'

'Tears are our friends,' said Ruth, wiping her eyes with her headscarf. 'We lived with just the same questions as you are asking. But we now see things so differently. There was an ancient prophecy about our descendent - that is, the baby born in Bethlehem who was revealed as the Christ. And the prophecy said that he would bear our griefs and carry our sorrows.

'Oh, yes, I know that,' said Mavis. 'Heard it sung by the choir once or twice. Very nice it was. Or would have been had Mr Trenchard sung in tune.'

Ruth politely acknowledged Mavis, then continued. 'Have you ever wondered, though Mavis, what that means?' Mavis looked like a child at school who was asked a question and had no idea of the correct answer. Mavis was relieved that Ruth decided to answer her own question, as she said, 'It means that there was something remarkable in his life. Or to be more precise in his death.'

'I understand,' said Alice. It's like many of us help support one another when we are hurting. In a way we carry each other's griefs and sorrows that way. But I get from what you are saying that there was a difference about how He carried it.'

'A big difference, Alice,' said Naomi. 'You see He carried it so much, that he died with it.'

'But he didn't just die with it,' said Ruth. 'He came back from the grave, you see, and opened the door to a whole new world.'

'So, what did he do with the grief and sorrows, then?' asked Alice.

Naomi looked over to Alice and said, 'Alice are you familiar with the concept of alchemy?'

'Hm,' said Alice thoughtfully. 'Well, I read Physics at University, not Chemistry. But I believe alchemy was something people believed in before they really got to know and understand basic chemistry.'

'Whatever are you talking about, Alice?' said Mavis. She looked at Ruth and Naomi and added, 'I swear, I don't know what the girl's talking about half the time.'

Alice ignored her aunt's protest and continued, 'So yes, I believe alchemy was a kind of magical transformation of an ordinary metal such as iron, into a precious metal like gold.'

'Yes,' said Naomi. 'So, you see there is a kind of divine alchemy. He took the raw material of our sufferings into the furnace of his own suffering and death. But then, on that Easter morning, he walked from the tomb carrying gold. '

'I'm sorry, I'm completely lost,' said Mavis shaking her head.

'I think I've got it,' said Alice. 'I've grieved so deeply for my lost father. So you are saying it's like the Christ also felt that loss so deeply that he took it into his soul when he was dying. And it went to the grave with him - that tomb in the rocks. Then, when he rose up on that sunshiny morning all those years ago, he came out carrying my grief still. Only it wasn't grief. It was something different. Something transformed.'

'Yes,' said Ruth. 'You see, he came out radiant in pure love. All your sorrows, which you felt so deeply, were transformed into a stream of love. Do you not see, Alice, that though you grieved so deeply, that aching heart of yours also started to love so much more? It did not protect you from all the struggles of life, but something was transformed in you. There was an alchemy on your grief. Little by little, the gold of love emerged from the tomb of sorrow within you.'

Mavis had been struggling with this conversation, but something in Ruth's comment made sense. 'Ah, I think I'm beginning to see what you mean,' she said thoughtfully. 'When my lovely Bert died, I was hurting so badly. But there was something about the way Douglas and Saoirse cared for me. I was hurting and angry and all the rest of it, but I did feel something tender inside of me coming to life. They helped bring it to life. And when I started going to church and got to know God a bit better, I could feel that alcho-watsit that you are talking about.'

'Yes, Mavis,' said Naomi. Mavis looked at the creased and dark skin of the face that was addressing her, and saw such a tender expression of kindness. Naomi continued, 'It certainly happened in your soul, and is continuing to happen. Let all your sorrows be turned to light. It may take time, but all things are possible.'

Mavis nodded as she looked at Naomi. And yes, she couldn't deny, that in some hitherto buried place of sorrow in her own soul, there was movement. A shifting. Some daylight. She reached out to Naomi and grasped the ancient hand. 'Thank you, Naomi,' she said, her voice quivering a little. 'I feel...' she looked out to the sea and paused for a few moments. 'I feel like something has woken up in me. It's been asleep far too long. Far too long. Yes, it's time I did a bit of waking up.'

'And the most precious gift he has given us all,' said Naomi, 'is the precious gift of hope. Look at this world you are in here today.' They all looked up as Naomi spoke the words and Mavis and Alice were taken aback by the utter beauty of the world around them. There were colours that were beyond their imaginings; sounds they had never heard before; fragrances so sweet they almost wept for the loveliness of them.

'Where are we?' asked Alice, her voice trembling and her eyes brimming with moisture.

'All will be this one day,' said Ruth. 'Paradise is never far from you, Alice. You have glimpsed your future. But His Spirit is here and it is her gift to breathe the future into your present. For the rest of your days you can remember this future and let it flower as hope in your souls.' She got to her feet and helped her mother to hers. 'But now,' she said. 'It is time for us to leave you.'

'Oh, but we are only just getting to know one another,' said Mavis, also standing up.

'Look,' said Naomi pointing to the inland hills. 'The dews of grace are falling now.' Alice also stood and with her good eyesight, she saw clearly the cloud of gold returning to them. As she realised this meant the end of the time with their new friends, she quickly hugged each woman and thanked them. Within a few moments the cloud was enveloping them.

'Oh, I'm feeling dozy, Alice,' said Mavis, sitting herself back on the velvety grass again. 'I think it's time for my afternoon nap. Wake me up, won't you, when it's time to go.'

But she received no answer because Alice was already lying on the grass. The golden mist was swirling around her and she was fast asleep and smiling the most contented of smiles.

CHAPTER 26

The Angel and his Friend

'Is this your doing, Dorch?' asked Douglas, who could just about make out the tall figure of Dorchadas through the dense golden mist.

'No, this is not my doing, Doug,' answered Dorchadas. 'But I suspect it's His.' He paused for a few moments as the mist started to lighten. 'It's not what I expected, though,' he added as he peered around him. 'Not what I expected at all.'

'Where exactly *is* this, Dorch?' said Douglas. 'And what *were* you expecting?' The mist was lifting quite quickly now, and Douglas could see they were standing on a sandy track. The air felt warm, and he could hear the sound of water nearby. There was something familiar about the place. 'I know this place, don't I, Dorch?' he said.

'Aye, that you do, Doug,' said Dorchadas, whose figure was completely clear now with the lifting of the mist. In fact, silky rays of sun were breaking through and Douglas could see that they were on a river bank, with tall reeds beside them swaying in a light breeze.

'Well, well...' said Douglas, smiling. 'We're back here again, Dorch.'

'Aye, that we are, Doug,' said Dorchadas, also smiling. 'We've come back to where we started.' Douglas looked around him and recognised various landmarks. He called to mind those cold days in early October, when he first met Dorchadas in *The Angel's Rest.* Was it only seven months ago? It was there that Dorchadas had spoken to Douglas about the power of the imagination. He somehow ignited Douglas' imagination in a way that lifted him into a completely different world. He "travelled", to use

Dorchadas' term for it. And the first travelling he experienced was to the land of ancient Egypt. And it was to this very place he had now returned. As Dorchadas said - back to where they started.

'Why have we come back here, Dorch?' asked Douglas, both pleased to be back, yet puzzled as well.

'I don't rightly know the answer to that, Doug,' said Dorchadas, who was casting his eyes over the scene around them. 'But I guess we just need to follow this path and see what's at the end of it.' And so the two friends made their way along the sandy path, which was wide enough for the two of them to walk side by side. Tall grass lay to their left, and on their right there was a river bank lined with a deep bed of large swaying rushes. Every now and again their presence would disturb a water fowl that would squawk in protest and clumsily fly off over the somnolent Nile.

'What's happened to the others, do you suppose?' asked Douglas. 'They'll be wondering where we've gone.'

Dorchadas stopped walking for a moment and, looking at Douglas with his dark eyes, said, 'I've been thinking about that too, Doug. I think all this is to do with Kathleen.'

'With Kath?' said Douglas. His eyes were half-closed as the sun was now blazing bright upon them.

'Aye,' said Dorchadas, pursing his lips and pulling at his beard thoughtfully. 'You could see today that she is very near her passing. Well, I'm thinking that it could be happening now.'

'What - now?' exclaimed Douglas. 'If that is the case, Dorch, I want to go back and be with her. She did ask me if I'd be with her, if possible, when her time came.'

'Aye, I know she did, Doug,' said Dorchadas. 'But don't worry about that. So much has happened in that heart of hers and she won't need too much help crossing over. You see, Doug, you, me,

Kath and Kev were very privileged to be there at His death, weren't we?'

'Yes...' said Douglas and the memory of that extraordinary time at Golgotha came easily to his mind.

'But it wasn't the whole story, Doug,' said Dorchadas. 'It was only the first part of the Great Story. Amongst us angels, it's known as that - the Great Story - because that's just what it is.' Douglas was listening carefully. 'I think we are now being taken to something to do with the second part of the story. And that part is about the Day of Great Wonder.'

'Is that another angel term?' asked Doug.

'No,' said Dorchadas smiling. 'No, actually that's my term for it. But it has all sorts of words doesn't it? *Resurrection* and *Easter* are the main ones. But no words do justice to what happened that day.'

'Did you ever get to see what happened on that Easter morning, Dorch?' asked Douglas.

'No,' answered Dorchadas. 'But I did meet one of the angels who were on duty that day. You'd call her a female angel. Oh, my, Doug. You should have heard her story.' Dorchadas shook his head and his face creased into its infectious smile. 'I've never seen an angel so beside herself with joy. As she told me the story - well, she kind of sang it to me really - she became a blaze of iridescence. It was utterly beautiful, Doug. I could never describe it to you. Your boys - Matthew, Mark, Luke and John - all tried to write about it. But, Doug, how can you honestly put such a thing into prose? Would have been better if they had written a poem or a song, I think.'

'I should like to have heard her song, Dorch,' said Douglas. 'But I'm still not quite sure why all that means we are here now. And it doesn't explain what's happened to our friends. And I'd still like to get back to Kath, even if she doesn't need me.'

'Ah, well, now, Doug,' said Dorchadas. 'I'm not really helping you, am I? What I'm trying to say in my usual befuddled way, is that I think all of us at the picnic may have stepped into a story that is to do with His rising from the grave. And my guess is that everyone will have their own tale to tell when we all get back together again. Or…' He hesitated for a while, then added, 'Or, maybe it will be when *you* all get back to them again.'

'Oh, Dorch,' said Douglas, and this time it was his turn to reach out and grasp Dorchadas' arm. 'You don't think this is the time for you to… to return. Surely not? We're not ready yet. And if Kath's really going to die today, then we need you, and…'

As Douglas was speaking, Dorchadas looked up. He put up his hand and, interrupting Douglas, said, 'Listen, Doug. What do you hear?'

Both of them were quiet and Dorchadas was right, there was a sound. It sounded like a sheet flapping in the wind. There was also a sound of creaking wood and some voices. It was coming from just a bit further down the path from where they were standing. They started walking towards the direction of the sounds and then saw the distinct shape of a mast and sail appearing over the reeds. As they walked a little further along, they found the reed bed came to an end and from the bank stretched a simple wooden jetty, to which a small sailing boat was carefully docking.

'Well, well,' said Dorchadas. 'Look who it is, Doug.' As they approached closer, Douglas did recognise the figure of the man who had jumped out of the boat on to the dock and was securing the boat with a rope.

'It's John!' said Douglas. 'Our friend, John the Baptist. He's alive, Dorch!'

As he spoke this, the bearded and somewhat dishevelled figure on the jetty turned round and waved at the two, who were now walking fast towards the boat. John ran down the jetty to the pathway and met the two visitors, greeting them warmly.

'Welcome, my dear friends,' said John. 'Come, come, come. The others are waiting in the boat.'

'Others?' said Douglas who was now in a state of near total confusion.

'Why, yes, Douglas,' said John. 'Your other friends. Look!' He ran up the jetty, beckoning Douglas and Dorchadas to follow. Douglas looked into the boat and there, sure enough, were the friends he had made during his moments of travelling. They were all smiling and waving at him.

Antonio, dressed in his Roman centurion uniform, stood up somewhat unsteadily in the boat and bowed towards Douglas and called, 'Welcome aboard, Douglas. And Dorchadas, old friend. Come...'

Antonio took Douglas' hand and helped him into the boat. Both Douglas and Dorchadas clambered aboard, and the occupants of the boat moved around to make space for the new arrivals. Mary Magdalen was there. Douglas remembered so well his conversation with her in the cool, night-time garden of Gethsemane. She was sitting in the stern of the boat next to Svetlana, the woman he had met in the playground who told Douglas her story of meeting the Christ at the well in Samaria.

'Sit here,' said a young Irish voice, and Douglas was both surprised and delighted to see young Grace, the girl whom he thought had been the stroppy Dingle teenager, but who turned out to be the daughter of Jairus. She ushered him to a place on a bench that was next to a young bearded man, whom Douglas immediately recognised as Joseph, the one he had recently met in Cairo.

As everyone settled, John said, 'And Douglas there are two others you have not yet greeted.' He stretched out his hand to a young woman, who removed her head covering and smiled at the two new arrivals in the boat. 'Here is Salome,' said John, and introduced him to the young dancer that Douglas had last seen when he and Dorchadas had found a mysterious doorway leading from the Gallarus Oratory to the lower chambers of Herod's palace.

He felt somewhat confused at the thought of seeing the very person, who was effectively responsible for John's death. She must have read his mind, for she reached forward from her seat and taking Douglas' hand said, 'Douglas and Dorchadas, it is so good to see you both again. I remember well our meeting.' Looking specifically at Douglas, she said, 'And Douglas, do not be confused by seeing me and John in the same place. We are living in a world now that is infused with the life of Risen One. All is safe in this world. All is healed.'

Douglas was about to respond, when a husky voice from the bow of the boat called out, 'Don't forget me! Dorch, you old rogue, how are you?' Douglas immediately recognised the voice that belonged to the great patriarch Jacob, the man he met the very first time he travelled with Dorchadas. Both Douglas and Dorchadas reached forward their arms and greeted the old man who shook their hands in turn.

So here Douglas was, in a boat with various people of old who had come alive to him in mysterious ways during these recent extraordinary months. He was grateful that Dorchadas chose to sit beside him in the boat. Though he was in many ways pleased to see again all these biblical figures, he was very unsure quite what to say to them all. Having individual conversations was one thing, but how was he supposed to interact with them all *en masse*? As if reading his mind, Dorchadas leaned towards him and said in a quiet voice, 'Don't feel you need to make conversation, Doug. I don't think they are here to talk to us. They just want to accompany us. That's all.'

'Accompany us where, Dorch?' said Douglas, as John pushed the boat away from the jetty and raised the sail.

'Let's see,' said Dorchadas. The boat drifted out into the river and, as it caught the breeze, it sailed quietly away from the jetty. 'I've not known this kind of thing happen before, Doug,' continued Dorchadas. 'But then, I've not known one person have as many meetings as you have. I mean look at them all, Doug. Quite a few, aren't there? Should make your sermons interesting in the future, don't you think?'

Douglas smiled in response, then asked, 'So, what do you think it's all about then?'

'Time, Doug,' said Dorchadas, adjusting his position so that he could stretch his legs a little. 'This is the difficulty. You have only a restricted view of time. But you see, all these characters here. Yes, they lived thousands of years back. But when the Day of Great Wonder happened, well it shook up time, you see. And death was defeated, Doug. Paradise, you see - it's all about the beauty of the healed world, and the beauty of the healed lives. It was the birth of a whole new beauty. Don't you feel it here, Doug?'

Douglas had been so preoccupied with his questions, that he had not really thought to look around at the scene in which he was currently living. Here he was, sailing down a tranquil River Nile. Everything around him - the water, the reeds, the green fields beside the river, the swaying palm trees on the river bank, the distant dusty brown hills, the tall sail catching the light breeze and above it, the cloudless blue sky - he could feel it all existing in a state of such rich harmony. And the people in the boat: they were all looking out over the waters to something in the distance. He was impressed by a remarkable sense of calmness in each one of them. He had never sat in such peaceful company. In some respects, he felt like he was in a deep sleep, and yet he could honestly say he had never felt so wide awake.

All his senses were sharpened. He felt he could hear the tiniest noise, see the farthest distance, smell the faintest of fragrances.

'Dorch,' he whispered. 'Are we.... Are we actually in Paradise, then? Have I died? Tell me honestly. I can take it.'

'No, Doug,' said Dorchadas answering him in a whisper. 'No, son, you haven't died. This is another bit of travelling. In fact, I am fairly certain it is your last bit of travelling. But, more than any of the others places you've been to, this is more permeated with Paradise than anywhere else you have been to.'

'So, why are we here, Dorch?' he whispered.

Dorchadas' eyebrows twitched for a while, before he answered. He looked at Douglas and said, 'I think this is my time, Doug. And you are here to help me.'

'Yes, you are right, Dorch,' said the husky voice of old Jacob from the bow of the boat. 'Douglas is your gift to help you during your final hours in human form. You've become so fond of humans, that you've been given one to help you with the final bit of the journey. During your days of walking the Earth as a human you have called on many of us to assist you in the work to which He called you. We in this boat are the ones who were called to help you friend, Douglas.' Douglas was aware of the people in the boat smiling, and Joseph reached out his hand and grasped Douglas' for a few moments.

'So, in a sense,' added Joseph, 'we represent all the people of old, who have been called to work with you, Dorchadas.'

'It has truly been an honour,' said Svetlana. 'And I think you learned one thing when I made my visit. And that is, you should not go spinning on one of those children's roundabouts!' She laughed at the memory, as did Douglas.

'Aye,' said Dorchadas. 'I certainly had much to learn when I lived my life as a human.'

'Here we are,' called John, and Douglas saw they were approaching another little jetty. John steered the boat to it and leaped out, securing the boat. He held out his hand to Douglas, who stepped off the boat.

As Dorchadas stepped out of the boat, he looked back and said, 'Thank you. Each one of you. Thank you.'

'Now just follow the path,' said John, and the two friends left the jetty and followed the path ahead of them.

Once again, they found themselves on a path with tall grasses either side of them. 'Where is this leading, Dorch?' asked Douglas.

'To be honest, Doug,' said Dorchadas. 'I have no idea. But I think we'll soon see.' After a while the grasses thinned until they were in open ground, and it was clear they had walked into a desert place. For a time, they followed the rough outline of a path, which became less and less distinct, so that it was not long before they were walking in the desert with no path and with no idea of where to go.

'Are we lost, Dorch?' asked Douglas, more out of curiosity than anxiety. It would not be possible to be anxious in this world.

'Aye, I think so, Doug,' said Dorchadas. 'And I suspect we are meant to be.' They carried on in silence for a while and, at one point, Dorchadas walked a little ahead. Douglas looked at him and smiled in great appreciation.

He looked at the tall figure with its thick dark hair, scruffy jumper, faded jeans and ex-army boots. He called out, 'Dorch.'

Dorchadas stopped and turned around. 'Sorry, son,' said Dorchadas. 'I didn't mean to be walking ahead of you. I was just lost in my thoughts. What is it, Doug?'

Douglas caught up with him and said, 'Dorch, I just want to say "thank you". I honestly don't know where I'd be in life if I hadn't met you. I really…'

'No, no, no, Doug,' said Dorchadas. 'There's no need to go thanking me. It's me who should be thanking you.'

'What for, Dorch?' asked Douglas.

Dorchadas pulled his hand out of his pocket and brought it up to his chin and scratched his beard for a few moments. He leaned his head to one side and said, 'Of all the humans I met in my travels, Doug, you were the one who was the most honest. Come, let's keep walking.' They continued on their trek through the wilderness, and Dorch said, 'We've had some grand times, haven't we?'

'We certainly have, Dorch,' said Douglas, and for some time they found themselves reminiscing of the months they had spent together. They spoke of the meetings they had had with the people back in the boat. They spoke of the people they had grown to love so much, especially Kath and her family. They both frowned as they remembered the wild storm on the seashore and the argument on the beach where all of Douglas' agonising questions about life tumbled out of his angry heart. They laughed as they remembered Dorchadas surprising Douglas that day in the church of Kilmalkedar and their eating rhubarb tart together afterwards in the little tea cottage on the hill. They remembered conversations in pubs and cafés and strolls on streets and seashores. And they remembered the frantic car chase which ended with them tumbling down the hill in Douglas' car, but opened the door to the wondrous scene of Golgotha.

'So here we are, Dorch,' said Douglas, 'After all our adventures, we've come to a place where neither of us knows where we are or where we are going.'

'Aye,' said Dorchadas, and they both paused for a while. 'But this is a wonderful place, Doug, don't you think? Maybe it's wonderful because we don't know. We've let go.' Douglas looked around him. The river was a long way behind them now, and all around them was a dry land with rocks and shrubs stretching out to distant, shimmering hills. The land seemed desolate, yet there was a powerful sense of vitality in it. The sun shone brightly upon them, but it did not burn them. There was no water nearby, yet they did not thirst. Both of them appreciated the stillness and silence. 'The land that loveth silence, Doug,' whispered Dorchadas, and Douglas slowly nodded his head.

For a time, they enjoyed the utter peace and deep tranquillity of the place until they both became aware of the sound of fluttering wings above them. They looked up and only a short distance above them a dove was flying. In fact, to Douglas' eye, it looked more like a pigeon.

'Remember John's story, Doug,' said Dorchadas. 'The dove at the baptism. The Holy Spirit is with us, Doug. We're in the right place.' The dove circled around them for a time and then flew off in the direction of the hills. Douglas and Dorchadas followed it and, in time, they spied an old man sitting on a stone. As they drew nearer to him, they watched him reach into his jacket pocket and pull out a handful of seed and throw it on the ground. The dove fluttered down and gratefully fed from the seed.

'Who is it?' asked Douglas.

'Well, Doug,' answered Dorchadas. 'This may surprise you, but it is one of my superiors. It is Raphael - one of the Archangels.'

Douglas had always pictured Archangels as mighty and huge creatures ablaze with light and majesty. But this gentleman looked much more like the kind of man whom he might find slumped in a shop doorway in Sheffield.

'Ah, there you are, Dorchadas,' said the old man. 'You made it. And I'm pleased to see that you brought Douglas with you. Come now.' He opened an old leather satchel next to him, and pulled out a bottle and a couple of mugs. He poured some red liquid from the bottle into the mugs and handed them to his visitors. 'Pull up a stone,' he said, chuckling.

Douglas and Dorchadas both found some rocks nearby and Douglas was surprised at how comfortable his was. Dorchadas took the mugs from Raphael and passed one to Douglas who, on taking a sip from the mug, was sure that he had never tasted such delicious wine ever in his life.

'So, Dorch,' said Raphael. 'This is it, then. You, the angel who has been called to fathom the dark things of God. You have completed your years spent as a human.'

'That I have, sir,' said Dorchadas. He took a sip of his wine, then placed the mug in the sand beside his rock.

'And you have met with Gabriel, and you know how much your work has been appreciated.'

'Yes,' said Dorchadas in a quiet voice.

'So,' said Raphael. 'Are you ready now to come home?'

Douglas looked at his angel friend to see his response. Dorchadas stared at his boots for quite a time with his head bowed low. Douglas was disturbed to see large drops of water fall from his eyes to the dry desert land beneath him. 'It's all right, Dorch,' Douglas found himself saying, even though he had no reason to offer reassurance.

Douglas watched as Dorchadas lifted up his face and looked at Raphael. It was a face creased by so much kindness, laughter and sorrow. It had about it, thought Douglas, a look of such humanity. Maybe humanity at its best. Dorchadas wiped the moisture form his face. Then, looking at Raphael, he responded to his question: 'But where is home, sir? I've become so at home in the world of humans now, I'm going to be lost in the world of angels.'

'You mean,' said Raphael, leaning his head to one side, 'you have come to prefer the world of mortals, to enjoying the glory of Paradise?

'Forgive me, sir,' replied Dorchadas, 'But, you see, I have found His glory is just as wonderful on Earth. I have seen it in the hills and valleys, the rivers and the seas, the light of the sky and beams of the moon. But most of all, I have seen it in the faces and hearts of the humans He made to dwell on His sweet Earth. I have walked with them a long time now, sir. I have... Well, I have grown to love them, I have. I'm sorry, but I suppose I have grown to love them a bit too much.'

Raphael frowned and got up from his stone and came over to Dorchadas, whose head was bowed to the ground again. Raphael crouched down in front of him and reached out his hand, placing it on Dorchadas' shoulder. He said, 'Dorchadas, you were made free and you will always be free. All His creatures are free. So, what is it that you desire?'

'To serve Him,' said Dorchadas without hesitation and looked up into the face of the Archangel. 'That has always been my desire.'

'And where do you wish to serve Him?' asked Raphael.

Dorchadas looked down at the ground again briefly, then back up at Raphael and said, 'On Earth, sir.'

Raphael, still crouched before Dorchadas, asked, 'And how do you want to serve Him on Earth. As an angel disguised in human form or in the form you were originally created to be?'

Dorchadas looked at Raphael and frowned in puzzlement. 'Well, sir. I really didn't know I had a choice. I thought it had all been decided - that my days serving in this way were fixed. But if there was to be a choice...' His expression quickly changed from frown to raised eyebrows. 'If there is a choice, then I'd sooner choose to live a little longer as a human. I mean, I know how beautiful them chambers of Paradise are, don't get me wrong. But, you see, something has got into my soul during my years living amongst the humans. I guess I'm just more at home now with the salty breeze from the sea on my face and with the smell of peat in my nostrils.'

'But your path is to return to Paradise and take up your work again as the celestial spirit you were created to be,' said Raphael.

'I know, I know,' said Dorchadas and his countenance fell as he looked down. 'And so, I will follow the path, sir. As I said…'

'No,' interrupted Raphael. 'Look at me, Dorchadas.' Dorchadas lifted his face to Raphael, who continued, 'Have you learned so little? The Kingdom of the Three is one where every wish is treasured. It is a Kingdom of freedom, not laws. It is a Kingdom of love, not obligation. The path can always turn. Love always moves things around. Surely you know that? So, Dorchadas, tell me. Where will you love most freely?

Dorchadas replied, 'Without doubt, I would love most freely by living on Earth for a little longer, as a foolish human with a tender heart.'

Raphael moved his face closer to Dorchadas' as if inspecting something deep inside him. 'But Dorchadas,' he said. 'You have found the sorrows of this world hard to bear. They have made you weary. You have seen how human hearts can be cruel and hard. You have wept many tears. These days of walking this world in the guise of a man have cost you, dear friend. Are you sure you can live with the pains and sorrows for a further time?'

Dorchadas looked back into the eyes that were searching his. 'To be honest, sir,' he said. 'I have asked myself that question many times. I have wondered if I can carry any more sorrow. There have been times when the pains of the world have all but overwhelmed me. But walking in this desert today and feeling the fluttering wings of His dove of glory, I realise that the pain is not for me to carry. To feel, yes. To carry, no. It is *His* burden. So, yes, sir. I am sure I can live with the sorrow. What is love if it is not prepared to be pained by sorrow? I am not a strong angel, as you know, sir. But I do try to be a loving one, because that is the way He made me.'

Raphael reached out his hand to Dorchadas and cupped his rugged cheek in the palm of his hand. 'Dorchadas. You, who have been called to befriend the darkness of God: take your freedom; follow your heart; serve your Lord.' Dorchadas closed his eyes and slowly nodded his head.

Douglas watched as Raphael now whispered some words into the ears of the angel. He watched Dorchadas look up briefly at Douglas, then bow his head again. When the Archangel finished delivering his message, he stood up, and Douglas and Dorchadas also stood. Raphael took a couple of steps towards Douglas and said, 'Douglas, you who dwell by the dark stream: you have heard your new calling through the beloved people you met in Cairo. So, it is now your time to step into the destiny that awaits you.'

'Thank you, sir,' said Douglas.

Raphael turned back to Dorchadas, and said, 'Now, Dorchadas. You have made a choice. You have chosen to serve your Lord for a further season disguised as a human, to live among them and serve according to His will. So that shall be your path. But first, it is time for you to withdraw for your retreat for a season. You are tired. You have carried much human sadness in your soul and you need restoration. Go and live under the beam of His love. Be refreshed in the streams of grace. Be nourished by His abundant goodness.'

'That I will, sir,' said Dorchadas, with a slight bow. 'Thank you, sir. Thank you'

'Well, off you go now,' said Raphael returning to his seat and gathering his satchel. 'I've got other things to be doing. God's peace go with you both.' And having said so, he was gone.

Douglas and Dorchadas simply stood for a while. The dove, which had been pecking happily at the seeds, took off from the ground and flew above them for a while, and then flew ahead of them, clearly beckoning them to follow. As they walked along, Douglas said, 'Well, Dorch. How do you feel about that?'

Dorchadas looked at Douglas and smiled his broad and winsome smile and said, 'Do you know, Doug. I never, for one moment, thought that I would be given that option. It just shows that I'm the eejit I always thought I was!' Both men laughed in delight. They walked on a bit further, then Dorchadas stopped and, looking at Douglas, said, 'But Doug, there is one sad thing. You saw Raphael whisper some words to me. Well, I'm sorry to say, but he told me that you and I won't be seeing each other again. At least, not until it is your time to cross over. I feel truly sad about that, Doug.'

Douglas felt the familiar grazing of grief against his soul and yet, in this blessed desert, sorrow was easier to bear. 'Well, Dorch,' he said. 'One thing I have learned in recent months is that grief, though horribly painful, is never without hope. If today is our last day of being together, then I must use this chance to say thank you. In these past months you have been my dearest friend. Literally, you have saved my life, and I shall always remember and be grateful. I shall miss you horribly, Dorch. But I shall never, ever forget you.'

'Aye, Doug,' said Dorchadas. 'And you know how much I want to thank you. As I said before, you have meant the world to me.' His countenance brightened a little as he said, 'And Doug, we've seen, haven't we, that the days every mortal is given to live on God's good Earth is only part of the whole, beautiful, glory-packed story. There's so much more isn't there? And that "much more" changes everything, don't you think? Even our sorrows.'

'Yes, Dorch,' said Douglas. 'Of that, I am now quite certain.' During their conversation the dove had alighted on the ground, but it now fluttered its wings and took to the air again and appeared to beckon them on. Dorchadas put his long arm around his friend as they followed its lead. Douglas, aware that this was to be his last journey with this friend, made the most of these moments of closeness, drawing into his soul, as deeply as he was able, the goodness, wisdom and love of his rugged angel friend. Then, after they had been silent for a while, Douglas paused and, stepping back, he looked up at Dorchadas and said, 'But Dorch, one thing. I never imagined an Archangel to be an old, dishevelled-looking man, sat in the desert, handing out mugs of wine.'

'You didn't?' said Dorchadas, raising one of his fulsome eyebrows. 'Well, Doug. We really are back where we started, aren't we? Back to imagination. Remember our first conversation in the pub: the wee lass, Emily Brontë, and her poem about imagination being the benignant power and all that. Yes?'

'Oh, yes, Dorch,' said Douglas. 'Of course. I do remember. But I think it really will take me a lifetime to learn to imagine with the kind of imagination you have.'

'Aye, lad,' said Dorchadas. 'It may do. That's not a bad project for a lifetime, though, when you come to think about it. But, my goodness, you have come a long, long way, Doug. Just look at where your imagination is now.' He put an arm around his shoulder and pulled him tight to himself.

At this point the dove stopped flying ahead of them and returned to the two friends and started to fly in circles around them. Douglas tried watching for a while, but to do so was making him dizzy. In fact, the dove was now starting to fly so fast that the breeze it created started to stir up the sand around them. It wasn't long before it felt like they were in a sandstorm. It was not a violent sandstorm, but in a curious way a very comforting storm, as if the sand was caressing and soothing them. Douglas closed his eyes and it felt as if he was now being caught up in the swirling sand. It was such an extraordinarily comforting feeling and, for a few moments, Douglas thought that it must be how a contented babe would feel in the womb.

He had not long to cherish that thought, because soon the sheer comfort of the experience led Douglas into a most blissful sleep. And because he was asleep, he never saw his angel friend plant a kiss on his forehead, then walk slowly away towards the distant hills, with his hands, as ever, firmly planted in the pockets of his faded jeans.

CHAPTER 27

The Priest

It was the smell of the thing which intrigued Pat. It was not unusual for a fog to suddenly breeze in from the sea, though he had never seen it come in as orange before. As it arrived and descended on the group, he stood up. He sensed it was something to greet, not fear. He noticed a brightness at the other side of the Reask compound and, feeling drawn to it, he left the group and made his way over to where the light was gathering - by the decorated standing stone that Alice had admired earlier. It was then that he became aware of the fragrance: a rich clover honey smell. Indeed, as he opened his mouth, he could also taste it. It truly was the most exquisite smell and flavour. In fact, it felt like all his senses were coming alive in a new intensity. Though the fog was dense, he felt he could see with great clarity. His listening was more acute and now he caught the soft sound of waves breaking on the seashore. He reached out his hand and the golden mist that was shimmering around the standing stone felt feathery soft. All this made him feel extraordinarily happy. No sea fog in his experience had ever affected him like this. It was most curious and most delightful.

He would gladly have stayed in this sensory mist for as long as it would have him, but it started to lift and he was both surprised and disturbed to see that he was no longer at Reask. The sound of the waves grew louder, and before long he saw their white flecked forms rolling in on the sand. As the air continued to clear, he could see exactly where he was. Quite how he had got here, he had no idea, but there was no doubt that he was standing at one end of Clogher Strand, the beautiful, open, wild sandy beach where once, when he was a teenager, he had come across the young Sarah Miles doing a recce before the filming of *Ryan's Daughter*. 'One of the most beautiful faces I have ever laid my eyes upon,' he said out loud, as he recalled the memory. 'Dear Lord, those eyes. Those dear, sad eyes.'

As the mist cleared completely, he noticed a sizeable gathering of people at the other end of the beach. He felt disappointed, as this was a place where he loved to be alone. Many a time he had come here. He only came out of season, when he would often be the only one here. Sometimes he would pace up and down on the sands as he wrestled with a pastoral issue. At other times, he would come just to take a break from his parish work, and he would clamber on to a rock and rest his eyes on the heaving surf. At other times, when he was sure he was alone, he stripped off and splashed and hollered in the crashing waves, delighting in the visceral vitality of the cold ocean. Yes, this was a beach for aloneness, not the encountering of a crowd of tourists. So, he turned around to walk in the opposite direction and there, walking towards him, ambled the familiar figure of Dorchadas.

'My, my, Dorch,' said Pat as they met. 'How, by all the saints, did we ever manage to make our way from the grass of Reask to the sands of Clogher Strand? And whatever was that golden cloud? I've never seen anything like it in these parts before. Do you have a clue as to what's going on? Because if anyone has a clue about this, it will be you, Dorch. Have I fallen into a dream?

'Well, Pat,' said Dorch, 'I can tell you one thing for sure, and that is, you are not in a dream. In fact, far from it.'

'Then, whatever are we in, Dorch?' he asked frowning. 'And what about the others? Are they still back at Reask, Dorch, or has the mist taken them off to other parts of the land? I'm especially worried for Kath, Dorch. She was looking none too well at the picnic.' For some reason, Dorchadas' arrival was causing many anxious questions to surface in Pat. The presence of this friend was giving him a live link to reality, which was making the whole experience more unnerving.

'Aye, Pat,' said Dorchadas. 'The others are back at Reask. And don't you be worried for Kath. But, Pat my friend, the truth is that this golden mist, as you call it, has opened doors for all of us. We've all been doing the travelling today.'

'Have you been somewhere then, Dorch?' asked Pat, slowly removing his glasses and pulling them to the rim of his jumper for their usual ineffective polish.

'Aye, I have, Pat,' said Dorchadas. 'Douglas and I found ourselves on a visit together...' Dorchadas paused as he spoke. Pat could see that he did not want to say much about whatever it was that had happened to him and Douglas. He watched the tall figure of his friend turn and look out to sea. 'Isn't the sea beautiful today, Pat?' he said.

'I'm sorry, Dorchadas,' said Pat, polishing his glasses hard on his jumper. 'I don't really understand all this. I'm really just a simple man, Dorch, you know. I wasn't cut out for all this mysterious business. I really wasn't.'

Pat returned his glasses to his face and looked at Dorchadas. He studied this friend, who seemed to be lost in his own thoughts, gazing out to sea. Pat felt he looked different, but couldn't quite say how. Dorchadas then turned to Pat and said, 'Pat, my dear friend. I just want to say thank you. Thank you for taking me in when you did. Without a shadow of hesitation, you took me into your home and gave me a warm meal and a bed. Thank you for allowing me to stay in your lovely home. You and Mrs McGarrigle have looked after me so well, you have. I couldn't have wanted for a better home. Truly.'

Pat could see there was a curious mix of joy and sadness in Dorchadas' eyes. 'Ah, I see,' said Pat. 'Dorch, my friend, you are on your way again, are you not?'

'That is the truth, Pat,' replied Dorchadas as he brushed back a lock of his hair that had blown into his face. 'In fact, to be fair,

I was on my way to somewhere else just now, but then I heard that you were visiting this shore.'

'Ah, so one last visit before you are off, then?' said Pat.

'That's it,' said Dorchadas.

'But you'll be back again, for sure, Dorch?' said Pat.

'No, Pat,' said Dorchadas. 'No, for you and me, my friend, today is goodbye.'

Pat frowned and he looked up at his friend through his furrowed brow and said, 'Oh, Dorch. You have become a dear, dear friend to me, you surely have. This is sad news indeed. I don't like to hear of such things. I'm surely going to miss you.' He paused for a few moments and then added, 'If the truth be told, Dorch, I think these last months with you lodging in my home, have been my happiest. I have you to thank for that, Dorch. I truly have.'

Dorchadas smiled at his priest friend and the two hugged each other as the breeze from the sea caused the sand to scurry past their feet. Then Dorchadas stepped back and said, 'Listen, my friend, I'm here because I have one last duty before I get on my way. So I best be getting on with it.'

'Och, don't let me be holding you up then, Dorch,' said Pat.

'Well, Pat,' said Dorchadas. 'The duty actually involves yourself.' He pulled at Pat's arm, and said, 'Come with me, old friend.' He turned and started to lead Pat in the direction of the crowd that was still gathered at the other end of the beach.

'Oh, no, Dorch,' protested Pat. 'I'm not really in the mood for meeting lots of new people today. I've never really been one for bantering with the tourists. I'd rather be getting back to the others up at Reask now, if you don't mind.'

'I know, Pat,' said Dorchadas. 'I know what you are like. But won't you just trust me for this?'

Pat looked at Dorchadas. Seldom had he known a truer and more honest friend. As he looked at the rugged, kindly face of the man who was gripping his arm, he knew this was a friend he could always trust. 'Very well,' he said. 'Whoever they all are, I'll say a quick "hello" to them and then be on my way.'

'Good man yourself, Pat,' said Dorchadas, and led Pat towards the group of people. As they got closer, the people turned to look at the two tall men walking towards them. Those in the crowd who had been sitting on the sand now stood up. Then, a man at the front started to clap. As soon as he did, others joined in and soon the whole crowd was clapping and cheering. Pat looked behind him to see who it was they were cheering. 'Dorch, is there some famous celebrity on this beach that I can't see? They seem mighty pleased with someone around here. Or is it you they're cheering? That must be it. And I don't blame them, Dorch.'

'Pat,' said Dorchadas chuckling. 'Don't you see? They are clapping and cheering *you*!'

'Cheering *me*?' said Pat, who stopped walking for a few moments. 'Now, why ever would anyone be wanting to clap an old shock of a priest like me?'

Dorchadas chuckled again, and led him on to the group. As they arrived at the assembly, the man who had started the applause, stepped forward and said, 'You remember me, Father?'

Pat looked at him and said, 'Why, in heaven's name, it's Pádraig! What in God's holy name are you doing here? I buried you over ten years ago!'

'Aye, that you did that, Father,' said Pádraig. 'And a fine job you made of it too. But do you remember how you came to me in hospital that day when I was so poorly. I was so afraid of the death, I was. I was in a terrible state. And in you came and sat on the bed, even though the matron had given you strict instructions not to. And you took my hand, you did. And you recited that twenty-third psalm and told me of the Shepherd that was Good, who was preparing something beautiful for me in Paradise. Then you leaned forward and placed your hand on my head - like this.' Pádraig lightly touched the top of his head, then continued, 'And you said a prayer, Father, that brought such light and peace to my troubled soul. And after your prayer, you got hold of me and held me tight while I sobbed out my fears and griefs on your shoulder. I swear, you left that hospital bed with your cassock half soaked in my tears. But when all the tears were shed, I was surely at peace. And less than ten minutes after you left, I stepped into the Glorious World and I was welcomed by the very Shepherd of that beautiful psalm. I can't thank you enough, Father.'

Pat was now struggling to hold back his own emotion, and simply grasped Pádraig's hand tight and smiled at him. Then a young woman came forward and said, 'Father Pat. You remember me, don't you?'

'Oh, aye,' said Pat. 'Dear Clare, how could I forget you, lass?'

'It was a long time ago now, Father,' said Clare. 'You were a young priest, but you came to my home when our Sarah was so sick.'

'Oh, little Sarah,' said Pat, his dark eyebrows furrowing in sorrow. 'She was such a sweet, wee thing. How we all sobbed our very hearts out at her wretched graveside that day. Oh, you poor soul, Clare.'

'Aye, we did, Father,' said Clare. 'But it was you who gave us comfort and such courage at that time. And look...' A young woman, who looked very much like Clare, came forward. 'Look, here is Sarah ,' said Clare.

The young woman came over and grasped the arm of her mother. 'I was that child, Father,' she said. 'I was desperately fearful, I was. For I knew my time on the Earth was coming to a close. But your visits to our home always gave me courage. You told such wonderful stories and always made me smile. And on the day when the angels came and took my hand, it was your voice I heard in my ears. And because it was a voice of love, I was able to make the crossing without fear. Thank you, Father.'

'And I have now joined our Sarah,' said Clare. 'We are together now in the world of Great Light that He opened for us.'

Clare and Sarah stepped back and others then stepped forward from the crowd, sharing similar testimonies of Pat's ministry to them. After about a dozen had spoken to Pat, Dorchadas said, 'And look, Pat. Look at all the others.' Pat looked at the crowd assembled on the beach, and he realised that it was no small crowd. Not by any means. 'Each one,' said Dorchadas, 'has come to say their thanks. Your ministry, dear friend, has worked wonders in this world. It truly has.' Dorchadas had known his own version of such unexpected accolades during his meeting with Gabriel at Golgotha. He therefore knew a little of how Pat was feeling.

Pat turned to Dorchadas and would have said something, had he not been stalled by the wretched pain in his chest, which always had a maddening habit of intruding into special moments such as these. Dorchadas took him by the arm again, and now led him away from the crowd towards the breaking surf of the incoming tide. 'Will I remember all this when I wake up, Dorch?' Pat asked, rubbing his chest. 'I sure would like to. That was a dear thing, that was, Dorch. I never thought... Well, well.'

'Of course,' said Dorchadas. 'But, Pat, you *are* awake, you know. The One you have served so faithfully sent all of them good people. It's not a dream. This is real. You have been a wonderful priest, my friend. You have served your Lord well. Have no fear.' For the first time in his life, Pat actually countenanced the thought that his ministry might have done some good in the lives of the people he was called to serve. Gone were all the voices that told him he was a failure. Instead, he nurtured an extraordinary sense of being valued. It was like being back at St.Seannach's isle on Easter Day, when he had met with Thomas. As they walked towards the sea, the fragrance of honey returned and the golden mist started to enfold them once more.

Pat inhaled the sweet fragrance, then said to his friend, 'We're returning, aren't we, Dorch?' The pain in his chest was growing more intense, so he reached out a hand and grasped the arm of Dorchadas.

'No,' said Dorchadas as the two stopped walking for a few moments. 'This journey is not about going back, Pat. We are going forward. That is what happened at that tomb on the day He burst out of it, showing the whole world that grim death would not have the last word in this beautiful and broken world. This is what we are touching today, Pat. We are touching the love that is stronger than death. So, my friend, this is your day of being born into glory. Can you feel it, Pat?'

'I can, Dorch,' said Pat, almost in a whisper. 'I can. I truly can. It's curious, Dorch. But I feel… I feel free, Dorch. Yes, it's a freedom, it is. And the pain in my chest has gone now, Dorch. You know, I think there has been a healing in this old chest of mine.' He chuckled for a few moments, then added, 'No, you are right. I'm feeling much better, I am.' He looked around him and was blinking hard, as if he had just walked from a dark room into bright sunlight. 'I'm glad we're not returning just yet, Dorch,' he said, nodding his head. 'This is the kind of place where I'd like to settle myself for a wee while. Yes, this is a settling place, it is. Let's get a bit closer to the waters over there.'

'Come, old friend,' said Dorchadas. Pat was still firmly grasping Dorchadas' arm. With his free hand, he took off his glasses and held them loosely by his side. He never noticed them dropping silently onto the sand beside him. Together the two friends walked through the feathery and fragrant mist of gold towards the welcoming, vibrant and endless ocean.

CHAPTER 28

The first thing Alice noticed when she woke up was the feel of the grass beneath her. It had lost its velvety loveliness. The second thing she noticed was that she had lost the clear eyesight that she had known in the enhanced form of her beloved Morwenstow that she had just visited with her aunt. She felt a sense of loss and sorrow as, once again, her view of the world was restricted. However, she could see well enough, and she noticed that the mysterious golden mist had dispersed. A seagull squawked overhead as it flew dreamily over the ancient ruins. There was no wind. The land was silent.

Alice sat up and realised that she had moved from the cell where they had all picnicked. She was in some open ground nearby. Mavis was fast asleep on the grass not far from her. Alice smiled at the gentle snores and noticed a look of contentment on the face of her aunt, that, more often than not ,presented as anxious. She got to her feet quietly so as to not disturb her and looked around. The mist had completely dispersed now and a warm sun was shining from a sky that was decorated with only a few clouds. She saw that the picnic site was deserted and the members of the group had scattered to different locations within the compound.

The first people she saw were the three Americans, who were lying near the outer wall of a large double clochán not far from where she was. She smiled at the sight of young Rosa, lying with her arm around Daisy. She walked to the other side of the compound and, at the remains of the oratory, she saw the figure of Kevin asleep in the doorway. She drew closer and peered inside, and there was the rest of the family - Kath, Peter, Elsie, Nancy and Brí - all asleep on the grass. She noticed that Kath's wheelchair was not there, and, knowing how weak she was at the picnic, wondered how she had made her way across the grass to this oratory.

She was keen to find the others, and as she surveyed the compound she noticed the tall decorated standing stone that she and Douglas had admired earlier. Lying peacefully next to it was Father Pat. She walked passed him quietly so as not to stir him. Then to her delight, she saw the figure of Douglas, asleep in a smaller clochán, not far from the gate through which they had entered just a few hours previously. She entered the low-walled clochán and rested her eyes on Douglas. To her, even with her limited eyesight, he looked more handsome, more at peace and, though sleeping, more alive than she had ever seen him. She tried not to disturb him as she sat down next to him on the shingle, but, as she settled herself down on the grass, he awoke. He blinked a few times and looked around him. When he saw Alice, he smiled, and pulled himself up.

'How did I get over here?' he asked.

'I've no idea,' said Alice. 'But we're all spread out around the place. None of us are in the cell where we had our picnic.'

'I've been…' said Douglas, still blinking a bit. 'I couldn't begin to explain it to you, Alice.'

'I know,' said Alice. 'Me too. Either there was something in those cakes that Elsie made for us, or we have been in one of Dorchadas' things. I wonder if the others have also been travelling? Sounds like some people are waking up.' They could hear the sound of Rosa's voice talking excitedly to Daisy and Frank.

Alice said, 'Douglas, my love?'

'What is it?' asked Douglas. He could see anxiety in Alice's eyes.

'I was the first to wake up, and I've been round the whole place,' said Alice. 'In the oratory just over that wall is Kath and her family.'

'Are they OK?' asked Douglas.

'Well, most of them are, I think,' said Alice. She lowered her voice and said, 'But I think maybe Kath has... you know... passed on.'

'Ah...' said Douglas, and he slowly nodded his head. 'Maybe this is why she wanted us all to come here for the picnic. Perhaps she had a premonition that this would be the place where she would leave us.'

'The others will be so shocked, though, when they wake up,' said Alice. She was going to say more, but was then distracted as she noticed the tall figure of Nancy standing up. Both Douglas and Alice watched her stretch for a few moments. Then, stepping over her sleeping brother, Nancy left the ancient oratory. When she saw Alice and Douglas, she made her way over to them.

'Are you all right, Nancy?' asked Alice.

'Sorry about the Prosecco,' said Nancy. 'Afraid it's gone.'

'What about your family?' asked Douglas. 'Are they OK?'

'Yea,' said Nancy. 'Still asleep, I think.'

'And what about your mother?' asked Alice, frowning with concern.

'Fast asleep,' said Nancy. She then caught sight of Rosa and galumphed over the grass to meet her.

Douglas and Alice looked at each other and Alice said, 'I think we had better check.' She took Douglas' hand and they walked somewhat nervously towards the oratory. As they arrived at the low-walled enclosure, they noticed Kevin stirring from his sleep.

'So, we're back,' he said as he pulled himself up. 'Did anything strange happen to you guys?' he asked.

Alice and Douglas were about to reply when they heard Brí calling anxiously to her mother, 'Ma! Mammy! Will you wake up? Please!'

The sound of Brí's voice was enough to wake Elsie, who opened her eyes wide and exclaimed, 'Holy mother of God, where are we now?'

Peter, who was lying next to Kath, also stirred suddenly and turned immediately to Kath and, placing his hand over hers, said, 'Oh, Kath, love.' He looked at Brí and said, 'Did we all have the same vision? Were you there at the tomb, Brí?'

'Aye, I was,' replied Brí.

'And me,' said Kevin, coming over to where his mother was lying on the grass.

'We all saw it, didn't we?' said Brí.

'Aye, we did,' said Peter and closed his eyes firmly for a few moments as he feared the worst for Kath.

'What's up with my sister?' said Elsie. 'Why is she not waking up? Oh, holy angels of God, have mercy…'

Douglas and Alice looked at each other. Clearly the family group had entered some kind of corporate vision. But what was becoming disturbingly clear was that Kath was not waking.

'You dudes all waking up?' came Frank's voice from behind them. Daisy, Rosa and Nancy were with him and they peered over the low walls of the oratory ruin.

Peter said, 'Yes, we are all waking up, but our Kath here is still resting.'

Peter was about to say more, when Kath's eyes opened and she said, 'Who says I'm still resting?' The first thing they all noticed was that she spoke with her normal voice, not with the hoarse whisper of recent weeks. 'Did you all think I was as dead as a leg of mutton, then?' she asked as she sat up.

'Oh, Kath, my darling,' said Peter and wrapped his arms around her. There was a flurry of activity around the seated Kath for a time and eventually Kevin said, 'Look, we need to be careful of Ma. We're crowding her. Mammy, tell us, please. How are you feeling? Can I fetch you your chair?'

Kath, still sitting on the shingle, looked around at them and said, 'Well, if you must know I'm feeling pretty good. To be fair, better than I've felt for some time.'

'But Mammy,' said Brí, 'we saw you and Peter go into that tomb, and we…'

Kath looked at Peter and smiled, then said, 'Oh, aye, we went into that tomb all right. Some tomb it was too, was it not, Peter?' Peter smiled at his wife.

'And what happened?' said Elsie. 'Will you tell us what went on in that tomb?' She was starting to get cramp, so she reached out her hand to Kevin who helped her to her feet.

'What tomb are we talking about?' asked Mavis who had also awoken and had come over to join the group. 'Whose been visiting a tomb, then? I'm none too keen on tombs, I have to say. They're not healthy by my reckoning. They're things to keep well clear off.'

Brí quickly reassured Mavis, then explained to the group the remarkable vision that her family had witnessed including the tomb in the Garden of the Resurrection. As each person present had also experienced their own vision, no-one found it hard to believe.

Kath looked at Peter and said, 'I'm not for sitting on this rough shingle much longer, Peter. This shingle is nipping at my backside. Help me up and then tell them all what happened.'

Peter helped Kath up and, much to the surprise of all those watching, she had no difficulty standing on her own two feet. She leaned back against the wall and said, 'Go on Peter, darling. Tell them what was in that shiny tomb.'

'Oh, Kath. I don't think I will ever be able to tell what we saw in that tomb,' he said. 'What words would you use to describe it? All I can say it was a place of… Well, what would you say, Kath?'

'You're right,' answered Kath. 'There's no point in chasing after the words, Peter, love. They won't be found. Not in this world at any rate. Let's just say it was something like the most perfect place you could ever imagine. Even that doesn't do it justice. But you can tell we liked it.'

'Aye. We certainly liked it, Kath,' said Peter. The sunlight glinted on his round-rimmed spectacles as he continued, 'And for those of you who weren't there, I have to tell you that there was this stunning, shining creature of light...'

'More than stunning,' interjected Nancy. 'Made me cry, it did. Couldn't help it.'

'Me too,' added Brí. 'I've just never, ever...' She shook her head at the memory of the wonder.

'Well,' continued Peter, 'I wanted to make a request of the creature of light, you see.'

'A request?' asked Daisy. 'What kind of request?'

'Peter,' piped up the young voice of Rosa who had been listening intently to the conversation. 'Did you ask the great shining creature to heal Kath?' asked Rosa. 'Like my Aunt Daisy was healed by the great light of heaven? Was that your request?'

'Yes, that's just it, Rosa,' said Peter, nodding at the girl. The glinting sun on his spectacles gave the impression that he was connected with some current of electricity. 'I wasn't sure if we were allowed to ask that kind of thing. But I had no doubts about where we were. I knew absolutely that we were in the garden where Christ rose up from his grave. And there we were - at the very grave where it all happened! I mean, it sounds impossible, doesn't it? But it felt... well, sort of natural when were there. Natural, but also awesome, of course. And I thought, "if there's anywhere you can ask for a miracle, this is surely the place."'

'Well, I agree with you there, Peter,' interjected Elsie. 'About the place being both natural and awesome. And I had also guessed it was the holy Garden our Lord's rising. But I wasn't thinking about miracles. I was thinking, that if we were at the grave of our Lord, then the only reason we would be there would be for the passing of our Kath from this world to the next. And, if I'm honest, I got to feeling mighty sad. But you know, it wasn't just the sadness, because for the first time in my life, I got to seeing that there was a real world to move on to after this one. And I thought, "Well, if that's where Kathleen is heading, she could be a lot worse off. She'll be all right, she will" I thought.' She then looked at Kath and added, 'But, by the look of you, it seems you're not heading there just yet, sister.'

'Aye,' responded Kath. 'Bad luck, Elsie, love. Looks like you've got to put up with me for a wee bit longer yet.'

There was a ripple of laughter in the group, after which Peter said, 'I believe, Elsie, that you were exactly right. That was what was supposed to happen. It was the appointed time for Kath to leave us. But, you see, as I looked at that extraordinary creature of light, I felt not afraid but, curiously, very safe. I really don't know what this creature was, but I knew it was somehow part of the story of His rising, and a question to the creature was a question that would be heard in Paradise. And I felt Paradise would not be offended if I asked it any question. In fact, I felt this strong sense that Paradise really wants to know all our requests, and that it would be wrong not to ask. So, once inside that tomb, I made my request. I asked if Kath could be made well and given longer in this world.'

'Aye, you certainly did, Peter, love,' said Kath. 'And given the situation, I thought you put it very well. You were very clear, you were. I was most impressed.'

'And so what happened?' asked Douglas.

'I don't rightly know,' said Peter. 'Do you remember, Kath?'

'No,' said Kath. 'No, actually, I don't really remember much after you made your little speech. I just felt... Well... I felt so peaceful. Yes... Just really peaceful. I guess I just went off to sleep. Next thing I knew I was being woken from my sleep by you lot hollering at me.'

'So, you better, then, Mammy?' asked Nancy. 'You not dying anymore?'

'I don't know, love,' answered Kath. 'All I know is that just at this minute, I feel a whole load better now than I have done for months. I'd best get down to the Doctor and get her to check me out, then we can see what's going on. But, I get the impression that you'll all have to reckon on me being around for a while yet.'

There was another flurry of excitement as Kath's family started to take in the real possibility that the mother, wife and sister they thought they were so close to losing, had been returned to them in good health. Brí was about to wrap her arms around her mother, but Kath said, 'Let me just say one thing, though, before you all suffocate me with your hugging. I've seen things today that means I will never be afraid to die now. When my time does come, I now know where I'm heading. And I can tell you it is some special place. And the One I used to mock and curse, is the One who will welcome us all home one day. That's something to look forward to, it surely is.' And as she said this, everyone nodded. Indeed, everyone had witnessed a world that had taken from them all fear of death. 'Mind you,' Kath added, turning her head to one side. 'I was hoping to see my friend Brigid. Couldn't spy her there. I guess I'll just have to wait 'til it really is my time to step over.'

'Whose Brigid?' asked Rosa.

'Oh, sorry, love,' said Kath, smiling at the young girl. 'I'll tell you about her one day. I think you'd love her, you would.'

'But where's Dorchadas, for goodness sakes?' said Kevin as he suddenly realised Dorchadas was missing.

'Ah,' said Douglas. 'I was with Dorch.'

'You were, son?' said Elsie. 'What's become of him, then? I didn't like the way he was talking in recent weeks.'

'I know, Elsie,' said Douglas. 'It is true. He did believe his time on Earth as a human was coming to an end. Well, I think that may now have changed. I don't honestly know. But it sounded to me like he was given more work to do in this world as the Dorch we know and love. But when he will return, who knows? And where, for that matter? Could be any place or any time. That's just who Dorch is.'

'Och, I wish he wouldn't just vanish like he does,' said Elsie. 'I'd like to wish the fella a proper farewell. He's done us all so much good he has. It's never the same when he's not around.'

Others were about to speak about Dorchadas, but they were interrupted by a call from the standing stone. They could only see the top part of it as their view was blocked by a low wall. But they could clearly see Daisy and Frank beside it. Frank was beckoning them. 'Father Pat's asleep there,' said Alice. The group made their way to the stone and, when they passed the low wall, they beheld the figure of the somnolent priest at the base of the stone.

As Kevin saw him, he said quietly, 'Oh that man works mighty hard, he does. I think we should let the poor man sleep for a while. He's exhausted, most likely. We can pack up the picnic in the meantime.'

Daisy was looking hard at him and frowning. She said, 'I'm not sure he's asleep...'

Frank knelt down next to him and touched his hand. He looked up at Douglas and said, 'Doug. I'm not sure this guy is with us anymore.' Douglas joined Frank on the grass and checked for a pulse, then, looking at Frank, shook his head slowly.'

'What's up with our priest?' asked Elsie, grasping hold of Brí's arm.

Daisy's eyes were filling up as she said, 'I think he may have left us, Elsie, sweetheart.'

'Oh, by all the holy saints of Ireland, that can't be,' said Elsie crossing herself. 'The man's our priest. He can't be leaving us now. He was perfectly well at the picnic. Oh, I hope to God it wasn't the cake!'

'Och, leave him alone,' said Kath, who was standing just behind Elsie. 'The dear man has a right to step over when his time's come. Look at his face, now.' They all studied the figure of the priest, lying on his back on the fresh, green turf. One arm was cradling the base of the standing stone. The other arm was laid across his chest, with his hand over his heart. There was no sign of his glasses. On his face, which was turned towards the soft hills beyond, was a smile. It was the kind of smile that he would so readily throw into a room, before some inner anxiety would cause him to quickly withdraw it. But this time, the smile had remained on his face. He looked like a man utterly at peace with himself, with his world, and with his God.

Elsie, who was now weeping freely, said through her tears, 'Such a dear man and wonderful priest. But I've caught a wee glimpse of the world he's stepped into. He'll take to that place, I'm sure of that. He'll have none of his worries, there.' She turned to Douglas and said, 'Douglas, love. Would you do a blessing for him? You loved his dear heart. The poor man needs a blessing, he does. The poor, dear man.' She pulled a hanky to her face and blew her nose loudly.

Douglas also felt deeply sad at the loss of this priest, for whom he had developed a great respect and fondness. He reached out and with his thumb, he made the sign of the cross on Pat's forehead. 'Patrick, our dear friend and priest,' he said. 'Go now from this broken world that you have loved so much. Go now, in the name of the Father your Creator, the Son who was your Friend, and the Spirit who was your delight. Be healed of all your fears and released from all your woes. Enter now into the joy of your Lord, you good and faithful servant.' He then bent over Pat and kissed him lightly on the forehead. Kevin also knelt down and embraced him, and others in the group followed.

Rosa watched with interest, then whispered to Daisy, 'Aunt Daisy, I ain't ever seen a dead man before.'

'No, honey?' said Rosa, putting an arm around her niece and holding her tight. 'So how does he look to you?'

'I'm not frightened,' said Rosa. 'I thought I would be. I thought it would be really spooky. But look at him. He looks like he has seen something so beautiful, that he would never want to turn around and come back to this world again.'

'I feel the same,' said Daisy. She then added, 'Darling, Rosa. What a day this is turning out to be.' Rosa nodded and squeezed herself closer to her aunt. She closed her eyes, and saw once again in her mind's eye the sequoia forest. She could smell the pine and hear the crunch of the snow. She felt that, as long as she could always bring this blessed scene back to mind, she would never have any reason to be afraid ever again.

It was a very different party that packed up the picnic to the one that arrived at Reask only a few hours earlier. Kevin had called for the ambulance which soon arrived, and the body of the deceased priest was placed on a stretcher and carried away.

Elsie distracted herself by packing up the remains of the sandwiches and cakes. But her constant sniffing betrayed her sadness.

'Well, at least he enjoyed a few of those cheese sandwiches of yours before he left us, Elsie,' said Kath to her sister as Brí picked up the last of the picnic boxes and took them to the car.

'Aye,' said Elsie. 'And he had a good helping of one of my pies too. I like to think of him going off on a full stomach.' She paused for a moment and then looked up at her sister and said, 'But look at you, Kathleen. There you are, standing up as right as rain. I can't believe what I'm looking at. I honestly thought it would be you that we'd be putting under the turf, not Father Pat here.'

'Well,' said Kath. 'It looks like you're not going to get rid of your younger sister that easily. I've been hit by a power today, Elsie. And that power sure has done wonders to this old body of mine.'

'Hm..' said Elsie looking at her as she placed a hand on her hip. 'That it might have. But whatever happened to you today, it's done nothing for that weight you're carrying. Work to be done yet, sister, I'd say. Work to be done.' Kath looked at her with a terse look. Then a broad smile spread across her face, which soon turned into a laugh that resonated around the ruins. And for the first time in many months, she was able to laugh without coughing. Elsie was also laughing, but soon the laughter was replaced by tears of relief, wonder and delight, and the two sisters clung tight to each other as the May sun shone warmly upon them and upon the dark stones of the ancient walls that enfolded them.

CHAPTER 29

News of Father's Pat's death within the ancient walls of Reask on Ascension Day spread fast around the town. There were conversations in shops and on the streets about the suddenness of his passing, and messages and tributes appeared on social media. There was a wide consensus that the town had lost a much-beloved priest. The bishop was immediately informed but regretted he could not take the service as he was on a sabbatical visit to Australia. Those close to Pat were relieved at this news as Pat never got on particularly well with the hierarchy. They were pleased to discover that Father Lucas, a neighbouring priest and good friend of Pat's was able to take the service. The funeral mass had been set for just a week and a day after Pat's death.

Alice had been due to return back to England only two days after the picnic, but she decided to stay with Douglas to be with him for the service. Mavis, not wanting to return on her own, also decided to remain in Ireland for a little longer. Frank was also in a quandary. He and the family were also due to fly home the weekend after the picnic, but he, Daisy and Rosa all wanted to stay around for Pat's funeral. After some hasty phone calls, texts and emails, they had managed to alter plans and change flights so that they could stay for the service. This put Elsie into something of a spin, as she had other guests booked into St.Raphael's. However, as she knew all the other Guest House proprietors in town, she was soon able to transfer them to different accommodation.

Thus it was that the group, that had experienced the extraordinary Ascension picnic together, were able to assemble at the church on a blustery May morning for Pat's service. The church was packed with people coming not just from the town, but from nearby villages to honour their priest. Pat was duly honoured by several tributes. After the service at the wake in a local hotel, Kath said, 'Well I didn't recognise the saint they were all heralding in them tributes. He was a good deal more human than they made him out to be, and thank God for that.'

'Aye, that's the truth, Ma,' agreed Kevin. 'He sure was a man who understood the stuff we mortals are made of.'

'He did that,' said Kath. 'But at the same time, he was a man in whose wounded eyes the shafts of heaven shone.'

'I can't disagree with that, sister,' said the sniffing Elsie. 'He was the most holy and most human priest I've known. And for my money, that's just what a priest should be.'

The wake continued long into the evening and they all felt that Pat would have gladly pardoned them for the hangovers most of them nursed the next day.

Kath's sudden and remarkable recovery was also the talk of the town. Some of the less charitable folk suggested that she hadn't been as ill as she had said she was. A few of pessimistic nature spoke eloquently of the risks of getting over-excited, and how this remission would soon pass. But, generally speaking, most people in Dingle were used to lives shaped by legend and touched with wonder, and were therefore not surprised that one of their own should have been visited by a miracle.

With most of the group leaving on Monday, Kath had the idea of a gathering together for a final lunch on Sunday which happened to be the feast of Pentecost. All agreed this would be an excellent idea and they duly booked a table for thirteen at *The Angel's Rest.* As it happened, this Sunday turned out to be another glorious sunny day, so Oonagh recruited Douglas, Frank and Kevin to set up a table in the beer garden, which was just big enough to manage the group. On a day of sunshine, the courtyard was the most enchanting place for a family lunch party. On a couple of sides of the courtyard rose the high red-brick walls of neighbouring buildings that reached up to weather-worn chimney stacks. A wild lemon-white rose with a sweet fragrance sprawled over much of one wall. On the other two sides of the courtyard there were lower walls mostly covered in ivy. Other plants clung to the mortar between the bricks . A somewhat dilapidated arbour shaded one corner, from which hung a flourishing wisteria. The courtyard was also filled with pots of every description, each one filled with bright geraniums, Oonagh's favourite flower.

After the Pentecost Mass, everyone made their way to the pub. Most of the group collected a Guinness on their way to the lunch table and they sat in the sunshine sipping from their glasses as they recollected the events of recent days. Oonagh brought in a steaming pot of stew and bowls full of mashed potato and vegetables, and Elsie served them all. Frank said a grace and they all set to work on the excellent lunch.

Towards the end of lunch, as they were scraping their plates from the range of sweets that Oonagh had provided, Douglas tapped on a glass and the group fell silent. 'I know I'm one of the visitors here...' he began.

He was interrupted by Kath who said, 'You most certainly are not, son. Like it or not, you are one of the family here and that's not going to change, I can assure you.' There were lots of ‘Hear, hear’s from the family.

Douglas felt full of emotion as he thanked Kath. 'I'll try to continue,' he said. 'Firstly, I think we should give a round of applause to Oonagh who has fixed us such a great meal today.' Oonagh was duly summoned and came out to the courtyard, red-faced from her labours in the kitchen and wiping her hands on her apron. She beamed at the group as they all cheered her.

'Next,' said Douglas, as Oonagh departed back to the bar, 'I thought each of us might just like to say something before - sadly - our group breaks up tomorrow when some of our friends have to leave us.'

'Shame!' called Kevin, banging his hand on the table. 'You must all stay here!' he cried, and others chimed in agreement with him.

Frank was the first to speak. He stood up and said, 'Guys, I don't know how to say this. But this trip for me has… well, let's just say I'm never going to be the same again. I know I look like a strong guy. I played pretty good as the Offensive Tackle and I can do mean and tough. But ask Daisy here, and she'll tell you that there's a little boy in here that's been pretty darned wounded. I don't mind telling you all, because I feel safe with each and every one of you. Now, I've had some experiences these past days that I will never forget. We all went somewhere special when that golden mist came down upon us and my, my… All I want to say is that in those precious moments I received a balm from heaven that has made its way to some of the most hurting places of my soul. And I sure give thanks for that.'

Douglas, who was sitting next to Frank, reached out and squeezed his large forearm. 'Thanks, Douglas, my man,' said Frank. 'But now I'm going to give you some bad news: I'm gonna preach a sermon.'

'Oh, no, honey,' said Daisy, who was sitting next to him. 'Do you honestly have to? You're still on holiday.'

Everyone chuckled as Frank replied with his big smile, 'Darling, the good news is that this is going to be the shortest sermon you ever heard me preach! What I want to say is this. Today is the feast of Pentecost, and Pentecost is when those followers of Christ got the Holy Ghost. And my, they got the Holy Ghost big time. And as far as I can see, the first thing that seems to have happened then is that they became a family. A *real* family. And my preach is this: that you know the Holy Ghost is working among you when you see the kind of family that we have become. 'Cos look at us: black and white; English, Irish and American; older, younger and some in the middle; female, male; straight, gay; rich, poor…'

'And people like me,' interrupted Nancy.

'Och, Nancy,' said Brí, grasping her hand.

'And each and every one of us, Nancy,' continued Frank. 'Each one of us so different, and yet bound together in this little back yard of a town that most of the world has never heard of. And here we have been visited by the Holy Ghost. And man, I feel this is how the world is truly meant to be, with none of those hurtful walls that we build against each other. Now what we have here is a whole heap of love, and that's worth something special. And that's the end of the sermon. Amen.' And with that, Franklin sat down, and there were cheers and applause.

Rosa put up her hand and asked, 'Uncle Frank?'

'Yes, sweetheart,' replied Frank.

'Uncle Dorchadas said that Reask was once a monastery which was a very special kind of family. Do you think we are now a monastery?'

'Rosa, my love,' said Frank. 'I think that's exactly what we are. Not the kind folks usually think of. But the kind that is the family of the Spirit.'

'I thought so,' said Rosa.

Then somewhat to people's surprise, it was Mavis who stood up next and said, 'Well, now. I'm not going to make a big speech and I am certainly no preacher, that's for sure. But all I know is that I came here a few days back with... well... my own worries and sorrows and what have you. But up at that Reask place when we were all... you know. Well, things changed for me, they did. And... Oh, Alice, I don't know how to say things like you do, but you understand, don't you?'

'Yes, Aunt,' said Alice smiling.

'Well,' continued Mavis. 'I just also want to say that these past days have been the happiest of my life. And I want to thank you all.' With that, she sat down, pulling a hanky from her sleeve and blew her nose hard. Elsie reached over and squeezed her shoulder.

It was Kevin who stood next and spoke. 'Dear God, what can I say about the recent months since Douglas breezed into our town last October? You all know, I've been a violent man in the past and I have done so much I shouldn't have. God knows where I'd be now if it wasn't for all of you - and Father Pat, of course, God rest him. And Dorch - oh, I wish that eejit were here now.'

'Och, I do too,' added Kath.

Kevin looked down for a few moments, scratching his head. He then continued, 'Me and Doug and Dorch had a chat a wee while ago, and it was something that Dorch said about heaven that touched me, it did. I mean, we all had a taste of it up at Reask, don't you think?' There were various nods and murmurs of affirmation. 'Well, in the curious and remarkable visits that Dorch has had a hand in arranging, something extraordinary has happened in this soul of mine. Dorch said it was something about coming home. Something about being who you're meant to be in this life. And I guess that's what's happening to me now. That can't be bad, can it?' He looked for reassurance to the group who were all nodding at him. 'But the thing is, I couldn't have got where I am now without each and every one of you here. You people have forgiven me and loved me back to life. Thanks a million to all of you. That's all I want to say.' He lifted his glass, smiling his wounded smile and all raised theirs to him.

Bríana was the next to get to her feet and she said, 'Oh, my! Where do I begin?'

'Keep it short, love,' said Kath, then winked at her daughter.

'Thanks Mother,' said Brí smiling. 'Like my brother, I've had troubles in my life. Many of mine are of my own making. And, as you all know, my Mammy and me have had our fights. But this last week all that has changed. We have much to thank Father Pat for, Mammy, don't we?'

Kath looked at her daughter and said, 'Aye, lass, we do. He gave us a hand up when we needed it.'

'Well,' continued Brí, briefly running her hand through her hair, 'I've also visited a place that had something to do with Paradise, and catching sight of that has made me realise that my view of this world has been, frankly, a very dull one. I now see so many new possibilities and I feel a sense of wonder has returned to my soul. Things that I once thought impossible, now look within reach. Now, to be truthful, I've never been that fond of God. And when I took to loving a woman rather than a man, well, I felt then that God and his followers would be done with me for good. But in recent days I've revised my views a little. I've discovered that in all those years when I wasn't fond of God He, in fact, was actually quite fond of me. And it wasn't the vision at Reask that taught me that. It was just being with all of you these few days. You've given me something so precious, and I'm so grateful.'

'So, do you like God now?' piped up the voice of Rosa.

'Why, Rosa,' said Brí looking at her little friend, 'Thanks to you all, I think that it is possible that me and God might just start getting along. Let's see. Bless you.' And with that, Brí reached across Peter to grasp her mother's hand for a few moments while the others clapped her.

Peter then stood up and, as he did so, he fiddled with his spectacles, then loosened his tie. 'I'm a shy man, I don't mind saying,' he said. 'So, my speech will be very short. But I agree with Franklin. There is without doubt a little child in me who is also "pretty darned wounded", as you put it, Frank. And he's been a lonely child, I don't mind admitting. In fact, in many ways I've felt alone most of my life. But by God's grace I have found my Kathleen again, and...' He paused to master the emotion that was rising in him. Then, looking at Kath, he said 'And I thought I had lost you... But my darling, you're back with us.' He removed his spectacles briefly, then said, 'But yes, Frank. I agree. This community is what it's all about. This is how it should be. I'm not lonely here. This is where we come sharing our broken humanity with each other. And it's where, together, we keep an eye on Paradise, which doesn't mind if we sometimes ask for a miracle to help us journey through this precious life of ours. This is indeed Pentecost. Thank you.' He quickly sat down, and Kath placed her arm around him and kissed him.

Rosa then put her hand up and said, 'Please may I speak?'

Almost everyone at the table said, 'Of course' or words to that effect. Rosa stood up and, for a moment, looked hard at the table, pressing her lips together. She then looked at Daisy and said, 'Aunt Daisy, I don't know what to say,' and giggled.

'Go on, honey' said Daisy, and gripped her hand. Nancy, who was sitting the other side of her, reached over and briefly rubbed her back.

'Well,' said Rosa after taking a deep breath. 'I've very much enjoyed my holiday.' She smiled her beguiling smile. 'I kinda want to stay here for rest of my life now, but I also want to go home. I know I've got things to do now. You all know that me and Aunt Daisy and Uncle Frank met with Rosa Parks who is the nicest lady you'll ever meet. And she said some cool things about me and my Mom and Papa. I'm never going to forget what she said. So I think that's all I need say, really.' She was just about to sit down, when she quickly added, looking around at all at the table, 'Oh, and of course, I love this monastery and I'll never forget any of you.' With that, she sat down and beamed at every one as they applauded her.

Daisy then stood up, continuing to hold Rosa's hand as she did. 'I don't know where to begin,' she said. 'Like Kath here, I was staring death in the face only a short time ago. But here I am on vacation in Ireland with my hair growing back and my body getting strong again. I have seen things these past months that I never knew existed. But among the wonders I have seen, is meeting you all. We will always be bound together because of our Ascension experience. Each one of you has given me something so precious. Oh, listen. I'm not one for speeches. All I want to do is to thank you all.' She waved at everyone and sat down. Rosa got off her seat and sat on her aunt's knee.

At that point Elsie and Kath, who were sitting next to each other, both started to stand up. They looked at each other and Kath said to her sister, 'Well, are you going to say something, or am I?'

'Oh, for God's sakes, you go,' said Elsie and sat down.

'Please yourself, then' said Kath, and got to her feet. 'Well, now. What does a woman who has pretty much returned from the grave say? I don't rightly know how to put this. But I'm going to pick on you now, Douglas. This English priest,' she said pointing across the table at Douglas, 'came over to Ireland last autumn and, for reasons I'll never know, I decided to tell him the story of me and Peter and all the stuff that happened after that. Now, Doug, I know your life was a busted wreck at the time. But you know, son, the thing is this: despite the fact that you were hurting so much yourself, you listened to me gobbing on about my troubles. You *really* listened. And later on, you helped me with that old Venerable Oakenham. You remember?'

Douglas smiled and said, 'Kath, how could I ever forget that day!'

'Aye,' said Kath chuckling. 'But the thing is this. I've had a mighty journey of healing, I have. Healing of mind, heart and body. And it took one person to stop and listen to get the whole thing started in me. So, I want to thank you for that, Douglas. And when we all say you are one of the family, we really mean it. You know that, don't you, son?'

Before Douglas could acknowledge Kath, Elsie stood up and said, 'Well, if anyone is going to grab Douglas for a son, it'll be me, thank you very much.' She reached over and clasped Douglas' hand. 'He's been staying in my home these past months,' she said, 'And as far as I'm concerned, you can stay here as long as you like. Mind you,' she added, 'I have noticed that a certain young lady from the County of Devon has been catching your attention of late, so I have my doubts that you'll be wanting to stay at my home for ever.' Douglas and Alice looked at each other and smiled.

'Anyway,' continued Elsie, 'Being as I'm now on my feet, let me have my say. These past few months - since you arrived in our wee town, Douglas - have been strange ones, they surely have. What with Douglas diving into the sea like he did, and the car chase up the hill, my sister getting back together with her childhood sweetheart and then getting the cancer and frightening us all to death. And then the wonders at Reask that we'll none of us ever forget. And then losing our priest. It's been quite a few months, has it not? But I just want to say through all the ups and downs of it, something has gone on in my heart that I can't rightly explain. But I know there's been a healing, and I'm mighty glad of it. And I look around this table and each one of you has had a part to play in it. I can't tell you how grateful I am. And...' Her eyes started to redden as she looked at Kath and continued, 'And, I have my sister back. God has given you back to us, sweetheart. I just want to say, for all my blather, I do love you so much and I thank God for the miracle I thought could never happen.' And with that she reached out and grasped Kath's hand and with much sniffing she sat down.

Alice wiped her mouth with her serviette, then stood up. Douglas squeezed her hand briefly and then she spoke. 'I'm a real outsider here.' There were several objections, after which Alice continued. 'Long, long ago,' she said, 'My pa and I had a favourite place we used to go to on the north Cornish coast. We would sit on the cliff top and he'd tell me about a young Irish girl called

Morwenna who came over to Cornwall from Ireland. Morwenna is my second name, and she is someone I have always loved. And my pa would often tell me that one day he would take me to Ireland, her homeland. Well, sadly my pa died young and he could never take me. But this man here,' she nudged Douglas, 'invited me over. And the moment I stepped foot in your beautiful land I felt at home. I came for the first time last autumn, and now I have been back here these past few weeks. There has been more healing in my soul these past few days than I ever thought possible. Thank you for making me so welcome. And yes, Frank, I so agree with you. I feel that beautiful Holy Spirit at work in us all, drawing us together. Wherever I'm taken in life, I shall always see Dingle as a place I can call home. Thank you.' She quickly sat down, and reached for Douglas' hand as everyone applauded.

'Well, I suppose I should say something, ' said Douglas.

'Don't feel you have to,' said Frank teasingly. 'You're a worse preacher than me, don't forget!' He laughed his heaving laugh and Douglas laughed with him.

'Frank,' said Douglas. 'You have done all the preaching that needs to be done today. I'm just going to say one thing.' He took a deep breath and reached down touching the table for a few moments. Then, looking back up, he said, 'Seven months ago I came here as a complete wreck. I'd lost my beloved wife, my faith and my mind. I arrived here on a rainy day in October. I had never been to Ireland before and I intended to knock on the door of my late wife's aunt. Only when I got here, I discovered she had been dead for almost a year.'

'God rest her soul,' said Elsie.

'Yes,' agreed Douglas. 'I then met Elsie, Kath and others of you. And of course, I met Dorchadas. I don't know about you, but I'm really missing Dorch today. He should be here.' There were lots of nods and comments of agreement. 'That he changed my life, there's no question. But he couldn't have done it on his own. I needed all of you. As I look around the table, each one of you has had a part to play in the extraordinary healing I have known these past months. We've had a few adventures between us, haven't we?'

'Aye, that we certainly have,' said Kath. 'And, for some of us, that included rolling topsy-turvy down a mountainside in that tin can of a motor of yours!'

'Yes, thank you, Kath,' said Douglas, chuckling. 'I can assure you that was not deliberate.' Laughter rippled around the table. 'But seriously, you friends here in Ireland have been my salvation. And Frank - you and Daisy have helped me more than I can say. And little Rosa - what an inspiration you are. And then Mavis, my dear faithful friend back in England. You stood by me so wonderfully during my troubles, and it is so right that you are here today.' Mavis looked down shyly, but could not hide her smile. 'And Mavis, I have something else to thank you for. And that is, you have a beautiful niece called Alice.' He reached out and held Alice's hand. 'I never imagined I would ever be able to love a woman again after the terrible pain of losing Saoirse. But the healing that has taken place in my heart in recent months has created space to breathe again. It has created space for love. And I have found someone who loves me in a way she has no right to. She is a remarkable woman. And…' He looked at Alice, who smiled and nodded at him. 'And Alice has given me permission to let you all know that last night she agreed to become my wife.'

'Oh! You two… Oh!' exclaimed Mavis and, with the words failing her, rose from her seat and made her way round the table and tearfully hugged her niece tight. Others also gathered round to congratulate the couple.

When all the congratulations were over and people had returned to their chairs, Brí said. 'Nancy, love. Did you want to say anything?'

Nancy didn't stand, but from her chair she said, 'I'm sorry about the Prosecco. I like Prosecco, I do, and I'm sorry the top shot off when it did, because it meant we couldn't have any.'

'Well, that's all right, love,' said Kath. 'We didn't really need the Prosecco that day, you know.'

'Hm' said Nancy. 'I liked it there, though,' she said. 'I liked it up there in that monastery place. I liked all the angels.'

'You referring to Dorchadas, love?' asked Elsie.

'No,' said Nancy.

'Well, what *did* you mean, Nancy?' asked Kevin.

'I mean the angel I met in a field once. That same angel - he was there. And a few of his friends. I had a nice chat with them. Nice things, angels are.

'You mean, you saw them when we were in that garden?' asked Brí.

'No,' said Nancy. 'They were on the walls with me and Rosa. We like angels, don't we, Rosa?'

'We do!' said Rosa with delight. 'Nancy sees them better than me, though,' she added. 'Are there some here today, Nancy?'

'There are,' said Nancy. 'They like it here - with all of us.'

'Can you see them here, Nancy?' asked Daisy, betraying some nervousness in her voice.

'Course I can,' said Nancy. 'Can't you?'

'Oh, dear,' said Elsie. 'I'd have put my best frock on, if I'd known that.'

Unbeknown to Nancy, Douglas had slipped out as she started to speak and he returned with a bottle of Prosecco in his hand, and behind him followed Oonagh with another bottle and some glasses. 'Nancy,' he said, 'Come and open your Prosecco.'

Nancy whooped with delight and came over to Oonagh and grabbed hold of the bottle. Soon the top flew off to the street outside, and Prosecco was being poured into the glasses. Rosa's glass was refilled with lemonade.

Nancy lifted up her glass and said, 'To friends, family, God and his angels,' and all lifted their glasses and drank.

Elsie then said, 'And to our Father Pat. The most beloved of priests.' Again, all responded.

Kevin then said, 'And to our dear friend, Dorchadas, without whom we'd not all be gathered here today.' Once more people cheered and sipped from their glasses.

'Finally,' said Kath.

'Get on with it sister,' interjected Elsie.

'Patience is a virtue,' replied Kath. 'My toast is to my dear friends Douglas and Alice. May God bless you, you darlings. And many congratulations. You both deserve a whole load of happiness.'

After the toasts, the company settled back into smaller conversations around the table. Oonagh supplied the group with tea and coffee, and eventually the sun started to sink in the sky, removing its warm beams from the courtyard. With great reluctance, the party eventually broke up and there was much embracing, laughter and weeping. Nancy, Brí and Kevin all remained behind to help Oonagh clear up and return the tables inside. Soon the musicians arrived and the sounds of music and song, chatter and laughter filled the pub that, only a few months back, had been the place where Douglas had first met the tall Guinness- sipping Irishman called Dorchadas, who claimed to be an angel from heaven. Douglas and Alice ate out at another pub that evening and spent the time making plans for their future. At one time, not so long ago, neither of them imagined that the future could be a world full of delight and possibility. But now their imaginations were reborn and their hearts were afire with hopes and dreams.

*

The next day was a sad day for Douglas when his friends returned to their homelands. Frank, Daisy and Rosa were the first to leave with a generous mix of both laughter and tears. They drove off soon after breakfast to catch their flight back to the States. No sooner had they left than Elsie was in their room clearing and cleaning in preparation for new guests. Douglas drove Alice and Mavis to Cork, where they caught their flight back to the UK. Douglas took the long route home, for he wanted an evening drive back over the Connor Pass, a drive that now held such precious memories for him. Once over the brow of the hill, he drove down to Dingle in the gentle evening light.

He met up with Kevin for a fish supper that evening, and then came back to his room. He was all for an early night, but noticed his journal on his desk. He realised he had not written in it for some time. Now he was so close to Alice and shared so much of his inner thoughts with her, there was less need to write. However, he was feeling a bit lonely, so he pulled up the creaking chair to his desk. He opened the notebook, and turned back many pages to his entry of 8th October. The first line read, 'It's a while since I've written in this pathetic book. There has been nothing to write - only misery.' How much had changed since then! He flicked the book to the most recent entry, which he wrote on 7 May, the eve of Alice and Mavis arriving in Ireland. What a few weeks it had been. What a few months it had been. How things had changed. He turned to a fresh page and smoothed it down. He chewed the end of his pen for a few moments, then started to write.

Journal 1 June

They've been and they've gone. It's been quite a few weeks. Too tired to say too much about it now. It was a big meal with Kev this evening, so have to go to sleep soon. But there are some very important things to report before I sleep.

The visit of Mavis and Alice, and Frank and his family was a great success. And it worked well that they all came together. We've had a great time exploring this part of Ireland. Kath has been really ill, but she insisted on us all going up to a place called Reask for a picnic on Ascension Day. It turned out to be much more than a picnic. A kind of golden cloud came on us. Nancy said it was the shekinah glory. She seems to know about these things. Anyway, it worked a kind of magic on all of us because we all went 'travelling' as Dorch calls it. All to different places, but the common theme seemed to be the Resurrection. Alice and Mavis went to somewhere like Alice's beloved Morwenstow (can't wait to visit that place with her one day). Frank and co went to the Giant Sequoia Forest in the States - or something like it. Sounded so beautiful. Rosa was really sweet telling me about it. Kath and all her family went to a place that I think must have been the garden of the Resurrection. Or at least a 'deep memory' version, like the Gethsemane and Golgotha places I visited before. The truly incredible thing is that Kath came back from that place well! Everyone thought she really only had days, possibly hours to live. But no, she's now fighting fit! I can't pretend to understand all of this, but I am so pleased. I was feeling so sad to think of losing Kath. She has become a dear, dear friend.

And I found myself travelling with Dorch. Dear old Dorch. What a friend he's been to me these past few months. Well, we found ourselves back in Egypt (deep memory version). And wonderfully we met up with all the bible people I've come across these past few months - John the B, old Jacob, Antonio, Mary Mag, Svetlana, Grace, Joseph, Salome. They were all in a boat together! And we sailed down the Nile together for a time. Oh, it was SUCH a beautiful experience. But then we had to get out, and Dorch and I found ourselves in a desert. But the dove was with us. The Holy Spirit dove. Such a sweet and gentle thing actually. And then we came across the archangel Raphael. I wasn't even sure such an Archangel existed. Anyway, he wasn't the great and mighty thing I expected an Archangel to be. He presented to us as an old man. Didn't faze Dorch at all. Well, it was clear that Dorch was about to be sent home - back as an angel again. But - and this was so touching - he asked if he could remain a human for a bit longer. I mean, I'm sure most angels sentenced to time as a human, would be longing to get back to their normal selves again. But not Dorch. He has absolutely loved being a human. So, I guess he may still pop up in this world somewhere. But he did say it was time for him and me to part. That was so sad. I shall so miss him.

The other sad thing is that dear Father Pat died on that day. I can only hope he had some experience or vision that helped him over. We have all grieved so deeply his passing. But it was Daisy who reminded me that death is not the end of things, but the doorway to a far greater life. Pat's work was done on this earth. I just hope he knows how much he helped people in this world.

And now the best bit of news: A couple of nights ago I took Alice out for a meal. There was a great band at the pub and we spent some time enjoying the music. Then we went for a walk. It was a beautiful evening and we wandered down to the shore. And there I plucked up courage and did the traditional thing of getting down on one knee and proposed. I wish I could describe her response. It was so beautiful. So touching.

When I lost my Saoirse, my heart broke into a thousand pieces. My nicely-honed faith collapsed and I lost touch with God. Well, in a way I was shedding a distorted idea of God. Here in Ireland, through Dorch and other friends (including friends in the bible!) I have discovered God to be very different to what I thought. Once I discovered this God, I started to heal. Even my broken heart started to mend, and space grew in my heart for a new love. I think I have loved Alice from the moment I first met her. I believe I am loving her already as much as I loved Saoirse. I can't believe a human heart can do this, but it can. I know I have Saoirse's blessing on this, and I know that Alice and I are going to be happy. So, what can I say? What a journey I've been on. I'm sure there's more to say, but Elsie's calling me.

*

Douglas closed the journal and put down his pen. He put on his slippers and made his way down the stairs. 'What is it Elsie?' he asked.

Elsie was in her dressing gown, and Douglas noticed a random array of grips in her hair. Her cat-eye spectacles sparkled as they reflected the hall light. 'Douglas, darling,' she said as he came down the stairs. 'I had a look out of my window, and would you believe the moon? She's an utter beauty this evening. Would you join me outside just for a few moments to have a look at her?'

'Of course,' said Douglas and followed her out into her little garden at the back of the house. It was a mild and still evening.

'Sit yourself here, love,' said Elsie, who had moved a couple of the garden chairs into place for a good viewing of the moon. Douglas sat in the chair and Elsie disappeared inside for a moment then returned with two glasses of whiskey. 'Here, Douglas,' she said, handing him a glass. She sat down and said, 'You've had some sad farewells today, son, so I thought a drop of this, plus a little sit under the glory of heaven would help you to rest well tonight.' She lifted her glass and said, 'Sláinte.'

'Sláinte,' responded Douglas and clinked his glass with Elsie's. She downed her glass in one, while Douglas took a careful sip from his.

Elsie savoured her whiskey for a while, then said, 'Would you look at all those stars, Douglas? Aren't they something beautiful? I never tire of looking at them. They do me a power of good, they do. Especially when my heart's a little tender.'

Sure enough, the indigo night sky was pierced with a myriad shimmering bright lights. And set in the midst of them was the slender arc of an exquisite new moon. Douglas rested his eyes on the glorious heavens above him. Then he recited,

> 'Heaven is not far, tho' far the sky
> Overarching earth and main.
> It takes not long to live and die,
> Die, revive, and rise again.
> Not long: how long? Oh, long re-echoing song!
> O Lord, how long?'

'What was that, love?' asked Elsie.

'Oh, just some lines by Christina Rossetti,' said Douglas.

'Oh aye?' said Elsie. 'I don't think I've ever met the lass. But sounds like she has a nice way with words.'

'Yes, she does,' replied Douglas. He reached out his hand and grasped Elsie's. 'Thank you, Elsie,' he said. 'Thank you. This is a truly beautiful evening. And you are right. The whiskey and the stars and the moon are just what I needed.'

The two sat together for some time without saying anything. Then Elsie slapped her knee and said, 'Well now, Douglas. I'll need to get back inside, else the damp will get my leg going. And I've got to be up early in the morning to get ready for the guests. More Japanese - and you know how they like their rooms spotless.' She got up from her chair somewhat unsteadily and, looking at Douglas, said, 'No hurry, Douglas. Stay here as long as you wish. But mind you don't get cold. You need to keep yourself in good health now, with that young lady of yours to care for.'

Douglas smiled as he watched the busy figure of Elsie gather up the glasses, then limp back into the house. He leaned back and looked at the expanse above him. Yes, the night sky could do anyone a power of good. A silvery cloud drifted languidly in front of the moon.

He enjoyed the silence for some moments, and then, in his mind, he imagined a voice. 'You alright, there, son?'

'Yes, thanks, Dorch,' he said out loud. 'Just enjoying the dark.'

'Ah, that you are, son,' he heard the voice reply. 'That you are. I always knew you'd get a liking for the dark stuff.'

Douglas chuckled, then slowly inhaled the briny sea air.

There was no doubt: his soul was at peace.

NOTES

The quotations from Pope Francis are from *Evangelii Guadium - The Joy of the Gospel* (Veritas Publications 2013) pp135f. They are produced by kind permission © Libreria Editrice Vaticana.

The Bible stories referred to in this book can be found in:

The raising of Jairus' daughter	Mark 5.21-43
Thomas and the Resurrection	John 20.24-29
Joseph's flight to Egypt	Matthew 2.13-15
Ruth and Naomi	The book of Ruth
The Resurrection	John 20.1-18

All non-biblical characters in this story are fictional.

Some features of the town of Dingle and the peninsula including names of pubs and Guest Houses are fictional.

Beauty Born Anew is the final part of the Dorchadas Trilogy.
Part 1 is *The Face of the Deep* (Amazon 2019)
Part 2 is *The Fairest of Dreams* (Amazon 2020)

Further details of the author's work can be found at michaelmitton.co.uk

APPENDIX 1

Summary of *The Fairest of Dreams*, Book 2 of the Dorchadas trilogy

Douglas Romer returns to the town of Dingle in the new year, following the dramatic storm and near-death experience that led him and his friend Dorchadas to a 'deep memory' encounter with the Garden of Gethsemane on the eve of Christ's death (see *The Face of the Deep*). This encounter was a profound experience for Douglas that led not only to a reforming of his faith, but also to a further stage of healing on his journey of grief. On his return to Dingle, Douglas soon meets up again with Dorchadas, who had mysteriously disappeared following the dramatic events in the storm. During an early conversation, Douglas reaches a clear conviction that Dorchadas' claim to be a retired angel is true. During the story, it becomes clear that Kath is also much reformed and has met up again with Peter, the man she once loved. Peter, a former priest, is now a Quaker and professional psychotherapist.

At the end of *The Face of the Deep,* Douglas was informed by British Intelligence that his wife's death was not a terrorist drive-by shooting, but a deliberate assassination by an agent acting on behalf of someone in Sheffield, who was anxious that Saoirse was close to uncovering this person's illegal arms-dealing activities. As the novel progresses, Douglas becomes increasingly concerned that this person will start focussing their sights on him, now that he has been informed of the reason for Saoirse's killing. He is right to be concerned, because the man who planned this murder is Gerald Bentley, a member of Douglas' congregation and a powerful figure in the Diocese where Douglas has worked. Gerald's alcohol-dependent wife, Angela, encourages Gerald to eliminate Douglas, as she fears he will unearth her husband's illegal arms dealing, and his arranging of

Saoirse's murder. She dreads losing the wealth for which she has so longed. She plots with Gerald a plan to kill him.

During these days, Douglas becomes increasingly aware of the dark powers that operate in the world, and also in the church. Through Dorchadas' angelic services, he has a 'meeting' with John the Baptist, a man who contested the religious and political powers of his day. He also is taken to the fortress where Herod has arranged the beheading of John. Both experiences introduce Douglas to very different and much more attractive forms of power.

Douglas decides to resign as Vicar of St.Philip's and meets with his bishop. While he is in England he also meets up with his good friend Mavis, whose recently divorced niece Alice now lives with her. Douglas and Alice get on well, but neither feels ready yet for a relationship.

Douglas also has a video call with his good friend, Franklin, an Anglican priest in the USA, who used to work in England in a neighbouring parish. Frank's wife, Daisy, recently experienced a miraculous healing of her cancer at a church meeting. As a thank you gesture, they decide to give a considerable sum of money to Douglas, which enables him to remain in Dingle for some time without having to worry about earning an income.

Father Pat, the local priest of the town, informs Douglas that there is to be a memorial mass for Saoirse's Aunt Ruby, and that Saoirse's parents, Niall and Orla Flynn, will be attending the service. Douglas is alarmed at the prospect of seeing them again. He knows how much Niall hates him, as Niall has a record of violent behaviour, and is bitterly opposed to the British and to Protestantism. He believes his daughter is in purgatory for her 'sin' of marrying a Protestant and not having a proper Catholic funeral.

Douglas therefore finds that there are now two people who have reason to kill him. The day of the mass is cold, with a light fall of snow. Gerald and Angela have made their way to Dingle under false names, with the express intention of eliminating Douglas. Niall and Orla have had a brief meeting with Douglas at the Presbytery, which showed Douglas that his former father-in-law had lost none his hatred. As it turns out, Niall is enraged by seeing Douglas again, and he becomes intent on seeking revenge by killing him. Thus, at the Mass, both Niall and Gerald are present, with murderous intent.

When Kevin sees a bulge in Niall's pocket, he knows he is carrying a gun. He urges Douglas to flee the church, and at the end of the service, Douglas drives fast out of Dingle, with Dorchadas, Kath and Kevin as passengers. Niall follows in hot pursuit, as does Gerald and Angela. There is a car chase out of the town. Douglas fails to see some black ice and his car skids out of control. The cars of Niall and Gerald collide with it, and they all tumble down an incline.

The next scene is of Douglas, Dorchadas, Kath, Kevin, Niall, Gerald and Angela who all find themselves in the 'deep memory' of Golgotha. Each one has a significant encounter with the cross of Christ, discovering it to be a place of extraordinary power, despite the fact that the man on the cross seems so powerless. Once again, Dorchadas disappears, although he has assured Douglas that he will be back in Dingle before long.

Gerald did not survive the accident, but the others did and spend some time in hospital recovering. When they are all out of hospital, Father Pat invites them to an afternoon at his Presbytery, where each person tells their personal story of their encounter with the cross at Golgotha.

For Douglas, this experience produces another powerful healing of his grief, and for the first time he feels a sense of hope about the future and a welcome sense of contentment. The novel ends with Douglas walking on the seafront when he meets up with a young girl called Grace. He has met her once or twice in Dingle before. On this occasion she gives him the disturbing information that Kath is seriously ill with cancer. Although Douglas is very shaken by this news, he realises that he is now strong enough to help others again, and so he resolves to remain in Dingle to help his good friend. The novel ends with Grace in conversation with Dorchadas. The two seem to know each other well.

APPENDIX 2

The main characters in the Dorchadas Trilogy

Dorchadas	An angel currently living in Dingle in human form
Douglas Romer	Anglican Vicar of St.Philip's Church, Sheffield, who resigns during the course of the trilogy.
Saoirse Romer	Deceased wife of Douglas, originally from Cork.
Elsie O'Connell	Proprietor of the *St.Raphael's Guest House*, Dingle
Kathleen Griffin	Proprietor of *Kathleen's Coffee Shop*, Dingle and sister of Elsie.
Kevin Griffin	Son of Kath, who runs the local garage.
Bríana Anderson	Daughter of Kath. Lives in USA with partner, Carol
Nancy Griffin	Daughter of Kath. Lives in Limerick
Peter O'Callaghan	Formerly a Catholic priest. Defrocked after affair with Kath when young. Now a retired psychotherapist living in Adare.
Father Pat	Parish priest of Dingle.
Mavis Treneer	Member of Douglas' congregation and good friend. Her husband, Bert, died a few years ago. Aunt of Alice.
Alice Fournier	Niece of Mavis. From Bideford, North Devon. Now lives in Sheffield with Mavis. Previously married to Georges and lived in France.

Niall Flynn	Father of Saoirse. Lives in Cork.
Orla Flynn	Mother of Saoirse. Lives in Cork.
Gerald Bentley	Member of Douglas' congregation and chair of Diocesan Board of Finance.
Angela Bentley	Wife of Gerald.
Franklin Oberman	Anglican priest in California. Spent a few years in neighbouring parish to Douglas in Sheffield
Daisy Oberman	Wife of Frank, and recently recovered from serious illness.
Rosa Chatterbury	Eight-year old daughter of Daisy's sister.
Brian Edge	Churchwarden of St.Philip's Church.
Bishop Pauline	Suffragan Bishop of Tankersley
Oonagh Kelly	Landlady of *The Angel's Rest* and church organist.